THE PIZZA DELIVERYMAN'S TALE

by Ronan Barbour

Green Gingerbread Press

Los Angeles, California

ISBN: 978-0-578-72290-0

Cover art by Thomas M. Baxa

www.baxaart.com

Cover design by Michael Calabria

THE PIZZA DELIVERYMAN'S TALE

DEDICATION

For Blair and Isobel ~ for being there for me too, when I wanted to hear voices on the other end of the line.

Listen to Roky Erickson to get the quote about ghosts...

Prologue

Santa was coming. . .

I didn't know what sort of surprise he'd bring me, only that I wouldn't like it.

I heard a sound and knew it was the woman. The clacking footsteps stopped. Then started up again on the hardwood floor, heading towards her.

She had said something, hadn't she? Something in a whisper.

Tried to think of what it was. . .

I saw an orange. Flashing. Blinking sun orange behind my eyes. I had closed them, hadn't I? It hurt.

My head hurt bad. Real bad headache bad.

I thought of how it would taste in my mouth, an orange. Cold vital fruit. Sweet.

An orange sounded good. Orange bursting in my mouth. If only I could ever have one again. In my mouth. That was my tongue moving. Slowly. Some old gray turtle, I imagined, in there, clawing clay away. Feeling out my teeth. They felt dirty, tasted dirty. And my mouth was dry. Black dry. This was my mouth and what I was going to die with.

I was going to die.

YOU HAVE ARRIVED!

I felt a hot rush at the sound of that familiar voice in my head and opened my eyes. They fixed on a blank white wall a couple of feet away from where I lay on the floor. From this position, lying on my side, I could see nothing but the wall. I raised my head to look around but could see nothing else. The room was dim. Slowly I lowered my head back down onto the hard floor.

I shut my eyes. My head hurt so much. Like the worst New Year's Day hangover, it was killing me.

No, *said one of my voices,* **He** is killing you. . .

I opened them again. It wouldn't do, I realized. He was going to come from the door that had to be behind me. I needed to see.

I needed to see Santa coming.

Vampire *Santa, I corrected myself.*

I lifted my head again and tried to roll over but didn't get far before I encountered resistance. I rolled back to my side.

My legs had been tied together and my wrists cuffed.

I took in several breaths, readying myself. I still had to see that door and I knew it was going to hurt. "Okay, okay," I whispered. "Here we go."

Tightening my abdominals, I jerked my left shoulder back and pushed with the right. I was halfway there. Pain shot through my wrist as my weight centered on it as I landed on my back, trapping both arms and lifting my ass off the ground, handcuffs digging into my lower back. I moved my legs to the left and pushed again with my upper body. I didn't think I'd make it, but the sudden cracking pain in my wrist motivated me to keep going, and I landed on my side.

I saw the door outlined by the light coming from the hallway. It was open, just a crack. Like the way my parents used to leave my bedroom door so that I would know they were not very far if the monsters should come.

My parents.

I saw their faces in my mind.

My heart began to pound. I heard myself moaning as I struggled like the helpless fish I was. My whole body felt strobe light panic. It was sinking in that I wasn't going to see my parents again, or anybody else for that matter.

Just Vampire Santa when he came to get me.

"Oh God," I whimpered. For the first time in my adult life I heard myself praying. "Oh God, oh God. Please. Help me, God."

I felt sick. Felt warmth spreading in my pants. I was pissing myself. I hadn't felt that feeling in a long time, not since the junior Olympics when I'd been standing in line with the other young runners waiting for my very first 75-yard dash. I'd been so nervous then.

What the hell was I going to do?

I closed my eyes for a moment to swallow back the panic, then took a deep breath before taking in the new view. I was in a bedroom. To the right of the door, a bed with a comforter was pushed up against the wall. There was a little table next to it with a lamp and some books.

To the left of the door I saw a semi-opened closet, one of the sliding door variety. I couldn't see much of what was inside, just vague shapes.

To my far left, a flat screen TV was mounted on the wall. Just below it was a dresser. Maybe there was something there that could—?

A dog woofed somewhere in the house.

The Dog. *I'd quite forgotten about him.*

The woman shrieked.

I almost yelled for help, but I caught myself, strangling the noise I had begun to make in my throat into a pained gurgle. There was no point to that. Only he would hear me. And it would only make him come sooner.

But Jesus Christ, I needed help. I needed

Orange *orange.*

Why did I keep thinking 'orange'?

Was my mind trying to tell me something? Or had he done some serious damage to my head?

Think…

But I could only think to try to get up. What then? What was I going to do with my hands and feet bound?

I could hop through a window?

Surely there was a window in the room.

But even if I could manage the momentum to break the glass, I'd likely only fall to break my neck. Or be so lucky as to bleed to death in shattered glass before he came.

Maybe that was better than waiting for Vampire Santa.

How the hell had I ended up here?

Chapter 1

The ad for a part-time pizza delivery driver in Grantwood had listed some basic requirements, but a GPS had not been one of them. So when I went in to fill out the paperwork, I was unprepared when they told me I would be taking deliveries right away.

All I needed besides my car and uniform for the job, they said, was a GPS system.

"I'm sorry," I told Dave the manager, a bald heavyset man with a blond mustache. "I don't actually have one."

"Do you have a Smartphone?" he asked.

"No."

Dave shook his head. "I got a GPS in my car you can borrow. Just be sure you get yours before your next shift."

The next day I had an audition for a play in Hollywood, and I planned to first go over to the used electronics shop across the street and buy myself the cheapest GPS I could find. I had to work my second delivery shift later that day, so I figured the audition would be my chance to test it out.

I drove over to the shop. The door was locked and everything was quiet inside, even though the opening hours in the window said 10:00 am and it was already past that.

I didn't have a lot of time to spare.

I figured I might as well take the plunge and buy my first Smartphone. I was due an upgrade and had been toying with the idea a while. The Horizon Wireless store was a few blocks up.

There were no customers in the store when I walked in, only a salesperson in a white shirt behind the register.

"Good morning!" I said to the Asian clerk, walking over. I

might have mistaken him for a boy if not for the eyebrow-thin mustache and tuft of hair growing from his chin.

I explained my situation to him, asking him to show me the least expensive Smartphone available with a GPS function.

He left the counter for the back area and re-emerged, showing me a phone, priced at $72 after tax.

Not bad, I thought. I could afford that with the $136 I had to my name.

But I was still curious to see what the used store might have to offer, so I told the salesman I'd be back for my upgrade sooner or later and thanked him. There was still enough time before I needed to get going to the audition that I could give the used store one more chance.

I drove back up the street. Pulling in to the parking lot, I could see the store was open.

The proprietor, a stocky dark-skinned fellow with grey hair, greeted me warmly when I approached the counter. I told him that I was looking for the cheapest GPS he had, the most basic features would do.

"This one," he said, pointing to a device without a box. "Sixty dollars."

"I'll take it," I said.

The man bent down and got it.

"Now, if I have any problems with it, can I bring it back?"

"Sure."

When I rushed in to the Horizon Wireless store that was still without customers I found the little Asian man in the white shirt still standing stoically behind the register, seeming to be waiting for me.

"You know that phone you showed me?" I said, a little out of breath, "The GPS on it does have voice directions, right?"

"Yes," he said.

"Can I get that now? I'm in a bit of a hurry." I was trying to stay cool, but was hot as hell. Whether the thing was damaged or the most primitive GPS ever, I was already done with what I'd just bought for $60. For only $12 more I could have gotten a modern working GPS and a new Smartphone to boot! What the hell had I been thinking? And I'd been back to the used electronics shop only to find the doors locked again, with no sign to indicate when the proprietor would be back. I'd stood outside and called the store's number that was painted on the glass door only to hear it ring and ring.

At this point I figured the chances of making my audition were slim. All because I'd had to check out that shop first thinking I'd get some kind of deal.

On top of that, buying the phone would leave me with only a few dollars left, and my car was almost on empty—by the time I got what little gas I could and went to Hollywood and back I'd probably have just enough to get to work. Of course I was supposed to show up with a full tank of gas.

The clerk came back with the phone and printed out a contract. I just signed my name and gave him the money.

After he had set up the phone, he showed me a few basics. "It's pretty straightforward," he said. "And your GPS? You just go to this icon, Navigation. I've made it appear on your screen. See?" He tilted the phone and I spotted an orange-colored arrowhead symbol on the screen. "I will now activate the voice. . ." He handed me the phone.

"Thanks," I said. I had sounded to myself like someone yelling next to his calm, soft voice. Despite the agitation I'd brought in with me, listening to him had made me feel at ease.

"Let me print you a receipt." As he did I looked at his nametag.

"Lance," I said. "Thanks again. Take care."

Lance's lips twitched with what must have passed for a smile. "You too."

Chapter 2

I awoke to a voice in the dark, coming from my phone.

I reached behind me and felt for the unfamiliar, heavy rectangle that I was sure I'd switched off before sleep.

The display lit up when I found it; it all looked the same. I tapped the text message icon to see if I had any new messages; I didn't. I checked the voicemail icon. (0)

So why did it keep doing that?

"Horizon Wireless!"

This had been happening all day; a happy-sounding female voice announcing *Horizon Wireless!*

I switched the phone off once more, knowing it was pointless.

I put the phone back on top of Vic's speaker, and closed my eyes. I was nearly asleep when I heard it again.

"Horizon Wireless!"

I sighed aloud.

At least Vic was a heavy sleeper.

Chapter 3

As soon as I sat up in the morning a big, shirtless Samoan greeted me. He looked at me, unsmiling.

"Dude. Who kept texting you all night?"

As usual, Vic was already up and working at his desk. Three blue cereal bowls were stacked with three spoon handles jutting from the top bowl. He'd already had his second and third breakfast.

"Nobody," I said, rubbing my eyes. "It woke me up too. I don't know why it keeps doing that. Some kind of alert, maybe."

"It better not do that again tonight, man."

Victor Mapu was one of my best friends. He'd come down to LA before me and was trying to make it as a comedy writer. When he wasn't writing, he was working as a bouncer at a club in West Hollywood. When he wasn't doing that, he was eating. I'd been crashing on the floor of his little studio apartment for the last three months. I didn't like seeing him unhappy. Vic and I had never had a fight and, for my own sake, I planned to keep it that way.

"Sorry," I said. "I'll figure out what's going on with that."

Vic turned back to his work.

I got up, gathered the bedding and stepped past Vic to the open closet.

"You working today?" Vic asked.

"Yeah, at twelve."

"Big Shits? Or the pizza place?"

"Both," I said, "Big Shits first."

"Ffthgh!"

Dave was at the register when I walked in. "What's up, Dylan?"

I saw a new guy in delivery uniform, holding a car topper. He was about my height, but bulkier, with a bristly black beard hiding half his face. He looked unsure of where to look.

"Hi bud," I said as I approached to collect my own topper.

He looked at me and nodded.

"Why don't you go ahead and put that on your car and then come back to me?" Dave called out to the new guy.

As I walked back out to the front, Dave counted out twenty from a register, and handed it to me for bank.

Outside, I found the new guy waiting for me.

"What was your name?" He held out a thick hand.

"Dylan Murray," I said, shaking it.

"Hooper Daniels."

"Hooper Daniels? That's a pretty cool name. What's your dad's, Jack?"

He didn't laugh. "Yeah, actually," he said. "It is."

"Your dad's name is Jack Daniels?"

"I am not kidding."

We walked around the corner, passing a waxing studio; we both looked in at the two gals sitting behind the counter, who smiled perfect whites at us. We looked at each other, Hooper with his eyebrows raised, then walked down the stairs to the garage.

I started walking in the direction of my car to set up the topper.

"I'm just going to go put mine on," he said behind me.

Once we were both done, Hooper met me halfway back to the stairs.

"Well, that was pretty easy," he said as we walked back up. "Have you been working here very long?"

"This is only my third day," I said.

"How do you like it?"

"So far, it's pretty great. You basically drive around with your deliveries, drop them off, take their money, get tipped, and come back. Easy. It's a pretty stress-free job."

"So…that's it? Just driving around, getting tipped?"

"Yeah, like I said. That's pretty much it."

"Wow," he said. "Good deal."

"Do you work another job?"

"Yeah," he said. "I work for a music venue downtown. Also this week I've got an interview for the VBMC. Which I don't know do you… it's a marijuana collective, in Venice."

"Oh." I said. "Cool."

"I'm pretty excited about that. Do you work another job?"

"I work at Junior Browne's."

"Bartending?"

"No, I'm a server. I hate it."

"You at least make good money, though?"

"Not really. That's why I'm working here."

"Really? I would've thought waiting tables near Beverly Hills and all would be pretty good money."

"Maybe at every other restaurant. Not at JB's."

Up ahead, another delivery guy was coming our way. I recognized the small skinny Latino with long, badly dyed orangey blond hair from the shift before. He and I had crossed paths a few times, but had never officially met; I nodded to him in greeting as we passed.

Hooper and I walked back to the pizza shop to start the shift. Dave was standing behind the register by himself.

"You guys can wait outside until we call you," he said. "We're slow right now."

Hooper and I sat outside the ice cream shop and a few minutes later, we saw the blond driver again. He was talking to another driver carrying one of the carrier bags, back from delivery. I recognized him from my first day. The portly guy was dough-pale and freckled, with curling red hair sprouting from the back of his hat. He'd seemed nice from the small talk we'd exchanged.

The portly driver came back from the shop alone and without the bag. He spotted us. "How's it going, gentlemen? What's up Dylan?" he greeted me.

"I don't think I've met you yet," he said, looking at Hooper and extending his hand. "I'm Joel."

Hooper introduced himself and they shook.

"How's business?" I asked Joel.

"Slow today, dude," he said. "I got on at four. Been out once so far."

"Where are you from?" I asked Joel.

"Long Beach."

"What brought you here?"

"I'm going to UCLA. You?"

"SF Bay Area."

"Trying to be an actor?"

"Yep."

"I'm from Orange County," Hooper said. "And I am not trying to be anything."

"Aw, whussup guys?" said the blond driver coming up. "Whussup, what's this, a meeting?" He cackled. He pulled out a cigarette and popped it into his mouth.

"I haven't properly met you yet," I said, leaning over the table and extending my hand to him. "I'm Dylan."

"Oh whussup man?" he said. "I'm Paul. Good to meet you, bro."

"Likewise, and this is Hooper," I said. "He's here because of Jack Daniels."

We talked until finally Hooper and I were called in. During that time, Joel and Paul clarified a few things for me; the business was family-owned and this location had been open less than a month. Joel and Paul had been hired at the same time two weeks ago (along with a third guy, who'd simply vanished by the end of his first shift). Our delivery area was a three-mile radius, covering all of Grantwood and some of West LA. Most importantly, since Grantwood was one of the most affluent areas of LA, people were pretty generous with tips.

"You're all set, Dylan," Dave said when I reached the counter. He had stacked two carrier bags. "Let me get your dispatch."

I walked to my car and set the heavy bags onto the backseat. Once in the driver's seat, I set aside the detail receipt and pulled out my phone and called out the address: "One, seven, two, two, Darby Street."

The screen indicating it was searching, I started the car and headed out of the car park.

"Turn left onto Gorman Avenue!" said the cheery female voice.

"You got it, Sally."

I had taken to calling my GPS voice Sally from the night before. I pictured a woman with thick blonde hair bobbed the length of Ronald McDonald's; with a smile that shaped her cheeks into shiny bunches.

I turned left and took particular care at the frequent stop signs. I'd noticed that people in Grantwood tended to step straight out onto the street without looking.

"In eight hundred feet. Turn right onto Darby Street!"

"If it'll make you happy…"

"In six hundred feet. Your destination is on the right!!"

Slowing, I looked for parking.

"You have arrived!"

The building's entrance was like a drawbridge door you could drive a truck through.

I pulled out the detail receipt from the plastic pocket at the top of the carrier bag.

Mary Dempsey. #P4.

At the callbox, I found Dempsey in the directory and tapped in the code.

"Hello?" said a female voice.

"Hi, it's Taste Testers," I said.

"Hi! I'll buzz you in."

Inside, a large ornate fountain stood in the middle of the archway. Twin statues of cherubs poured thin streams of water from casks onto the tier below, where the face of a lion was framed between the streams, frothy water bubbling out from its mouth. Several pebble-shaped lights gave the water a warm golden glow, the bottom of the pool peppered with the dark pennies of dropped wishes.

I continued on into a large courtyard, the layers of apartments framing the sky.

I took the elevator to the penthouse level and found apartment 4 with the door already open.

"Hi there!" said the woman, giving me a smile of perfect white teeth. She had shoulder-length brunette hair, and looked slim and fit.

"Hi yourself," I said. "How are you this evening?"

"We're great! We're so glad you moved in to the neighborhood. We love you guys."

"Oh, thanks," I said. "Thanks for giving us a try."

"We've given you guys several tries. It's great."

"Pee-*zhah,"* said a little voice from behind the woman.

"Pizza!" agreed the woman. "Pizza man is here!"

"Pee-*zhah,"* said the little voice again, and I looked down to see a toddler as I removed the box from the bag. The little girl was in pink pajamas, holding a small stuffed animal between both hands. She stepped closer to the door and looked up at me with curious brown eyes, her open mouth. "Pee-*zhah*."

I smiled at the girl and chuckled as I handed the box to the woman.

I pulled a pen from my shirt pocket and asked for her autograph on the card receipt, which she signed against the doorframe.

"Pee-*zhaaah.*"

"Pizza, Evelyn." Mary handed me the receipt.

"Thank you, I really appreciate it," I said. "Hope you ladies enjoy."

"We will, thanks again."

She closed the door. I heard Evelyn behind it one more time.

Walking away from the door, I glanced at the receipt. She'd written $7.00 under the tip line.

Nice.

The next guy was an Aaron Feldman of 871 Acorn Lane.

I read the address out to my phone and started the car, waiting for Sally to start directing.

"In a quarter mile. Turn right!"

The route to Acorn Lane took me to the other side of Sunset Boulevard. This was where the fancy apartment complexes and condominiums ended, and the big houses began.

At Sally's order, I turned off Sunset and onto Mannerville Canyon. As I went along the tree-lined road, I tried to get a look at some of the looming houses. Some of these were *mansions.* No doubt there were some famous movie stars or big-name directors behind those gates (I'd heard from Vic that Arnold Schwarzenegger and Steven Spielberg lived somewhere hereabouts).

Bright white lights came up behind; I glanced in the mirror and winced. I pushed some more on the gas.

The lights didn't pull back. I was being tailgated.

I signaled to the right and slowed down. Pulling off to the side to let them pass. A black SUV cut into the lane just in front of me and sped off.

"Continue on Mannerville Canyon for one mile!"

I took the opportunity to slow down again to try and catch some views of the amazing houses, but again, lights came up behind me. Despite the private-looking neighborhood, it was a busy road.

I sped up again. This time, I wouldn't be pulling over.

"In eight hundred feet. *Turn right onto Acorn Lane.*"

I glanced down at my phone.

That was a different voice I'd just heard.

The cheery, if commanding, Sally had suddenly changed to a huskier, British female voice.

What was that about?

In any case, I followed the instructions of the new voice.

Ringing the doorbell hadn't done anything, so I knocked hard on the green door.

A yelp from inside was followed by a crash.

A moment later, a light flicked on above the door and I heard the snap of a lock. The door opened inward to reveal a large bespectacled man wearing an aqua blue and black striped shirt and a pair of white briefs. His protruding gut was a perfect sphere, like he'd somehow swallowed the world's biggest jawbreaker. Wild tufts of dark hair stuck up from the back of his otherwise bald head.

"Hi," I greeted him.

The man stepped to the doorframe and glowered at me, his mouth open.

"Pizza?" I asked.

The man stuck his tongue out.

I looked from the quivering tongue, to the man's unblinking eyes. "I'm sorry," I said, as his tongue began to slowly retract. "Is this…?"

The tongue flicked out several times in rapid succession, before the man closed his mouth and seemed to chew. He swallowed, and finally blinked. "You scared me," he croaked.

"Is this eight-seven-one?"

"Mmph," he assented.

"I have the right house?"

"Mmph!" The man beckoned impatiently with a meaty hand.

I opened my bag, hoping he only meant for me to give him the pizzas.

"Here's the first two," I said, handing them over.

The man accepted them. He looked down at the two large pizza boxes in his hands. "Mmm…"

"And here's…two more."

The man held out the boxes as I stacked them. "Mmm!"

"There you go, sir," I said. "Now, if you could please just

sign this…" I took out the credit card receipt and my pen. The man balanced the four large pizzas in one hand and took the pen and paper with the other.

"Thank you, sir," I said, taking the pen and receipt back. "Hope you enjoy."

"Mmm!" The man flicked his tongue out at me again, making wet sounds.

I turned and began walking down through the garden to my car.

The door slammed behind me.

Chapter 4

I stepped out into the warm sunlight and began walking towards Santa Monica Boulevard.

I had the day off from both jobs, and my first order of business was to be rid of the useless GPS and get my money back.

Inside the shop I found a young Hispanic woman behind the counter.

"Good morning," I said setting the bag onto the counter. "I need to return this. The man I bought it from said I could return it if I had any problems."

"Oh," she said. "I'm sorry. But he is not here right now. He is the owner and I can't."

"Is he here later today?"

"I don't know. If you like, you can write down your number and I give it to him."

"Please," I said.

She handed me a pad of yellow stickie paper and a pen. I wrote down my info and handed it to the woman.

Leaving the shop, I had a sneaking feeling I was going to have trouble getting my money back.

I called my dad to tell him about my new job.

"Isn't that kind of dangerous?"

"Not where I'm working," I said. "Grantwood has to be one of the safest places in LA. But yeah, you wouldn't want to do this job in some places, that's for sure."

"Have you met any strange characters yet?"

I told him about the pants-less tongue-flicker from the night before: Mr. Blue Bumblebee, as I now thought of him.

"He tip you at least?"

"Three bucks."

"Asshole."

I laughed.

"Oh well, anyway, that's good you found another job. So, what else have you got planned for the day?"

"Well today's my only full day off," I said. "JB's usually schedules me five shifts a week, and I've asked Taste Testers to give me three, so I won't be having many days off for a while. Right now, I'm doing laundry and waiting on that guy from the used shop to call me back so I can get my refund.

"Speak of the Devil," I said, hearing a beep. "There's someone calling on the other line now. Hopefully it's him."

"Get the money back from that fucker."

"I will, gotta go. Talk to you soon."

"Take care now. *Asshole,"* I heard him mutter.

My dad wasn't so sure about the used guy either.

"Hi, you left me your number," said a voice I recognized, sounding impatient. "Now, what is the problem?"

"I need to return the GPS I bought from you."

"No sir. Everything in my shop works fine."

"No, I mean I guess it does work, but it doesn't have the voice-activated directions, which is really what I needed for my job."

"Okay, sir, no problem. Just come back and you can exchange for something. But I am not giving money back."

"Well, hold on," I said. "I'd like my money back. You said I could bring it back if for any reason it wasn't working for me."

"Sir, no!" he said. "I said you could bring it back if there any *problem* with it. But I know it works fine. Maybe you misunderstand English."

"I understand English *fine,"* I said, raising my voice. His condescending manner was pushing me now. "And I understood you when you said I could return it if I had any problem with it. Well, I do, and I want my money back."

"Sir, I don't know what you are trying to do here. I love my customers and my business and—"

"Hey I'm not trying to do anything! I just want my money back. I needed a GPS for my work for that day and I had to go out and buy a phone with a GPS. I came back to you, but you were not there!"

"Sir. I am not going to argue over the phone with you. I said no problem, come in and I can exchange for you another one. But that is all I can do."

"But I don't need anything else."

"That is all I can do."

"That is all you can do. Jesus, *Christ,*" I muttered, not caring if he heard. I took a deep breath and sighed. "Okay, I will be right in."

What do I need? So far, I didn't see much in the shop that would cost around $60, and I sure wasn't going to give the proprietor a penny more of my money.

I looked around impatiently. Went over to where I saw some videogame systems stacked by the display window. I hadn't played videogames in years, but maybe Vic would appreciate something as a gift. I checked the closest box for a price tag.

The proprietor shuffled towards me, his slippered feet making whisking noises across the floor.

"Can I help you with something?"

"How much is this?" I asked.

"One forty five," he said.

I put the box back.

I was going to step past him without saying a word and keep looking, but I found myself looking at my phone instead. I had to get back to check my washing and I wasn't in the mood for this.

"I really can't find anything here I need," I told him.

He nodded and looked up at me. "Do you want me to make you a receipt so you come back another time?"

"Yeah," I said. "Would you please?" I handed him the GPS.

He walked off, returning a moment later, holding out a small white envelope to me.

"This is good, anytime," he said.

"Thank you," I said, taking it.

He licked his lips. "I'm sorry what happened," he said. "Sometime you know, my English. I mean to say you can return for anything in the store when I talk to you."

He offered me his hand. I shook it.

"It's not a total loss," I said to Carter, reclined on his couch. "At some point I'm going to really need something. I'll go in and maybe he'll have it. Then we'll be even."

"Still, man. It's not that. It's the *principle* of the thing."

Carter was one of my co-workers from the restaurant. In the last few months, he and I had become pretty good friends, despite our age difference (he was only twenty two) and what I sometimes also thought was a significant difference in maturity. He also happened to live only a few blocks up the street.

"I think he should have just given you your money back. That's fucking robbery, man."

"Well. I'm going to cut my losses for now."

"You working at Big Shits tonight?"

"No man I'm off, but I tell you what, I think I'm ready to put my two weeks in."

"Really? Aw shit man, no! You can't fucking do that to me! Why?"

"Why? Why wouldn't I? Do *you* like working there?"

"Everybody hates working there!"

"See, there you go. Everybody. It's a horrible place to work. When I worked at my last restaurant a lot of people hated it too, but we stayed on because the money was good at least. The money sucks here. Man, I sometimes made more in one night than I make in three at JB's. And then the fucking management..."

"No no I agree with you man a hundred percent! But that's why you got to stay on! Don't leave me in that shitty place by myself! We've got to work through this."

He patted my leg.

Carter was a funny guy.

"I can't stand that fucker John," I said.

"John's an asshole," Carter agreed, sounding serious for the first time. "He's only nice if you've got a coochie."

"And he's a fucking *dick* if you've got a dick."

"Seriously. I see that fat bastard everyday trying to cozy up to all the ladies and I just want to walk up and tell him—you're a fucking GM! And you're fucking sexist."

"He really is," I said. "He's a genuine creep. Doesn't he look like Bob's Big Boy, only older?"

"He's socially awkward and doesn't give a shit. The dude's from old Hollywood money."

"And Ella..."

"What's wrong with Ella?"

"You like Ella?"

"I mean. She's all right, I guess."

"She's a real bitch to me," I said. "You know, she hired me, so I had a real soft spot for her for a while. She was nice to me, and I thought, you know...well, she is kinda hot. But then one night, like my second week there, for some reason an order never went through to the system and the people were waiting like forty-five minutes before they complained to me."

"That system, dude..."

"I know. So anyway, they complain to her. Long story short they end up walking out just as all the food comes out. And then she tells me, smiling that sharky smile of hers, that I just cost her eighty-whatever dollars. And ever since then she treats me like crap."

"Ella's bipolar I think."

"I really don't care," I said. "Bottom line for me is, between her and that asshole John I don't feel at all respected or appreciated. And since the money sucks I had to go out and get a second job. And you know what? I've only worked this pizza job for a couple of days. So far, I'm nearly making more a night there! So, I'm going to wait and see how my next few nights are. And then, because these guys are actually short staffed, I'm going to see if I can get all the nights I want. If I think I can work this job like five or six nights a week and make enough to get by, I'm out of Big Shits."

"I feel ya." Carter sighed. "Well man I hate to say it..." He stood up, stretched, and picked up his phone. "But I gotta get ready. I'm on at four."

"Do you have GPS on that thing?" I asked, pointing to his phone.

"Why?"

"Do you have one that gives you directions with a voice?"

"No. Why?"

"I'm hearing weird voices on mine."

Chapter 5

I thought I had found my temporary solution to JB's.

But when the office door opened and I saw Ella and her unsmiling eyes and John the Big Boy himself hunched at his desk, I realized I was in for a fight.

"Dylan what's up?" Ella asked.

"I just wanted to let you know that I'm starting a full-time job next week. So I have new availability now," I said, pulling out the folded slip of paper from my ass pocket. I handed it to Ella.

Ella opened the paper and looked down. She furrowed her brow, then made a surprised face that seemed to make the hairline of her dyed-red mop flinch back from her forehead. "Ooh," she said, slightly shaking a no-no. She looked up at me.

"Okay," she said. "JB's requires you to be available for four shifts a week. It doesn't matter lunch or dinner, but it has to be four. And two of them have to be on a weekend."

"I'm sorry," I said. "But I'm only going to be available for those three."

"Here's what you do. I need you to write down four shifts, any four shifts."

"I can't," I said. "I'm going to be working more than forty hours a week at this other job. This is the best I can do."

"Only three night shifts? Ooh. . ." She did a quick half-spin to John. "Tuesday, Wednesday, and Friday?"

"Lemme see," John mumbled, sticking out his hand. Ella passed him the paper.

I looked at John's big back, his cream-colored dress shirt taut. I looked at the back of his head. On the other side of that thing, I could imagine his heavy-lidded eyes, regarding what I'd written with little care.

"I'm not going to change your availability," he said. "You

can go online to our schedules and request your days you want off. You can do that every week. But I'm not changing your availability." He stuck his hand back out with the paper. Ella took it and turned to me.

"Okay, but…if you're not changing my availability," I said. "Then you're not guaranteeing I'll get the time off I need."

Ella pushed the paper back at me. "Write down the four days you're available. I can schedule you three a week, but write down the four you are available for."

I took the paper from her. "Here," she said, and snatched up a pen from her own desk.

"All right," I said, taking the pen.

But I realized what they were really trying to have me do. "I can write down any availability right now, but if I get scheduled, I'm telling you now and in writing I can't work it."

"Uh…" Ella did her turn again at John, who hadn't budged, then back at me. She shrugged.

Going nowhere.

"Well…we'll see what we can do," Ella said.

I bet you will, I thought.

I left them to start my shift; sure that John had not turned to watch me go.

Chapter 6

I walked towards the house, passing a plastic skeleton in the grass. At the edge of the lawn another skeleton was made to look like it was climbing out from a grave, the mock tombstone behind it reading R.I.P. in red letters.

With it getting closer to Halloween, I was seeing more and more decorations going up in Grantwood, particularly in the neighborhoods with the big houses.

I rang the doorbell. On the other side of the door I could hear a piano being played. As I waited, I took a closer look at the thing under the alcove to the left of the large door: A life-sized scarecrow statue sitting on an attached chair.

The door finally opened on a dark-haired man with a 5 o'clock shadow. He gave a slight nod and smile. He looked about my age, and he looked the male model type.

I handed him his pizza, with the little bag of pepper and Parmesan toppings.

"Could you sign this, please?" I asked, taking out the pen from my top pocket. I handed him the pen together with the credit card slip. "I like your decorations."

"Thank you," he said, handing me back my pen and paper. "They're for the kids."

"I bet they love them," I said. "I love Halloween."

"Yeah. It's fun."

"Thank you very much sir. I hope you enjoy."

"You too," he said. "Good bye."

I heard the door close behind me. *Nice man,* I thought. I looked at the slip before putting it away. The man had tipped me $5.

As I walked, I looked up at the view the man had from his place. The houses all looked spacious and well ordered. The sun was going down, making the colors of the day appear to glow in that magic halfway point. The big trees were dropping leaves onto the sidewalk and street. I could hear the sounds of kids playing somewhere close by, that happy playground sound. I liked that sound, though it was making me feel a sudden longing.

It must be nice to live in such a pleasant place, I thought, as I opened my car door, taking one more look around. With a wife and kids. Like that man had.

Wife and kids.

"Goddamnit," I whispered inside the car with my hand on the wheel.

My watery eyes had begun to blur my vision.

Joel was sitting outside the ice cream shop. He turned his head as I approached. I nodded at him, hoping my eyes didn't still look puffy.

"Slow again tonight," he said.

"Is it usually like this?" I asked him.

"No, bro," he said. "This is really slow for a Friday. We've been slow the last week. When we first opened? Dude, we were so busy. There were fewer drivers. We made bank."

"Well, sorry to ruin it," I said.

He laughed. "It's all good. It'll pick back up I'm sure."

"Do you mind if I ask, what's your paycheck usually like every week?"

"It's all right," he said, and shrugged. "I've been working six days a week, on average. My check's like one-fifty, and that's not even counting tips. That's anywhere between thirty to a hundred dollars a night."

Even with only $30 in tips, that was comparable to JB's.

And here I didn't have to give back half my tips to cranky bussers and bartenders.

"Do you like working here?" I asked.

"I do," he said. "Dude, this is like the easiest job I've ever had. It's like zero-stress. All we do is drive around, man. The people here are cool, everybody's nice to you."

"I'm actually thinking of asking for more…" My voice trailed off as a blond woman in a halter-top and short jeans passed by on the sidewalk.

I turned back to Joel and saw that he too had noticed; his

head was still turned.

He turned it back, mouth open. "What were you saying again, bro?" He grinned.

"Hey," I said. "Is it usually like that?"

"All the time. *All* the time. Dude. This is Grantwood." He gestured like it was self-explanatory. "They've been breeding hot here for generations."

Good money, no stress, hot chicks, and all the flexibility I needed as an actor?

Sold—to the man in the yellow pizza hat.

Sitting in bumper-to-bumper traffic on Barrel Road (usually a busy narrow stretch, I'd discovered), I looked out my window.

A young gal was walking on the sidewalk wearing oversized red earmuffs. The rest of her dainty figure was all in black. She had a strange bounce to her walk. I watched her disappear behind a large parked truck.

Someone honked.

I glanced at the rearview mirror, then saw the growing space between me and the car in front. I let up on the brake.

Moving forward, I looked for the young woman and saw her again, her long ponytail of reddish-blonde hair swishing behind her as she bopped along. I passed her.

The traffic slowed. I stopped a few cars short of the traffic light.

Looking back through my driver-side mirror I spotted the gal again, bouncing my way. Watched her getting closer, hoping the light would hold so that I could get a good look at her.

"Come on, come on baby," I said. "Just a little closer. . ."

Ahead the light changed.

"Damnit," I muttered.

Damn it.

The familiar sound of Vic's keys in the door meant the end of my video festivities. *So much for getting through Universal Soldier,* I thought, closing my window on his monitor. I picked up my near empty beer can and swiveled the chair around as he walked in.

"Howdy," I said. "How was work? Any celebrities in tonight?"

"Madonna and Lindsay Lohan."

"No shit? They came in together?"

"Yep."

"What were they like?"

He shrugged his big shoulders. "They were in the VIP area."

I got up off his chair as he came towards me. We stepped around each other as I went over to the little fridge to get another beer.

Sitting on Vic's futon with my beer, I turned towards where he stood at the open closet, his large layered back to me as he got out of his work clothes.

"You coming with me to Mike's Halloween party tomorrow?" I asked him.

"I don't know. We'll see."

I could tell by his tone that Vic was in another one of his dour moods. He often came home with these. He resented working a job while he thought he should be writing.

"I don't have anything to wear," I mused aloud. "Have to try and swing by one of those Halloween costume shops before Big Shits tomorrow. By the way, I've decided I'm quitting JB's. I'm putting in my two week's notice tomorrow."

Vic, now in a pair of red gym shorts, sat down heavily on the swivel chair, which squeaked like he'd crushed some small animal. "Why even give them notice, do you really think they'll give you a reference?"

"Maybe not a glowing one," I said. "But I'd like to quit properly anyway."

Vic didn't say anything. After a moment, he got up and walked over to our kitchen area. He got out the cornflakes and poured himself a bowl. He munched a few spoonfuls.

"I see you fixed that thing with your phone," he said. "What was it?"

"Oh that Horizon Wireless alert? I don't know exactly, but I played around with the settings. I think it was some kind of roaming alert."

"Mmph." Vic turned around and set down his empty bowl. He got out a clean bowl from the top cabinet, poured himself another bowlful and got himself a new spoon.

"But you know what? Now my GPS is acting weird. I hear different voices on it sometimes. That kind of trips me out."

Vic munched, looking down at me. As he got ready to

swallow he held up one pudgy hand, indicating that I should hold on and not talk before he did. “Dude,” he said in a voice thickened by milk. He gave a smirk that lit up his eyes. “Your phone is haunted.”

Chapter 7

The phone rang while I was driving to JB's. It was Mike; I picked the phone up from the nook after doing a quick scan around for cops.

"Hey Mike."

"Yo," he said. "What time do you think you're getting to the party tonight?"

"Aw man," I said, "I don't know if I'm going to be able to make it tonight. I'm sorry." I was, too. I had rushed to the Halloween store on Wilshire, hoping to find a cheap skeleton costume like the one I had in storage back home in the Bay Area. I had found one that came with an inflatable 'boner,' and had stood in line anxiously checking the time as it counted closer towards the start of my shift while also debating in my head whether or not I could really afford to be spending $45 on a Halloween costume. Before I got to the counter, I had realized that I really couldn't. I still owed Vic $150 in rent. I'd put the costume back on the rail on my way out.

"Why not?" Mike asked.

"I don't have a costume."

"That's why you're not coming? Oh dude, don't worry about that. Just come. Trust me, you don't want to miss this. The party last year was *epic!*"

"I'm not going to be that one guy who shows up without a costume looking like a dumb-ass."

"Just improvise something. Come on! I'm sure you've got something at home you could put together."

"Man, I really don't," I said. Earlier in the day I'd gone looking through the two suitcases I kept in the trunk of my car, hoping to find that I had somehow included my skeleton costume among all my clothes that Vic's studio apartment had no room for.

I'd only found my winter bathrobe I'd forgotten I had.

Wait. Bathrobe. Who wore a bathrobe?

"Actually," I said. "I just got an idea. I have a bathrobe. I could just go out and buy a cheap pipe and I'd be Hugh Hefner."

"There you go," Mike said. "That's actually good. I like it!"

I did too, the more I thought about it.

"Maybe I will come," I said.

"No, you're coming. How about Vic? Is he working tonight?"

"I don't think so," I said. "I'll see if I can get him to come too."

"All right. Shoot me a text when you think you're getting out. Maybe we can carpool."

"All right," I said. "Talk to you later."

Hugh Hefner. Not bad for improvising.

I drove towards Century City feeling perky, now that I had a Halloween party to look forward to.

An *epic* Halloween party.

I walked in to JB's with a weird flutter in my stomach.

Don't be nervous. You're almost done here, two more weeks and you never have to step foot in here again.

Ella came out from the swinging kitchen doors up ahead and went over to the computer terminals to assist two other uniformed employees.

Of course, of all the managers it has to be Ella tonight. Fucking Ella...

Walking towards them, I put my hand into my back pocket, feeling for the folded piece of paper on which I'd written my notice.

"D-Man!"

I turned and saw Andy coming towards me with an empty tray in one hand. With his other he made the hand gesture for a shake-five and a fist-bump. I pulled my hand from my pocket and gave him a shake-five and a fist-bump.

"You going to Mike's party tonight?"

"Think so," I said. "You?"

"I think I am too."

I'd believe that when I saw it. Andy was a nice guy, but possibly the biggest flake in LA.

"Hi Dylan!"

I turned towards Ella, surprised at the warm greeting. "Hi

Ella, how are you?"

"I'm great, thank you."

I couldn't help but smile. She had answered me in a soft tone I wasn't used to hearing and appeared genuine for once; no condescending darts aiming at me from out of her shiny black-brown eyes. She actually looked good when she gave a real smile. *Too bad she couldn't be like this more often.* I reached for my back pocket, but she had already turned and walked away.

"Whoa there boy, look at you," Andy said. "Somebody's getting it on with the management."

I walked back to the office hoping to find Ella by herself, but when I looked in through the window there was still no one in there. "Damnit," I muttered. I only had one table, but the dinner rush would be on soon. I wanted to give my notice to Ella sooner rather than later into the shift, but if I waited till the end I risked an audience, as the other servers would be checking out with her too. Better to give her the notice in private, in case it somehow got awkward.

I entered the kitchen on my way out to the dining area, but was waylaid by Eduardo, the kitchen manager. He handed me two tickets. I looked to see what I needed, then got the plates from the line. Balancing three, I took them out with me through the swinging doors. I dropped the food off at the tables.

Looking around the restaurant, I spotted Ella helping out behind the bar while at the same time the hostess was seating my section again. So much for giving my notice at the start of the shift. Oh well, I thought. All I had to do was get through the shift and then I'd be giving my notice, audience or not.

I checked my phone. It was just after seven.

The rush was already over. Now I only had one table. There was a good chance I'd be cut soon, which was fine with me. I'd been low-balled on my tips a couple of times and figured I stood to make less than $40 for the night—another typical night at Big Shits.

I couldn't wait to hand Ella my notice.

I was heading to the back, thinking now was a good time to try and catch her, when I met her coming out from the kitchen.

"I need you to food-run for me," she said.

"What?"

"I had to send Robert home, I've only got Claire. You've only got one table, and they've already got their food, right?"

"Yeah."

"Great, so keep an eye on them until they're closed out and food-run for me."

She turned to go.

"Wait," I said.

"What?" She stood close. Ella was in her speed mode.

"Why am I food-running? I was scheduled section eight."

"Yes you were," she said, "And I need you to food-run. I don't have a food-runner two. So you're my man tonight. Meet up with Claire. Just till the rush dies down—kay?" She turned, her hair almost swatting me in the face.

"When will I be cut, then?"

Ella glanced over her shoulder, not looking at me. "Probably ten."

I watched her big booty as she walked it away from me. Now I wanted to kick it.

Ten? *Fucking Ella!*

"Sir?"

I looked towards my table and saw that the elderly man had his hand up. I walked over.

"We're ready to go now," he said.

"So am I..." I dug in to my apron for the check presenter.

They laughed. This time I didn't.

I met Claire at the line (after accepting a few tickets from the ever-thrusting hand of Eduardo). She looked up at me with her slow-regarding blue eyes. She sniffed. "I don't know why they sent Robert home. I'm the one with the cold."

"I'm trying to get out of here too," I said. "It's so slow, and Ella said she wants me to stay till ten, and..." *I have to get to an epic Halloween party*, I wanted to say. But I already sounded like I was complaining, and felt a little bad. I liked Claire, and I knew they had recently been scheduling her food-running shifts to punish her for whatever reason.

"Ella's being a bitch," she said.

"Yeah she is."

We got our plates off the line and went out the door together, me kicking the door open first and letting her through before I followed.

"Mac Daddy Dylan," Andy said, meeting me at the computer station. I was closing out my last table. "Are you cut?"

"No. Are you?"

"Indeed I am. I'm about to kick this shit. So I'll see you at the party?"

"Sure."

"Dude, I just figured out what I'm going to be tonight. I'm going to be the guy from Breaking Bad."

"Walt?"

Andy grinned. *"Heisenburg.* I've got the goatee and the glasses. I just need to find a bald cap to wear at a Halloween store and I'm set. I've got the hat already. When are you getting cut?"

"Not till ten, Ella said. She has me food-running now."

"What?"

"Robert went home for some reason."

"She has you *food*-running? What did you do?"

"Are you boys on my clock?" Ella had come out from the kitchen.

"I'm not!" Andy said.

Ella walked on. I shook my head. "I got to get back to it. Take it easy."

"That's bullshit, man," Andy said. He gave me a sad look. "Bullshit..."

"Everything about Junior Browne's is bullshit," I muttered, walking in to the kitchen. "That's why we call it Big Shits."

"Here amigo, here," said Eduardo, thrusting more tickets at me.

I wanted to smack Ella. *Of all nights I really want to get out early, she has to decide I'm 'her man' tonight and keep me here. Don't bother* asking *me.*

Outside at the patio area I greeted the table, a well-dressed young couple, and set their plates down.

"This isn't right, no," said the lady, immediately lifting the big plate. "I asked for baked potato, not mashed."

"Oh, I'm sorry," I said, taking back the plate. "So, baked potato. I'll be right back. Everything else look okay?"

The woman scrunched her face, as if I'd said the stupidest thing.

Like a spoiled child.

"Why don't you just go get that first, and then we'll let you know."

"And I'd like another Daiquiri," said the man, turning to me. He shook his empty glass.

"I'll tell your server," I said, knowing from the ticket that it was Monica.

"Going to take this?" said the man, lifting his glass.

"Nope."

I went in through the swinging kitchen doors. "Eduardo," I said, showing him the plate, "This is supposed to have baked potato, not mashed."

"Where's the ticket, amigo, where's the ticket?"

I uncrumpled the ticket and handed it over.

"It says *mashed* potato, amigo! Can you see?" He held up the ticket, with a look on his face that made me want to throw a fist at it.

"It's not my table, I didn't take their order. Can you fix this? I have to go find Monica because the table wants to order more drinks."

"Pinche wedo," he muttered, grabbing the plate off me. He turned towards the line. "Miguel!"

I don't have to put up with this bullshit, I thought.

Why even give them two weeks notice?

I pulled out my phone to check the time and saw that I had gotten a text. Probably from Mike wondering when I was going to get off.

Time for a little bathroom break.

"I'll be right back," I told Claire. I turned the corner. Realizing I hadn't actually registered the time, I pulled out my phone.

"Are you on my clock?"

I looked up and saw Ella ahead walking towards me.

"I'm just checking the time."

"Are you on my clock?"

"I'm just checking the *time*, Ella."

"We have clocks on the computer terminals. Teams members are not allowed to have their phones out while on the floor. It's a rule here."

I knew it was a rule. And I knew that I had seen Eduardo checking his phone constantly.

"Is it okay for managers?"

"I'm sorry?" Ella was walking back up to me with a squinty look on her face.

"Is it okay for managers to use their phones? Because I've

seen Eduardo on his all night."

"You're asking me if a *manager*, who has to check for updates for the *company*...?"

"You sure that's all he's doing?"

Ella showed me her white teeth, blood rising in her tanned cheeks. I realized I no longer cared what she was doing.

"You know what?" she said, giving the air between us a sharp jab with her finger. "If you seriously feel *that* strongly that *managers. . ."*

I wasn't listening. I was focusing instead on her mouth. Chomping.

"...we can discuss it. But while..."

I looked into her black eyes. Looking at me like I was plankton. I pulled out my phone and held it up.

"...on *my* time..."

I tapped the screen. "You know what?" I said, interrupting. "Now you're on *my* time." I dropped the phone back into my pocket and stepped past her.

"We are not finished."

I untied my apron and let it fall as I walked towards the door, knowing that I had my tips secured in my back pocket.

Cash me out.

"Come back. Dylan. Hey! *Dylan!*"

I stepped through the swinging doors. Walked through the dining area, looking straight ahead, and out the front door. I was mad, was sure that I looked mad and blushing, but I also felt myself getting lighter as I descended to the lower level of the parking garage via the escalator. I found my car and got in, realizing I only had one job now. Already I was feeling so much the better for it.

On my iPod I found Saxon's cover of *Ride Like the Wind*, hit play, and turned up the volume.

Chapter 8

"Come on man, it's a house party! There's going to be tons of chicks there. You really rather sit in here on your computer all night?"

Vic slowly turned away from his monitor. The look on his big face was one I was getting used to and didn't like. His jowls seemed to frown more so than his mouth.

"Dude. I have work to do."

"You've always got work to do, but what kind of writer are you going to be if you never get out? Come on man. How long has it been since we went out together? Everybody's in costume—what more of an icebreaker do you want?"

"I don't have a costume," he said, turning his big naked back to me.

"Well let's improvise something, I did! Come on. Surely you got something in your wardrobe."

"Like what?"

Like usual, Vic was looking for every negative.

"You've got the cowboy hat."

"You want me to be a fucking cowboy?"

"Then...why don't you just wear shorts and let your hair down and you can be a wrestler? You'll be half naked already, the chicks'll love it!"

"It's all right," he said. "You go. I'll pass."

"How about your work uniform? Looking all sharp-dressed, why don't you just do that and wear my shades and tie your hair back and you can be one of the men in black?"

"No one's going to think I'm one of the men in black."

"No one's going to *care* what you are anyway! It's a Halloween party—it's just supposed to be fun!"

"I'm not in the mood."

"Fine," I said, giving up. "I'm going to take a shower."

Toweling myself dry, I realized I'd been pushing Vic. Though I only wanted the big guy to have a good time with me, you had to want to go to a party. At this point it was probably best to drop my case and just let him do his thing.

I opened the door.

Vic was standing a few feet away, scowling. Wearing a sailor's cap, a black vest and light blue pajama pants.

"What the fuck?" I laughed, looking at his cap. "Where the hell did you get that?"

He grinned. "It was my grandfather's. I'll get a pipe too. I'll be Popeye, the Samoan Sailor Man."

I laughed, clapping my hands. "I love it!"

Mike came out of his house wearing jeans and a black T-shirt with playing cards taped to the front. He was carrying a case of beer.

"I'm a card shark!" he said, sitting awkwardly in the passenger seat. "See?" Leaning forward, he turned, showing the fin-shaped piece of cardboard that he had painted black and taped to his back.

"So how do we get to your friend's place?" I asked him.

"I have the address. You got GPS?"

"Sure do."

He gave me the address and I put it into my phone.

While Sally instructed us, I told Mike about my exit from JB's.

"Ella's gotta be pissed," he said. "Good for you man. I gotta get outta there next, soon as I can find myself a better serving job."

"In one thousand feet. *Turn right onto Pico Boulevard."*

"Did you guys hear that?" I asked.

"Holy *shit,"* said Mike.

"Daaamn!" exclaimed Vic from the backseat.

"It's weird, huh?" I said, glad to have someone witnessing my GPS voice changing from Sally to the slower, sultrier-sounding British voice (who I'd been referring to in my head as 'Elizabeth').

"It's freakin *hot,"* Mike said.

"She's looking at us!"

"What are you—?" I had looked to my left and I saw the

woman in the car driving alongside us. She was wearing a black hood, but I could see some of her long dark hair flowing out behind her ears.

She was looking at me.

She narrowed her cat-like eyes and smiled, showing vampire fangs beneath thin red lips.

I looked ahead and saw that we were approaching a green light.

"Turn red, turn red, turn red..."

The light turned yellow. I slowed down, looked over and saw that she was doing the same.

I pulled up alongside her and lowered my window.

"Invite her to the party!"

"All right, shut the fuck up," I hissed. "I'm about to."

I turned to our neighbor, reached out with my arm and, pushing my hand against the car door, pulled myself a little towards her.

"Excuse me!" I yelled, indicating that she should roll her window down. As she did, I reached back and took the pipe out from my mouth. I held it out to her in what I thought was a 'father knows best' gesture. "Do you know where you're going, Miss?"

She looked at my pipe and gave it thumbs up. "I like it," she said. She smiled again, showing us her real-looking fangs.

I winked at her, slightly turning my head to exaggerate the gesture. "Where art thou going, Lady of the Night?"

"To a party."

"Follow us then! We'll show you the way."

"Hey," Mike said nudging me. I turned to look at him. "Ask her if it's Rich and Dean's party."

I turned back to the young woman, but her window was already going up.

"Hey!"

The window closed, but I saw the woman inside smiling. Her tongue beckoned out the side of her mouth and glided over a fang.

Ahead the light had turned green.

"Follow her!" Vic called from the backseat.

I kept my eye on the silver car as we moved further up Pico Boulevard towards the gold-glittered skyline of Century City, watching for openings in the lane next to us. When I saw one I signaled, but seeing the silver car already four cars ahead, changed my mind.

"She's getting away," Vic said, sounding annoyed and spoiled.

"Forget her," I said, starting to feel stupid. "What do you wanna do, follow her till she parks somewhere and then we gangbang her? She's either going to another party or she's going to ours, and if she's going to ours, great, we'll see her there. If not, there'll be a lot more like that where we're going. Right Mike?"

"Oh yeah."

We drove further up Pico, losing sight of the vampire girl in the silver car.

The GPS voice switched back to Sally, who told us to turn right. I went as ordered, not knowing I would later have reason to wonder what might have happened if I'd kept following the car to the tune of Elizabeth's voice.

Costumed people passed us as we turned up the driveway towards the house. I could already hear laughter and the bass of music from inside. We went under a stucco archway decorated with fake cobwebs and little glowing jack o' lantern lights and found ourselves in an enclosed lawn area, the cement path turning right and leading to the front entrance. A couple framed in the bright light from inside the open doorway were gesturing at one another; a lanky shape with a homburg hat and a curvaceous female in a sprouted tutu dress.

"Excuse me folks," Mike said, "Pardon me…"

I nodded at the tall man masked like the Green Hornet.

The three of us inside, we stood together.

"Well," I said, looking around at the groups of people standing or sitting around the living room, "this looks like my kind of place."

"Yep, yep," Mike said. "Let's head outside and see who's here."

We followed Mike around throngs of costumed people, passing a kitchen and a moving full-body cow suit.

The large backyard was packed with people, reminding me of an outdoor concert, and in contrast to the inside of the house, where the dimmer lighting made it seem festively moody, the bright lights put everyone in the spotlight. The energy was ramped up as well.

I turned around to see if Vic was still following me, and he was standing right behind, surveying the scene with his usual grim focus. I was going to ask him what he thought, but all of a sudden, the absurdity of seeing my ever-serious Samoan friend looking like a sailor going out for a night at the S & M club got me laughing.

"What's up?" he asked, beginning to grin.

I coughed. "Did you see that guy in the cow costume?"

"No."

"He's back there in the kitchen. You should go check it out."

I turned and saw Mike being greeted by people he knew, recognizing Rob, one of his housemates whom I had met once before. Rob saw me at the same time and lifted his beer in salute.

"And who's Hugh?" asked a tall Wonder Woman.

"I'm Hugh," I said, extending my hand. We shook and she told me her real name. I told her it was nice to meet her.

Mike introduced me to the rest.

"Where's the beer?"

Mike bent down, took out a beer from the case at his feet, and handed it to me. I popped the top.

"Listen," he said, speaking close to my ear. "I'm going to hide this case somewhere. Otherwise we'll never see any of these beers."

"Okay," I said, though I wasn't sure why we needed to hide them. There seemed to be plenty of beer; I'd noticed a keg. Our beer was only Pabst.

Mike went off.

After tossing my empty in a garbage can, I walked back inside the house.

A few gals stood to my immediate left: A Nurse, a Vampiress, and a School Girl. School Girl was looking at me while listening to her friend. I winked. She gave an involuntary twitch of the mouth towards a smile. I made a show of putting my pipe to my mouth and taking a long, considering puff before picking it out from my lips and holding it out to her.

"Excuse me," I said. "How old are you?"

"Eighteen," she said.

I held her gaze for a few seconds, then looked to Nurse, to Vampiress.

"Too old," I said, turning away.

The gals burst out laughing behind me as I walked towards

the kitchen.

I got to the fridge and pulled it open.

Chock full of beer like I'd been hoping, the middle shelves were nothing but green Rolling Rocks, silver Coors Lites, white Modellos, and blue Bud Lites. *No Pabst, though*. Maybe Mike had something after all. I picked out a Coors Lite.

Suddenly I seemed to be hearing the bittersweet theme from *Phantasm*. I moved through the crowd.

Near where School Girl and her gals were standing a door opened into another room where the lights were off. I saw a few people moving. The *Phantasm* theme had been invaded by a beat, and was now a dance song.

I went in and saw a DJ standing behind a turntable sandwiched between two large speakers. He was wearing a Cat-in-the-Hat top hat and pink-rimmed sunglasses that were too large for his face. He smiled bright whites that seemed to glow under the purple-black lighting. People stood around in a loose cluster to allow the dancers room in the middle. I watched the gyrating until the *Phantasm* theme returned to the mix, and then I needed to leave the room.

Concentrating on getting that musical pattern that reminded of loss and longing out of my head, I found my way back to Mike and his buddies. Mike saw me set down my can next to a collection of empties that had gathered by a lawn chair and handed me a Pabst.

"The beer is behind the trashcan in the alley, near the front of the house," he said into my ear.

I nodded as I saw the same Vampiress I had approached inside joining the group.

She began talking to the Wonder Woman gal as though they already knew each other. Watching the two, I found my eyes being drawn more to the luscious form in the tight black dress. The way Vampiress was standing, I could see the crease of her rump. From there I followed what I could see of her legs down to her pale ankles. Looking up at her face, she looked young and so fresh, even though the streaks of white hair extensions she had added to her black hair were meant to make her look like an ancient Countess.

Wonder Woman caught me looking. "Hey!"

"Hey what?"

"Have you met Hugh?"

Vampiress turned and stepped forward. "What's your

name?"

"I'm Dylan," I said.

She passed the glass she was holding into her other and extended her hand.

"Roxanne."

She put her soft hand into my grip.

"We're taking off, babe," Wonder Woman said, putting her hand on Roxanne's shoulder. Roxanne turned around. They kissed each other on the lips. "See you at The Circle."

Wonder Woman left.

Roxanne turned back to me.

"Cheers," she said.

"Cheers," I said, tapping her glass with my Pabst. "What are you drinking?"

"I don't know," she said. "Red wine?"

"Nice."

"I didn't know you liked Pabst."

"Huh?"

"*Hugh.*"

"Yeah, well. Every now and then I like to have a drink with the boys."

Roxanne laughed and looked away. A lot of the group had left. She looked back up at me, eyes expecting. I was starting to think she was a little drunk. Or a little in to me.

"So what was she talking about, your friend? You guys going out tonight?"

Roxanne summoned me closer. I bent forward, turning my ear to her mouth so she could shout into it.

"We're going to Santa Monica!"

"Nice. You driving?"

"No, Hell no," she mouthed. She put her glass to her lips.

"You need another drink?" I asked.

"I should probably go find my friends."

"All right."

"You going in?" she asked.

I followed her in to the house.

"So where's your friends?" I asked.

She was looking around. I noticed bottles of wine accompanied with clear plastic wine glasses, a couple of which were half-filled, left out on one of the snack tables. "I'm going to get another beer," I said. "Do you want some more wine?"

"Sure."

I went in to the kitchen and got another beer. When I returned Roxanne had already switched her empty glass for a full one.

We toasted.

Roxanne was doing a lot of looking around, while I was trying to think of things to say to lead to my getting her phone number. That clock of opportunity was ticking. I was wondering whether it was a good idea to recite my graveyard poem when a gal dressed up like Storm from the X-Men came up and Roxanne suddenly became animated. I couldn't hear what they were saying, but when I caught Storm's eye, I winked. She didn't wink back but gestured with her head to Roxanne, and the two turned to go.

I followed the girls around the corner and in to the living room, now cast in a warm orangey glow because someone had lit a fire. To the left of the fireplace there was an open door to another room, where the girls were headed. Just then I happened to spot Vic standing against the wall across the room. He wasn't talking to anyone (no surprise there), just standing and looking around like he was looking for someone in particular, his head held high as he turned it. Scanning like the Terminator, and not seeing anything.

The clock was probably ticking there too. Knowing Vic as I did, he'd come find me within the hour and want to go home.

Nobody likes to leave a good party. Except my buddy Vic.

Inside the small room beyond the fireplace a few people sat around a little coffee table on a black loveseat and matching sofa chairs. Roxanne greeted a few people while I stood back, grinning at nothing. I couldn't hear anyone over the music and voices. My eyes wandered to a gal sitting alone in one of the chairs. She looked gothic and pissed off. She looked up at me, then down and straight ahead to whatever she was thinking. I thought of giving her my Hugh Hefner line, as I stared at her red lipstick-coated lips, puckered like a little valentine heart.

Gothic gal got up and left the room. Roxanne moved to the empty chair before I did and sat down, Storm taking a seat across from her on the loveseat. Wondering whether Roxanne realized I was still there, I moved to the chair.

I tapped Roxanne on the shoulder and she looked up.

"Scoot over," I said.

She did and I sat down. Our legs pressed together.

Storm gave me a wary look.

"Oh, this is Hugh," Roxanne said.

Storm flicked her eyes back to me and bent forward, extending her hand while smiling; painfully, it seemed. "Hi," she said.

Her hand felt thin and cold.

Leaning back, I took the room in as the two continued their conversation without me. The place might've been a study that had been cleared out. I looked at the other people. Two gals sat close together in between Storm and a big black guy who was obviously a body builder. The guy was wearing a toga and a laurel wreath.

We met eyes.

He smiled. "What's happening over there? *Hugh?*" He laughed.

"Hail," I said, lifting my drink. "Caesar."

"Cheers," he said. "But I don't have a glass. I'm already drunk."

"Good for you," I said. "That's what I'm working up to."

"Yeh it's hard work."

Storm got up and left. I turned to Roxanne. "Hey, how ya doin'?" I asked in my Rocky impression.

She nodded, her plastic glass to her lips.

I couldn't tell if I was being a pest. Though her leg was still pressed against mine.

"Lots of drama," she said.

"What's the drama?"

"One of my friends is drunk off her ass."

"Is she here?"

"No, Santa Monica. One of my friends called her and she sounded so drunk my friend could hardly understand her. All she got for sure was something about having slapped a guy in the face. She recently broke up with her boyfriend."

"I see," I said. "How's yours?"

"My boyfriend?"

"I meant your wine, but sure. How's he?"

"I don't have a boyfriend," she said.

"Really? Why not?"

"Hey I ain't complaining. It's fun to be free."

"I don't like em either. Wanna feel free with me sometime?"

"What do you mean?"

"I mean, give me your phone number now and I'll call you up for some free time later."

"I'll give you my number."

Putting my arm around the back of the chair, I moved the front of my robe over and found my phone in the big pocket. As I pulled it out, I happened to look over at Caesar. He was staring with tired eyes and without lifting a hand, he blew me a kiss.

"Here, I'll give it to you and you call me."

I tapped in the numbers and hit the call button. Roxanne took out a ringing phone from her purse. "I got it," she said.

Someone tapped me on the shoulder and I looked up. It was Vic, the Sailor Man, grinning. "Hey," I said, "What's happenin Boss? Good party. Hey." I leaned over to him and he turned his ear as I asked, lowering my voice, "Are you enjoying yourself?"

"I'm not feeling it," he said. "You ready to go soon?"

"Already? No."

"So you want me to walk home?"

"No, but...why don't you hang out a while? This place is full of chicks."

"Stuck-up bitches."

"Someone say something to you?"

"Look man, I didn't want to come out tonight."

"Look, give it another half-hour at least. You're still not feeling it then, I'll give you a ride home. Fair enough?"

"Half-hour? Sure, man."

"Why don't you get a drink?"

"Nah." He stood up.

I turned to Roxanne as Vic was leaving the room.

"Who was that?" Roxanne asked.

"His name is Ganley Smitherwick. Do you need another drink?"

"No, I'm going." She bent forward and picked up her purse. Pressing her leg almost painfully against mine, she tried to stand up. She grunted, and fell back into the seat as I laughed.

She looked at me. I leaned in and kissed her.

After a moment she broke from our kiss and turned away. She had kissed me back, but only slightly.

Putting her hand on my shoulder, she pushed down and got up. "It was nice to meet you."

"Same here," I said. "Call you later."

Roxanne left.

I looked over at Caesar, who appeared to be snoozing, then got up and left the room.

I saw someone dressed like Walt in his Heisenberg guise

from *Breaking Bad*, and remembered Andy.

No, it *was* Andy. He'd actually made it.

"Walt!"

Andy saw me coming and smiled. I had to laugh at the sight of him. He had found a bald cap somewhere and really looked the part.

"Dyl-laaan…" His eyes looked glassy as he gave my hand a good shake.

We caught up as we went in to the kitchen to get more beers. I told Andy about how I had walked out on Ella and JB's. Like Mike, he found the whole thing very amusing.

We went outside to find Mike.

I was leading the way back to the corner to where I'd last spied Mike and some of his friends, drifting through skunky-smelling patches of pot smoke, when I saw a gal dressed like Red Riding Hood coming my way. She grinned at me, looking wicked beneath her red hood. I winked at her. She kept her eyes locked on me as we moved towards each other.

"Are you lost?" I asked her.

She was a petite blonde with big boobs. She didn't blink but stared up at me, not changing her grin.

"I am," she said. "Are you the wolf?"

"Yes, I'm Hugh Hefner," I said. I clamped the pipe in my mouth and found her hand. It was warm. I brought it up to my mouth and gave it a light peck from the side.

"You looking for girls, Hugh?"

"No, I'm looking for *ladies*, Hon—young and attractive ones. Where were you going?"

"Nowhere."

"Nowhere?"

She just stared up at me, still grinning, her thin eyebrows arching. I wondered if she was drunk. I wondered if I was. I kissed her. She kissed back, opening her mouth enough for a little tongue. I hoped my friends were seeing, particularly Vic.

We broke away, and I put my arm around her waist, turning her with me. I saw that Andy had joined up with Mike and was talking. Mike looked over at me.

I looked at my Red Riding Hood, and kissed her again. This time she didn't seem so into it.

"I have to go to the bathroom," she said.

"You want me to go in with you?"

"No."

"Well I meant...okay. You coming out here again?"

"Yeah."

"All right, see you in a few." She turned and left.

I went over to Mike and Andy.

"Whoa there," Mike said.

"Where'd your little Red Riding Hood go?" Andy asked.

"I let her go take a piss," I said. "You got any Pabst left?" I asked Mike.

"I told you, in the alley near the front of the house."

"Oh that's right. You want one?"

"Sure."

I went back into the house. Near the front door I saw my sexy Red Riding Hood talking to a cop. I saw the drink in his hand and knew he wasn't a real one. The guy was taller than me and pretty big. I walked past them and out the door.

"Motha-*fuckah!*"

I had stepped off the front step and saw two figures in the middle of the lawn. As I walked down the walkway, I saw that one was a short black female dressed in white stockings and a pink skirt. On her head was a gold-colored crown. She was standing with her hands on her hips and looking down at a kneeling figure in oversized red pants. When I got close, I could see that the kneeling figure was somebody dressed as a clown, with a polka dotted shirt and curly orange wig, and looked about to be getting sick.

The clown turned his head, the white make-up lugubrious with the smeared red around the mouth.

The clown spat into the grass. *"What?"* he said in a strained voice. "Pttgh...*what?"*

I walked past and turned to go under the stucco archway.

Found the alleyway and saw the trash can at the end by the fence. Behind the trashcan I found Mike's case of Pabst. I pulled out a couple of cans.

I had passed the couple on the grass on my way back up to the house when I heard "BLUUURRRGH" behind me, followed by the voice of the princess: "Motha-*fuckah!"*

Red Riding Hood and the cop appeared to be in deep conversation. I went out back and found Mike and Andy.

Vic joined us.

"So what's up with this dance floor over here?" Mike said, indicating the open patio doors to the room with the DJ. Purple light pulsed out at us.

"You down to get jiggy with it?" I asked Vic.

"Let's get down!" Andy yelled.

Mike led the way.

There were more people inside the room now standing around the circle with a few dancing within. Mike and Andy stood at the edge looking on, Mike bobbing his head, Andy drunkenly swaying his hips. After a moment Andy stepped in and started shaking at one of the girls dancing. Mike jumped in too, rhythmically raising a leg up while clapping his hands towards the opposite. Even Vic began to move on the outskirt of the circle.

I gulped my beer, finishing the can, and set it down on a table.

I jumped in and began to dance. In a matter of seconds, the others all cleared out, leaving me in the empty center. I untied my robe and opened it, showing everybody my boxer shorts. I got cheers. I pulled the belt from the loops of my robe and whipped it.

I saw Andy on the outside of the circle. I whipped it at him.

Saw a gal and whipped it at her.

"Go Dylan!"

I lassoed it above my head.

"Go Dylan!"

I fully opened my robe to more cheers, letting it fall behind me. Spreading my arms in a Karate stance, I dropped down into the push-up position and started doing push-ups on the floor.

"Go Dylan! Go Dylan!"

I heard my friends laughing while I kept at it.

When the song ended I got up and did my version of the Rocky-at-the-top-of-the-steps dance, and got applause from Andy and Mike.

"Dude. That was fucking *awesome*," Andy said, laughing.

"I don't know about you guys, but I need another beer," I said.

"Fucking Dylan!"

I got my robe back on, leaving it open in the front, and left the room.

Vic found me in the kitchen.

"How's it going, fella?" I asked.

"You ready to go?"

"Not really."

"That's fine dude. I'll walk."

"No I'm giving you a ride."

"Dude! You said in a half-hour. That was almost an *hour*

ago."

I cracked open my beer. "All right, let me finish this beer and we'll go."

"Forget it." Vic turned.

"Vic. Wait."

He kept going.

After a couple of seconds, I started to follow. "Vic! Hey!"

He turned around and waited at the front door.

"Okay, okay," I said, catching up. I put my beer down.

"You okay to drive?" he asked at the car.

"I'm good."

Vic didn't say anything along the ride, and I was glad. I wanted to look calm and unconcerned, even though I was really pissed at him. I gritted my teeth on the stem of the pipe.

As soon as I pulled up to his place, he thanked me (actually sounding appreciative) and got out.

I hurried off into the night again.

Fucking Vic has to take me away from a good party!

I had already passed the lights of Century City when I realized I didn't know when I was turning off Pico.

At a stoplight I pulled out my phone and tapped the Navigation icon and selected the last address used. I dropped the phone into the nook and awaited Sally's instruction.

Instead, a guttural voice barked out.

"What the. . .?" I slowed the car.

"Go-*ink* leffgh..." the low voice said, trailing off into static.

Sounded like it meant *Turn Left*, so that's what I did at the next light.

Seeing no immediate traffic, I looked down again at the phone.

The voice had spoken with the grunting of a pig, but sounded more like a human voice when played back at an unnaturally low speed. Like demon cartoon characters or evil robots on TV. And unlike the other two commanding voices I'd heard on the GPS, this one was undeniably masculine. Though it didn't make me think of a man.

The arrows on the screen instructed me to go another 1000 feet, then I was to turn right.

Wait a second, I thought. *I don't remember turning left off Pico…*

Up about a block, the voice barked, "**Go-*ink* roighttt…**"

I turned right at the light, then looked down at the phone to see what it was doing. The arrow on the screen indicated I should continue on Western for 1.5 miles. That sounded more like it.

But what was up with the new voice? It was *creepy*.

As I went along, I thought of the possibilities. Some kind of glitch when the phone was in the middle of rerouting. A signal that my battery was low. Or, like Sally and Elizabeth, this was just another voice utilized for giving commands. Whoever the phone makers were, maybe they thought switching up the voices every now and then made things somehow more interesting.

I kept driving, waiting for more instruction, glancing down at the phone every so often to see how close I was getting to my turn.

At 0.2 distance I slowed, anticipating turning at one of the next traffic lights.

After passing a couple, I looked down at the phone.

It said to continue for 2.5 miles on Western.

Two and a half more miles? That seemed too far.

But then again, what exactly did I remember? I had been busy following a girl dressed like a vampire while listening to the hoots and hollers of my passengers. How much attention had I even paid to where I was going?

"**Go-*ink* leffgh…**"

I turned left, onto Manchester.

The area I was going through looked very run-down. Compared to what I was used to on the west side, these streets were so quiet.

Then again, I wasn't in the west side of LA anymore was I?

Where was I?

I was on a street lined with low buildings that were all shuttered up and closed. Except for a couple liquor stores I had passed, nothing looked open out here. Just abandoned or shut for the night.

Was this some kind of back-way back?

What if I had picked the wrong address in my phone after all?

What if the Demon Voice was leading me astray?

I wanted to laugh at that idea, but instead I put up my window.

I stopped at a red light. At the corner to my left there was a small gray building of a liquor store, and along the wall furthest from the entrance I saw a group of guys standing around. They all looked thuggish to me, and they were all looking *at* me. The lone car in the road.

One guy wearing a long checkered flannel suddenly straightened up. I looked away to see if the light had turned, but it was still red.

When I looked back, flannel man was bolting toward me.

Ducking, I turned and hit the gas. A few seconds later I heard the sound of shattering glass.

No denying it now. I was in a bad area.

My heart still hammering, I came up to the next light as it went red, but I had no intention of stopping. I was going to turn a left at the intersection and floor it back up to more familiar territory.

I slowed down to make the turn, looking both ways for oncoming traffic.

"Go-*ink* leffgh..."

This time I obeyed the command only because I was already turning.

How the hell did I get out here?

I had turned onto a narrow street and wanted to speed up but the riding was bumpy, thanks to so many potholes.

Up ahead I saw a shopping cart left in the middle of the road.

Turning my head from left to right, I realized I was still hunching. I straightened up in my seat. As rough as the area looked, I was surely safer now that it was residential. No one was out and about.

The homes on either side of the street looked small and dark and had bars on the windows.

I'll just go up a few more blocks then turn a left and swing back onto Manchester and fly back the way I came. That way I'd come out having bypassed the liquor store and the broken glass on the road.

"Go-*ink* leffgh..."

"Yeah fuckin right!"

Now I *knew* which direction I needed to go at the intersection ahead.

I slowed, seeing that I was actually approaching a T, my headlights lighting on a tall chain link fence and graffiti-covered wall. As I got closer to the wall, I began to make out a glowing white shape in the midst of all the scrawled tagging.

I stopped, staring at a large Donald Duck caricature somebody had artfully spray-painted. This Donald had an evil look on its face and appeared to be butt-fucking one of the fry kids from McDonald's.

"Go-*ink* leffgh..."

"Shut up," I said.

I slowly began inching out and to the right, seeing that the turn looked pretty sharp. I heard what sounded like a glass pop.

"Shit," I whispered, feeling my heart begin to race.

All I need now is a flat tire.

Just as I realized I was only turning in to a dark alleyway littered with trash, the ground an obstacle course of shopping carts and old crates, a dog started barking.

I turned and looked behind to see a bank of yellow light at the other end of the alley coming from the open mouth of what looked like an old shed, in front of which I saw the shadowed form of a large tethered dog.

"Christ!" I turned and faced front.

Up ahead a figure was ambling towards me.

I hit the brake.

It looked like a man with an oblong head, a spiky tuft of hair sprouting from the top like a pineapple. It walked with one thin arm outstretched to flag me down.

I hit my fist against the horn. The figure didn't flinch.

The man that stepped into the glare of my headlights had a long sagging face beneath the fabric binding up his dreadlocks. His dirty blue trench coat was open, revealing taut brown skin lined with muscle and bone, the matted mass of pubic hair the only thing visible between his legs. I looked back up at the face and saw it shaking slowly from side to side, the eyes rolled back and mouth open. His other arm was behind his back.

I found reverse and took my foot off the brake. Keeping my eyes on the bum in front, I lightly stepped on the gas.

The light behind got brighter a second before I heard the start of an engine.

I looked over my shoulder and saw the front of a car emerging from the shed.

Turning back to front while at the same time moving my foot to the brake, I jerked to a stop.

The bum was rushing towards me brandishing a tennis racket.

I turned my wheel to the right.

The bum ran past the front of my car. Just as I saw his hand reaching the door handle I flipped the switch. The door locked and I ducked.

I felt the pull at the door, followed by loud tapping at the window.

Head down, I turned the wheel all the way, then sat up.

The bum had gone around to the other side and was blocking me. He stood ready to swing the racket, his eyes wide and mouth foaming.

More afraid of being pushed into the alley and trapped by the car behind, I stepped on the gas and lurched towards the street.

The bum leapt onto my hood and somersaulted up the windshield. I heard the body thump off the back and kept going.

"In eight hundred feet. . ."

I swerved at the sound of Sally's voice, knocking aside the shopping cart.

"Where the *fuck* were you?"

Chapter 9

"I think you're crazy."

I took another sip from my coffee and closed my eyes, savoring the magic hot liquid.

Listening to myself as I had described to Vic my night ride into south central LA; how I had been led there by a demonic-sounding voice on my phone, I realized how loopy it sounded.

But Vic and I had gone out to my car. Neither of us imagined the dents on the roof and hood, left there by the creepy Tennis Bum.

"So, what happened to that car that was trying to block you in the alley?"

"I didn't look back until I was at the top of the street, and only saw their headlights from a distance. Luckily, they didn't follow. They must have stopped at the Tennis Bum."

"You might have really hurt him."

"What was I supposed to do? For all I knew, he was trying to get me trapped in that alley so they could rob me, do god-knows-what."

"How do you know they were trying to trap you in that alleyway? What if it was just some regular people coming out of their garage?"

The thought had occurred to me too, but I didn't see how it made much difference. "You weren't there, man. Trust me, you would have done the same. Place had a very bad vibe."

Vic swiveled around in his chair to face the monitor on his desk once more. He was going back to his work.

Finishing my coffee, I decided I was going to go out for a walk before I had to leave for work. It would do my body some good. And Vic was annoying me.

"That's really weird."

Hooper and I were on the wall. I'd just told him about my bizarre night. He was looking through my phone, checking the settings for anything unusual. Finding nothing amiss, he handed it back to me.

"You going out again tonight?" he asked.

"For what?"

"Halloween."

I had forgotten tonight was actually Halloween. Last night had been Devil's Night, as my Dad called it: The night of pranks.

"I don't really plan on it. Got my fix last night, I think. You?"

"Me and the girlfriend are going to stay in for the trick-or-treaters." He shrugged. "Smoke lots of pot?"

I was wondering what I might do with my evening when my phone rang.

"You're up."

I had parked in the first spot next to the podium where one of the valet attendants always stood by the alleyway exit. As I walked to my car, I passed Jorge, the valet attendant, standing at the entrance to the car park.

He turned his head in my direction. "Amigo!"

"Hola Jorge!" I said, leaning the pizza bag against the rear door as I unlocked the front. "How are you?"

"Okay! Kind of tired."

"I hear you."

I got in my car.

"One-one-nine-two," I said into the phone, looking at the dispatch. "Ohio Street."

I put the phone into the nook as it calculated, wondering what I would do if I heard the Demon Voice again.

"Turn left onto Gorman Avenue!" Sally said.

There she is again!

The young gal was up ahead, dressed the same way as before: All in black with big fuzzy red earmuffs, though it wasn't the slightest bit cold outside in the early evening. She was bopping down the road facing my direction.

I looked over at her as she approached.

She walked with her head down, her small oval face pale. I thought I could make out a spattering of freckles on her cheeks. Her thin eyebrows were slightly arched, and the shape of her mouth showed amusement. She didn't look up at all as she passed.

I stopped the car.

Was that a grin of mischief or pleasure?

Looking in the driver's side mirror, I watched the retreating figure. The gal had turned. She was now walking up a shrub-lined path leading behind a big house.

Going to her boyfriend's? Was that why she was grinning? Or was she coming *back* from her boyfriend's?

The gal was gone.

Damn it.

The new driver, Jeffrey, a barrel-shaped guy with a black flattop, sauntered up and silently sat down next to Paul, who was busy texting on his phone. There was now a line of us on the wall, waiting to be called. Hooper was the only one out on delivery.

"I think you're lucky, man," Joel said, shaking his head. "That could have been way, way worse."

"Oh what's this, bro?" Paul asked, suddenly listening.

"Dude, this guy got lost in the ghetto last night. He ended up stuck in an alleyway."

"Ho-OH shit, bro! What happened?"

I repeated the story for Paul and Jeffrey. Like Joel, neither of them seemed particularly impressed that I had been led by an evil-sounding voice from my phone.

Everybody seemed to think I was making that part up.

"Damn, bro!" Paul said. "Hey though you know what, bro? You were lucky, bro."

Joel chimed in. "Right? That's what I said."

"Naw. Seriously. You know the thing about those areas, bro, is that you're all right to drive through em during the day, like on the main street? You'll be fine. It's when you go into the residential, bro, where there's a lot of alleyways? That's how you get punked. You got fools there just waiting for that shit, bro. They see a new car? Dude, you're fucked."

"That's the thing about LA," Jeffrey added. "It's mostly nice, but you go into a bad area, it's like, all of a sudden, it's *bad.*"

"Yeah, you're lucky," Joel said. "I'm glad you got out of that one all right, Dylan. I'm real glad. Oh, but how's your car?"

"It's got a nice few dents in it now."

"That sucks."

"What bro, that's a brand-new car bro!"

"Don't I know?"

"Shiiit..."

Joel was getting a call on his phone. He got up. "All right, gentlemen..."

He soon reappeared around the corner.

"Hey guys," he hollered. "Everybody's up."

"It's gonna be busy tonight bro," Paul said, walking besides me.

I'd been on Barrel Road for more than a half-hour and had barely gone a few blocks.

There goes your tip, bro, said Paul's mocking voice in my head. *Ho-ho-hah!*

I watched costumed children and adults walking up and down the sidewalks. There was a little light left in the sky, but the trick-or-treating was on.

I wondered what sort of party Earmuff Girl would be going to tonight. What she'd be dressed as.

A family of four Bella Lugosi-inspired vampires came walking down the street. The older boy was leading his little sister by the hand, both with dark capes and grinning with cheap plastic vampire teeth. The parents followed, resembling Lily Munster and a younger Al Lewis. I smiled, reminded of my own family of four I had grown up with (Now only three) and felt my lips begin to twitch. I looked away, to the bumper in front. Cleared my throat.

"Come on," I said. "Move it."

As the night wore on the traffic on the main roads gradually thinned, though it remained busier than usual. This, I had learned from Joel, was thanks to a huge section of Santa Monica Boulevard being blocked off for the night over in West Hollywood. Thousands of costumed people would be there. It was one of the biggest public Halloween parties in the country.

Tonight though I just wanted to get home. I was tired of all the driving and all the politely pissed people I delivered to. I didn't like the way my body reacted whenever I was on a darker street and saw car lights suddenly appear in the rear-view mirror. And I kept thinking of the Tennis Bum.

I had that bastard's mark on my car now.

The thought made me feel a little sick.

I was driving up one of the streets that ran through the apartment complexes. I had my window down and the cool night breeze blew in, minting my damp hair. Leaves were sailing off some of the trees. Up ahead a man dressed as Robin the Boy Wonder was walking on the side of the road carrying a brown paper sack. The guy was Burt Ward. Only, *the* Burt Ward was much older now, and there was something melancholy about this Robin walking alone on a dark street, head down.

I turned in to the parking lot, passing a valet attendant I was not yet acquainted with and went under to the garage. As I drove down the ramp, I saw Jorge walking over from the back by the elevator, a black beanie now covering his shaved head. He stepped to the side to give me room, and I pulled in to the first spot next to the podium.

He raised his arm in my direction as I got out of the car. "See you later, my friend."

"You're going home?" I asked.

"Si."

"Okay Jorge. See you tonight in my dreams." I winked at him.

Jorge's eyes went wide and his cheeks puffed, then his face exploded into laughter.

He continued to laugh as I walked off.

"We'll go ahead and cash you out," Dave said as soon I walked in. I gave him my credit receipts and then counted out the cash I owed him. I said I'd be right back with the topper from my car.

On my way down the stairs I realized I was whistling. Vic was out working tonight, so I'd have the apartment to myself when I got in – a cheery thought.

Jorge was coming back from the alleyway, his face now covered. What I'd thought was a beanie on his head earlier had been pulled down over this face. A balaclava.

Very Halloweenish of you, Jorge.

I waved him a final salute, walking around to the passenger side of the car.

I pulled off the topper from the roof. Turned around.

Jorge had come up behind me.

He pointed at me and said something, but his voice was muffled now because of the balaclava.

"What's that?" I asked.

He said the same thing again.

I repeated what I thought I'd heard. "Night?"

He nodded.

"Good night, Jorge."

He shook his head. He pointed again, and I looked down at the cash I carried in one hand.

Now I understood.

"Was it a good night? Yeah, it was pretty good."

He nodded. Pointed again, and said something different and incomprehensible.

"About seventy dollars," I said.

He nodded, as if to say, *that's pretty good.* He held out his hand for a handshake.

"All right, Jorge," I said, pulling the topper up to my chest, hugging it while I switched the cash into my other hand. I held out my hand to Jorge's while noticing his other hand was missing from his jacket sleeve, like he was cold, or had something—

GOD MY EYES!

My hands slapped up to my face and I heard the clattering of my topper, then I was being shoved back and off my feet. I felt the ground hit me like a solid wave.

I couldn't open my eyes. They were being eaten alive by hot sand.

My hands, slick with tears and snot, crawled up and down my face, as the footfalls and laughter faded into the alleyway.

"Yee-hee-hee-hee!"

Chapter 10

"Pepper spray! Are you kidding me?"

"Nope."

Carter was in an almost-splits position in the middle of his living room. He stared up at me with incredulity.

"So," I continued. "The guy runs off before anybody sees him."

"He take the money?"

"Course. And I can't identify him because I never got a good look. All I could say to the police is that he looked like one of our valet attendants. That he was wearing a similar jacket."

"How long did the pepper spray last?"

"About an hour. Even after washing my eyes out it was still kind of stinging for a while after. The cops were a blur when they were talking to me."

I lifted my beer to my lips and finished it. Set the bottle down onto the coffee table with the rest of my empties.

Three more to go.

I got up.

"I'm really sorry," Carter said as I stepped around him and the sea-green yoga mat. "I shouldn't have left you alone for two nights."

"No, you shouldn't have." I went into the kitchen. "I had no one to protect me. I was like, where's my skinny little Chinese friend?"

"That's why we train, that's why we train man!"

"Train this," I said, popping the top off a new bottle. "Sure you don't want one?"

"Told you, I ain't drinking no more."

I returned to the sofa.

"So that's about it. That concludes my epic Halloween

weekend. Kind of eventful, huh?"

"I'll say. All I did was get hammered at some fancy hotel party."

"Yeah, how was that?"

"Eh."

"Did you catch anyone humping in the bathroom?"

"I don't remember anything so interesting happening."

"You probably don't remember anything."

"Oh my Gosh."

"Did you miss Doc-tah Jones, Shorty?"

"Course, baby."

I put my feet onto the table, pillowing them on the pile of assorted junk mail that was the only clear spot between my empties and somebody else's. I sat back, feeling a slight pain still from where the guy had shoved me. I watched as Carter got into some kind of Tai Chi pose. He breathed in through his nose, making sharp airy sounds.

"Whoo," he exhaled. "Head's clearer now."

"That clear your headache?"

"Are you kidding me? You have no idea how much I drank last night." Carter rolled up the mat and carried it off into the room.

He came back and sat down onto the couch.

"I can't believe I got robbed," I said.

"I'm sorry to hear about all that, man, I really am. You've had some bum luck."

"I'll say." I took a good swig of my beer. Nearly finished, I knocked back the rest of it. "Ah. Can't believe I got robbed. I feel like a...fucking pussy."

"You are a fucking pussy. That's why I like you." Carter patted my leg. "I like fucking pussies."

"And I know it could have been a lot worse, you know?"

"I feel ya."

"It's just..."

"I feel ya."

"No, but I'm—"

"I feel ya."

I looked at Carter. The concerned look on his face vanished.

"Wanna get stoned?"

"You got maced! In the *face!"*

I couldn't stop laughing at Carter. He'd gone into his room and somehow come out wearing a red fez.

"Watch me!" He stood in the middle of the room. "You were like in *Bloodsport!"*

Mocking slow motion, Carter opened his eyes and mouth wide in imitation of Jean-Claude Van Damme at the film's climatic moment when his character is blinded by salt thrown to the face. "YAAAAAH*ghaah..."*

"Stop—" I said, almost choking.

"YAAAAAH*ghaah..."*

"This is...seriously hurting my chest."

Carter laughed, sitting back down on the couch.

"Oh man," I said. "Thanks. I seriously needed that."

"I'm just sayin," Carter said, sounding serious again. "You should have Van Dammed his ass."

"You know," I said. "I don't know what pisses me off more—that he pepper sprayed me, or that he pushed me like a little high school bitch and ran off. I don't care so much about the money. Any guy feels he has to rob a pizza delivery guy...ah fuck it."

"Fuck that guy."

"Yeah."

"You know what you got to do the next time he robs you?"

"Actually," I said. "I think I know exactly what I'm going to do."

Chapter 11

"You looking for stun gun?"

"I'm looking for a Taser," I repeated.

My old friend at the used shop licked his lips and shook his head. "You can't buy Taser here. But I have stun gun and pepper spray."

"What's the stun gun like? Isn't that the same as a Taser?"

"Not the same, but it work similar. I show you."

He produced a black rectangular device the size of a wallet from under the counter. "So with this, you hold button with your thumb and touch this end to the person and they get shocked. One million volts."

"Million?"

"Very effective. Forty-five dollar. It also come with flashlight."

I imagined the man in the mask coming at me again; only this time I had one of these.

A Taser would be better, though—you wouldn't have to be touching the person to use it. . .

But something like this would still be good to have. I might have to get up close and personal, but at least the next time someone tried to rob me. . .

And you might as well use up that store credit.

"And what's this?" I asked, pointing to another box under the glass counter.

"This is stun gun made to look like Smartphone."

"I'll take it."

Chapter 12

The next day I was called in to work fifteen minutes early.

Jeffrey and I walked in together. Joel, Paul, and Hooper were already sitting at a table.

"Here they are," said a man I didn't recognize behind the counter. He was big, with a head that was bald and shiny. In the back by the oven I saw Dave with the cooks. "You guys clock in and then join your buddies. I'll be with you in a sec, okay?" The man turned and walked to the back.

A moment later the man came out of the swinging doors.

"Hey guys. How you all doing today? My name's Elliot. I'm one of the owners." He sat down next to me and put his hand on my shoulder.

"The reason I called you in a little early today is because of what happened on Halloween. I have to say that I was really shocked when I got the call. This is the first time any of our employees at any of our stores has ever been attacked."

"Lucky me!" I said.

Everyone laughed.

Elliot patted me, then took his hand off my shoulder.

"Dylan turned out to be the lucky one this time, but if it's at all possible I'd like him to be the last."

Elliot continued. "It could have happened to any one of us. But even though you guys are in a safe area, it goes to show that even here you can run into scumbags. So, what I'd like for you guys to do is stick together when you're downstairs at night, especially after nine when the valet guys go home and there's no one downstairs."

"For how long?" Hooper asked.

"Forever. And you know, I really hate to say this, but..." Elliot's voice dropped to almost a whisper. "It might not be a bad idea if you guys want to carry some protection. Just in case."

"You saying we should carry condoms, Elliot?" Joel asked.

We all laughed.

"That too, but you know. . . I'm not saying go around with a loaded gun, *ever*, but maybe your own pepper spray or something. Get my drift?"

"We got you," Joel said.

"All right guys. That's really all I had to say. You guys look out for one another and keep up the good work."

Elliot put his hand on my shoulder again. "One second, Dylan."

He waited till the last of the drivers were out the door and then turned to me.

"I'm real sorry that happened," he said. "This may not be the right way to earn a bonus..." He pulled something out from his back pocket. "But here."

He handed me a one hundred dollar bill.

"Oh wow," I said, taking the bill. "Thanks Elliot. That's really very nice of you."

"You got it, bud. If I ever found that guy, I'd beat his ass for you."

I laughed. "You and me both!"

"Make a pizza of his face."

We got up. Dave was at the register looking at us.

"See what a nice boss we have Dylan? I wanna get robbed, Elliot."

"No, you want someone to take off your clothes, there's a difference."

"Your mom didn't think there was a difference."

I laughed as I stepped aside for the couple walking in through the door.

"Hi, welcome to Taste Testers!" Dave said.

The boys were waiting for me around the corner.

"Way to go Dylan!" Joel yelled. "Let's hear it for the first Taste Testers employee to ever get robbed!"

Joel and Jeffrey mock applauded while Paul laughed and Hooper grinned.

"Yeah, fuck you guys."

"It's all right, Dylan," Joel said. "I sometimes give to charity."

Paul laughed. "HO-HO-*HAW!*"

"We were just saying that that guy Elliot's cool," Hooper said.

"He is," I said. "He gave me a hundred bucks."

Hooper's eyes went wide. "He gave you a hundred bucks?"

"Bro, you actually made money out of this deal," Paul said.

"He probably wants to keep you as an employee, too," Jeffrey said. "I don't know if I'd want to keep working at a place where I got maced."

Paul's phone rang. "Hello? For sure. Hey bro," he said to Joel, "they want us both up."

Jeffrey wandered into the ice cream shop, leaving Hooper and I on the wall.

Hooper scooted closer to me. *"Hey,"* he said in a whisper, bumping my shoulder with his. "You wanna smoke some pot?"

"Thanks Hoop, but no. I could never smoke before work."

"I do it all the time."

"You've probably got a high tolerance. Not me. I'm not really a smoker."

"No? Hmph."

We sat together on the wall for a moment in awkward silence. Then Hooper said, "Well, I'm going to go downstairs then."

"All right bud," I said, wondering if I'd actually offended him.

Jeffrey came out from the ice cream shop with a double scoop cone in his hand. He slowly walked towards the wall, glancing up a few times at me as he licked at the top scoop, which was pink.

"What'd you get?" I asked him.

"Ice cream." He held out the cone to me. "Want a lick?"

"No thanks," I said with a chuckle.

Jeffrey didn't chuckle with me, or even grin. Just kept licking. And staring.

I wondered if it had been a serious question.

"Well," I said. "I'm going to go downstairs then."

"We got a double for you," said the cashier as I walked up.

"Nice," I said.

"Here you go," he said, handing me the long receipts nicely folded in the right order. "You're all set."

Downstairs, I felt a momentary flutter in my stomach as I walked to my car and looked around the lot, watching for cars and
(robbers)
people.

One of the valet attendants, a twenty-something who looked like he trained for the MMA in his free time, was sitting at the podium. I'd seen the guy around but never spoken to him.

"Hey man," he said, nodding his head.

No doubt I was the talk of all the attendants now.

There he goes, the guy who got attacked.

The guy who'd tried to put the blame on one of us.

I got in to my car with the bags in back.

I looked at my first dispatch and said the address into my phone. Fastened my seatbelt while it routed.

"Turn left onto Gorman Avenue!" Sally trilled.

Here comes Jorge…

I had noticed him on my way to and from deliveries, but he'd kept his distance up until now.

Now he was outside my car, waiting for me to open the door.

I felt a wave of unwelcome adrenaline.

Had to remember that Jorge had nothing to do with it.

"Hi Jorge."

"Amigo," Jorge said, speaking in a softer tone than usual. "I heard about what happen. I'm so sorry."

"Thanks."

"You thought it was me?"

"I only told the police that I thought it was you at first. Because that's how it happened, that's how the guy got close. He had the same sort of jacket, same build. But I didn't say I thought it actually was you."

"Amigo. I would never…"

"I know, Jorge, I know."

Jorge frowned, his mouth looking weighted down by his jowls. "I'm so sorry that I was not here. You are good person. If I was here…" He raised his hand in a gesture of grappling with words.

"Jorge, don't worry, I'm fine, thank you."

"Okay, amigo."

"You're a good person too."

Jorge's mouth turned up in a grin.

At the stairs, I turned and yelled back "Next time, Jorge, we fight them together!"

Jorge's laugh echoed as I went up.

I was out on a double and on the second delivery south of Santa Monica Boulevard, when a familiar voice suddenly spoke up from the nook where I kept my phone.

"In a half mile. **Go-*ink* leffgh**..."

I groaned. "You've gotta be kidding me."

As if in answer, the Demon Voice repeated its order.

"**Go-*ink* leffgh**..."

My instinct was to go the opposite way of wherever the Demon Voice said. But then, I thought, where's the shacks and alleyways with tennis bums here? What's the worst that could happen?

"**Go-*ink* leffgh**..."

I turned left.

I was on Colorado Avenue, where I was supposed to be. I looked at the apartment numbers as I went along. They were going up: I appeared to be going in the right direction.

The phone said 300 ft. to my destination.

I pulled up and parked when I reached the building number on my dispatch and GPS.

I started to get up from my seat, then sat back, wondering if the Demon Voice had really misled me on my phone the other night.

You drank a lot that night.

You shouldn't have been driving in the first place.

I got the pizza from the backseat and locked my door.

Crossing the sidewalk, I looked at the small building probably housing no more than a half dozen units. It looked old and run-down, the once baby blue paint of the front peeling and chipped away in white swatches. A little black gate off to the side was hanging open on a square of dirt lined with bike tire tracks and patches of dead grass. Leaning against the bars of the gate was an old dirt-covered plush doll that might've once been SpongeBob SquarePants. The thing looked eerily decayed. It reminded me of the many rain-destroyed plush dolls and stuffed animals I'd seen haunting the children's section on my one walk-through of the Hollywood Forever cemetery.

I went up the scruffy stairs, guessing it might lead to door number one. At the top, I found myself in the dark, the light bulb overhead out. Turning the corner, I walked to the lone door. Squinting, I could just make out the numeral on the front. I pulled aside the front screen and knocked.

What if it's the wrong building? the sceptic in my head asked.

So I knock on the wrong door and say sorry excuse me. No big deal.

And it wasn't the wrong building, I reminded myself. The numbers matched up.

The door opened on a big black man framed in orange light, smelling strongly of marijuana.

He waited for me to speak.

"Hi," I said. "How are you?"

"Sup," he said. "What you doin?"

"Hey, not much." I opened the flap of the carrier bag and slid the big pizza box out.

The man stared at me as I held the box out for him to take, his mouth set in a tight line. After a few seconds without breaking eye contact, he took the box from me.

"We didn't order no pizza," he said.

"What?"

The man just stared.

What the hell is he looking at?

"Hey who dat?" said a higher-pitched voice inside the apartment.

The big man finally broke off the stare and turned towards the voice, revealing a shirtless man sitting at a table, looking over his shoulder at me, his face scrunched in anger. Tattoos arched across the rippled contours of his back. He looked younger, leaner, and meaner-looking than the hulk in the doorway. "What *you* want?" he said.

The hulk turned back, glancing down at me, then looked back into the apartment.

"D! Yo! You know about this?"

"Aw yeah, that's that pizza I ordered," answered another voice.

"You ordered pizza?" The hulk raised a fist to his mouth and suddenly bent forward, laughing.

The hulk straightened and turned back to me. "All right, man," he said. "Late."

The door began to close.

"Hey!" I blocked the door from closing with my foot.

"Hey, what?"

"You still got to pay for it," I said.

The hulk glared, his lip curled in a sneer. "Get your foot out the door, man."

I stepped back.

So did the hulk. He turned. "D! Yo!" he yelled. "Come pay for this shit, nigga!"

A young man appeared in the doorframe, smiling but not looking at me. He wore a wife-beater that hung off his thin frame, a black beanie on his head, with long dreadlocks spilling out the back.

"How much is it?" he asked the floor, smiling.

I quoted the number on my dispatch.

He held out a wallet. The hulk snatched it off him, digging through it and handing me a stack of ones.

"Thank you," I said, turning to leave.

"Hey yo, what's this man?" a voice called out. I saw the other man who'd been at the table walking up to the door. He was holding a little white bag.

"Pepper and Parmesan." I told him.

"You got any more?"

I was about to explain that we only brought one per order when I was interrupted by shrill yelps that sounded like they were coming from another room. Or a closet.

The man's face scrunched in fury as he whirled around, lunging off in the direction D had gone.

The hulk again filled the doorway.

"Bounce."

I thought I heard the shrill voice say *"Gemme up off this—"* before the door slammed in my face.

"I owe you five dollars and three cents," Bill, the new cashier said. I watched him dig into the register for the pennies. He dropped them into the bill and handed it to me.

"Cashed out."

"Thanks," I said. Rolling the pennies out from the bill into my hand, I noticed that one of them was gray.

Bill must have given me a dime, I thought, as I held it up to my face.

No. . .

It said One Cent on the back.

I turned the coin over. Next to Lincoln's profile I saw the date.

"Holy shit," I said.

Bill looked up. "What?"

"Do you know what you just gave me?"

I showed him the penny.

"Oh," he said. "It's gray."

"That's because it's made of steel. Look at the date."

He looked. Then straightened up in surprise. "Nineteen-forty-four?"

"You just gave me a rare penny," I said, smiling. "It's a wheat penny from World War Two. My Dad has one of these in his old coin collection. For a brief while during the war, copper got rare, so they started making pennies out of steel."

"Whoa! Is it worth money?"

"More than a penny, anyway."

"Give it back, then. I only owed you three cents."

I laughed. "Not a chance. If there's such a thing as a real lucky penny, you just gave it to me."

Chapter 13

Almost midnight. I'd been sitting in my car for nearly two hours.

I didn't want to go inside. Just thinking of moody Vic hunched over at his desk...

An unspoken tension between us had developed since the party. It angered me that he'd seemed nonplussed by what happened. I'd been attacked twice, and he seemed to act as though it were my fault. Like I'd gone out looking for trouble. Like I deserved it.

Jerk.

I took a swig from my tall can.

Pretty soon I'd have to piss.

I picked up my phone and stared at the screen.

Carter was closing at JB's.

Mike and Andy hadn't returned my texts, and neither had my lady friend from the Halloween party. I took another swig from my beer.

Fuck Roxanne. Fuck them all.

Here I was in Los Angeles, with no acting gigs, no luck with the ladies and dwindling luck with my friends, it seemed.

And here I was, getting drunk in my car.

The night was quiet. Dark, except for the streetlights—bright and blurry pinpoints through my windshield. Across the street was the elementary school. I looked at the big empty yard through the chain-link fence.

I wanted to be somewhere else, but didn't want to go anywhere.

Thinking about the last several days, my life seemed to be bordering on the surreal.

I kept thinking about that voice I'd heard on the phone.

You mean the Demon Voice that no one believes?

Was there any way I could be imagining it?

If I *was* imagining it, I was nuts.

No. I'd heard it twice now, and what was worse was that on both occasions I'd been in danger. I hadn't imagined any of that.

Those guys in that run-down apartment had been straight up gangsters. I'd heard somebody's voice in the background, somebody sounding like they were in trouble. I hadn't done anything. I'd simply driven away, convincing myself that it was somebody just messing around. Telling myself that that was just the way those guys talked.

Did that make me irresponsible? Did that make me a coward?

A sudden pattering made me sit up from my reclined seat, expecting to see a crazie looking in.

It had started to rain.

I leaned back and put my hands to my face, feeling it tighten.

"What am I doing?"

I needed to talk to someone. Someone who cared.

I picked up my phone and stared at the screen.

Hell. I couldn't wake my parents at this hour.

I thought of my buddies and ex-coworkers up in the Bay Area. But again, at this hour, even if I got anybody they wouldn't want to hear about my problems.

I gulped the last of my beer, putting the can with the rest in the plastic bag. I reached my hand into my pocket and pulled out the small object my fingers had found.

The wheat penny.

My new good luck penny.

Need all the luck I can get these days.

I looked at the little gray Lincoln, and then to the side of the wheel at the little gray space there. Same color as the penny.

Why don't I tape it to the dashboard? It'll look cool. Might even bring me good luck. Might even ward off any—

My phone chirped:

What are you doing

I didn't recognize the number. But I recognized the significance of the three numbers in the middle of the series.

666

A message from The Demon Voice?

I immediately hit the call button and put the phone to my ear.

"Hi," a female voice answered.

"Who's this?"

"You already deleted my number?" A bitter chuckle. "It's Roxanne."

Chapter 14

"I feel ya."

"So in the meantime," I said, "I'm laying low around Vic. I get up in the morning and take my laptop over to that coffee shop around the corner and hang out there."

"But you can't always be outside while he's inside. That's your place too!"

"No, that's *his* place. And he doesn't for a second let me forget it."

"But you're paying half the rent!"

"It's meant to be only temporary. You see the size of that place—it's not for two people. His moodiness is getting on my nerves, but having me around his workspace is surely getting on his nerves too, you know?"

"His workspace?"

"You know, he writes."

Carter shook his head. "You gotta get out of there, man."

"Oh I know. But until I can afford my own place, I'm just laying low to minimize tension."

"I think it's bullshit."

"It is bullshit."

"I think it's bullshit that you don't move in with me, raise some kids." Carter put his hand on my knee.

"Be Poppa Smurf?"

"Be my Gargamel daddy."

"I am your daddy, and you're my little bitch son."

"Oh-ho!" Carter took his hand off my knee and stood up. "Your little bitch son can kick your ass!"

"That's why I don't let you live out on the streets."

"You wanna go?" He got into his fighting stance.

"No."

"You wanna see who's daddy around here?"

"No, but you can get me another beer. Hey, that rhymed."

Carter crouched, leapt up and did the Van Damme helicopter kick.

"YAAAAAH*ghaah. . ."*

I laughed, my hands up in mock surrender.

"All talky, no walky." He went to the kitchen, and came back out with a beer.

"Like a good little son."

"No, seriously," Carter said. "You gotta get another serving job."

"I'm taking a little break from serving."

"How are you going to afford to move out just on that?"

"I'm working six days a week now, averaging fifty bucks a night. Get a paycheck every Friday and there's no bullshit with tipping out bussers and food runners. I think I'll be in good shape in about a month. People are nice in Grantwood and they tip well. I wouldn't do it in a bad area. The only thing I've had to deal with so far is, well, getting robbed."

Carter laughed. "That's all?"

"Yeah, but that was just me in the wrong place at the wrong time."

"Speaking of time, what time is it?"

I pulled out my phone.

"You still having issues with that thing?"

"Two-oh-four. Yeah, that's another thing. I think I better take this thing back to Horizon."

"Why?"

"I told you about how I hear voices on it."

"Dude! Are you really being serious about that whole thing?"

"Yes!"

"I thought you were kidding."

"I am not kidding! I hear different voices when I use my GPS and one of them, the one I call the Demon Voice, actually misled me to that place in south central. And I heard it again last night."

"Did it take you back to Harlem or wherever?"

"No, it actually took me to the right place. But the thing is, there was something wrong about it too."

"What do you mean?"

While I told Carter the story, he packed and smoked a bowl

in his ceramic pipe. He silently interrupted me twice by holding out the pipe, but I waved it away. I had to work in a little over two hours.

"So what do you think of that?" I asked him.

"I think your phone's racist."

"What would you do, though?"

"I'd switch to AT and T."

"You're a big help."

Carter laughed. "I really don't know what to tell you. Go take it back to the shop and get it looked at. That weird voice you say you hear is probably just something faulty."

"Yeah." I downed the last of my beer. "Do you ever wonder where technology's going to take us in the next couple of years? I got this new Smartphone. What does it do? I speak into it and it tells me where to go. And I follow. This thing's a walking computer, camera and tracking device. God knows what else. It's kind of freaky. Do you know what I'm saying?"

Carter just looked at me.

"I remember computers growing up. If you had told me then that by the time I was thirty that everyone would have one of these things, I would have said it sounded like a science fiction movie. Or nineteen eighty-four.

"How long til this so-called smart technology starts developing on its own and turning on us? Like Skynet from the Terminator movies?"

Carter blinked and shook his head. "I'm fucking stoned as shit."

Chapter 15

I walked in to the Horizon Wireless store. There were two young men behind the counter, one showing the other how to do something on the computer. A woman stood on the other side of the counter. As I approached, she looked at me.

The taller of the two employees looked up. “We’ll be right with you, sir.”

“Problems with your phone?” the woman asked.

“Yeah. How about you?”

The woman rolled her eyes and shook her head. “It’s ridiculous.”

“What’s wrong with yours?”

“It just went dead on me! I’ve been here an hour waiting for them to charge it, but it doesn’t seem to make any difference. Of course, *they* don’t know what’s going on either.”

“How can I help you?” the tall man asked, stepping out from the counter.

“I’d like you to take a look at my phone. I seem to be having problems with the GPS system.”

“What’s wrong with it?”

“It works fine for the most part. But uh, I’ve been hearing weird voices.”

“Weird voices?”

“Like I put in an address and the main voice will come on, right? But then all of a sudden the voice will change to another one.”

“Okay.” The man looked at me expectantly, his eyebrows raised.

“So, what is that?”

The man’s eyes darted to his right and back, like they’d instantly retrieved some information. “I’m not sure what you’re getting at, sir. Do you not like the sound of the voice?"

"No, I don't care. I mean, is that normal? Could that be a glitch or something?"

"It can depend where you're going. There are regional variants, for example. So if you were to let's say drive to Alabama, you might hear a southern accent."

"I haven't been going anywhere very far, though. Mostly just around Grantwood."

"I do know that again it might depend on where you go. There are less common street names for example or new developments in areas that might not have shown up at the time of the initial recordings, so then the computer takes over and reads them."

"Oh."

"But it works just the same, so don't worry!" the man said brightening his tone. He patted me on the arm. "You're not hearing voices in your head."

"One of the voices has been misdirecting me."

"Misdirecting you?"

"Yeah and it doesn't sound like the other voices. It sounds male and kind of…scary." I chuckled for effect. "Like it's a demon cartoon character or something. You know?"

The man stared at me. "I'm not sure I'm following you. You said it misdirects you? The voices you hear aren't going to deliberately mislead you. There are glitches, of course, as with any software, but most the time you end up heading in the wrong direction it's because you didn't put in the zip code, for example, or it picked up a similar-sounding street that is almost spelled the same."

"I understand," I said. "But I don't think that's the case here. I think whenever I hear this voice there's something wrong going on. This voice doesn't seem to be working with the others whenever I hear it."

"You said it sounds like a cartoon character? You know, there are dozens of apps out there. People can download the voices of cartoon characters and celebrities to give them directions."

"But I haven't downloaded anything. This came with it."

"Where did you get your phone?"

"Here."

"May I see it?"

I handed him the phone.

The man tapped at it. “I don’t see anything but the normal Navigation installed here.”

“Could it be a bug or something?”

He shrugged. “It’s possible. How often do you turn the phone off?”

“I don’t think it ever goes off completely.”

“It’s a good idea for you to turn the phone completely off every now and then.”

“How?”

“Here.” He pressed the screen off button at the top of the phone. He held the button down, and a window popped up on the screen.

“Oh,” I said. “You know, my phone didn’t come with any instructions or anything.”

The man shrugged. “Well, like I said, it’s a good idea to just completely turn the phone off every now and then, like maybe once a week. It lets the phone charge and reboot. If you think you have any bugs, that’s the first thing to do.”

“That’s good to know,” I said. “Could my phone be used? Is it possible that a prior owner or somebody put something into my phone that is doing this?”

“If you bought it here, it’s been certified by the factory.”

“Uh huh.”

The man shrugged once again. “I would leave that off for five minutes, then turn it on again. Do that about once a week, like I said. If you still have troubles with the GPS after that, I can give you a corporate number to call.”

“Fine,” I said.

“I’ll be right back.” The man turned and walked behind the counter.

Great, I thought. *Now I’ll also have a corporate number to call if I have any issues and want to spend an hour wading through automated messages.*

The woman turned to me.

“Sounds to *me* like your phone needs psychiatric help.”

Chapter 16

I knocked and entered the apartment.

Vic was standing at the sink eating a bowl of cereal.

"What's up?" he said through a mouthful.

I shut the door and took my backpack off. "Where is Studio City?" I asked.

"It's in the valley. Why?"

"Got a date with Roxanne tonight after work."

"Who's Roxanne?"

"You remember that chick you saw me talking to at the party? She lives in Studio City, and we're going to have a drink at some place near her."

"Oh. Cool. Where are you taking her?"

"Some English pub."

"You taking her to The Slaughtered Lamb?"

"Ha, I wish. Hear the food's good there."

When Vic was referencing movies, he was in a good mood.

I took out my laptop from my backpack and put it on the futon. I heard clinking as Vic set his bowl with spoon onto the counter, followed by the squeak of the overhead cupboard being opened. He was fueling up.

"You heading off to work soon?" I asked.

"I'm about to take a shower after this." He took out a clean bowl.

"Before you go, do you have any tape? The see-through kind?"

"Should have some in there," he said, pointing to the container of office supplies he kept on the lower shelf of his desk. "Just be sure to put everything back *exactly* the way it was."

As soon as Vic had closed the door of the bathroom I got

up and went over to the desk. Finding the roll of scotch tape, I went out to my car.

I picked up the wheat penny from the nook.

My lucky penny.

After a few tries, I measured out a neat square of tape and laminated the penny to the side of the steering wheel.

Now I had luck riding with me wherever I went.

It had gotten me the date with Roxanne so far, hadn't it?

I was staring at the lucky penny when the phone rang.

"Delivery."

Walking towards the stairs, I noticed Paul sitting in his car, looking down at his phone.

That kid's always on his damn phone, I thought.

And everything's *bro*-this, *bro*-that. *For sure, for sure.*

Anyone who said *for sure* that much was someone I couldn't take at his word.

"Here's Dylan!" Taylor said as I walked in. Lewis the cashier turned and headed back to grab a carrier bag. "We're going to send you on a double, my friend."

I gave Taylor the thumbs up. Taylor was the other manager I liked working with.

Lewis packed the bags, then handed me my dispatches. "You're all set."

Taylor yelled as I opened the door. "If you see Paul down there, will you send him up?"

Downstairs, I walked over to Paul's car.

"You're up, Paul," I said.

"All right, for sure bro," Paul said, not looking up.

Stacey Noeltner.

I saw the entry code and dialed it on the keypad.

Cunck. "Hello?"

I took in a deep breath. Blew out, then said in a dry whisper, *"It's the man you've been waiting for. . ."*

"Who is this?"

"The pizza guy!" I said with cheer.

The woman laughed. "Come on up to the suite," she said, "It's the door at the end of the hall."

The door buzzed and I pushed it open.

Inside, it felt less like a lobby than a small room. The ceiling was low and the white-painted walls seemed to catch more shadow than light from outside. Facing me was an elevator. To the right an armchair leaned against the wall next to a potted plant, staring at the rectangular mirror mounted halfway up the wall across from it.

My footsteps sounded muffled as I crossed the space to the elevator.

I took the elevator up, the door opening on to a long hallway.

A woman peeked out from the open door at the end. "Over here!" she called, waving.

I walked over.

"That was pretty smooth," she said, tying her long blonde hair back. "And I'm glad you were the man I *was* waiting for." She dropped her arms.

I grinned, thinking she looked pretty smooth herself. She looked about thirty-five, and in great shape. She'd obviously had plastic surgery done to her lips and nose, and probably her breasts, which jutted out like cantaloupes under her white tank top.

When I handed her the box, she turned and bent over, setting it on something low down just out of my sight.

I stared at her behind in tight black sweatpants.

Thank you, Stacey.

Stacey straightened and turned back around.

"If you would just give me your autograph, I'd be an even happier man," I said, holding out the slip.

Stacey smirked. She took the slip from me, keeping eye contact. "You're a bit of a jokester, aren't you?" Her eyes told me she didn't mind.

She held the slip up to the doorframe, again showing off very round breasts. I looked away, trying not to obviously show interest.

"All right," she said, handing back the slip and pen. "Well, you have a good day."

"I will," I said. "Thanks."

"What's your name?"

"Dylan."

"Dylan. I'm Stacey."

"Nice to meet you."

"Well, I'm glad. Have a good day."

"Thank you Stacey."

Stacey grinned.

Walking down the hall, I almost expected to hear Stacey's voice call me back.

I reached the elevator and hit the button.

Going down, I looked at the slip of paper in my hand.

She had tipped me $5.

I remembered the dispatch, and uncrumpled it.

Stacey Noeltner. Followed by her address and phone number. Followed by a description of her order and the amount owed and paid via her credit card.

I thought of that look on her face, and felt something stir inside me.

"Got a hot date tonight," I said to Joel.

"Where you guys going?"

"An English pub in Studio City called Geoffrey's. Have you been there?"

"I've heard of it. Spelled with a G? It's supposed to be pretty nice. That's good man. Got a hot date to look forward to."

I heard a jingling noise that sounded like Paul, and looked towards the stairs to see Paul and Hooper coming back from delivery.

"What's up, fellas?" Joel asked.

"Chillin bro, chillin." Paul said, without turning.

Hooper looked at us. He waved at me.

When they were around the corner, Joel said, "That guy's weird."

"Who? Paul?"

"Hooper."

A minute later Paul came out. "Thank God bro, they asked that cat to fold some boxes in there, cause I didn't want him following me out here. That guy Hooper's a fucking creeper, bro."

"Dude! I was just saying the same thing to Dylan," Joel said.

"That fool freaks me the fuck out," Paul said, tapping on his phone.

"Why?" I asked.

Paul looked up. "Bro, just the way that guy follows you around, says weird shit."

"The way he's always staring," Joel added.

"Yeah bro. You know most people can usually take a hint. You know what I'm sayin, bro? And yeah, bro. The way he looks at you." Paul made a show of trembling. "Gives me the straight-up willies, bro."

I didn't say anything.

I didn't particularly like Hooper, but I didn't see anything really wrong with the guy. He was a bit odd, sure.

(For sure, bro)

But at least he tried to be friendly.

I looked at Paul tapping at his phone, at the many bracelets hanging off his skinny wrists. Almost every finger of his hand was adorned with a ring. What was he trying to look like with all that jewelry? Were all those rings supposed to mean something? Was that supposed to say he had some kind of class?

I looked at his orangey dyed hair.

From head to foot, the guy looked of cheap artificiality; the way he walked, the way he talked. All of it put-on.

And he was criticizing Hooper.

A few minutes later Hooper appeared around the corner. "Hey, you guys! Joel and Paul! You're about to be up!" He waved.

"Thanks Hooper, we're coming bud!" Joel yelled.

Joel pushed off from the wall. Paul followed with his head down still looking at his phone, his legs in his tight jeans moving as if by their own mind.

Hooper walked up.

"You're going to be up soon too," he said. "We just got a bunch of orders in."

He sat down next to me on the wall.

His face looked red and sweaty. He wiped his brow.

"What's got you so worked up?" I asked.

"It's hot by that oven."

"Yeah it is. Did you have to fold a lot of boxes?"

"Just some that they needed. Have you noticed all the cats disappearing around here?"

"Huh?"

"You haven't noticed?"

"What are you talking about? How would I notice?"

"You know how everyone in Grantwood seems to have pets?"

"I see a lot of people out walking dogs, yeah?"

"But have you noticed all the signs up for missing cats? Like on poles and stuff?"

"I have seen a few fliers, yeah. I've seen some for dogs too."

"But they're predominately for cats. Pay attention. It's not just the same cat with a lot of fliers, either. You'll see different cats are missing. There's a lot of them missing around here."

"Oh," I said. "Weird."

"Poor little pussies."

"Was that supposed to be a joke?"

"What?"

"All that you just said. Was that all just supposed to be a joke?"

"Why would I joke about all that?"

I shrugged.

Hooper stared. "What," he said. "What is it?"

"You're up Dylan!" Joel was coming around the corner, followed by Paul. They were both carrying double loads.

I got up, leaving Hooper alone on the wall.

Going up Barrel Road towards Sunset I kept glancing at the time. It was almost nine now, and I still had to run back to Vic's for a shower before I could leave for Studio City.

At least traffic wasn't bad this time of night.

I made it to Sunset, then continued straight on. Maplewood Road was the first right.

I turned.

"In a half mile. Your destination will be on the right!"

I'd been on Maplewood a few times already. It was narrow and winding as it climbed the hills. My furthest delivery had taken me about a mile and a half up. That was during the day, and I'd marveled at the view coming back down, where I could see the huddle of skyscrapers that was Century City and then out towards the ocean. Now it was dark, I was looking at only the gravel road lit by the glow of my headlights, and the trees in the sparse lighting from the houses on either side.

"You have arrived!"

I pulled to the side.

"All right, let's make this quick," I said, grabbing up the dispatch papers.

Outside, the night was alive with the sound of crickets.

I took the carrier bag out from the backseat and slammed the door.

Past my car, I looked to the curb for the house number. I was passing a big wooden gate. The house beyond it was too far back, if it had a number on it.

I kept going, passing what appeared to be a vacant area between houses. It was too dark to see the corresponding house numbers across the street.

I came up to another gate (this one open), and searched for the painted square and number.

Found it. Couldn't see it.

The darkened house beyond the gate was no help either.

Hearing a car coming up behind, I stayed far in, looking down at the rectangular painted box on the curb as the beams lit the ground.

The numbers were faded and unreadable.

Hurry up!

I looked at my dispatch slip in the glow of my phone. The phone number was listed. I could just call.

Or I could chance knocking on the door of the house in front of me. If it turned out to be the wrong one, at least I could ask them to point me in the right direction.

The driveway was large enough to park a tank. I walked up, triggering the sensor light.

The driveway wound to the left, where it led to two parked cars, an old brown Mazda and a shiny emerald Lexus beneath a canopy overhang.

I followed the path, towards the looming shade of the house. Another sensor light came on, illuminating the front of a modern building the color of obsidian.

I knocked on the door. My eyes drifted up to the familiar shape of a mezuzah affixed to the right corner of the frame.

A moment later, I heard the sound of someone coming down stairs.

I looked at the name on the dispatch: Adeline Frankmeyer.

"Just a minute," chirruped a female voice from within.

Seconds later the door opened inward on a short woman in a light-colored bathrobe. The woman's dyed cherry-red hair was in rollers. Her plump face wrinkled as she smiled at me. I guessed her age to be in the upper sixties.

"Mrs. Frankmeyer?"

"Yes?"

"How are you this evening?"

"I'm very good," she said, still smiling. "And how are you,

young man? Did you have trouble finding the place? Most people do. That's why we left the gate open."

"It's hard to see the numbers on the curb," I said.

"And it's so dark out there at night."

I nodded, and opened the flap. I pulled out the heavy box. "Here you go," I said. "You got it?"

Mrs. Frankmeyer nodded as she took it from me.

"Whoo, that's hot." She stepped over to a winding stairway and set it down on one of the lower steps.

She shuffled back to me; I looked down at her pink bunny slippers as they whisked across the hardwood floor, the stitched-on bunny heads looking like they were in a race. "How much do we owe you?"

Before I could answer, she held up a hand. "Aw jeez." She put her hands behind her, like she was groping for her own rump. "Wait a second."

She turned and stepped towards the winding staircase, both hands clasped to her bulging behind. "Mervin!" she yelled. "MERV!"

"What?" yelled a stung voice.

"I NEED MONEY FOR THE PIZZA!"

Mrs. Frankmeyer turned to me. She rolled her eyes, shaking her head.

I grinned.

"MERV! DID YOU HEAR ME?"

"Yes!"

"He'll be right down," she said. She picked up the pizza box from the step. "Thank you young man, for coming out here."

"You're welcome!"

Mrs. Frankmeyer smiled, then went off.

A moment later, legs dressed in baby blue pajama bottoms appeared, coming down the stairs.

The man who I presumed to be Mervin and Mr. Frankmeyer came towards me, holding a stack of cash.

The man was tall and very thin. He walked very slowly, billowing his blue pajamas with each leg forward. Above his wrinkled brow he bore several liver spots on his hairless head. He looked like he had a good twenty years on Adeline, as well.

And he looked unblinking at me the whole time he was coming towards me.

He stopped about a foot away, and lowered his eyes. He had a good foot on my height.

"Hi," I said.

He looked down. Licked his lips. "How much?" he said. His voice was papery, barely above a whisper.

I told him.

He flipped through the bills.

"Here you go," he said.

I took the offered bills. "Thank you very much."

Mervin Frankmeyer's eyes stared. He lifted his right arm. Opened his palm. His lips remained impassive.

Somehow, though, I got the feeling that he was regarding me with amiability.

"Bye," he said.

"Thanks again," I said. I turned with my empty carrier bag.

Going down the driveway, I pulled out my phone, hearing again the crickets. I hurried back to my car.

I was almost to Sunset when I saw her.

The gal with the red earmuffs.

Walking ahead, to my right.

I stepped on the brake too hard.

She turned around.

I looked in the rearview mirror. Luckily, there were no cars behind me.

"Idiot," I muttered, meaning me.

Looking forward, I saw Earmuff Girl turning her back.

She probably thought I was a lunatic.

She turned the corner at the last intersection before Sunset, down another residential street.

I had to give her a moment to get a little ahead of me.

And I had to give myself one, to figure out how I was going to approach this.

What do you say from a car to a gal walking home at night? When you're a pizza delivery guy?

Hey Babe, nice muffs!

She might be running up the block right now. Getting away.

Can't let her get away—you might not see her again!

I took my foot off the brake and turned the corner.

I could just see the gal at the edge of my headlight's glare. She was walking while looking behind her.

She's probably afraid you're following her—which you are.

I drove forward.

What are you doing, you idiot? You're already going to be late for Roxanne!

The gal looked right at me as I approached, her face seeming to glow even paler in the glare. I saw her freckles. Saw her lips locked in a small pink oval, her eyes looking wide and scared.

I almost hit the brake, then my foot found the gas and my car shot forward.

I drove on.

Feeling guilty and stupid.

Chapter 17

As the highway reached the vista, showing me the sprawling glitter of lights that was the San Fernando Valley, my car picked up speed.

"In a half mile. Take the one-oh-one freeway exit south!"

I was drumming my hands on the stirring wheel, not liking to be late and a little nervous. Roxanne, as I remembered, looked smoking hot.

"In two miles. Take the Coldwater Canyon exit!"

"Please still be hot," I said. "Please God. Grant us luck with the ladies."

A sudden green glint caught my eye and made me look to the wheat penny.

"Give me some luck, Lincoln."

In answer, Elizabeth spoke.

"In one thousand feet. Exit onto Coldwater Canyon."

I did as the seductive voice told.

"Continue on Coldwater Canyon for one mile."

The phone chirped. Another text.

The lady was getting impatient.

"In five hundred feet. Turn right onto Ventura Boulevard."

It occurred to me that I was being *led* by Elizabeth. She hadn't just interrupted Sally for one or two directives like she usually did—she had taken over navigational duty.

What did that mean?

What could that have to do with new areas on the map, as the retail clerk had suggested?

What if the sound of Elizabeth navigating, like the sound of the Demon Voice, was a bad thing?

"In six hundred feet. Your destination will be on the right."

I picked up the phone and ended Navigation, shutting off

Elizabeth.

Spotting the bar, I pulled over to a metered space and parked. Picked up my phone.

Let me know when you arrive

I looked up, hoping I'd see the green glint from the wheat penny again, but it just looked dull against the backdrop.

I texted back:

Just parkin

I clicked on the overhead light and checked myself in the mirror.

"Here goes," I said, giving myself the thumbs up. Then I put my thumb onto the soft plastic of the laminated wheat penny and pressed lightly, just enough to feel the cold press of it back.

Give me luck.

Geoffrey's had a patio with tables and heat lamps fenced in by a knee-high brick wall that opened in the middle. There were no lit candles on any of the tables, making the few clusters of people I saw from the street look like they were sitting in gloom. As I turned in, a glowing eye opened in the dark as someone dragged off a smoke, passing the bookish aroma of a clove cigarette.

Inside was boisterous with the sounds of men yelling. I looked up to the row of flat screens mounted above the bar. To the left I saw the larger space of the dining area in the dominating colors of red and blue. There was only one couple seated, with the remnants of dinner on the table.

Most of the chairs at the bar were filled. The pack of men in jerseys watching the TVs gave a sudden roar of approval, some standing up. I looked among their tables. I didn't see a lone woman among them or anyone who matched my memory of Roxanne.

She must be waiting in her car, waiting for me to come in first.

I stepped up to an opening at the bar and pulled out my phone.

"Help ya darlin?"

I looked up. "What do you have on tap?"

The portly woman gave a nod that indicated the line of tap handles she was standing directly behind.

"Sorry," I said, putting my phone back into my pocket. The bar was busy and the woman already looked impatient. "Speckled Hen."

"Here you go. Hiya Roxy!" the woman said, setting my pint down on the bar.

I turned and saw Roxanne a few steps behind me.

She didn't look at me, but said to the bartender, "Hi Mags."

"Hi," I said, stepping towards her with my arms out.

"How's it going?" she asked, stepping in for a brief embrace.

"What'll it be?"

"Here ya go, honey." I turned to see Mags already pushing a filled tumbler next to my own pint, the ice cubes clicking.

"Thanks Mags."

Mags looked at me, then turned and went to the other side of the bar.

"Do you want to take these over there?" I asked Roxanne, indicating the dining area.

"Let's go," she said.

Following Roxanne into the dining area, I marveled at the back of her.

Christ, she looked gorgeous.

There was little of the vampire look about her now. Her long hair was chestnut-brown, full and shiny, curling near the bottom. She was wearing a flutter-sleeve top the color of bright sapphire and dark blue denim jeans that looked painted onto her shapely legs. Her rump swayed from side to side as she walked.

Was I looking like the luckiest guy in the bar!

Roxanne went straight to the back, where there was a barren fireplace. She set her purse onto a table to the right of it, slid around and sat down. I had been planning on asking her if she'd been waiting long.

Instead, I said, "So where were you? I thought you'd said you were already here."

"I was giving head in the bathroom," she said, looking down as though rummaging through her purse.

"What?"

Roxanne looked up, seeming to actually look at me for the first time. I noticed too that her eyes were actually green.

"Fffthgh," she blew out her lips.

She was the first person in a while to give me the raspberry, besides Vic.

"That's what you were doing in the bathroom?"

Roxanne rolled her eyes.

"So," she said, looking bored. "How've you been?"

I already felt awkward, with the impression Roxanne wasn't approving. She looked great, and I could tell she'd put real effort into her appearance. She was wearing classy-looking bracelets around both wrists. Large hoop earrings. Her complexion looked impeccable. Her lips, glazed.

Only the looks she was giving me and the strange answers so far made me wonder if she thought she'd wasted all her time.

"You know the bartender's name," I said.

"Yep."

"So you come here a lot."

"That's Maggins."

"Maggins? What kind of name is Maggins?"

"Short for Maggie and Baggins."

"Maggie *Baggins?"* I looked towards the bar area where I happened to see the short portly lady with curly, ear-length red hair, polishing a glass in her hand with a rag.

I laughed, turning back to Roxanne. "That what everybody calls her around here?"

"No, only me."

"Well you're a cleva cunt!" I said in my Cockney accent. "Cheers!"

Roxanne gave me a mean look.

"I was just joking," I said.

Roxanne picked up her glass and tilted it to her mouth, ignoring the two thin plastic straws.

"I know you were," she said, setting the glass back down. "You'd have your dick in your mouth if I thought you were calling me a cunt for real."

I didn't know what to say. The Roxanne I remembered from the party had been talkative and friendly, if a little drunk. Hot or not, though, if this was going to be a verbal tug of war all night, maybe this was one to bail.

I still had a pint to drink. Might as well try.

"How'd the rest of your night go," I asked, "after the party that night?"

"I don't really remember it too well."

"I remember mine just fine."

"Yeah? You get laid?"

"Almost got killed."

"So what do you do?"

"I'm an actor."

"Which restaurant?"

"I have worked at many restaurants but this is kind of a new place in Grantwood. I'm actually a delivery driver."

"What kind of place?"

"It's kind of a fancy pizza place."

"So you're a pizza delivery boy?"

I picked up my glass, took a gulp of the bitter liquid. "Pizza delivery *man,"* I said.

Roxanne smiled, showing me rows of straight white teeth. It was a nice smile. It made her look suddenly very girlish, and delighted.

"Are you for real?" she asked.

"About as real as you."

Roxanne looked away and laughed. Like she was breaking fourth wall or laughing with an imaginary friend. Maybe she was. I took another gulp from my drink as she did the same.

"Hey," I said. "It's actually a great gig. Ideal for an actor. I don't have three quarters of the stress and shit you have to deal with as a waiter, and the pay's about the same. And it's kind of fun work. All I do is drive around, listen to music in my car, go up to people's places and give people what they ordered and get tipped. That's it. People are always very happy to see me. I meet interesting people and Grantwood's a nice area. I have a great flexibility too."

"I thought you were a writer, or something."

"Oh yeah, that's right. Well, not really. I think I told you at the party about a poem I had published somewhere. It's called Wandering in the Graveyard at Night. It's the only thing I ever had published. But I think it's pretty good. I like to recite it at Halloween parties whenever I get the chance."

"Can you still recite it?"

"Of course."

"Let's hear it."

"It's kind of long. It tends to test people's attention spans."

She nodded.

"I'm going to go outside and have a cigarette," she said. "Do you smoke?"

"Yes," I lied.

"I am the wanderer of graveyards
Frolicking in the black night at large

Chasing the spiritual residue
Of forgotten souls come before you

The shades of buried husbands and wives
Noble good-doers and wasted lives

That are ever moving unnoticed
Like invisible swarms of locusts

Searching for the world from whence they came
A door out of death where they remain

Writhing like thirsty fish on the land
And trampled by living feet like sand

"Alas, there's no respect for the dead!"
Laments the boy to trees overhead

To weeping willows bent in sadness
To great gnarling oaks wrapped in madness

Rising from out of the hallowed ground
Where worm-riddled skulls reside year 'round

Towards the inky vastness of space
As if deformed giants lay encased

Below the blanket of mossy earth
Their arms reaching up from crawling dirt

The boy picks his way through rows of stone
Age-worn monuments of corpses sown

Into the soil that forever thirsts
For life after the bubble has burst

Reading aloud the names of the dead

Stepping above their eternal beds

As wide-eyed owls hoot nocturnal song
Echoing throughout the shadow's throng

He kneels down in front of an old tomb
Glowing silver in light of the moon

And bows to the midnight gods of old
And the shorn sheep of the shepherd's fold

Whispers: "I heard your voices call me
O spirits of haunted memory

Like red embers in the autumn breeze
Carrying the spark of smoldered dream

As if a gale had blown them on me
And burned my skin so that I would see

The voice crying to be heard, and said
To one who would listen to the dead

Perhaps life is but one lucid daze
And death is a long unconscious maze

That has no ending; infinite road
To wander friendless and all alone

Know that I would accompany you
In limbo, for I am lonely too

So if you're listening, now is the time
To reach out to me and show a sign!"

And shutting his eyes prepares to wait
Long inside the cemetery gates

The wind swirls dry leaves on the ground
Phantom fog creeps in all around

Uh

Shit

"I always screw this part up. Sorry, one second. . .

"Okay, I'm just going to have to paraphrase this bit to get to the part I know I remember, okay? So yada-yada. . .dark witch-cat walks past meditating boy on the grass, the dark chameleon of the night turns once before drifting from sight. . .

And then a noise! His heart skips a beat
To dead leaves cracking; the tread of feet!

Out of the mist a neckless head flies
An evil face with deep sunken eyes

And baggy, yellow flesh like toffee
After being chewed and all soggy

With an oozing nose that's shaped porcine
And long, sharp teeth bared like a canine

The boy's lust for death turns to fear
His rapid heart thudding in his ear

As the ghoulish face opens its mouth
And says in an angry voice, "Get out!"

In a flash, he's gone, pumping his feet
Running for his dear life down the street

Leaving the ancient grave keeper there
All alone in the cool morning air

"Don't you ever come back boy, stay far!
Our ghosts are better left where they are."

"That's it," I said. I took a drag off the cigarette Roxanne had given me.

Roxanne took a drag off hers, still looking at me. Her eyes were green, I noticed again. Emerald. The smoke came out her nose.

"You're not inhaling," she said.

"I'm not really a smoker."

"I like it."

"What?"

"Your poem."

"Yeah? Thanks."

"Why don't you write more?"

I shrugged. "I thought I wanted to be a writer. Even went to college and majored in English."

"You graduate?"

"Yes. But everybody who majors in English seems to go straight into teaching, and that was one thing I knew I didn't want to do. What was I going to do, teach creative writing when I couldn't even do it myself, make a living? And teach people how they might? Didn't make sense to me. Most my writing heroes never went to college anyway—they just wrote their asses off."

"So why didn't you?"

"Write my ass off?"

"Yeah."

"I guess I tried. I spent about two years after college working as an office temp and trying to write at night. But it just didn't work. It was hard for me to be sitting all day, then get off work and try and write the rest of the night. Sitting alone, in the dark. When sitting was the last thing I felt like doing. I'd think of guys like Stephen King or Charles Bukowski, drinking their way through ten pages a night, sheets of paper that they maybe later couldn't remember even writing. That all sounded pretty good to me. But I just ended up sitting there and drinking every night. Drinking to get ready to write, then drinking more because I couldn't. Part of my problem was I just didn't have enough to say. Not for lack of wanting to, but really because I felt lacking in life experience for the things I wanted to write about. That wasn't easy to admit to myself.

"I took an acting class one summer, more for the purpose of just getting out and meeting people than anything else. I'd always fantasized about acting, fantasized about being my favorite characters. And you know what? I'm not saying a light came on and I suddenly felt destined to be the next Marlon Brando, but I came to realize that I'd always, secretly, dreamed of being a performer. I just never took it seriously. Never thought that I actually could do it. But after one class turned into several, I really started to say, you know, why not? Why *couldn't* I be an actor? I saw all types in the movies. Why couldn't there be room for me?

"That was the start of it. After a while I decided that my

idea of a writer's life just wasn't good for my health. I was happier acting. Acting gave me a license to be anything. You know, in a more physical sense. Physicality became important. It made me more aware of these things. Are you bored?"

"Let's go back inside," Roxanne said. She stubbed out her cigarette. "I'm ready for another drink."

"So you're an actor. Have you actually been in anything?"

"Do you watch the Reel Knowledge Channel?"

"Yeah."

"You know the show *I Fought the Law and Lost*? I was the main guy for one episode. We shot it up in the Bay Area."

"That's one of those reenactment shows."

"Yeah. It was a lot of fun to do. Other than that I've been in a few things. Mostly small bits on TV and student films and such. Done a few plays too. What about you?"

"I'm a bartender. Used to be a bartender here."

"No kidding? Why'd you leave?"

"I was working two jobs at the time. Here was cool, but I make more money where I'm at now and they asked me to work full-time. So."

"Where do you bartend now?"

"It's actually a bar in an Elk's Lodge in Sherman Oaks."

"And they have you working as a full-time bartender?"

"Not exactly. I do a couple hours of secretarial work before my shifts."

"What's it like working for them?"

"It's fine. They're a pretty good crowd. It's nice too because I'm always working by myself, unless it's some kind of big event."

"Good for you. And do you live in Sherman Oaks?"

"Yep."

"By yourself?"

She shook her head as she took in a drink. She set her glass back down. "What about you?"

"I have a roommate, yeah. Actually, I'm more just crashing with him until I can afford my own place. I'm pretty new to LA. *He's* a writer though."

"What's his name?"

"Victor Mapu."

"Haven't heard of him."

"You wouldn't have. He hasn't published anything yet, or

performed much. He's a comedy writer. He writes short stories and skits. But he's done some standup."

"Like open mic?"

"Yeah. He's pretty good. I think he'll definitely make a living off it eventually."

"Why doesn't he get his stuff published?"

I took a drink from my beer, shrugging as I did.

"He's a bit of a perfectionist. I think he's just more focused on his craft at the moment and wants to wait until he has a lot of stuff before he starts submitting. Bombard the market then."

"Was he at the Halloween party?"

"Was for a short time. Actually, you met him. He came up to us while we were sitting together. Remember a big Samoan guy dressed like a sailor?"

Roxanne made a sad grin with her mouth. "I don't remember much. Like I said."

"But you remembered me." I grinned.

"Not really. But anyway. How'd you meet him?"

"In college we had a couple classes together. Stayed in touch after and got to be great friends."

"That's bromantic."

Roxanne sat back in her chair. She looked away, her eyes narrowing like she was seeing something strange.

I turned and looked behind us. Saw nothing but the now mostly empty bar.

I turned back and Roxanne was looking down, tapping at her phone.

Probably texting someone.

"What's the matter, you getting bored?"

After a moment, she looked up. "What's that?"

"Nevermind. I guess they're going to kick us out soon."

"You're good to stay here as long as you're with me."

"Lucky me."

"You want another drink?"

"Um. . .you want one?"

"Why not?"

"I thought maybe you'd like to get going soon, or." *Might as well say it*. "You look like maybe you don't really want to be out."

Roxanne's eyes narrowed. "I wouldn't have come out if I didn't want to."

"Nobody's forcing you to stay, either."

"Do you want me to go?"

"I'm just saying you look like maybe you'd rather be elsewhere."

"Well, yeah. I'm thinking we can't stay here all night. I thought maybe you'd want to hit one more bar."

I looked at Roxanne, trying to read between her eyes.

"That's fine," I said. "But I got to be honest with you. I am kind of on a budget."

"You haven't spent a penny yet."

"I haven't settled up yet."

"You're not going to have to. I told you I worked here. I got connections." She stood up. "Why do you think I suggested here? Now do you want one more for the road or not?"

"Where to now?" I said. "I'm not familiar with this area."

"You like dive bars?"

"I was made in one."

Roxanne smiled. "There's a place up the road about a mile."

"Where'd you park?"

"I cabbed it."

"You don't have a car?"

"I do, but it's got a breathalyzer."

Roxanne explained the built-in device as we walked to my car. I thought she was joking, but after asking if she were really being serious, she said, "Trust me, this hasn't been my year."

On that, I did, and decided not to ask. The year before last hadn't been mine.

"Well," I said. "Let me introduce you to Ozzy."

"Ozzy?"

"My car," I said, pointing. "I named her that cause the dealership listed her as being iron man silver."

Pulling out my keys, I was about to step towards the passenger door to open it for Roxanne, then remembered that my Hyundai didn't have a keyhole on the passenger side—the Hyundai Accent was not a gentleman's car.

I went around and opened the car and we got in.

"You navigate," I said.

The bar was my kind of place: Small, with a pool table, free popcorn in a glowing corner, and a jukebox preoccupied with

AC/DC, Ratt, Cheap Trick, and Pantera.

Roxanne and I played pool. We seemed evenly matched (that or she was going easy on me), but the best part was watching her whenever she leaned over to inspect for an angle. I don't know if she knew it or not, but she tended to shake her rump ever so slightly. I gave her plenty of room.

Of course, she had the attention of every other guy in the bar too.

I felt good about that, until the guys came over.

Three bikers sauntered past on their way to the bathroom as Roxanne bent over, lining up her shot. Each of them made a point to stare at her behind, two of them whistling. The last one stopped, lifted his shades, then looked over at me.

He held my gaze. Then dropped the shades back, his thick black mustache seeming to frown.

When I saw the guys again, Roxanne and I were seated in chairs against the back wall.

The guy with the shades walked up, flanked by his two buddies.

"Are you a model?" he asked Roxanne.

"She is," I said.

The guy turned to me. "Why you gotta lie?"

"Huh?"

"I said. You're lying to me. Why do you feel you gotta do that?"

"I'm not lying to you."

The guy didn't move.

"She looks like a model to me," I said.

The smile was slow to spread on his face. "What's your name?"

"Dylan."

He held out his hand. "Rick."

We shook, Rick's hand swallowing my own.

"You have yourself a good night," he said, smiling with teeth too white.

They walked back to the bar.

"You're popular," I said, turning to Roxanne.

She smiled towards her drink.

"LAST CALL!" the barmaid yelled.

"You about ready to go?" I asked, taking up my beer.

"Yeah."

I knocked back my Rolling Rock, glancing towards the

men. They had their backs to us.

"Bye Sadie!" Roxanne called as we walked towards the door.

"Bye Doll!"

Now I was glad we had parked just outside, right on the street.

Key out, I went to open the door for Roxanne.

"Keep forgetting this thing only has one lock."

I turned around to see Roxanne's hand coming towards me.

Grabbing the side of my head, she pulled me towards her, and I leaned down into her lips.

Something like a minute later, I put my hands on her hips and we unlocked.

Roxanne looked away. I looked towards the bar's entrance.

The barmaid had come out. She was holding a lit cigarette in one hand and her phone up in the other.

"Come on," I said. "I'll take you home."

The road began to climb.

"How far up these hills we going?" I asked.

"You're going to be making a right coming up. . .right here."

"These are nice houses. How many roommates do you have?"

"I live with my parents."

"This is your parents place we're going to?"

"I moved back in with them last month."

"That must be kinda nice. You get to work and save a bit of money."

"Not really."

"You don't get on with your parents?"

"They're all right. Obviously I'd rather have my own place. Like I said. It hasn't exactly been my year.

"The road's going to end up here," she said, pointing. "You can turn around at the fence and just park."

She apparently didn't trust me enough to tell me which house was hers.

So much for asking to use the bathroom.

I did as she instructed. Flicked off the lights, and turned the key.

Opening my seatbelt, I leaned over. Roxanne's lips moved against mine.

I slipped my hand in between her arm and her side, meeting the curve of her breast. I pressed, feeling the thick fabric of her bra beneath the silky top. Then felt the entrance of her tongue in my mouth.

I turned more in my seat as Roxanne put her hand on the side of my head just above my ear. The soft press of her fingertips set off a tingling down my back.

She moaned into my mouth as I took hold of her shoulder and gently edged it forward, so that I would have room to slip my arm around and pull her in closer. I felt the scrape of her nails as I got it around, my other hand leaving her breast and going further around her side.

She broke from our kiss, turning her cheek.

"Should probably get going."

"Okay," I said.

I put my hand up to the side of her face and turned it back to me. I kissed her.

"See you soon?" I asked.

"Maybe. We'll see." She reached to get her purse, then realized she was still buckled in. With an annoyed grunt, she unbuckled her belt. "Not really into the idea of dating anyone right now."

She put her purse on her lap.

I picked up her purse and flung it into the backseat. "Then wait a second."

Putting my hand between my legs, I levered back my seat as far as it would go.

I reached for Roxanne, but her hands shot out.

"Guh!"

Her thumbs pressed my Adam's apple.

Then released.

I saw her hand come up, and like a slow slap land on the side of my head.

She held it there, looking me in the eyes.

Then she leaned in, pulling me forward, and kissed me.

I wrapped my arms around her.

With a sigh, Roxanne pushed me back and began to climb over.

The horn honked as her ass pressed on the wheel.

I laughed.

Above me, Roxanne cracked a smile. Again showing me that girlish look.

Lowering, she straddled me.

"This car's small," she muttered.

My erection mashed against the rough thrusting barrier of her jeans.

I pushed her back.

"Take this off," I whispered.

Roxanne shook her head.

I began to pull up her top as her hands found my throat again and pushed me back.

I brushed off her hands.

"What's the matter?" I asked.

Roxanne looked down at me, her face set. She was breathing hard.

She sat back. Brushed up her long hair with one arm. I noticed her necklace for the first time.

She seemed to look out the back window, like she was watching for something. Though I knew she couldn't see anything—the windshield behind her was fogged.

"I'm not going to bone you," she said.

"Okay."

"I'm going to go in."

"All right."

My fingers trembled just below her blouse. I felt them go under, feeling her hot bare skin.

She let me crawl up as far as her bra before she moved her hands forward and guided me down.

I went along behind her, feeling her back in massaging little circles.

Her spine arched. *"Sss."*

"You like that?"

She said nothing.

She took off her shirt.

I stared up at a half-naked Roxanne, but for the black bra that was barely holding back her breasts.

Lady Luck was with me indeed, I thought. I was about to break Ozzy in.

Roxanne didn't object as I reached behind to find the clasp.

Then the phone rang.

Roxanne climbed off and got back into the passenger seat with her purse. The light from her phone shined out from the partially unzipped top. She pulled it out and brought it to her face without checking who was calling.

Booty call?

"Yeah?" she said.

"Where are you?" The voice on the line was loud, and female.

"I'm at a friend's," she said.

"Where. Are. You."

"At a friend's."

"At a friend's?"

"Yeah."

I noticed Roxanne's voice had softened, whether by tactic or out of fear.

"Your curfew is at one! It is now two!"

Roxanne said nothing.

"Roxanne?"

"Yeah."

"Your curfew is at ONE! It is now TWO!"

"I heard you."

"You. . .ungth."

"Gimme that," said another voice. "GODDAMNIT WOMAN I'LL TELL YOU WHAT. YOU LISTENING TO ME? YOU GET YOUR SWEET BUTT HOME NOW! GODDAMNIT YOU GOT ME UP ALL GODDAMN NIGHT!"

"I can't hear you!" Roxanne said. "You're shouting!"

"YA LIL BRAT! I SWEAR TO THE ALLMIGHTY I DON'T SEE YA TRAILIN UP THIS WALK HERE NOW ANY MINUTE—"

"Put Mom back on!"

"YA LIL BRAT!"

"Put her on, or I'm hanging up."

"Jesus," I muttered. The man sounded like Yosemite Sam gone wrong. An old grizzled cranker I pictured wearing a cowboy hat.

"Roxanne. You heard your father."

"He was yelling at me!"

"He's been up all night with me worried sick. Now why didn't you come home? You know you have a one o' clock curfew. You know you have to go by our rules. Why didn't you come home?"

"I'm on the way now. We're in the canyon. I'll see you soon."

"You get home right now! Where are you?"

"I'm going to hang up."

"You get home! Now."

Roxanne ended the call. She stared forward in her seat.

"Guess you better go, huh?"

"Yeah."

She put her top back on.

God damn it.

I reached for the key.

"Wait," I said. "Do you really live on this street?"

"Yes," she said. "I'll just walk over."

"Do you want me to wait?"

"For what?"

I just looked at her, not sure what else to say.

"All right," she said. "Have a good night."

I leaned over for one more kiss.

Then she left.

Chapter 18

I woke up on the floor. Again.

Vic's big form hunched at the computer, his skin lit by the florescent glow. I closed my eyes and rolled onto my side, facing the dark beneath his futon.

"What's up snatch grabber?"

But now he knew I was awake. Might as well get up.

"What's up?" I said, rolling onto my back.

"How'd it go?"

"It went well. She was a lot of fun."

"Did you hit it?"

"No. But there's potential."

"Uh oh! Why not?"

I told Vic the story as I got up, put my bedding in the closet, and made myself a mug of coffee.

"So what do you make of that?" I asked.

"Somebody's got *issues*," he said, pouring a third bowl of cereal into a new bowl.

"I think she's going through a transition period. I mean, who would want to live with parents like that when they're already grown and making money?"

"You said she got a DUI."

"There's that. And I think something else must've happened, maybe on the same night she got her DUI. She definitely wasn't ready to talk about it, and I don't blame her. I'm still going through my own transition that, uh. . .I'm not exactly eager to talk about, with anybody."

"You're doing fine, though."

I looked at my coffee as a nervous gust came up from my gut. His words became tickling hairs at the bottom of my throat. All of a sudden I wanted to cry.

"What's up man?"

All of a sudden I did.

"Hey man," Vic said. "Come on. Time to talk."

I wiped my eyes. Cleared my throat. "I know it's been more than two years. But sometimes I see flashes of their faces, in happy times, and I remember what I've lost. What was *taken*. Sometimes that night, that moment comes rushing back. I feel that dread."

I cleared my throat some more.

"I don't think you have any idea. . .if you hadn't answered that call, I don't know what I would have done."

"I remember," Vic said. "I don't think I'll ever forget the way you sounded on the phone, man. The pain I heard in your voice. It was haunting."

Haunted was the word I felt.

"But you were there for me," I said. "At four in the morning. At the moment it felt like my world had come to an end. I want you to know that I always appreciate that."

"Of course. That's what friends are for man. I'm glad you called."

"I'm glad you answered."

At that, my phone rang.

"Morning Dad," I said, stepping out into the sun.

"What's happening?"

"Nothing much, just got up. Just having my coffee."

"You sick?"

"What?"

"You sound all congested."

"Nah," I said, sitting down on the stairway. "Just got up. Let me remind you that Vic's a writer. Which means that floor isn't vacuumed everyday."

"What is he, trying to keep the essence in, or something?"

"Something like that. So, what's going on with you?"

"Oh, nothing much. Your mother and I are going out to dinner tonight."

"Nice."

"Yeah, so. . .how did your date go, didn't you have a date?"

"I did, it went well. She was nice."

"You taking her out again?"

"I don't know. We'll see."

"Yeah? And. . .how's the job?" Dad sounded doubtful asking this, as he had ever since the attack.

"It's going fine, Dad."

"Well, that's good. You working today?"

"Working every night now except Mondays."

"Will you be getting any time off for the holidays?"

"No, but I'll be taking time off."

"You going to be able to make it up here, or."

"Of course. I'm going to request a few days off. Which reminds me, I should actually do that tonight when I go in."

"Think they'll give it to you?"

"They're going to be closed Christmas day, so I'm just going to ask for two more days. I'll try for Christmas Eve and the day after. That way I can head up after I get off the last night, get up to the Bay Area late, but then I'll have three full days after."

"Great! I wasn't sure if you'd want to stay down there, or."

"Why the hell would I want to stay down here?"

"And how about Vic?"

"I'm not sure what Vic is doing yet. He'll probably fly out to see his Mom."

"Okay. Well, that's good, I'm glad to hear you'll be able to make it up."

"Course. I look forward to it."

"Any auditions?"

I swallowed involuntarily.

"Hello?"

"Nope."

I opened the car door. Something lay coiled on the passenger floor.

It was Roxanne's necklace.

Must have came off with her shirt, and she'd forgotten about it.

I smiled.

Second date guaranteed.

Chapter 19

I walked in to Taste Testers to see three new people behind the registers, two guys and one gal. All three were listening to Taylor as he instructed them.

I stepped in through the swinging double doors.

Taylor turned. "Ryan and Joey," he said to me.

"Hi guys," I said. "I'm Dylan."

Ryan was tall and apple-bellied, with brown whiskers above his lips. His eyebrows flicked up in acknowledgment. He looked bored. Next to him Joey was short, fat, and cheery-looking. He smiled with baby teeth, a rivulet of sweat trailing from the dark curling hair beneath his cap.

"Melissa," Taylor said, pointing to the gal.

Melissa was small with rather flat features, but her smile was cute.

"Dylan's one of our drivers," Taylor continued. "Anyway, so. . ."

I walked to the back to get my topper.

Inside my car, I pulled out my phone and opened my last conversation with Roxanne.

I typed:

> Good morning. I believe I have a necklace of yours?

and hit send.

Wondering whether I wanted to try and catch a nap or if I should join Joel and Jeffrey upstairs, Hooper's big white truck pulled in to the space next to me, and that decided that.

Levering back my seat, I closed my eyes.

Heard a door shut. The heavy step of his work boots.

The breezy sounds of cars nearby.

Boots clacking up the stairs. And fading.

Knock-knock!

I opened my eyes.

The face of the Tennis Bum was pressed against the window, his milk-coated pupils round and excited. His trembling mouth opened and a crab came out.

BRIIINNG!

I bolted up awake, gasping.

BRIIINNG! BRIIINNG!

Heart pounding, I picked up the vibrating phone.

A voice I didn't recognize said, "Yeah, um. You've got a delivery?"

"Okay."

I ended the call and returned the phone to its nook.

"Jesus," I whispered.

I levered the seat up, then opened the door.

Walked up the stairs feeling tired and sluggish.

Shouldn't have scarfed all that food on the way here.

The boys were on the wall.

"Have a nice nap?" Hooper asked.

Back in my car, I pulled out my phone.

I had gotten a text from Roxanne.

I thought I lost it thank u. What you doing?

I texted her back

Working. Want to meet up again for a drink?

Pulling out of the parking garage into the alley, drizzle began to speckle my windshield. I flicked on my windshield wipers and went slower for fear of Grantwoodians who loved to step onto the road like they were car-proof.

"You have arrived!"

The dispatch said I was delivering to a D Santos on 900 Amelia Court, Apt. 207.

Apartment? There were houses on either side of the street.

I got out. Walked up the street towards an alleyway. Driving past, I'd seen what looked like little garages or bungalows—maybe there was a building with units tucked away there?

The alleyway wasn't lit, so the building numbers, if there were any, were hard to see. I saw a row of six buildings, three on each side.

These are probably just garages, I thought.

I took a few steps into the alleyway.

A tumbleweed crossed the path ahead as a breeze blew a cold trickling of water onto my back.

No, this can't be right.

Turning around, I walked back to the sidewalk. Seeing only houses, most of which were single storey and relatively small for Grantwood, I walked back to the car.

Inside, I again said the address into the phone's mic.

This time I didn't hear Sally or see the green screen of new directions, but the dark screen that usually showed a picture of the building only revealed a white blank square with text telling me that I had arrived.

What the hell?

"Thank you for calling Taste Testers in Grantwood, this is Taylor, can you please hold?"

"Hey Taylor!" I said. "It's Dylan."

"What's up Dylan?"

"I'm sorry man but I'm having real trouble finding this one address. My GPS is taking me in circles."

"Okay, where are you now?"

"I'm at the corner of Amelia Court and Sampson."

"Gimme a sec while I pull up the map. . .Amelia and Sampson you said?"

"Yeah."

"Did you cross over Wilshire?"

"No, I wasn't. . .I mean, I'm close to Wilshire."

"Well I see it here. You gotta cross over Wilshire, head down Amelia towards Texas Ave and it should be there. Give me a call back in five minutes if you still can't find it and I'll call them and see if they gave us the right address."

"Okay." I hung up.

I wiped sweat off my brow, despite the rain and air-conditioned car. Whoever this D. Santos guy was, he was probably wondering what was taking so long, and would probably factor that in when tipping me. *If* he tipped.

I headed off towards Wilshire.

After crossing over, I followed Mundy until I hit Texas.

"In six hundred feet. Turn right onto Amelia Court! Then your destination is on the left!"

I traveled the short distance and turned onto Amelia.

"Your destination is on the left."

Parked, I looked down at my phone. This time it showed a picture of the apartment building.

I shook my head.

Wonky-ass phone.

D Santos was not listed on the directory.

I dialed the phone number on the dispatch, and immediately recognized the voice of the woman who answered.

"You have reached a number that has been disconnected, or is no longer in service."

Great.

Just then a woman exited the building, letting the door fall back. I grabbed the handle.

I took the elevator up to the second floor.

The elevator doors opened and I was facing a doorway.

201

I turned right and began walking down the hallway.

The walls were bruised with grease smudges and the pen-line scratches of moved furniture. The carpet was the color of cigarette ash and smelled like the inside of a vacuum that needed emptying. I stepped over black spots that had to be very old gum.

At the top, the hallway continued on to the left. I looked to the right and saw 204.

I knocked on the door and stepped back.

*Wait a second. . .*I pulled out my dispatch and checked the number.

207

"Whoops!"

I turned and hurried away from the door before it could open, chuckling to myself: It had been a really long time since I played ding-dong ditch.

Someone might think there are ghosts in the hall.

Around the corner I found 207, and knocked.

Heavy footfalls came towards the door.

The door opened and a big guy stood there.

"Hey," I said, "I'm really sorry for being late."

"No!" he said. "No worries at all."

The guy had an open, kind face. He was about my height but stocky, with longish black hair and a trimmed black beard. He looked to be in his thirties.

"Appreciate it," he said, taking the pizza box off me. "That smells so good." He turned into his dim apartment. It looked like he had just moved in. I saw stacks of large boxes on the otherwise empty carpet.

He came back, and I noticed for the first time the familiar white logo on his black T-shirt.

"I like your shirt," I said. "I'm a big fan of AC/DC." Then I noticed the actual letters. "Oh, AD/*HD*." I laughed. "That's funny. Where'd you get that?"

The guy blinked. "Huh? Oh!" He looked down at his shirt, the fabric stretched over his soft stomach. "You know I. . .I can't remember. I've had it a while. I've got a lot of goofy shirts I've collected over the years."

"That's cool."

"How much do I owe you, boss?"

"That'll be twenty-six, seventy," I said.

He nodded, pulling out his wallet.

He handed me $35. "Thank you man, I appreciate it," he said.

"Hey, I really appreciate it," I said. "And sorry again for being late."

"Hey man, really, it's cool!" He seemed to be on the verge of saying something. Then he stepped towards me. His hand shot out. "What's your name?"

"Dylan," I said.

He told me his as we shook hands. It sounded like Deige.

"DJ?" I asked.

"Dee-Gee. D. And then G."

"DG. All right, nice meeting you."

"Likewise. See you again!"

"Take care!" I turned and walked away as his door shut behind me.

What a nice guy, I thought.

To think I'd been expecting an irate customer, only to get the gentle giant.

I turned the corner.

An elderly man in spectacles was peering out from behind the door to 204. He looked small and fragile behind the shield of the door.

"Oh, hello," he said as I approached, his voice soft and shaky.

"Hello," I said.

I stopped. "Are you okay?"

The man's eyes blinked behind the glasses. "I thought it was. . .someone knocking on the door."

I opened my mouth to tell him that it had only been me by mistake, but instead I nodded my understanding, and continued walking.

Before I stepped into the elevator I looked back. I couldn't see around the corner from where I was, but I had a feeling the old man was still there, leaning slightly out from the door.

Waiting.

The store was full with dine-in customers when I returned and I was immediately sent out again. As soon as I was back in my car I checked my phone. No word yet from Roxanne.

I started the car.

Chirrp!

All right, here we go with her answer, I thought.

This was the make or break moment. I felt good, though—I had a feeling Roxanne was hot for my bod.

My rumination was interrupted by the sudden change to Elizabeth's voice.

"Turn right onto Westlake Avenue. Then your destination will be on the right."

I did as the sultry voice instructed.

"You have arrived," Elizabeth purred.

I exited out of Navigation and checked my text message.

OK. Geoffs again? For starters

For starters. I liked the sound of that.

I texted back:

Sounds good. See you and Maggins there at 10 ;)

A young blonde woman in a pink bathrobe answered the door. "How are you?" she asked, smiling.

She was an *attractive* young blonde woman in a pink bathrobe.

"I am very good," I said. "Hope I didn't get you out of the shower."

"No," she said, and chuckled. "This is me in relax-mode."

She reached for the box, the bottom of her robe lifting to her knees. "Thank you—hey!"

A little dog had appeared and was now trying to scurry up my legs.

"Rocky! He's friendly."

"I can tell," I said.

"Sorry."

"It's okay." I bent down and petted the little guy. "Hiya Rocky. How ya doin?"

Rocky sniffed my hand, and licked.

"What is he?"

"He's a Shih Tzu. Uh oh." She had opened the pizza box and was looking in. "I'm sorry. I think there's been a mistake. This has mushrooms on it."

"Oh no."

"I mean, it's okay. I'll still eat it, I'm not allergic or anything. It's just that it wasn't supposed to."

"I'm very sorry," I said. "Do you want me to have them make you another one?"

"Um. . .you know what, it's fine. Really."

"It won't take long. I can just phone it in and they'll rush it out to you."

"I don't want to be a pain."

"You're not a pain in the slightest." I pulled out my phone. "Tell you what, so long as you don't mind waiting just a little longer, let me call these guys now and have them make you a new one, and we'll send it straight out. Okay?"

She put a finger to her pursed lips, turning her body while keeping her gaze locked on. Her eyes were big and blue.

"Okay," she said, smiling.

God *damn,* she looked incredibly cute.

"Why don't you come in?" she asked. "Get out of the rain

while you wait."

She held the door open.

"Rocky! Come!"

I followed Rocky inside to the rosy glow of her living room. It was lit by candlelight.

I held the phone to my ear while I waited for someone to pick up.

"Thank you for calling Taste Testers, can you please hold?"

"Sure," I said.

As I pretended to be listening to the automated spiel about how good our baked wings were, I looked around. The place was full of ornaments and knickknacks. On the mantelpiece two families of Matryoshka dolls stood in opposing lines of height hierarchy flanked by twin nutcrackers. On the walls I saw several paintings.

"Because we're *the Taste Testers. You've* gotta *try us. Our pizza dough is—"*

"You've a very nice place," I said. "It's like a cozy Christmas in here."

She laughed. "By the way, what's your name?"

"Dylan."

"I'm Adrian."

"Adrian? That's funny. You and Rocky."

"All my friends thought it was a good idea too."

"Very nice to meet you." I took Adrian's warm hand in mine.

"Can you wait here a moment?"

"Sure."

"Be right back." She turned. My eyes went to her smooth calves as they walked away. She went around the corner.

I heard what sounded like cereal being poured into a bowl.

"Here you go, Big Boy!"

I looked up, wondering if she meant me. Then I noticed Rocky was nowhere in sight.

She came back out from the kitchen, smiling.

I smiled back.

And noticed her robe was more open. A thick arrow point of skin now showed below her neck.

Must be because she'd had to bend down to pour the dog food.

Too bad I'd missed that.

Adrian went to her coffee table. Bending at the knees, she picked up a glass of red wine. She carried it to an armchair facing me where I stood.

She sat on the armrest, the front of her robe sagging forward.

Sorry, she mouthed. She lifted the glass as though to toast me, then took a sip.

As I listened to the actor on the line telling me for the second time about the Chicago-styled meat pizza, I heard Adrian with the other. "Mmm," she purred, having lowered the glass from her lips. She tilted her head back, closing her eyes. I noticed a partial stain of maroon on her lips.

As though she read my mind, her tongue came out and did a slow, circular glaze.

"Thank you for holding, this is Taylor, how may I help you?"

"Hey," I said. "I'm calling for Adrian. I got a mistake for order number one ninety-one. There wasn't supposed to be any mushrooms on their pizza and there's mushrooms."

"Ninety-one? One second, pulling it up. . ."

I heard a muttered curse from Taylor. "So there wasn't supposed to be any mushrooms?"

"No."

"Okay. I'll have the guys remake it."

"Thanks," I said, and ended the call.

"Okay," I said, looking back at Adrian.

Adrian had crossed one leg over the other, lifting the bottom of her robe to her lap. She was showing me a full view of her bare thigh. Below it I saw a faint trim of golden hair.

"Well?" she asked.

I looked up to her face.

"They're going to remake it now and someone will bring it out to you soon."

Adrian smiled. "I really appreciate it."

"No problem at all. I'm sorry for the inconvenience. Why don't we leave you with this pizza? So now you'll have two. Maybe Rocky can get some?"

"No, Rocky doesn't get pizza. Thanks. I'll never eat it all by myself though."

She uncrossed her legs and stood up, the robe falling back to below her knees. "I guess I'd better pay ya."

She set her glass onto the coffee table, and walked over to me. I took the pen from my pocket and handed it to her along with the credit card slip.

She signed it, and handed it back with the pen.

"It was really nice meeting you, Dylan." She gave me a big smile.

"You too. Good night."

I turned and walked to the door.

"Bye," she purred behind me.

Sitting in my car, I looked to the door of Adrian's first floor apartment, half-expecting to see her framed in the rosy glow from within, her pink bathrobe now hanging open, waiting for me to come back. But the door was closed.

That gal had *wanted* me.

And I'd just walked out. Without taking the cue.

"Man!"

I looked at the dispatch.

Adrian Schwerz. Followed by her address and phone number.

I put the slip into the space below my audio setup where I kept my iPod and sunglasses, not sure what I planned to do with it.

Maybe I'd want to hold onto it so I could contact her.

Maybe if you hurry your ass back, you'll be the one to take the second pizza out!

I fastened my seatbelt. Turned on the car, the headlights.

She bats those bedroom eyes at me this time, I ain't hesitating.

All three of the boys in yellow hats were standing by the wall as I hurried up. It had stopped raining.

Joel turned and shook his head. "What a night," he said.

"Slowed down?"

"Stalled, is more like it," Jeffrey said.

"What do you mean?"

"Been getting any mistakes?" Hooper asked.

"Yeah, just got one."

"It's the new people," Joel said. "They've been fucking up all night."

"Especially that girl," Jeffrey said. "What's her name?"

"Melissa," Joel said. "What a ditz."

"She's the reason we're all sitting here right now," Jeffrey said. "Every one of us is back because an order got screwed up."

"Wow," I said. "Anyway, I gotta go in now."

"See if any of us are up," Joel said.

A phone rang, and I heard Hooper say, "Guess I am."

When I walked in Taylor was behind the register, red-faced and sweating. He was doing something on the computer while Melissa and Ryan watched.

He whizzed past as I stepped in through the doors.

"Hey guys, where's one-twenty-six already? Come on!"

"Hey Taylor?" I asked.

"You gotta give me a second," he said. "Hooper! Here's your one-ten. Double-check the dispatch! And can you send the rest in? I need these orders out now!"

Chaos in here.

"Everybody keeps fucking up tonight," he muttered, wiping sweat from his brow. "What you need?"

"So about that last order I took out?"

"Ninety-one's all good."

"I know they're remaking it, I was just wondering if I could be the one to take it out, because—"

"It's all good. The lady with the mushrooms, right? She called back and said she was fine."

"Oh."

"Don't worry about it. Why don't you go grab me a bag, I'm sending you right out in a sec."

I drove off again into the night.

Damned if I didn't feel like a loser.

"Adrian. . ."

Hot gal like that invites me inside, shows me up her legs, knowing I can see she's wearing nothing underneath. Gives me the signs, and what do I do? I blow it.

"ADRIAAAN!"

"Continue on Sunset for one mile!"

I felt hot and sticky beneath my uniform and undershirt. Now that it was no longer raining, I lowered my window, welcoming in the cool breeze.

"In one thousand feet. Turn right onto Glennmeadow Canyon!"

Glennmeadow was a new one.

I signaled and turned.

"Continue on Glennmeadow for one and a half miles!"

From what I could see, Glennmeadow looked like Mannerville Canyon, being a two-lane road with rich foliage on either side. But unlike Mannerville, which ran flat and mostly straight for as long as I'd been on it, Glennmeadow was winding and seemed to be steadily climbing.

Headlights appeared behind me.

I continued, slowing as I took each curve, anticipating deer.

The lights behind got brighter.

On a straight stretch, I looked in the rearview mirror.

It was a white truck.

With a lit Taste Testers top.

Hooper?

Funny that he should be on the same road.

We continued on, Hooper staying close behind. I kept glancing at my mirror. I couldn't actually see Hooper, but I kept expecting him to start honking or flash me with his high beams or something in friendly acknowledgment.

But he just kept following.

There was something a little creepy about Hooper following. We were headed up the hills at night. There were no other cars on the road. No one else seemed around.

I glanced down at my phone. Still a little over half a mile away.

Looked up and found myself approaching a fork in the road too quickly.

"Shit!"

I went right.

The road continued up. I waited to hear the voice of Sally correcting me, but she stayed silent. Apparently I'd stayed the course.

So had Hooper.

"What the hell is he—?"

Wait a second. . .don't tell me one of the new people dispatched us both to the same place?

That seemed more likely now.

"Guess we'll find out who brought the right order," I muttered.

"In nine hundred feet. Your destination will be on the right!"

On either side of the road I saw houses, spaced well apart.

Each seemed to have old-fashioned mailboxes.

I glanced down.

250 ft to go.

"Your destination is on the right!"

Ahead I saw a red mailbox. Above it a sign that said 51.

This was the place.

I pulled to the side of the road, noticing the open gate for the first time. I passed the gate and parked.

Looked in the rearview mirror.

I didn't see Hooper.

He hadn't passed me either.

Strange.

Must've been delivering to another house after all. Right below me.

With these orders being so close, why the hell hadn't they just sent me out on a double?

Must be the new people.

I got out from the car to the chorus of crickets.

Got the carrier bag, and shut the door.

I walked over to the wooden gate.

The path went down, then wound out of view. It was large enough for one car, but wasn't paved.

I started down the path.

The sand was now effectively mud, thanks to the rain. I had to watch where I was going; the many littered leaves were slippery too.

I turned the corner by a big tree, and saw more path.

The crickets seemed to get even louder.

I continued on, my shoes squelching.

Man it's dark.

No lights out here.

Something snapped behind me.

I whirled and looked.

Didn't see anything.

I waited, listening to the crickets and the thumping of my heart, but I heard nothing else as I stared up the dark trail, expecting to see a sudden shadowy figure descending down.

Hooper maybe. Following me out into the woods. For no good reason.

Whatever it was, it had sounded like a tree branch snapping underfoot.

I waited some more. Then I turned and continued on.

Probably just a deer.

Or a mountain lion.

It occurred to me then that I *was* in mountain lion country. They liked to hunt at night, didn't they? And I was a walking aroma with three hot pizzas in a bag.

I imagined myself getting jumped by a giant cat. My bones and yellow hat would be found a few days later.

Better watch them shadows. . .

To my left was an upward slope. The attack would most likely come from there, if not from behind.

The path wound to the right, up a slight incline, then down, and I saw nothing but darker path ahead.

"What the hell?"

Is this a driveway or a hiking trail?

The house is probably just around the next corner, I told myself.

But what if it wasn't? What if the wooden gate was left open because the house was *miles* back?

The GPS could be wrong, once again.

I walked faster.

I was approaching another bend. If I didn't see anything beyond it this time, I was turning back.

I turned the corner and saw lights.

Not just the lights from the house. The tree line opened up ahead, revealing the glittering lights of the urban sprawl far below.

I walked up to the house, following the path in between an old dusty blue pick-up truck and black range rover, the way lit by the bright porch light.

The house front was modern, like a giant windowless white square. The door was gold-colored. I pressed the glowing button to the side of it.

The door was opened by a tall middle-aged man with thinning red hair, his face and arms heavily freckled.

"Hey, pizza guy!"

"Good evening," I said.

"Come on in, won't cha?"

Wiping my shoes first on the welcome mat, I followed him in.

The inside was as white as the front, with shiny hardwood floors that squeaked beneath my shoes.

I followed the man up a step into a modern kitchen.

"You can just set it down right here," the man said,

indicating the marbled counter.

As I stepped over I noticed the black-carpeted area that was another step below the kitchen. There were two people there, both sitting with their backs to me at desks.

One of them was a young woman with short shiny auburn hair. She turned and looked up at me.

"Pizza guy," she said, giving me a warm smile. "Yay!"

The other, a very pale man judging from the Eminem haircut and bulk beneath the dark shirt, didn't turn from the computer.

I opened the bag and pulled out the large boxes one by one, stacking them.

The man walked over and opened the boxes. I stood aside. Turning my head past the studious two, I noticed for the first time the far wall was entirely glass; the lights of the city below winking like an ocean of glitter.

"Wow," I said. "You folks have an amazing view."

"What's that?" the man asked.

I turned to him. "You have an amazing view," I repeated.

"No, what is *that?"* he said, frowning at the pizza.

I walked over and looked down.

It looked like the thin crust barbeque chicken pizza to me.

"Honey, can you come here?"

The woman swiveled around on her seat and got up.

She had a slender body and graceful walk. She joined us in the kitchen.

"What's what, honey?"

"Did you order anchovies?"

"No."

"Then what the jumpin flapjacks is that?"

"Mmm," she said, peering in to the rising steam. Stepping back, she turned to me and smiled. "Smells delicious."

"What are those fried wormy-lookin things?"

"Those are red onions."

"Red onions? Did you order red onions on this?"

"It comes with it."

"Oh."

"Is it okay?" I asked.

"It's fine," the woman said. "How much do we owe you? Or Sanders, did you already—?"

"I already paid, yes."

"If I could just have your signature," I said, pulling out my pen and the slip.

"I got a pen," Sanders said, whipping one out from his shirt pocket.

The woman walked back towards the living room area. "Bobby? Are you ready for the pizza?"

"Sure," Bob said to his computer monitor.

"Here you go," Sanders said, handing me back the slip. "Thanks a lot." He smiled, showing real warmth on his face. He reminded me of Fred Gwyne.

I smiled back. "You're very welcome, sir."

"Thank you!" the woman called from the living room. She had gone back in, but now she was coming back towards the kitchen.

She put her hand on Bob's shoulder.

"Come on Bobby. Let's eat."

"Thanks again for coming out here. We know it's a bit of a hike."

"Sure is," I said. "But it was a nice walk."

"Walked?"

"I mean, I parked at the gate and walked in," I said.

"Oh jeez," the woman said. "That's a creepy way to go at night."

"We leave that gate open so people know to drive up," Sanders said.

"It's a nice starlit night," I said.

"No, it's *not!"* Bob whirled around in his chair, with transparent skin and glowing eyes. "It's not a starlit night, or do you see me out there with my instruments?"

Bob got up and trotted towards me, like an angry dough man, the hair on his head looking like cream.

"Bobby loves the stars," said the woman. "We have our own little observatory room."

"This summer I saw Ophiuchus," Bob said. He looked up with a furrowed brow, his incredibly pale face a jigsaw of blue veins, his pink eyes seeming to stare through me.

I didn't know what to say to that.

"Do you know why he wrestles? It's because he wishes to be alone. We all know the snake is linked to Asclepius. But what he's doing, if he could only break through the loop binding, he could sever the head from the tail, he could undo what is and take the medicine and leave off the refractive armament, breaking free and we could never observe him again. That would be freedom."

I *really* didn't know what to say to that.

Bob said, "It's also known for its beautiful globular clusters."

With that, he turned and trotted over to the kitchen.

"It's been really nice meeting you," said the woman. "Would you like Sanders to drive you to the gate so you don't have to walk it again?"

"Oh, no," I said. "But thank you. That's really nice of you."

"You sure?"

"Sure he's sure!" Sanders said. He turned to me. "Come on, I'll walk you to the door."

"Nice meeting all of you," I said.

"Bye," said the woman, smiling. Then she turned her head. "Bobby! We're not using the Waterford crystal."

Sanders opened the door. "Well." He put out his hand.

I shook it.

"You have yourself a good one." He looked again like Fred Gwyne.

"You too sir."

I stepped out into the night.

"Take *care!"* Bob yelled, as the door closed.

I looked at the credit card slip as I walked forward in the glow of the porch light.

Sanders had tipped me $30.

"Wow."

What an odd bunch of nice people.

Thanks to Sanders, I thought, I'll be able to buy Roxanne a few drinks tomorrow.

"Bless you and your family."

I was well up the path before I remembered I could still get eaten by mountain lions.

Chapter 20

"I feel ya."

Carter shivered. "Man, I wouldna put up with that shit. If I know a guy is following me in the woods, I'm layin a trap for him."

"Well he didn't," I said. "It just seemed like he was. I followed the trail back to my car and he never showed."

"Do you really think he was following you though?"

"No. It was just weird being up on that windy road in the middle of nowhere and the weirdo from my work happens to be on the same route right behind me the whole way."

"I woulda been trippin."

"I was. But then when I got back to the store I saw him, and the first thing he says is, *man that was really weird seeing you up there*. And he showed me his dispatch slip. He was delivering only a few houses down the road. It was just a mistake made by one of our new employees. They should've dispatched those two orders to one driver."

"That's a lie."

"What?"

Carter's eyes bored into me. "I think that's a lie. I think you really got jumped in the forest and raped and now you're trying to justify why you've been skimping on our workouts together. So that you could meet with your illegal lover, the Cat Burglar, in the forest."

"You mean illicit lover, you illiterate fuck."

Carter laughed.

"Wait," I said. "Where did you get that?"

"Get what?"

"Cat burglar. Why did you just joke about me meeting with a cat burglar?"

"The Cat Burglar."

"What the fuck are you talking about?"

"The fucking Cat Burglar! You haven't heard? There's some guy going around robbing people's places in Grantwood when they're not home. He takes their cats, if the people have cats. It's his traitmark."

I decided to let this grammar slip of Carter's go.

"Really?"

"Don't you pay attention to the news?"

"That's what I come to you for. That and your philosophical digression."

"Do you wanna smoke some pot?"

"No man, I'm good. I've got to work in two hours."

"You're fucking drinking beer!"

"Two beers, that's all. And what are you talking about, aren't you working later too? You going in to work stoned?"

"I can talk to people at their tables stoned, that's not uncommon. You're a fucking driver."

"It's only two beers," I said. "Your fridge needed cleaning out."

"Yeah get that shit outta there."

"You quitting drinking again?"

Carter nodded. "For at least the month of November. I really gotta start focusing man."

"I hear that," I said. I finished off my beer. "Seriously, that whole Cat Burglar thing, I'm going to have to look into that. Somebody had mentioned it at work. I thought they were only joking."

"It's for real," Carter said. "It's fucked up. Somebody took my cat I'd be pissed. I don't know what I'd do."

"You don't have a cat."

"Because SOMEONE TOOK IT!"

I laughed.

"I actually do though, back home. His name's Dylan. He likes to be stroked."

"Carter!"

"WHAT!"

Oh Jesus, here we go. I hadn't known Maddy was here.

Madeline and Annabelle were Carter's roommates, who also happened to be cousins. They were nice gals. They were always nice to me, at least. But Maddy was always clashing with Carter whenever they were all around together; usually on the grounds that Carter was being too loud. Annabelle worked a graveyard shift and was usually asleep and out of sight during the day. Maddy was pretty protective of her cousin's beauty rest.

The way they would argue, you'd think they were always less than a step from coming to blows. Which I always thought was an interesting scenario to imagine, Maddy being almost twice the size of Carter.

"WHAT?" Carter yelled again.

The door at the end of the hall opened.

The hardwood floors groaned like they were being fucked.

Maddy filled the corner.

"CARTER! HOW MANY TIMES DO I HAVE TO TELL YOU TO KEEP IT DOWN DURING THE DAY? Hi Dylan."

"Hi Mads."

"Keep *your* voice down, she's sleeping!" Carter hissed.

"SHE'S NOT SLEEPING NOW BECAUSE YOU WOKE HER UP, YOU ASSHOLE!"

"Don't call me an asshole!" Carter hissed.

Then, as an afterthought, he jumped off the couch. He took several angry steps towards her. Maddy put her hands on her considerable hips.

"Don't get aggressive with me, Carter."

"Hey guys," I said, standing up. "I think I'm going to go. I'll see you guys later."

"DON'T CALL ME AN ASSHOLE! I DON'T EVER CALL YOU A CORNPONED HUSSY, DO I?"

As I was walking towards the door, the ceiling thumped with the stomping of the tenant upstairs. "SHUTTUP" *"FUCK YOU!"* Maddy and Carter yelled together.

I opened the door, wincing at the brightness.

I closed the door, and heard a crash from inside as I stepped off the stoop.

Chapter 21

Walking back to Vic's, I thought about getting more beer. I was feeling good, why not?

Because you're a driver, replied Carter's voice in my head.

He had a point there.

I checked the time on my phone. I had a little over an hour and a half to go before my shift started.

I could just get a can of something light, chug it back in my car in about fifteen minutes while listening to some tunes, then go back to Vic's and take a quick nap.

Quick cup of coffee before you're out the door, and you're as good as new.

That was my voice.

I decided it had a better point.

Because I was feeling *great*. Despite all the shit that had been happening, I was in LA, city of my dreams. I had friends, a job, and my whole acting career ahead of me. And tonight, I had Roxanne.

Ah, Roxanne. . .

I had a feeling I would be getting lucky soon.

Why? Because a little bird named Elizabeth tells me so.

I stopped in my tracks.

"Wait a second. . ."

Elizabeth. That sexy voice on my GPS.

I ran through my mind all the times I could remember hearing it; the vampire chick on the way to the Halloween party, on the way to meet Roxanne, on the way to Adrian's last night, who had been obvious as to what was on her mind. . .

"Holy shit."

Here I've been telling everyone about this Demon Voice that misleads me, but what about the other *one?*

What if Elizabeth also leads me to places?

Sexy places.

I was still thinking about it when I found myself outside Vic's apartment.

I decided I'd keep walking a while.

Chapter 22

Turning the corner, I saw Melissa out front, holding a tray of pizza samples.

"Hi!" Melissa said.

"Hi there. How you liking the job so far?"

Melissa shrugged. "Eh. You want to do this?"

"Do what?"

She held up the spatula. "Sample?"

Only the management ever had me sample, and that was only when there were no deliveries or it was very busy and all the cashiers were dealing with customers.

"No."

Melissa gave me a pout as I went in to the store.

Lewis and Bill were behind the counter.

"Bring me two bags," Lewis said. "We're sending you out on a double."

I went to the back, passing Dave by the oven, and exchanged my bag for two hot ones.

Lewis loaded the bags.

"That new gal?" I said. "She just asked me if I wanted to sample."

Lewis shook his head. "She keeps trying to get out of sampling for some reason."

"I don't know is that chick lazy or stupid or both," Dave mumbled, coming up to the front.

"I heard last night was fun," said Bill.

Dave shrugged. "I wasn't here, but that's what Taylor told me. There were so many fuck-ups with the new people. Were you here?" he asked me.

"There were a few mistakes," I said, picking up the loaded bags and dispatch slips from Lewis.

"You have arrived!"

I got out of the car and walked across the street towards the apartment building I had passed.

Just ahead, a man suddenly stepped onto the sidewalk from the other side of a tree.

He turned to me. "Oh my god, have you tried these?"

"What's that?" I asked.

The man nodded to the branches above, at the big berries hanging there.

I looked at the man. He had his fist to his mouth, like he was shoving in a mouthful.

Was he serious?

The guy was either dressed in his working clothes or his only clothes. He looked very dirty and worn, though the greasy hair curling out from behind his grimed-darkened baseball cap was colored a youthful brown. The thin arms sticking out from his T-shirt were sunburned to lobster-red and lined, like the man had shrunk from a larger bulk.

The man took his fist away, chewing.

"Try them," he said.

The berries didn't look appetizing. I wasn't even sure they were edible.

The fallen ones on the ground looked like crushed cockroaches.

"They're good?"

The guy nodded. "They're *so* good. They're great on your cereal."

I'll have to try them, I almost said.

Instead, I said, "Okay."

And kept walking.

The way the man's eyes looked, all wide and frozen. . .

I looked over my shoulder after I had passed a distance.

The man was not following or watching me. He was reaching for more berries.

I walked up the steps and found the glass doors wide open.

I stepped in and immediately knew why.

The place *smelled.*

"Man," I muttered. "What is that?"

The hallway was wide, the walls white and the carpet a light blue. *Clean colors*, I thought. The place smelled anything but.

Miss Paula R, as she'd listed herself on the dispatch, was on the first floor, number 109.

The apartments had to be fairly spacious. It was a long hallway, and I passed only four doors before the hallway turned a corner.

The smell got worse.

It smelled like the worst body odor.

I breathed in through my mouth, pretending my nose was corked.

I passed a large shut window in the middle of the hallway, the airy sunlight coming in warm and mocking.

At the end of the hallway I found 109, the lone doorway facing the hall.

I knocked.

After a few beats, I heard the door being unlocked from the inside.

The door opened.

"Hi, how're y—?"

My head fell forward as I coughed, having inadvertently taken in the smell as soon as I started to talk.

Pretending to cork my nose again as I straightened up, I looked at the young woman and said, "I'm sorry, excuse me."

"That's all right," the young woman said. She looked to be in her early twenties. She was small, slender, and pale.

A sour gust of air nearly knocked me flat.

What the Christ does she have in there?

"Here you go," I said, sounding like someone was pinching my nose. The woman took the box.

She handed me a ready stack of bills. "Thank you," I said, eagerly nodding my head (what came out sounded like Thagg ghou).

The woman smiled and shut the door.

I got the hell out of there.

Outside, the air actually smelled sweet.

Walking back towards my car approaching the overhanging tree with the berries, I imagined the Berry-Eater suddenly appearing again from behind the tree, but this time to grab me. *Try them, they're good, they're good*, he'd say, shoving handfuls into my mouth.

But whoever he was, he was now gone.

I looked down as I approached the stained part of the sidewalk, trying not to get any gunk on my shoes.

I sped down Sunset on my last delivery for the night.

"In a quarter mile. Turn right onto Mannerville Canyon Road!"

*"Manor*ville," I said. "Lifestyles of the rich and famous-rich. Here we go."

"In eight hundred feet. *Turn right onto Acorn Lane."*

Elizabeth.

"Yes!"

Here we go, Big Boy, said Adrian's voice in my head. *Time to test out your theory. . .*

I looked at the wheat penny and imagined I again saw that green glint.

Elizabeth and my lucky penny: Two forces at work for me.

I turned onto Acorn Lane.

"In one thousand feet. Your destination will be on the right."

"Thank you, Elizabeth, you silver-tongued matchmaker!"

Parked, I got out from my car.

Greeted by the sound of crickets, I looked up at the house. It sat back from the road atop a little hill of a garden. I couldn't see much of it in the dark, but I saw two glowing windows on either side of what had to be the door.

I rang the doorbell, my heart beating fast.

The green door swung open.

My eyes lit on a familiar aqua blue and black striped shirt stretched over a very fat stomach. The face of the bespectacled man was all too familiar as well.

Mr. Blue Bumblebee.

"Mmm."

"Hello sir," I said.

He was still in his underwear.

"How are you?"

"Mmph!"

I opened the flap of the bag, letting out the hot steam.

It had never occurred to me to check the name on the dispatch to see if it was male.

Should've recognized that I'd been to this house on Acorn Lane before.

Well, there goes my theory. I pulled out the large boxes one by one and handed them over.

"Mmm." Bumblebee looked down at the boxes in his hands, then up at me. His tongue poked out and did a slow circle of his lips.

"Aaron, who's there?"

The tongue retreated, and the man turned at the sound of padding feet.

"What are you. . .oh!"

Bumblebee stepped aside.

My mouth dropped open at the sight of a young woman wearing nothing but a pearl necklace and garter belt. My eyes went to the large tanned breasts, to the trimmed patch of dark hair between her legs. "Babe! Come here and look at what Aaron ordered us!"

"Huh?"

The woman turned back to me, smiling. She took a step into the doorframe. Putting her hand on her hip, she struck a pose. "Well, hello there, and look at you. . ." she said, eyeing me up and down. "Mmm. Handsome!"

"What's going on?" asked the other female voice.

"Look at what we got here, Chloe. A pizza boy!"

The dark-haired woman made room for the other woman to see.

Chloe's eyes went wide. "Oh, he's *cute!"*

Chloe was naked as well. She was almost half the height of the other woman, and pale in contrast. Her hair was dyed the color of French vanilla, and was cut in a flattop. Both of her nipples were pierced with rings. A tribal sun tattoo circled her pierced bellybutton, with one longer ray pointing towards her shaved vagina.

"Looks like you brought us something hot to get us cooking!" said the dark-haired woman, laughing. She put her hand up to her mouth and shook her head. "I gotta say," she said, taking a more serious tone. "Fucking love the uniform. It even looks worn."

"I like the boxes!" Chloe said.

"Aaron," said the dark-haired one, turning to Bumblebee. "You shouldn't. . ."

The woman looked at me. Then back at Bumblebee.

"Wait Aaron. He *is* a pizza boy?"

Bumblebee turned, sticking out one meaty hand.

I handed him the pen and credit card receipt.

"Oh, my God." The dark-haired woman turned. I watched her bare oval behind framed in the garter belt as it walked off.

"Aw-unh!" Chloe stomped one foot. "You could have at least told us you were ordering takeout! What kind of fucked-up shit is that?"

"*Mmph!*"

Chloe whirled and scampered off.

Bumblebee handed back the pen and credit card slip.

"Mmm," he said.

I stared at him.

He stared back.

Then raised his bushy eyebrows, twice. "Heh-heh!"

And closed the door in my face.

Chapter 23

"Do you believe in God?"

"Hell no," I said. "That's dumb-dumb shit."

Roxanne smiled. "Seriously."

"Not in the Christian sense, if that's what you mean. Or any religious sense, like as in a deity called God that has a face and personality and temperament that gets pissed off if we don't do exactly as it says. I think that's all too human. But I might say yes in the obvious way that, hey, I know *I* didn't create any of this. I didn't invent the planet or you or anything else in the natural world. I just woke up one day and here I was. So yeah, obviously there's a higher power."

"So you do then. Believe in a higher power."

"Yeah, sure."

"So you believe in God."

"It's not like I got a choice in the matter."

"How you mean?"

"Most people, they ask you do you believe in God, I usually answer no, because the way that's phrased, it sounds to me like a Christian or somebody religious asking do I have faith in *their* idea of their deity. And in most religions, which are only organized human corporations and clubs as far as I'm concerned, it is a choice for them. They see it like you're a true believer, or you're a non-believer, infidel, whatever. You know what I mean? But what I'm trying to say is that I am a spiritual person. Not like I meditate with crystals, but in that I feel connected to the grand scheme of things. And I feel enlivened by Nature and the little things and so forth. I just don't feel a connection with religion to spirituality. Do you know what I'm saying?"

"Have you been to rehab?"

I laughed. "Whoa, where'd that come from?"

Roxanne stared with the hint of a smirk, her green eyes looking feline in our corner of the dark bar.

"Oh well, obviously," I said, lifting my pint. I took two long swallows for effect.

When I put the glass down Roxanne was looking at one of her bracelets.

"No, actually," I said. "I just read The Artist's Way."

That got me another smile.

"That's one of the books they give you," she said.

"Good book," I said. "So you have, I take it?"

"What?"

"Been to rehab."

Roxanne looked up, but not at me. She didn't say anything.

After a moment I said, "I ain't judging."

"I'm not worried about you judging," she said.

"I've never been to rehab, but I've been to therapy."

Roxanne smiled again. "I'm going to therapy."

"Right now?"

She nodded.

"That's good," I said. "I remember when I was going, I really needed it at the time. It was the one thing I looked forward to the whole week."

Roxanne chuckled. "Yeah that's kind of how it is."

"Is that why you asked me about God? Are you reading The Artist's Way?"

"Um. I don't know. I mean, I've read it, yeah."

"Funny you should bring it up. I remember doing the morning pages, you know? At that time it really helped with my writing. I enjoyed keeping a sort of diary. It was nice to look through later. But you know what that made me realize? You know the way we often wonder why bad things happen to good people? Why there are natural disasters and accidents that happen out of nowhere? Why there are some really, truly, *bad* people? It occurred to me that, as a creator, as a writer of fiction, I made bad things happen and bad people to give the story something to do.

"So if I have to visualize God in a personal sense, to me he's a writer. He's the Author. And just as an author sits having to come up with something, he makes all of us, good and bad and everything weird in between, to amuse himself."

"Huh."

"Don't we read stories and go to movies and like to see

characters having to rise up and overcome dire circumstances? Does anybody ever read a story that is nothing but everybody having a good time all day and that was it? Wouldn't that get boring?"

"That's interesting."

"So if you ask me do I believe in God again, I'm going to say yes. He's the Author, and he's enjoying it."

I finished my beer.

"Do you want to play another game?" Roxanne asked, indicating the pool table.

"I don't know," I said. "The drinks are catching up and I'm getting tired. Of losing."

"One more," she said, "Then we'll go."

"All right." I put my hand in my pocket.

"I got it," she said. She walked over to the bar.

That girl sure likes to drink.

Then again she wasn't doing the driving.

You better be careful tonight, man. You get pulled over, you're fucked.

We were on the way back to Roxanne's with Lynch Mob's *Tangled in the Web* playing when I got an idea.

"Why don't we just GPS it?" I said. "That way you don't have to give me directions."

"I think I know how to get back to my own home."

"I know you do, I'm just saying. . .here." Taking one hand off the steering wheel, I pulled out my phone.

Glancing down, I unlocked and hit the Navigation icon.

"Here, can you—?"

"Yellow."

"Huh?"

I looked forward.

"Shit!" I stepped on the gas just as the light turned red.

Red lights flashed behind us.

"What the fuck man!"

"Goddamnit," I muttered, signaling right. The flashing lights filled the rearview mirror.

Roxanne smiled without any joy in her face. "You're about to get a DUI."

"Relax," I said.

"What are you going tell him, that you were making out

with me, that's why you smell like alcohol?"

"Not a bad idea," I said.

Roxanne let out a frustrated sigh.

I lowered our windows. Put both hands on my steering wheel.

I had a mint in my mouth that Roxanne had given me after we left the bar. I chewed it to pieces, spreading it around as much as I could with my tongue.

My heart was pounding.

This is it. . .

"Hi there," said a man in uniform peering in. He shone his light in my face.

"Hi," I said, wincing.

"Do you know why I stopped you?"

"I'm not sure."

"You're not sure? I just see you run a red light?"

"I was cutting it pretty close," I said.

"Really? Cause from where I was I thought I saw you run it."

"It was pretty close."

"Hi there!" he said to Roxanne.

"Hey."

"Who's this guy to you?"

"My boyfriend."

"Yeah? Where you guys coming from?"

"The Moon Lite."

"How much did you have to drink there?" he asked me.

"Three beers."

"License and registration?"

The officer stepped away after I gave it to him. Roxanne and I sat still, listening to the voices on the police radio.

The officer came back.

"Where do you live?"

"I'm in West L.A.," I said.

"Why is this a different address?" he asked, indicating my license. "You know you're supposed to notify the DMV soon as you move."

"I'm staying with a friend," I said. "I'm living here now, but I wasn't sure how long I was going to stay. I'm going to be getting my own place soon, so I was just waiting."

"You say you didn't run the red light? That you had only three beers tonight?"

I didn't say anything.

"Correct?"

"Yes sir."

The officer stared at me a moment.

"To my eyes it looked like you ran that light. But, I could be wrong. I'm going to cut you a break tonight. But I want you to know, I can take you in for having three beers. You look all right to drive, but that's not the point. I don't have to tell you the legal limit. You get me?"

"Yes sir. Thank you."

He handed me back my license and registration.

"You drive safe."

"I will sir. Thank you."

He left.

"My God," Roxanne said, shaking her head. "Are *you* lucky."

The lights of the passing police car reflected on the plastic mounting of the wheat penny.

"Seriously," Roxanne slurred, the evening's drinks clearly catching up with her. "How'd you do that?"

"Magic."

"Magic my ass. You told him three beers. That's retarded."

"No, it was smart. Everyone always says two. You say three, it sounds closer to honest."

"You never admit to a cop you been drinking. That gives em prob. . .probable cause."

"Not in this case," I said.

"I can't fucking believe you didn't get a DUI."

We drove on.

"Boyfriend, huh?" I glanced at Roxanne, grinning.

"Just keep your eyes on the road, asshole."

I turned a left as she instructed, and parked part way up the hill.

"Well," I said, turning to her. "How you feeling?"

"Good," Roxanne said, her eyelids looking heavy.

"Yeah? Oh! I almost forgot." I slid the necklace off from the rearview mirror. Neither one of us had noticed it the whole time we'd been in my car. "Here you go."

"Thanks."

We sat without speaking.

"All right," I said. I pulled the key from the ignition, and opened my door.

Went around to the passenger side.

Through the glass I saw Roxanne bent forward, her lush hair obscuring her face, as she appeared to be making sure she had everything.

I pulled open the door and stepped back.

She stepped up to me, her eyes slightly dazed. Her hand went to the side of my face.

I leaned in.

After a moment we broke off.

"I really gotta go to the bathroom," I said.

"All right," Roxanne said. "Let's go."

We walked up the street, the heels of her boots clacking.

She turned in to a driveway.

There was one car on the driveway I assumed to be Roxanne's, as she'd mentioned earlier that her parents were away for a few days visiting her aunt in San Diego.

At the top we turned a corner and continued on a little walkway up to the front door, passing a lawn and a row of potted plants.

She unlocked the door and stepped in. I followed.

I stood in the dark after Roxanne shut the door behind me. Her boots clacked a few times, then bright light suddenly filled the room.

I was facing a sleepy-looking living room, a deer head mounted on the wall. On either side of the trophy were framed paintings, all of which seemed to have a Western theme. The carpet was shaggy and nutmeg brown.

Comfy, I thought.

(Though I could never be completely comfortable with a deer head on the wall—not after *Evil Dead* 2)

Roxanne went into the kitchen. I followed as far as the doorframe and watched her pour a glass of water from a filter jug.

She took a long drink, then handed me the glass.

The cool water was good, cleansing the dry sticky layer coating my throat.

Roxanne took the glass and refilled it. She handed it back. "Come on, this way."

I followed her into the hallway where the shaggy carpet began. Roxanne hadn't removed her footwear, but I stopped to remove mine, as I always felt bad about walking on a clean carpet with the bottoms of my shoes. The place smelled of sandalwood.

She opened the first door to the right.

I turned and saw a queen-sized bed beneath the window.

She flicked on a lava lamp, giving the room a black-light glow.

"Oh, Hell no!" I said. "No, you do *not*. . ."

But somehow she did.

Somehow I was looking at a large framed poster of the album cover of Black Sabbath's *Heaven and Hell*.

"You!" I took the glass from Roxanne's hand and put my arm around her, pulling her against me. "You just got even sexier."

On my knees between her legs, I pulled my shirt up over my head and threw it aside.

Roxanne bent her knees, giving me a marvelous view of her inner thighs and her black thong.

She crossed her arms over her breasts and turned her head.

"I'm not boning you."

I backed off the bed and stood up. Opened the button of my jeans.

"I'm not. You're not gettin any."

I pulled down my zipper, pushed my pants down my legs.

"I'm not boning you."

"Yes you are," I said, stepping out.

I got back onto the bed and in between Roxanne's legs. Leaning over, my erection poking out from my boxers, I gently took hold her wrists.

"Stop," she said.

"What?"

"Not happenin."

"Why not?"

"Cause I says so."

"All right." I took my hands off her wrists. Then put my hand to the side of her face, gently urging her to turn her head back.

When she did, something about the look on her face, the rawness of it, got my heart racing.

Suddenly she uncrossed her arms and wrapped them around me, her nails digging into my back as she pulled me down. I felt the soft mounds of her large breasts and my nipples met her own, felt their circling warmth and a chill go up my spine as they went hard against hers. Hungrily, she kissed me.

I straightened my legs, feeling the spot of warmth through

the thin fabric covering her crotch as I lay on top, my erection pushing against that last barrier.

Roxanne moaned into my mouth as I rubbed against her.

We're going to make it, I thought, staring into the galaxy of my closed eyelids.

I imagined the closet door suddenly bursting open, her father yelling *tarnations!* as he drew twin guns.

No such luck tonight, Pops.

"Mmph!"

Roxanne broke from our kiss.

Her hands shot out to my throat.

She didn't squeeze like last time, but she held them there as she shook her head.

"What?" I whispered. "What's the matter?"

Her eyes rolled, and she closed them. She took one hand off my throat and put the back of her wrist to her forehead, covering her eyes. She groaned.

"Goddamnit," she said, lowering her arm. "All right."

She used her other hand to push me onto my side, then onto my back.

She climbed on top.

She arched her back and began to rub against me.

I slapped my hands to her hips.

"Unh!"

The phone rang.

"Unngh. . ." Roxanne climbed off.

She found her phone.

I heard myself groan—I had a pretty good idea who it was.

"Yeah?"

"*Roxanne. What. Are. You doing?*"

"What?"

"I just got a call from Missus Singleton. You've got somebody in our HOUSE!"

As I waited for Roxanne to come back, hearing the faint murmur of her voice from the other side of the closed bathroom door, I stared at the angels on the poster.

Finally I got up and put on my clothes.

Roxanne came back into the room. She bent down to pick up a shirt off the floor.

"Well," I said. "Big trouble, huh?"

Now wearing a black T-shirt, she looked very tired. “It’s fine.” She sat onto the bed, then fell back. She moaned. “I’m gonna be so fucked at work tomorrow.” She turned onto her side, her back to me.

“I’ll get going then. What did the parents say?”

“Nng?”

Knees bent to her chest, her pale legs glowed in the black light, the dark thong making the crevice of her rump look wider.

Just looking, I felt myself getting excited again. I wanted to put my hands on her ass and knead it, slip one hand around to her soft belly, up to those mounds. . .

Such a near miss!

Again!

I came around to her side of the bed and crouched. Her eyes were closed.

“I’m going to go,” I said.

“Nng. All right. I’ll walk you out.”

“You don’t have to.”

I gave her a quick kiss on the lips.

“Night,” I said, standing up.

“Hey.” Her eyes were slightly open. “I wanna go to Santa Monica.”

“What?”

“Santa Monica. Let’s go.”

“Now? What are you talking about?”

“Take me. To a hotel in Santa Monica. Stay the night. On a weekend.”

“Oh. Sure.”

“Then I’ll bone you.”

Chapter 24

Sitting on the wall, I lifted my head to the cool breeze, sunning my face.

Life was good.

Here I was in Grantwood, one of the nicest parts of LA, working an easy job that allowed me to sit for moments like this and watch people walk by smiling and greeting each other; some in business suits, some pushing tykes in strollers, out jogging, or walking their dogs.

They all looked pretty happy.

I think I'd be happy too if I lived here.

It wouldn't be long before I could afford to move up from Vic's floor and into my own room somewhere. I would land some good acting gigs. Then one day I'd be able to live here.

"Hello."

It was Hooper.

"Hi Hoop. What's shaking?"

"What is shaking? Um. I don't know. Not much?" He shrugged.

"Enjoying the day? It's gorgeous out."

"That it is. I'll be right back, I just gotta go clock in."

Hooper went around the corner.

A few minutes later he came back with his topper.

"There's one ticket up," he said. "I think you'll be up in about five minutes. Do you wanna walk with me while I go put this on downstairs?"

"Sure." I stood up.

"Just in case I get jumped by the valet?"

"That's right, we're supposed to stick together down there."

I followed Hooper down the stairs.

"You hear about Tom Hanks?"

"What?"

Hooper looked back at me. "You don't watch the news? His cat got stolen."

I wanted to laugh, but then realized what Hooper was referring to.

"That Cat Burglar guy got Tom Hanks' *cat?"*

"Yep."

"You're kidding me?"

"I am not. It's really gotten serious that whole thing. That guy's now hitting the mansions. I think when he gets caught, he's in serious shit."

"Wow, I'll bet. That's bizarre!"

Hooper lifted the topper to his roof. "There's something I've been wanting to ask you. Would you like to come over sometime? For a few beers? Smoke some pot if you want?" Hooper shrugged. "Hang out?"

"Uh, sure," I said. "When?"

"I'm off Mondays and Sunday during the day. Let me get your number."

As I was giving Hooper my number, I saw Paul's car come around the corner. He turned around and backed into a parking spot a few up from where we stood.

"What's going on Paul?" I said as Hooper and I were passing on our way back towards the stairs.

"Sup."

We went back up.

Just as we sitting down on the wall, my phone rang.

"Time to deliver."

Ryan and Melissa were behind the counter, Ryan staring up at one of the many TV monitors with a sour look on his face.

Melissa looked at me, then darted her eyes away.

"What's up?" I said.

"Hi!"

"Hi. You guys rang?"

"You have a delivery."

"Where?"

"Huh?"

"Usually when I get a call, I come in and there's a delivery packed."

"Oh yeah. . ." Melissa turned and went to the line.

I could see why everybody had been complaining about her.

"Eighty-six?" She turned towards Ryan. "Right?"

"Uh-huh."

Melissa walked towards the counter with the box.

"Oh, uh, grab me a bag."

"The bags are behind you," I said.

"I know, but I don't wanna go back."

"I'll get it!" Dave yelled from the cook station. He unplugged a bag from the shelf and walked as far as the oven. "Catch!" He swung it towards me as Melissa scrambled out of the way. I caught it.

I put it onto the counter and opened the flap for Melissa. She put it in.

"There you go."

"Needs pepper and parm," I said.

"Oh!" She went and got it.

"Dispatch?"

"Huh? Oh, yeah!" She stepped to the computer. "Now how do I do this again?"

Ryan turned. "Here," he said, stepping over. He punched a few buttons on the screen and the dispatch printed out.

"In five hundred feet. *Turn left onto Linden Way."*

Elizabeth!

Linden Way was only a little street and ended not very far up ahead.

"Your destination is on the left."

I parked and got out of the car with the bag.

The chirping of birds made me stop and look around. Linden was a nice street. Most of the houses were white or bright pastel. They all had lawns with multicolored flowers and plants growing.

Thomas Kincaid-y, I thought, crossing the street.

The house had a white picket fence with an open gate. I walked up the brick path to the shaded alcove and knocked.

After a while I knocked again and rang the doorbell.

I called the number.

"Hello," said a posh female voice after the sixth ring, *"This is the Sandsworth's residence. . ."*

Ending the call, I looked again at the dispatch slip.

Ron Sandsworth.

Probably had his phone on silent.

I hammered on the door.

"Just a moment," said a female voice from inside.

The door trembled while I heard the unlatching of a lock.

The older woman who opened the door was well-dressed. My eyes went to her pearl necklace before they were pulled to her smiling white teeth.

"Oh, hello," she said. "You must be the pizza man."

"I'm glad you heard me that time," I said. "I was just about to walk away."

"Oh, *nooo,*" she said. She covered her mouth and raised her thinned orangey eyebrows, her blue eyes looking alarmed.

The gesture was comical.

Taking her hand away, she said, "I'm dreadfully *sorry.* I was in the back having a ciggy."

"It's okay," I said.

"Oh, I'm *sorry.*"

I couldn't help but smile. Despite the practiced manner in which she talked, there was something likeable about this woman. I had to admit too, she looked good for her age. She obviously came from "good stock" as my granddad would've said. Her vanilla blond hair was coifed in a way that reminded me of Mary Tyler Moore.

Must've been a knockout forty years ago.

I opened the flap of the carrier bag.

"No no no, love. Do come in with that."

She turned and began walking. I followed her in, shutting the door behind me.

"Now this way, darling. Follow me."

Halfway up the hall, the woman stopped to pick up a wine glass left on a little table.

We entered the kitchen.

I walked up to the counter top.

"There is fine, dear. Thank you."

"You're very welcome," I said, pulling the pizza box out from the bag.

"You're polite," the woman said.

"Thank you."

"Did they train you to be that way?"

"My parents?"

"Your parents, of course. I meant your people at the

pizzeria."

"No," I said, shrugging. "Just the way we are."

The woman raised her glass to her lips, holding my gaze as she tilted it back. When she lowered the glass, the wine drained, she lowered her chin and raised one eyebrow. "And you're rather charming."

"You're not too bad yourself."

"Hah! Dah-ha-ling! The ladies must *love* you."

I smiled and shrugged.

"Oh now you're blushing, you *dote!* Tell me, what is your name, young man?"

"Dylan."

The woman held out her hand. "Harriett," she said.

I took Harriett's hand in mind. It felt soft but strong. "Very nice to meet you, Harriett."

"You too, love. Now, I suppose you have something for me to sing?"

"Pardon?"

Harriett suddenly stood very straight, her feet together. She clasped her hands, tilted her head, and fluttered her eyes while pouting her lips.

"I'm sorry, I don't know what you're talking about."

Harriet regained her normal composure. "Oh, it's just something we used to do in our family. We used to be excused from our dinner table with a brief showcase of our talents. It was Daddy's idea. I loved it. I was the singer in the family."

"Oh," I said. "Nice."

Harriet gave a tired wave. "That was before your iPads and iPods and godknows what-the-crumb you young people have these days."

"I think it sounds nice," I said.

"It was nice." She sighed. "Well, young man, I really don't mean to hold you. I'd better sign your thing. But it's been very nice talking to you."

"You as well." I handed Harriet the slip and pen.

She signed it and handed it back.

"You're welcome here."

"Thank you," I said.

"Do you like wine, Dylan?"

"Yes," I said.

Harriet turned and picked up her wine glass and walked over to the counter. She poured herself some more.

She came back to me. "Taste this."

"Oh, I shouldn't. I'm a driver."

Harriet laughed, giving me that lovely open-mouth smile again. "Just a taste, you dote!"

"All right." I took a drink.

"Mmm," I said, handing it back.

Looking at me with her big blue eyes, Harriett swiveled the glass around and took a drink from the same spot where my lips had touched.

She licked her lips.

"Well I hope you enjoy," I said.

Harriet grinned and raised her eyebrows.

We walked to the front door.

"Thanks very much again, Harriet," I said.

"Thank *you*, darling. You're a breath of fresh air. I'll be seeing you again soon."

"I hope so."

"You will so."

She blew me a kiss as I left.

The phone chirped as I was driving down the ramp into the garage.

The text message was from an unlisted number.

Thank you Dylan lovely x

Harriett.

I had called the number she'd given on the dispatch. Despite her formal greeting, I'd been calling a cell phone after all.

Now she had my number and was texting to let me know.

Interesting.

Maybe there was something to my theory, I thought, walking up the stairs. Even if it was Harriett.

Apparently she was *Horny* Harriett.

"What did Hooper want?" Joel asked.

"What you mean?"

"Saw you talkin to that cat Hooper bro," Paul said.

"Yeah?"

"So what'd he want with you Dylan?" Joel asked.

"He invited me over to his place for a few beers."

Paul jerked up, looking up from his phone for the first time. "HO HO shit, bro!"

"Are you serious?" Joel asked. "I hope you said fuck no."

"Actually I said sure."

"What? Dude, why?"

"I don't know. Why not?"

"Uh. Cause it's like, fucking Hooper? Fucking psycho?"

"For reals dog."

"I don't think he's a psycho," I said. "Think maybe he was just being friendly."

"Psssh. Yeah? Maybe."

"Fuck bro, that fuckin cat asks me over I'm saying Fuck You bro," Paul said to his phone screen.

What a couple of dicks, I thought.

Jeffrey joined us.

"Did you guys hear about Tom Hanks?"

"Dude, yeah," Joel said. "Poor Tom!"

"Poor everybody that's had that happen," Jeffrey said. "Stealing people's pets." He shook his head.

"That's like stealing somebody's children for some people bro."

"Yeah, somebody told me," I said. "I wasn't sure if it was a joke."

"Dude. It's for real. Is that fucked up or what?"

"That's fucked-up bro. I like Tom Hanks. This shit gonna affect business."

I turned to Paul. "How so?

"Bro, you noticed people already not giving us the access codes to their buildings?

"I guess?"

"That's how he's getting in the apartment buildings," Joel said. "He must have the codes."

"Yeah," Jeffrey said. "It could be one of the drivers."

"Shit. Don't look at me bro."

We sat together in silence.

"Way to make things awkward Jeffrey." Joel laughed.

"Don't go far," Dave told me, "we've got another one coming right up."

Standing at the side of the register, I glanced at the family I had passed on the way in—I thought one of them had given me a strange look. Now I saw the smaller of the two boys looking around.

There was no one at the registers. I decided I'd get a drink of water and leave before anyone asked me for anything.

"Excuse me?"

The smaller of the two boys was holding his hand up, like he was in class.

"Hi," he said. "Weren't you on that show, *I Fought the Law and Lost*?"

"Yes," I said, gulping involuntarily. "Yes, I was."

"Oh, wow!"

The big man next to him leaned towards me. "We just love that show!"

The wife grinned at me even as she was sucking through a straw.

The other boy looked up with big eyes.

"Thanks," I said. "Yeah, we filmed that one up in the San Francisco Bay Area. A lot of those shows are produced up there. It was really fun to shoot."

"Wow," the little boy said again. "I thought you were a real criminal."

"That's his favorite show," the wife said.

"Well, he is a real criminal," I said. "I was only portraying him."

"You were playing a real bad guy!"

"Yeah." I chuckled. "Thanks for watching."

"You bet!" the man said.

I nodded at them all, the little boy last. "Thanks," I said again.

Outside, I looked down at whatever I was holding and saw that I was crushing a small plastic cup.

My phone rang.

It was the store.

I answered the call even as I was turning towards the windows.

"I'm waving at you. . ." Dave said.

Speeding down Montana Avenue, my phone rang.

My parents, calling me back.

"Mom!" I yelled. "I just got recognized!"

"What?"

"Can you hear me? I just—"

"Dylan, what's that wind? Oh my God. . .you're not *driving?"*

"No," I lied. "Listen! Someone just came in to the store and they recognized me from the show!"

"Really?"

"Can you believe it?"

"Oh my God Dylan, that's so. . .*haha!"*

I smiled at the genuine delight in my mother's laugh.

"Oh, wait till I tell your father. Dylan, that's brilliant!"

"I just had to tell you Mom. It feels so great to have a complete stranger come up to you and say they liked your work, you know?"

"How exciting!"

"Ah, it really is," I said. "I'm really over the moon at the moment."

"I'll bet you are. And you know what Dylan? You deserve it."

"Thanks."

"You know, your—"

"In a half mile," interrupted Sally's voice. "Continue on to Stratford Street!"

"What was that?"

"I gotta let you go now Mom, I got my work calling me."

"All right, thanks so much for ringing. I'll tell your father. I'm very happy for you."

"Thanks Mom."

"We're so very proud of you."

The text read:

Dylan would you be a gent and visit me tonight? x

I was about to tap OK, but hesitated.

What about Ron Sandsworth? That was her husband, surely.

What about Roxanne?

We're not an official couple.

Come on man, you like her. She wants you to take her for a getaway so you can consummate your relationship.

Yeah, if her fucking parents don't have us followed out there. I can just see us on the bed in some rented hotel room and then the phone rings. . .

My phone rang.

"You're up," said Ryan's curt voice.

I ended the call and texted back

I'm off about 9. What is yr address again?

Chapter 25

Harriett was waiting at the door. The bright light surrounding her looked warm and inviting.

"Good evening, dear." Harriett grinned.

Her brow furrowed as I walked up the steps. "What's that?" she asked, nodding towards the brown paper bag.

"A little blueberry beer."

"Blueberry? *Beer?"*

Not wanting to show up to Harriet's empty-handed, I'd gone across the street to Whole Foods after work.

Harriett puckered her lips, gliding her hand up my arm.

I leaned down, not sure if I should be turning my cheek.

Harriet closed the distance, pressing her lips to mine. Her tongue went into my mouth.

The hand on my shoulder squeezed, and Harriett broke away. "Do come in now, dear."

I followed her inside and stepped past as she closed the door. A row of tea lights on the floor illuminated the hallway to the kitchen. More tea lights were arranged around a coffee table in front of a sofa.

"Will you have some wine then?"

"Sure."

"Then make yourself comfy in there. I'll be out in a jiffy, you tiffy."

I watched as she walked down the hallway.

Had she been drinking the whole time?

I took off my shoes, then stepped towards the carpeted living room.

A piano stood in the corner between the window and fireplace. Rows of framed photographs were lined on top. The one in the center was a black and white and appeared to be a family portrait. A man with a hat and a black mustache sat on a chair in the center, looking very serious. On his right stood a young woman with her hand on his shoulder, looking patient and tired. On the other side of the man stood a lanky boy. On the man's lap sat two little girls who could've been twins. They were blond and smiling, looking secure wrapped in the man's arms.

Could one of these little girls be Harriett?

I leaned closer to the photograph, looking for a resemblance.

Up-close the features on the little girls were grainy. The photo looked overexposed: Bad lighting in a time where you couldn't just check the photo on your phone and keep trying as many times as you liked. Back then getting a photograph had to be a pretty big deal.

Back then. Hell. Harriett wasn't *that* old.

I looked at the other photographs and saw a boy reappearing, often alongside Harriett and a man. This had to be Harriett's son. And the man had to be. . .

"Are you looking at my family, darling?"

I turned and saw Harriett coming towards me with a glass of wine.

"Thank you, yes." I took the offered glass.

"Come sit down."

We sat on the couch.

"Cheers," I said.

"Cheers, darling."

I tried the wine.

"Lovely and fruity, isn't it? Do you taste the maple?"

"I think so." I drank again. Circled my tongue behind my closed lips. "I don't have the biggest taste for wine," I admitted.

"That's okay, darling. You'll learn." She patted my leg. "You'll learn with Harriett. Ha ha."

I nodded.

"Awful name, isn't it? Harriett. Makes me sound like an old hag. And you can't very well call me Harry, can you?"

"I'm sure you're not hairy."

"Certainly not."

I looked to the window, blocked by pink curtains.

I heard the tick of a clock somewhere.

"Peaceful, isn't it?"

"It is," I said. "You have a lovely home."

Harriett purred. "You really are quite the charmer. So good

of you to agree to spend some of your time with me."

Harriett leaned back against the armrest on her side, raising her legs onto the couch. She rested her heels against my leg.

She stared at me.

I stared back. In the dim light it was hard to read her expression.

"How was the pizza?" I asked.

Harriett's head twitched. "What? Oh. Oh, it was *fine*, darling. Would you like some?"

"Oh no thanks," I said.

"Mmm." Harriett continued to stare. "Sorry for not being such a conversationalist. I'm simply enthralled by you. And I'm a bit drunk."

"Have you been drinking the whole time since I delivered to you?"

Harriet sat up. "Heavens no! What are you saying about me?"

"Nothing."

"I took a *nap."*

She put her glass to her lips and knocked the rest back. Swiveled her legs around and sighed, leaning back into the couch.

"Oh but I'm tired again. I had to stay up and wait for *you."*

"Well. I hope I was worth the wait."

Harriett turned her head. *"You're* not too tired, are you?"

"No," I began as Harriett leaned towards me. She rested her head against my shoulder and sighed. Her hair felt hard through my shirt. It smelled faintly of vanilla.

I'll be good to drive, I'd been about to say. Now I decided to say nothing as Harriett raised her chin, puckering her lips. I gave her a kiss.

It was meant to be a light brushing of lips, but Harriett pushed with her tongue. It felt dry and tasted of soured grapes. She groaned into my mouth and brought her hand to the side of my head, pressing her fingers into my hair.

I pulled away as gently as I could.

"Shall we?" Harriett put a steadying hand on my shoulder as she stood up.

"Do you require a last glass? Or are you good?"

"I'm good," I said, raising the glass to show there was still liquid in it.

Harriett smiled, her head looking slightly unstable as she

showed me her white teeth. They seemed to glow in the dark.

She raised her index finger, and went off.

Alone again in the living room, I listened to the ticking clock and looked at my wine. I swallowed the last of it, and put the glass on the coffee table.

Though I wondered about Harriet, I already felt like I'd spent enough time with her.

I looked over at the pictures on top of the piano.

That little boy in the photographs was probably now the same age as me. And here I was with his mother.

Who may even still be married.

I hadn't thought to look for a wedding ring on Harriett's hand, but I supposed it didn't really matter now: I was going to leave as soon as Harriett came back. I felt a little guilty, realizing she was drunk. She was lonely and excited at the prospect of a young man for the night, but she'd wake the next morning with a headache and the impression that I'd taken advantage of her.

Besides, knowing that Harriett was drunk made her a lot less attractive.

I pulled out my phone and looked at the time. I stood up.

Music came on in another room.

Setting the mood?

Sorry Harriett.

Harriett reappeared in a dark Kimono.

My eyes looked over the robe, not being able to help my curiosity at the intricate designs on it.

"Nice," I said.

"Do you like it?" Harriett came with her arms outstretched. She stood on her toes and pulled me to her, pressing her mouth to mine. I felt the eager press of her tongue, but this time I kept my mouth shut, barring its entry.

I put my hands to her hips and gently pushed her back.

"Thank you for having me," I said. "I better let you get some rest."

Harriett looked at me quizzically.

"Rest?"

I nodded.

"Oh, *nooo. . .*don't you like me, darling?"

"I do," I said. "Very much."

"Well, then. How about a little oinky-boinky?"

"What?"

Harriett pressed her palms to my chest and leaned with her

weight, steering me back to my sitting position.

Suddenly she pushed hard and I fell onto the couch.

"Whoa! What the—?"

"Oinky-boinky!"

Harriett opened the Kimono, barring the front of her pale naked body, and flung the robe aside.

She was wearing nothing but a black garter belt.

I stared at her lean, surprisingly fit body, offset by the pair of tetherball-sized breast implants. My eyes dropped to the silvery strip of her pubic hair as she came towards me.

Harriett leaned down, her legs pressing my knees.

She bared her teeth in an animal grin, her eyes shining.

I sat up, but Harriett pushed me right back down.

"Hey now," I said, giving Harriett a hard look.

"Oinky-boinky!"

I sat up again with my hands around Harriett's waist, but she grabbed my wrists and pushed my arms back with ferocious strength, pinning me to the back of the couch. Her fingernails dug into my wrists as I looked up.

Harriet held both my wrists as she lowered her face to my lap.

Those grinning teeth!

Before I thought to sandwich her head between my knees, my fly had been pulled down.

Harriett put one hand to my throat, yanking my pants down with the other.

My whole body tensed as the crawling fingernails of Harriett's hand entered my underwear through the leg hole.

I sucked in a breath as they found my balls.

They tickled.

The hand around my throat disappeared, and I leaned my head back.

"Is that nice, darling?"

The fingers of her other hand entered through the other leg hole. They tickled up my inner thigh, around my growing penis, closed, and began to stroke.

The rest of my body relaxed as I felt her fingers go up to the waistband of my briefs.

She lowered my underwear.

My hard-on flicked up.

"Ooh!"

She lowered my underwear down my legs.

She stood up, looking at my hard penis. She took hold of it and put her other hand on my shoulder, lifting one leg onto the couch and then the other, squatting over me.

Slowly, she lowered herself.

I felt the hot ring of warmth, and closed my eyes as it enveloped me.

Harriett moaned as she sat onto my cock. "Yes! *Yes!*"

She bounced, furiously.

"Oinky-boinky! Oinky-boinky!"

Chapter 26

I opened my eyes. Again, the bronze light. Harriet's bed. I looked at the dripping candle on the bedside table.

A toilet flushed. I saw light behind the closed bathroom door.

Rolling onto my back, my abdominal muscles sore, I stared at the TV on the wall, where the soundscape was coming from. The image on the screen was of a moss-covered forest after a rain.

Christ, how long have I been here?

Harriett was insatiable. After each time she came back at me with even more energy. I was so tired I could barely move.

I felt drained. Used.

The bathroom door opened.

"Oh, darling," Harriett said, her steps spritely. "You have got me just *tingling."*

"I'm glad," I croaked.

She leapt onto the bed. My whole body tensed.

"What shall we do now?" she asked, lowering her spine in a stretch, raising her heart-shaped tail. Wagging it, she grinned.

What was there left?

I raised my hand to my face and covered my eyes, not being able to suppress a groan.

"Darling?"

Harriett's fingers encircled my wrist. Gently, she pulled my hand back. "What is it?"

"I can't," I said. "Harriett. I'm *tired."*

Harriett's look of concern evaporated.

She leaned back. "I see."

She got off the bed. She shrugged, then shook her head. *"I'm* sorry. Sorry I was so nice to you."

Unbelievable. Now I was insulting her.

Harriett's hand flew at my face, the slap shutting my eyes to exploding fireworks.

Then my arms were being yanked up.

Harriett's hot grip around my wrists turned to ice.

I opened my eyes, glaring up at Harriett standing over me, meeting her blue-fire gaze.

I jerked towards her.

Only to realize I'd been handcuffed to the bedpost.

"Well now, Mister," Harriett said, all the posh gone from her voice. "If we can't treat you right, we're just gonna have to treat you rough. . ."

Chapter 27

Daylight.

The candle was melted to nothing.

Harriett was gone.

I was still handcuffed to the bedpost.

Panic ripped through me.

I was Harriett's prisoner. At the mercy of an insatiable sex-fiend.

And nobody knew I was here.

"Hey!" I yelled. "HEY!"

"Just a moment!" Harriett called from another room.

A few minutes later she entered carrying a loaded breakfast tray.

"Good morning, darling!" She was in clothes. "Sorry to make you wait. Are you famished?"

I glared at Harriett. "Get me the fuck out of these cuffs."

She came to my side of the bed and set the tray onto the little dresser next to me.

"But I thought I'd spoon-feed you. Like the little pet that you are."

"Harriett. . ."

"Oh you're blushing, you *dote!"* She laughed.

Then produced the key and unlocked the cuffs.

After breakfast, Harriett walked me to the door.

"Thank you for sharing your time with me." She put her hand to the side of my face, stood on her toes and puckered her lips.

I gave her a quick peck.

"You're welcome here," she said.

I nodded.
"You have my number, so anytime you're lonely, darling."
I nodded.
"Or want someone to talk to. . ."
I nodded.
"Or, if you just want a little. . .you know."
Oinky-boinky.
She unlocked the door and opened it for me.
"Ta, Dylan."
"Thanks," I said, and quickly stepped outside.

Chapter 28

"You fucked a *customer?"*

Carter dropped his head and pushed back into the couch, lifting his legs. His sandaled feet pumped the air. "HAHAHAHA!"

I had to laugh too.

"Who would've thought you could get some action as a pizza delivery guy? I wonder how they do at McDonald's.

"So wait, was she good? You going to see her again?"

"I don't think so," I said.

"Oh, she wasn't that hot?"

"You see this?" I turned my head to show Carter the welt on my left cheek.

"What the fuck! What happened?"

I told Carter the whole story.

By the end he was laughing so loud, Maddy came out.

"CARTER! Oh, hi Dylan. Whoa! What happened to your face?"

"Dylan got raped by one of his customers!"

"Whaaat?"

"It's kinda true," I said.

"You guys are weird." Maddy went into the kitchen.

"YOU WANNA HEAR THE STORY?" Carter yelled.

"Keep it down Carter. No."

"CAN YOU GET ME A BEER?"

"Get it yourself."

"Goddamnit, all I ask is a simple thing. . ."

Carter came back with two beers. He set one on the table for me and sat back down, twisting the top off his own.

Maddy came out from the kitchen with something she'd microwaved. "Please keep it down guys."

"Sorry Mads," I said.

I turned to Carter after she'd left. "She seems a little subdued?"

Carter looked serious. "You upset her. Talking about getting raped n' shit. She likes you."

"Actually, you said all that."

"You two could get together while I go out for a walk. Why don't you try some of those tricks you learned from that woman?"

"Hey, speaking of tricks. I never told you. Remember how I said I've been hearing weird voices on my phone?"

"Yeah yeah, one sounds like Darth Vader and you get scared."

"I'm serious. Sometimes I hear a voice on my GPS that sounds like a sexy lady. A couple times when I heard that voice while out on delivery I delivered to ladies who seemed, well, horny."

Carter laughed with a mouthful of beer, squirting some out through his mouth.

"I decided to test out my theory—that's how I met Horny Harriett. I heard that voice right before and she flirted her ass off, invited me over, and I thought I'd try it to see what happens."

Carter looked at me shaking his head, his face slightly red. He still thought I was joking.

"I'm telling you, I no longer think I'm tripping. There is something in my phone."

Carter coughed. He held out his hand. "Lemme see it," he said hoarsely.

"Why?"

"I wanna borrow it."

"Why?"

"I need to get laid."

I shook my head. "I need it for work."

Chapter 29

Stacey Noeltner.

The name rang a bell.

I dialed the code on the callbox.

"Hello?"

"Pizza guy," I said.

Cunck.

I didn't hear a buzz, so I pushed at the door. It didn't budge. I pulled at the handle.

Dialed the code again.

Cunck. "Hello?"

"Hi," I said, "the door didn't open."

"Oh, but that's because all I heard was a piercing shriek. Do you hear it?"

"Pardon?"

"AAAAAAAAAAAH!"

I stepped back from the callbox.

Cunck.

"What the fuck?"

Then I heard the door being buzzed open.

Inside the small lobby, the sounds from outside were shut out with the closing of the door.

"That had to be a joke," I muttered, taking the elevator up.

The door opened and I recognized the long hall. Stacey was at the end, peering around the corner. "Over here!" she waved.

I grinned as I walked towards the end of the hall. Now I remembered her.

"Oh look if it isn't the man I've been waiting for," she said from her doorway. She smiled. "Did I get ya?"

"Nearly fell on my ass when you screamed. Thank you."

"Well, you're welcome. Figured I owed you for last time."

Like last time, Stacey was in a white tank top and tight black sweats.

"Thank you." She turned and slowly bent down, setting the pizza box onto something low just out of my sight.

Christ, I thought, if she didn't have the most amazing ass on the planet, my name wasn't

"Dylan, right?"

"You remembered."

She came back carrying a black leather purse and I noticed a ring on her finger.

Stacey was married.

Damn. Some lucky Devil gets to see her without clothes.

"Here you go," she said, handing me some bills. "You have a good night now, Dylan."

"You too, Stacey."

I walked down the hall towards the elevator whistling.

Lionel Maywaithe.

Did that name ring a bell too?

As I drove up Sparrow, I tried to recall any customers up this way.

There had been that nice old couple with the big modern house, that big blocky thing. That sleepy gentleman had had a 'proper' sounding name hadn't he?

(Merv! Merv!)

Mervin Frankmeyer.

But they'd been on Maplewood. I was past that now.

"Continue on Sparrow Canyon Road for one mile!"

I remembered Dave saying to me on my first day: *You're going to get a lot of repeat customers, people will come to know you and your name, and after a while you're going to know a lot of people here too, so you gotta make an effort to be personable. . .*

Maybe this Lionel had already made an impression. And if I couldn't remember, that wasn't such a bad thing: When dealing with so many customers you tended to remember the bad ones more than the good.

"In five hundred feet. Turn right onto Greenridge Road!"

Greenridge was exceptionally narrow—dangerously so, with the way most people drove in Grantwood.

"You have arrived!"

After turning around and parking, I walked up the road.

Lionel's driveway was unfinished and without cement paving, the dirt leading to a garage that was either being built or taken down.

Stepping around a wheelbarrow that was on its side, I nearly walked straight into a large spider web.

A walnut-sized spider lurked in the middle of the web. I ducked under. If I hadn't just then glanced towards the house and had the benefit of the light shining down from the windows, I would have met Mr. Spider face-to-face.

I stepped onto the misaligned flat steps jutting up from the earth I took for the path. Aside from what light came down from the house, there was no illumination. The owner of the house apparently figured a sprained ankle in the dark was my problem.

"Thanks, Lionel."

I reached a deck that faced sliding glass doors darkened by closed blinds.

Not sure which way to go, I went off to the left.

And nearly stepped into a hole.

"Jesus!"

I walked back towards the center of the unfinished deck. Off to the right it was too dark for me to venture without risking my health, I decided.

Needing the use of both hands so that I could illuminate the number on the slip with my phone, I put the hefty carrier bag down.

The voice that answered sounded youthful and nasal. "Hello?"

"It's the pizza guy. I'm having trouble getting up to your house. It's dark and I can't see."

"You're having trouble?"

Above, I saw someone look out the window on the far right.

"Oh," the voice said. "You went the back way."

I waited.

"Hello?"

"Yes," I said.

"All right. Come over to the side door and I'll be right out."

"Which way is that?" I asked even as I heard the click of the call ending.

After a moment I saw a pale light flick on to my left. "Hello?" I heard the voice call out.

Shaking my head with annoyance, I walked around the hole and carefully to a small set of wooden steps leading off the deck that I hadn't been able to see before.

At the bottom there was only a narrow lane between a fence and the side of the house. I looked to my right and saw the figure peering out from a doorway.

"Hello?" he called again.

"I'm here," I said, walking up.

The light from the bulb above the doorway showed me a plump and boyish figure in a wrinkled T-shirt, shorts and sandals.

"It's really hard to see without any light," I told the man/boy.

"That's actually the back of the house," he said. "The front is around the corner. I wanna put it in the notes section when I order online but they don't give me enough room." He splayed his hands in a helpless gesture.

"Here you go," I said handing him the pizza boxes. "And if you would just sign this, please."

"Here," he said taking the pen and paper. "Let me go over here where there's more light so that I can see."

I watched him hold the slip of paper up to the light, bring it close to his face, then scribble onto it against the top of the boxes. He took his time, seeming to have some trouble adding up the figures.

He handed back the slip and pen.

"Thank you," he said.

"Thank you," I repeated. "Have a good one."

I turned and went up the stairs to the deck. The outside light went off as I was approaching the hole. Luckily I'd been watching for it. I stepped around, found the steps leading off the deck, and began my descent in the dark.

Lucky too I remembered the spider at the bottom.

Back inside my car I looked at the credit card slip.

I held it up to my face like I couldn't see it, though I could.

Maywaithe had tipped me .89 on the $42 order.

"Thanks, Lionel."

Chapter 30

Two days later I was walking over to Carter's to borrow a pair of his dress shoes for my date with Roxanne. The one pair of dress shoes I did have, tucked away in one of the suitcases I kept in the trunk of my car, I didn't plan to wear ever again.

My steps felt light. Here we were in the middle of November and the sun was warming my arms and the back of my neck. I felt it sitting between my shoulder blades. I felt grateful too for having Carter as my friend.

My plan for the rest of the afternoon was to get my car professionally washed and cleaned inside, get a haircut, and then, if I had time, maybe knock back a brew or two at Vic's before heading out to pick up Roxanne. I had an overnight bag already stowed in my car.

I knocked on Carter's door and waited.

Knocked again.

Called his number. After six rings it went to voicemail.

"Come on, Carter." I knocked hard with the side of my fist.

I tapped out a text on my phone and sent it.

A minute passed and he still didn't come to the door.

"CARTER!" I yelled. I hammered the door with my fist.

"HEY!"

I jumped at the sudden bark of the voice overhead.

"I'M GONNA CALL THE POLICE!"

The door in front of me swung open and there was Carter, eyes wide and comical, but he was mad.

"Now you got him going," he hissed. *"Get in here!"*

I stepped into the dim living room. The place smelled of teriyaki chicken.

"Hey," Carter called up to the man on the second storey. "You're not calling the police. Stop harassing me." I heard the man say something unintelligible, to which Carter replied, "Stop harassing us or I'm calling them on you right now and we can do this whole thing again."

He closed the door.

"Fuck! What you doing hammering the door like that? You know that asshole upstairs calls the police every fucking day on us?"

"Really?"

"Yes! Haven't you been here when it's happened?"

"No."

Carter rolled his eyes. *"Any bit of noise we make he calls the fucking police. He does it nearly every night."*

"Why?"

"Him and his girlfriend have a baby. And that fucker's an ex-con. He's a fucking shit and I've already had to have a meeting with him and the landlord with Maddy and Annabelle."

"All right all right, I'm sorry," I said. "Calm the hell down. Why you whispering? And why did it take you forever to answer the door?"

"I was taking the kids to the pool."

"What?"

"I was taking a fucking shit!"

"You got those shoes for me?"

"They're over there."

I looked at the love seat and saw the box. "Thanks," I said walking over. I took the lid off.

"Try em on."

I picked up the shoebox. "So long as they're size ten and a half I'm good. I really gotta get going. Still got a few errands to run before I pick her up."

"Hold up. I got something else for you."

Carter went in to his room. He came back out with a small package.

"What's this?"

Carter grinned. "A little dessert for you and your lady."

I took the package. "What?"

"There's two cookies in there. Pot cookies."

"No kidding? You know, I've never tried these."

"Oh dude. They're great. But listen, you said you're staying the night at a hotel, right?"

"That's what I'm aiming for."

"Those things are strong. Take one and share it with her

when you're in your room. You might only want to even take like a fourth of it yourself."

"All right. Thanks man. That's real nice of you. Wow." I held the package up to my nose. I could smell the pungent marijuana through the paper. "They do smell strong."

"You'll like it man. If you've never had an edible before, it's a totally different high. Perfect way to top off your date after you've buried your willie in her snatchy-poo."

I laughed. "You're a pal."

"I'm more than that and you know it."

I opened the door. "I'll shoot you a text later and let you know how I get on."

"I wanna know how you get *off."*

Now this'll be interesting.

I sat on Vic's futon looking down at the package in my hand.

Carter had said there were two. One for me to share with Roxanne.

And one for me.

But they were strong. Carter had warned me to take just a little bit.

Just a taste, then. Just to try it. I'd been curious about edibles.

But did I have time?

I looked at Vic's clock. I had nearly two and a half hours.

Plenty.

I opened the package and took one out.

Tried to break it neatly in half, but part of the cookie crumbled off. Crumbs and a chocolate chip spilled off the package and onto Vic's futon.

I picked up a piece and put it into my mouth.

Putting the package aside, I got down onto my knees and swept the bits I'd spilled off the comforter into my other hand, and into my mouth; they hadn't been on Vic's futon for more than a few seconds.

"There now," I said, standing up. "All better." Then realized I had a bit of a problem.

I couldn't put the partially eaten cookie back into the same package, it would crumble and make a mess. I wanted to be able to pull out a fresh-looking, whole cookie for Roxanne. And besides, I didn't want Roxanne to know that I'd partially eaten one before the date.

Where then would I put the rest of this one?

I stepped over to the cabinets above the sink.

Of course, Vic had no foil or saran-wrap.

For a moment I considered crumbling the rest into Vic's open cereal box.

Then decided I'd better just eat it myself.

So it was strong, Carter said. I'd had enough marijuana before to know I could handle myself. So I'd go out having "smoked" two joints instead of one. I'd live.

I ate the rest of the cookie.

Chapter 31

Clack-clack-clack. . .

I look up as Stacey Noeltner enters the dining room on a large brown horse.

"Hello!" she calls out. "Don't be afraid!"

The horse walks past the long table, its hooves clacking on the hardwood floor. Stacey ducks as they pass through the open door and under the glittering chandelier hanging above the front entrance of the house, raising her derriere up at me as they round the corner. She is wearing white riding pants and black boots.

The horse comes in again with Stacey on top.

"Oop!" Stacey beams at me, bobbing up and down in the saddle.

As she and the horse again near the door, Stacey calls over her shoulder, "I'll be right with you!" Then they're gone.

I look around the lavish room wondering when dinner is to be served, and why the horse is in the house—surely it brings in muck from outside?

There is tea set on the table. The teakettle looks white gold. I reach out to touch it and it's cold.

"Oooh. . ."

I look up to again see Stacey coming in, but the horse has changed. The head is human. The head of a middle-aged man with long limp hair and a glaze of weariness over his features.

Stacey leans forward paying me no attention, a look of concentration on her face as she holds the reins.

"Oooh," moans the perspiring man-head. "Unng. . ."

There is a tap on my shoulder, followed by a timid voice. "Excuse me?"

I turn and look up to the rotting face of my deceased wife acting as butler, maggots waving like sea anemones as she leans down.

"What will you have sir, what will you haAAAVVVE?"

Heavy hands shook me awake, and I saw a man standing over me in a black suit.

"Wake up!" Vic said.

Moaning, I rolled over.

And fell off the futon.

"We need to have a serious talk, man. What the hell are you doing sleeping on *my* futon with your filthy shoes?"

Staring at the blurry carpet, part of my body still felt as though it were falling.

"What time is it?" I croaked.

"It's twelve-thirty. I got off early. Thought you were going out on a date."

"I am so sorry," I said.

Roxanne waited.

"I passed out. I was all ready to go out tonight and I just passed out. I've been out for hours. I only just woke up. I'm so, so sorry."

"Okay."

"I feel really fucking awful."

"That it?"

"What do you mean?"

"I mean, is that really it? Nothing else you want to tell me?"

"I mean. . .I don't have any good excuse to tell you."

"You're telling me you just got a little tired right before our date and you took a little nap only to find out that you were really tired and woke up five hours later? There anything else you want to tell me?"

I sighed. "I ate a marijuana cookie."

"What?"

"A friend gave me one as a sort of gift if we were to spend the night in Santa Monica, and I got curious and tried one."

"You ate a pot cookie right before a date?"

"I honestly didn't know what it would do."

"What did you *think*...?" Roxanne chuckled, bitterly.

"I know how incredibly stupid it sounds. There's no way I can tell you without making me look like a real idiot."

"That does sound stupid," Roxanne said. "That sounds really stupid."

"I'm sorry," I said. "It's the truth. I'm really, really sorry."

"I don't do this, you know."

"Do what?"

"I don't normally go on dates."

I heard genuine hurt behind her words. "Roxanne, I really like you. I was really looking forward to tonight. I'm so sorry I let you down."

Christ, my voice was beginning to crack.

Hold it together, man.

I sat forward in my car seat and touched my index finger to the wheat penny, making my wish.

I closed my eyes as I asked, "Will you give me another chance?"

"Yeah. Fine."

"Yeah?"

"You want to come out now and make it up to me?"

"Huh?"

"I'm at Geoff's. With Stephen," she added.

"Who's Stephen?"

"A friend. You want to join us?"

"I don't know if I can."

"Why not?"

"It's just I feel damn shitty still." It was the truth. The thought of driving over the hill now sounded like a walk up Mount Everest. "I mean I'm awake now, but I could pass out again soon. I still feel the effects. If I was to get pulled over again, I'm not sure my luck would last."

"I see."

"I'm sorry Roxanne."

"It's all right."

"Talk soon?"

She hung up.

I walked back to Vic's with the intention of sleeping a long time.

Chapter 32

"I feel ya man, I really do."

But Carter couldn't possibly know the extent of what I'd been feeling.

After telling him how I'd blown my night with Roxanne, I'd come back to talking about Horny Harriett; about how I suspected she was still married. I had never wanted to be *that* guy. No matter the circumstance.

I didn't want to be the thing that came between any man and his wife.

I began to cry.

"Hey hey, whoa Charlie! *Charlie."* Carter got up and sat down next to me. He patted my shoulder as I leaned forward, sobbing into my hands.

"Dylan," he said, "What's happening here, bud? Tell me what's going on."

"I never told you," I said. "About what happened to me a couple years ago."

I sat on the bed with the phone pressed to my ear, glaring at myself in the dresser mirror as I heard the dial tone again, my face aglow with splashes of color from the Christmas lights Darlene had wrapped around our room.

If I had to hear Darlene's apologetic voicemail greeting one more time. . .

There was a glaring rush of air, then Darlene said, "Dylan I'm driving! Can't you hang on?"

"Where were you?" I shouted, standing up.

"We're nearly home. We got—"

"I've been calling for the last two hours!"

"It's been on silent! Look can you just calm down? We're nearly there."

I walked over to our little dining area where two covered plates still sat at a table set for three. The candles had long been snuffed out and I'd eaten my own portion. "Yeah, I'll calm down, now that I know YOU'RE BOTH OKAY!"

"Stop shouting!" *Darlene yelled back.* "We'll be home in five minutes, do you really have to—?"

"Do I have to wonder if my wife is okay when I don't hear from her after she's supposed to have been back from taking my sister to court more than five hours ago—yes! You said you'd call as soon as you were out and then we were going to have dinner. Well, I went and made dinner, expecting you home when you said. But instead I'm left waiting while your phone just rings and rings, and I get to think well my wife and sister were in downtown San Jose last I heard—"

"SHAAAAAAAD!"

I jerked at the interruption of my sister's voice screaming and the sound of screeching brakes, and dropped the phone.

I quickly picked it up.

"Darlene, you okay? Hello?"

I took the phone away from my ear and looked at the screen that showed a picture I'd taken months back of Darlene at the gym pushing the leg press and laughing with a joyous look of surprise at the camera.

It meant the call had ended.

My normally irreverent friend was speechless.

Now that I'd finished he looked away from me, staring at some part of the floor towards the kitchen with his mouth open.

I'd gotten my tears under control and continued. "I'll never know what held them up. There's no record of them spending money. I like to think that Darlene took my sister out somewhere in nature, maybe for a long drive up to the hills where they went for a walk at our favorite hiking spot. Maybe talked and came to some kind of understanding. It had been Darlene's idea to drive my sister to court. I think she only wanted to try and be a supportive sister-in-law. I think she wanted to see if she could do anything different, if somehow her approach could help my sister with her drug problem. I don't know. I don't know what took them so long to get home, and God knows I don't care. I'd have waited decades more if I knew they would come back to me safe. I'd wait the rest of my life if I knew there was any way they could come back at all.

"You see, man. My coming to LA is me trying to move on. I spent so much time wanting to kill myself, hating myself. Sometimes I think the only thing that kept me going were my parents. They'd lost their daughter and their daughter-in-law. Killing myself would just be me killing me too. They were going through hell already and I couldn't. . . kill them too. HAHA!"

I saw my laugh startle Carter from the corner of my eye.

"Then I would've killed everyone I love! *Ha-ha ha—"*

"Hey!" Carter was staring at me, his small stomach pulsing beneath his white shirt. "Stop that shit," he said.

I put my fist to my mouth, pushing my lips against it. After a moment, I took my hand away. "What I mean is, coming to LA is me trying to redeem myself. Darlene and I met in acting class. It was our plan to come down here when we were ready. So coming here is me trying to make something of myself. If not for me, for my parents, and for them.

"But. . ." I felt the tears coming again, like ants in my throat. "I don't think it'll *ever* be enough. There's nothing I can *ever* do. . ."

"Look, man." Carter swung his head in a half-circle. Then slowly, he brought it back. He held up his hand as if to stop or calm me. "You didn't kill anyone. You phoned your wife trying to reach her. That's all *you* were trying to do. She picked up. She did. Now I'm not saying that it's her fault. I'm just saying. . .dude, it was an *accident.* Your sister happened to be in the car too. You didn't plan any of it, my friend. So as awful as you have to feel, and I'm, God. . .I'm so *sorry*. But you are not responsible!"

"I don't know if I am," I said. "But I know I'm haunted by it. I'm always going to be haunted by it."

Chapter 33

"The number you have dialed has been changed, disconnected, or is no longer in service."

Not only was the GPS taking me in circles, now I couldn't even call for directions.

The name listed on the dispatch was Monique Debbenfield.

Either she was an idiot, or one of the new staff members had fucked up again.

I drove back to the store.

"Lew, I can't find this address and the phone number isn't working."

Lewis pulled it up on the map screen.

"Oh. I think this is that weird one. I know Paul's had it before. Ask him if he's downstairs. Look at the map here, see?"

There was a pink line showing the directive route from the store, but it didn't make sense. It was leading to the Veteran's Complex and back as far as I could tell. "I've been there already," I said.

"Try and find Paul if he's downstairs. Otherwise if you can't find it just come back."

I got back in my car. Again I put in the address. And again, Sally was directing me towards the VC.

"Fuck this!" I turned right onto Barrel Road instead of left.

In the parking lot I saw Jeffrey and Joel.

"Guys seen Paul?"

"He's upstairs," Jeffrey said. "He got called up."

Joel saw me carrying the bag and asked what was wrong. I told him.

Looking at the slip he said, "That eleven's probably a mistake. They probably added an extra one. Or it's four-six-zero."

Paul came down. I showed him the ticket and asked if he recalled the address.

"No, bro."

Back in the store I explained the situation to Dave. He looked at the dispatch.

"Who took this order?" he asked the front. "The phone number starts with one-five-six? That's not a number."

"I think Melissa took it," Lewis said. He pulled something up on his screen.

"One-six-five sounds more like it. Do you want me to try calling them?"

I watched Lewis as he greeted the person on the line and explained that he was calling from the store. I thought he had the wrong number until he began explaining that we had a new employee, correcting my dispatch with his pen.

"I'm so sorry." Lewis looked at me, pointing out the corrected address on the dispatch. "How long will it take you to get there?"

"I'll leave right now."

On my way out I heard Lewis trying to comfort the customer. She was probably irate that the delivery had taken so long and would probably take it out on me when I arrived, thanks to Melissa.

I drove over, very close to where I'd originally been directed by my GPS.

I pressed the apartment number and waited.

The door buzzed open.

Entering the courtyard, the first door in the downstairs right opened. I saw a short woman in the light of the doorway.

"Over here," she said.

I walked over.

"I'm really sorry," I said. *I'm just the messenger* I was prepared to say, or *Hey, I didn't take your order.* I showed the dispatch slip with the correction. "I was given the wrong address and phone number."

The woman with waist-length hair the color of stone parted in the middle grinned. She wore a long aqua-blue shirt with a pattern that made me think of a glowing aquarium. "It's okay. The guy on the phone told me. He said you had a new girl."

"How are you?" I asked.

"Well. It's life. It's great." She spoke slowly and softly, her round pale face lined and tired-looking as she continued to grin at me. I thought she could be stoned.

I pulled the pizza out and handed it to her.

She went to get her money, leaving me with a glimpse of the inside of her apartment. It was filled with lit candles on small tables, many of which also had small statues and other artifacts. I smelled incense. *Somebody's keeping the Psychic Eye Bookstore in business*, I thought.

She came back, counting out the money from a green pouch, including five dollars.

"Thank you so much," I said. "And again, I apologize. If you'd like, you really should email or call the store and tell them about the delay and I'm sure they'll send you out a coupon. Just, whenever, your leisure."

"What's your name?"

"Dylan."

The lady stared at me, the grin gone.

"Well, thanks again," I said. "You know what, I'll tell them now when I get back and they'll send out some kind of discount for you."

"Dylan," she said.

"Dylan. Like Matt Dillon, the movie actor."

"But it's spelled D-Y-L-A-N."

"Yeah. I just say that sometimes cause I figure people might remember."

"When I look at you I don't think Matt Dillon at all. I'm good at seeing the soul behind people's eyes. I think you've got something more magnificent than that."

"Oh. . .thank you."

The woman's grin returned. "See you again," she said.

Back in my car I fastened my seatbelt and turned the ignition. The lights of my display came on with the slam of layered guitars and blast beats. I reached for the volume dial and turned the music off.

I rode off listening to the silence, feeling a great tingling between my shoulders as though someone massaged me, opening a green window of space there.

Chapter 34

Phone to my ear, I listened to it ring.

A week had gone by since I ate the cookie, and so had Thanksgiving. I'd been wondering what I might do to win back Roxanne's favor. After Vic suggested I do something out of the ordinary, something a little adventurous, I thought I had come up with just the thing.

"Hello?"

"Hey," I said. "It's me."

"What's up?"

"What you doing later?"

"Why, what's up?"

"Let's go out tonight," I said, looking at the wheat penny. In the daylight, it looked dull and almost blended in with my dashboard. A light coating of dust had settled on the tape.

"You want to meet at Geoff's?"

"No, I meant let's go out to dinner tonight."

"No."

"No?"

"I said no."

"Why not?"

"Forget it. I'm not doing that again."

I paused, considering the undercurrent of hurt that came with her words.

She must have really dressed up for our date. She must have looked gorgeous.

And to think I'd missed that for a fucking cookie that'd had made me feel like I was on acid.

"How about just a casual dinner then? I'm going to be hungry when I get off work."

"How bout you fill up your stomach after work and then you

can take me out for a drink?"

I closed my eyes and reached for the penny, touching it with my index finger.

"Well, that's fine," I said, measuring my tone. "It's just that what I have planned is out here on the west side."

"You want me to come out to the west side?"

"I'll pick you up right after work. Traffic at least won't be bad."

"Why don't you just come out here and we can drink out here? Why go all the way out there and back?"

"Because. I've got a little something planned."

"What?"

"Just a little adventure." I shrugged. "Guess you'll just have to agree to see me now, won't you?"

Roxanne said nothing for a moment. Then, "Whatever. I gotta go."

"Wait!" I said.

"I gotta go, I'm working. Text me when you get off."

She hung up.

I looked over at my gray Lincoln, and smiled.

Chapter 35

I stepped in dog shit.

Not only had I stepped in a big pile (I'd felt the yielding cushion before seeing it, of course), but they were the non-slip shoes I'd used for serving, the only pair I wore. The shit was inside the tiny pockets of the crisscrossing grip.

I tried scraping along the curb, then walked over to a patch of grass. Rubbed, then looked again at the bottom of my shoe.

The shit was sporting green hair.

"Shit!"

I found a puddle by the curb and dipped my shoe in, jerking my foot from side to side.

Now the muck in the clogged pockets merely looked damp.

I took my shoe off and dropped it in the puddle. Hopped back to my car.

What was I going to do now? I could hardly work the rest of my shift with only one shoe.

I didn't have time to go out now and buy a new pair.

And I'd already given Carter his shoes back.

No, I thought, before the voice in my head could even ask. You're not wearing those shoes now. You're not wearing those shoes ever.

Why not? the needling voice countered. *They're shoes. They're* just *shoes. You need them.*

So you happened to be wearing them when you got married, to the funeral. So what? Why keep them then?

My heart felt like a throbbing lime.

I keep them because I haven't been able to let them go, even if I'll never wear them again. I was happy when I first stood in them.

Just wear them for the rest of today. For chrissake, what's going to happen?

I looked at the overcast sky. The day was looking bruised and getting darker.

"Whatever," I said, opening the door. "They're just fucking shoes."

"You're looking a little glum, chum," Joey said. "What's the matter, your woman stop putting out?"

As I looked at Joey I saw my wife's face, remembering the way it had looked whenever she showed concern.

Joey smiled with his tongue between his teeth, like he was showing me a big red berry in his mouth.

"Shut the fuck up kid," I said, taking the dispatch, "or I'll knock you on your dumpy ass."

Back in my car I almost started crying.

The shoes felt cool and soft on my feet. Airy and spacious.

They felt good to wear. They weren't supposed to.

The phone once again misdirected me to a dead end.

Fortunately it was a dead end I recognized, having been to the corner of Amelia and Sampson before. Rather than calling, I ventured across Wilshire to where Amelia continued. The next time I tried the address I ended up in front of an old apartment building on the corner of Texas and Amelia.

I looked at the dispatch slip.

D Santos

I remembered the guy with the AD/HD shirt—a big cheery fellow with a black beard. He'd been nice.

The side door to the building opened and a man stepped out.

"Wait, can you hold that?" I asked.

The man turned, and seemed to blink in surprise.

"Oh, it's *you,"* he said. He held out his hand to stop me, closing his eyes. "Um. Dylan, right?"

Now it was my turn to look surprised. "That's right. And you're DG."

"Glad you caught me, I was just stepping out for a few minutes. You're real quick this time!"

While DG kept the door open with one of his sandaled feet, I opened the carrier bag and slid out the large pizza and smaller box of wings.

"Oh, yeah," DG moaned, taking the boxes. "Thank you boss. You don't know how good this smells right now."

"I've got a good idea. After a night of delivering my car smells like a pizza oven."

"Must make you hungry!"

"It does."

"How much do I owe?"

I looked at the receipt and told him.

Balancing the boxes with one hand, he reached down to the side pocket of his shorts. He made a clicking noise with his tongue and teeth. "You know what, my wallet's in my car. Can you hold these a sec?"

"Sure."

He handed me the boxes, and I watched him walk over to the curb and open the door of an old brown Mazda. He reached in, shut the door, and walked back over while going through his wallet.

"Here you go bud!" He handed me the cash, then took the pizza boxes from me.

"Thank you DG," I said. "Nice to see you again."

"Hey!" He slapped me on the shoulder. "Pleasure's all mine, man. You keep a hopeless bachelor like me well-fed."

"Joey, here." I handed him the bag of freshly baked chocolate chip mini-cookies I'd bought from the ice cream shop.

He looked at it like he thought it might explode, then quizzically at me.

"Sorry for snapping at you," I said. "I've been having a bad day. But that's not your fault."

"Oh, it's cool Dylan, thanks!"

"No hard feelings?"

"Naw."

Outside, I pulled out the other bag of cookies I'd gotten for myself, and sat down.

I was about to pull out one when I saw Melissa, looking timid as she approached.

"Hi!" I said.

"Hi."

"How you doing?"

She shrugged. "Erm."

She looked at her shoes, the over-sized yellow hat seeming to swallow her head. "You got a cigarette?"

"Don't smoke, but I got something better. Just for you."

I handed her the bag, open side to her. "Cookie love."

"For me? *Aww.*" Looking delighted, she reached in and brought out a cookie.

"There you go," I said. "Cheers."

Her eyes gleamed as she brought the cookie to her face. Looking at me, she bit in to it.

I pulled out one for myself and took a bite.

"Mm," I said.

"Can I ask you something? Does everybody here hate me?"

"Why you asking me?" I said. "I don't hate you."

"Everyone else does!"

"What makes you think that?"

"Because. . .I mess up a lot. I've already been warned by the managers."

"You're new. You're still learning. Just relax and give it time. Help your co-workers, and they'll help you."

"You're right. I just hope I don't get fired. Thanks for the cookie." She turned.

"You're welcome."

She stopped. "Hey, do you smoke pot?"

No, I eat it. "Every now and then," I said.

"I'll smoke you out."

"Okay," I said. "Not tonight though."

Melissa nodded. She raised her arm in a wave as she turned her back.

I watched her walk back to the store, a new bounce to her steps. I had to smile as I pulled out another cookie.

555 was one of the largest apartment complexes on Barrel Road. The front of the rosewood building looked flat and nondescript, except for the three large golden numerals, but inside and beyond the greeting area you entered a lush courtyard that featured replicas of Greek statues and two large fountains on either end that colored the air with the sounds of rushing streams. I'd been here several times before, usually delivering to Shelton Burkel.

I walked up to the digital callbox. Mr. Burkel was one of the trusting few who provided me with the code to the building. As I let myself in, my eyes immediately went to the large fireplace. It wasn't real wood burning, but the effect was cozy and welcoming.

"How you doing?" I called to the man sitting behind the desk. I saw this same older gentleman every time, and the ritual was also the same: The man looked up from the newspaper he was reading, his drooping face impassive as he nodded and said a perfunctory good evening in a tone that sounded more like good night.

The courtyard was lit well enough to see where you were walking, but had a dark and shadowy feel because of the tall plants and statues.

It's perfect, I thought.

Mr. Burkel was on ground level, the last apartment to the left in the corner.

I knocked, then waited, knowing that he had heard me. The man had keen ears, if nothing else.

The door slowly opened.

"Good evening Mr. Burkel."

The old man looked up at me with eyes that looked glued-on behind his spectacles. "Hello," he whispered.

"How are you?" I asked, opening the carrier bag that felt deflated in my hand. I groped inside for the small box.

"Knees still hurt. Haven't been able to go for my walks. All I can do is just sit around here. Terrible."

"I'm sorry," I said, holding his personal pizza in my hand. I didn't immediately hand it over on purpose. "I think you said last time that you were going to get them looked at. Has that happened yet?"

Mr. Burkel licked his lips. I noticed the liver-spotted hand resting on his cane was trembling. "Yeah, but. Unnh. There's not a whole lot they can do. They just give me more damn pills."

"I'm real sorry to hear that. I hope you feel better soon."

"Yehnn. . .and how you feeling? Are you recovered?"

"I'm feeling fine now, thanks." He inquired the same thing every time.

"Well." His hand reached into the pocket of his checkered smoking jacket. He brought out a ten. "Here you go. Young whippersnapper."

I smiled as I took the bill from him, then handed him the pizza.

"You know, you might consider trying to use the hot tub. Maybe just sitting on the steps with your legs in the water might soothe the joints a bit?"

"Ehnn. . .been years since I was in that pool. Chore enough these days to get into the goddamn bath. Good night."

"Good night Mr. Burkel. Take care."

In the courtyard I walked towards the pool and hot tub. It was only from this side of the courtyard, walking back as I usually did from Mr. Burkel's, that I would even notice. The many tall potted plants and shrubs walled in the area.

Making it nice and secluded.

I approached the gate and looked in. The bean-shaped pool glowed blue, the small round hot tub beyond glowing green.

Reaching over the placard warning that no lifeguard was on duty, I unlocked the gate. Pushed the little door open and aside.

I dipped my hand in the pool. It was heated. Looked up and couldn't see any of the apartment windows, which meant no one from above could see down. Unless somebody was to walk right along the cement wall and peer down, no one from above would take notice.

I stood up, grinning as I shook my wet hand.

"One more, Dylan," Taylor said, indicating the two bags waiting for me on the counter. "I'll cash you out after this, okay?"

I picked up the folded slips on top, put my wrist through the handles of the plastic bag with the salad, and hefted the loaded carrier bags.

In my car I looked at the dispatch.

And groaned.

Lionel Maywaithe.

"You have arrived!"

I pulled up to a driveway and turned around. With parking only on one side of the narrow road, it wasn't surprising that it was packed. I'd have to go back down the road a bit.

I was more than a quarter mile down before I finally found a space.

"This'll be a grand waste of time," I said as I hefted the heavy bags from the backseat. I closed the door with the nudge of my backside.

Facing the road, I realized it was going to be an uphill walk.

Shaking my head, I began.

I soon felt myself sweating, even though I could see my breath.

And this little fucker isn't even going to tip worth—

Clack-clack-clack!

I stopped in my tracks.

An elk was trotting towards me on the road.

The antlered creature stopped.

We stared at each other.

The elk began to trot towards me.

My heart sped up as I readied myself for the charge, but the elk went behind a car and up onto the sidewalk. From there it climbed a slope of ground ivy between two houses, turned and looked down. As big as it was, it felt threatened by me.

Thing's nearly the size of a reindeer, I thought.

I stared up at the magnificent creature a moment longer, then continued, feeling the weight of the load I carried.

As soon as I came upon the dark bombed-out rubble that was Lionel Maywaithe's garage, I cursed, recalling the awkward climb in the dark. Now I remembered the little fucker saying something about a front way to the house, which he neglected to include in his delivery notes.

I started up what passed for a driveway.

At least the spider web was gone.

I climbed to the deck, careful to mind the hole. I went up the side of the house where Lionel had appeared the last time, and knocked on the door.

A light came on from the other side of the fence. I heard another door open.

"Hello?"

"I'm over here!" I called out.

"Oh."

The light over the side door flicked on.

I opened the flap of the carrier bag as the door opened.

As I was tugging out the stack of boxes, Lionel said hi in his short nasally voice. It sounded like a grunt from a penguin.

"Here you go," I said, handing him the boxes. He set them onto a crate next to the door. Then I gave him the salad bags.

I handed him the credit card slip and pen. His face looked confused as it squinted.

"Can't see," he muttered.

Lionel took his time, seeming to need it to add up an equation.

The bill was over sixty dollars.

Maybe he's going to tip me a percentage after all.

"Thanks," he said, handing me back the slip and pen.

"Thank you," I said.

As quick as I could I walked to where I could see the hole in the deck before he shut the light off.

I made it just in time.

On Lionel Maywaithe's driveway I held the slip up to my face.

Lionel had tipped me .87. He'd done the math in order to make the total a round number.

"Son of a *bitch.*"

I stopped and looked back up at the house sitting on the dark hill, shaking my head.

What kind of douchebag can afford to live in a house like that and not tip the pizza guy even two bucks?

"Lionel Maywaithe may fucking *wait* the next time he gets me."

When I neared my car, I saw the elk, still at the top of the little hillside covered in ground ivy, looking down at me.

I unlocked my car and threw the carrier bag in.

The elk looked from side to side, seeming confused and trapped.

I drove away, wondering why it seemed so scared.

Chapter 36

"What's this?" Roxanne asked as I shut off the engine.

"Just parking," I said. "We're going around the corner."

"To what?"

I leaned over and ventured a kiss. Roxanne let me, but the response was tepid. "To our destination."

I opened the door and retrieved my backpack from the backseat.

Roxanne eyed my bag. "You taking us camping or something?"

"Nope. This way."

We walked towards Barrel.

"We're just up here," I pointed, stepping onto the sidewalk.

"Wait. Are you trying to take me to your place?"

"Nope."

"This is all residential."

"You speak the obvious, my dear."

"So, what. Are you taking me to a fucking party?"

"Sort of."

In front of the rosewood building, I pulled out the slip of paper that had been Shelton Burkel's dispatch slip, and put in the code.

"This way," I whispered, beckoning Roxanne while my other hand grasped the large wooden door handle. "And please be quiet once you're inside."

Roxanne looked at me, then stepped inside.

My heart began to race as I followed, seeing first the fake fire, then the empty clerk's desk.

He's out, good!

Roxanne's boots clacked on the shiny brown tiles, the echo of her footfalls the only sound. I pulled open the door to the courtyard, letting in the sound of rushing fountains.

The many statues gave the illusion of a presence in the shadowy court. Looking up, I saw no one looking down.

Taking her hand, I guided Roxanne around the heavy foliage to where it parted. Beyond the gate, the pool water glowed.

"We're going in here," I said.

"What? *Why?"*

"Because I want to go in for a dip."

Letting go of Roxanne's hand, I reached over and unlocked the gate. "Come on."

Roxanne stayed put. She crossed her arms. "Who lives here?"

"Lots of people."

"This isn't where you live?"

"Nope."

"How did you know the code?"

"I got it from one of my customers. People give me the codes to their buildings all the time. You coming, or what?"

"No."

"You just going to stand there while I use the hot tub?"

"Is this supposed to be some stupid joke?"

"No joke. Coming?"

Roxanne eyed my backpack. "What do you have in there?"

"Towels, and the best mead in California."

"The best what?"

I turned away, letting go of the gate.

Lawn chairs were arranged to the left of the pool, tables with pulled umbrellas spaced on the right. A life preserver hung by the back wall of shrubbery. I walked to the nearest table and set down my backpack. Looked over my shoulder, and Roxanne was standing behind me.

She stepped into my arms. My hands felt the soft fabric of her sweater, offset by the abrasive ribbon of her bra strap. The top of her head smelled like some kind of rare berry. Her hair brushed me as she moved back and her eyes narrowed as I leaned down and kissed her. Closing my eyes, I felt the welcome brush of her tongue.

She trembled as we pulled our lips apart.

"Excited?"

"It's cold!" she said.

"Then we'd better get in."

"I'm not swimming."

"Neither am I. I'm going in the hot tub."

I opened my backpack. Pulled out the towels and the bottle of mead.

"What if someone comes out?"

"There's no security clerk. A place this big, no one's going to know everyone. Anyone does come, we're friends staying with Shelton. What are they going to do? Here." I handed her the bottle. "Check it out."

I walked to the hot tub. Crouching, I put my hand in.

All it needs is bubbles.

My eyes went to the life preserver, then noticed the small box near the ground. I walked over and pushed the button. The water came alive with large bubbles and froth.

"Interesting," Roxanne said, still eyeing the bottle of mead. "Does it taste like honey?"

"I think you're about to find out."

"You didn't bring any glasses."

"You know I don't have cooties."

As I was unbuckling my belt I heard a clink, and looked to see that Roxanne had taken out the last thing from my backpack: My wine key. She cut at the bottle's seal.

I took off the rest of my clothes, save my boxers, and left them folded on the chair.

Roxanne handed me the bottle.

"Coming in?"

"Someone really might see us," she said, looking up.

"Kinda exciting, ain't it?"

Not willing to wait while she made up her mind, I walked to the tub and stepped in.

Facing the wall with the life preserver, I backed up till my feet found the step. Reaching behind, I set the bottle down, then submerged to my neck in the bubbling hot water.

I looked up the rectangle of night sky framed by the upper floors of the complex. The layer of clouds from earlier had broken, leaving the remainders looking like scrapes of purple icing among the glittering stars.

This is the life, I thought.

Reaching for the bottle, I caught Roxanne in the corner of my eye. She was coming over.

And she was naked.

She sucked in a breath as her feet stepped into the bubbling tub, the jerking movement of her upper body making her breasts bounce. I looked from there to the dark patch between her creamy legs as they moved in to the water towards me.

"Ah." She opened her mouth as she rolled her head back and closed her eyes.

"Nice?"

"Hot."

"Sure is."

I moved to where she stood in the center of the tub. Glided my hands up her arms to her shoulders, feeling her skin, still cold and goose-bumped.

She rolled her head forward with her eyes still closed. We kissed.

My hands moved up and down her back, drawing warm rivulets of water onto her.

We seemed to float in golden carbonation. Lowering my hands, they entered the water, finding the fullness of her rump. I felt one leg lift and brush across my waist, then the other until both her legs were around me. On the other side of the fabric, she was pressed against my erection.

Breaking from our kiss, I said, "Could you get off me for a second?"

Her legs unwrapped and her hands fell away.

I backed up.

Bending down, I lowered my boxer shorts and stepped out of them. I flung them out of the water.

Roxanne laughed. "I was wondering why'd you keep those on when you're going to have to take them off anyway!"

"It was pretty stupid."

"Where's that bottle of honey stuff?"

I handed her the bottle. "You might want to sip it, it's pretty rich."

Roxanne carefully angled it up with her lips over the top. Her breasts lifted out of the water, the nipples hard.

She quickly lowered the bottle.

"Good?" I asked, taking the bottle. Her cheeks were puffed as though she were trying to hold in her breath. She nodded, and swallowed.

I lifted the bottle and took a good drink.

Roxanne was wiping her mouth. I couldn't tell if any of the clear drops on the hollow of her throat or migrating between the cleft of her breasts were drops of mead or water.

"It's sweet," she said.

"Do you like it?"

"Yeah, it's all right. Like a dessert wine."

"I can't picture the Vikings ever having dessert, but there you go."

"You're fucking random."

"You fucking like it."

Roxanne beckoned with her fingers. I handed her the bottle.

When she was done I took it back, had a swig, then wrapped my arms around her still holding the bottle.

"Am I forgiven?"

"I'm here with you," she said.

I set the bottle down.

Putting my arms around her, I lowered myself and lifted her partially out of the water. Her legs wrapped around me again.

This time, I felt my erection meet her.

Her arm came up, and she put her hand to the side of my face.

I felt the tip of my penis enter new warmth under the water.

"Sss. . ." Roxanne's hand came off my cheek as she rolled her head back and lifted her arms.

Then she moved forward, sliding onto me, her hands on my back, nails scraping my skin.

The bubbles stopped.

Roxanne smiled, closing her eyes. "You need the bubbles?"

"I don't care."

Her nails dug into my back, as Roxanne rolled her head and brought my weight forward. I put one hand above the water to buoy myself as I sank towards it. Roxanne reached, as though pushing into a backstroke. Her waist lifted, and I saw the dark mound of her pubic hair rise near the surface before she shot forward.

She was going towards the steps.

I straightened up.

Roxanne's legs drifted straight out, then her knees bent as her upper body lifted. Her breasts came out of the water and shook as she adjusted herself onto one of the steps. She looked behind her for the rail. A hand came out of the water and beckoned.

Her legs parted.

"Fuck me here," she whispered, pulling me in. My penis

entered.

I leaned forward, my hands spaced apart on the step below her shoulders.

I slid back.

"Ooh…"

And in.

"Ah!"

"Shh," I whispered. "There are still people sleeping around us, you know?"

Roxanne's whole face smiled. "Okay. Maybe we do need more bubbles."

"That seems like a good idea."

"Get up."

Arching my back, I slid out. Roxanne grabbed hold of my shoulder and used it to leverage herself as she stood up. She turned and walked up the steps.

I watched her dripping naked body leisurely walk towards the control box, her footsteps making wet smacks on the cement as her pale skin glowed in the green light from the tub. I stared at her rump, watching as weight shifted from one leg to the other.

The bubbles came back on. She turned and came back down the steps, grinning.

Our lips met, then our tongues.

There was a wonderful tugging on my penis under the water. It was her other hand.

Lowering myself, I caught her opening legs as she stretched underwater, grabbing hold of my shoulders. She pulled herself against me, found the spot, and impaled herself.

She wrapped her arms around me as I held her tight, making slow upward thrusts.

For a while there was nothing but Roxanne's soft moans and warm caresses.

Then the bubbles went off again.

I opened my eyes, blinking from the sting of dripping sweat.

Roxanne got louder as she held on, grinding furiously. I held her as close as I could, waiting for the pressure to give.

Suddenly, her arms released my back and were pushing at my chest. *"Here."*

Climbing onto the step with her knees, she looked behind her and backed up. Dropping her lower back, she raised her rump.

Putting one hand on her soft waist, I guided myself in.

Roxanne moaned.

"Oh...oh...OH! *WHAT THE FUCK MAN?"*

I pulled out. "Sorry! You okay?"

"LOOK!"

I followed Roxanne's pointing finger to the seating area.

The umbrella above the table furthest from us had been opened. Below it, in a chair facing us sat the unmistakable form of a person, slouching.

"Oh shit," I said.

"I'm getting the fuck out of here!"

"Wait," I said, trying my best to see the stranger's face. The shadows where he sat were too thick, but I thought I could just make out the shape of a bald head.

Shelton Burkel?

"Roxanne."

"What?"

"Shh," I said, lowering my voice. "I know that guy. He lives here. He's an old man, and I'm pretty sure he's legally blind."

"I don't care! We're getting the fuck outta here RIGHT NOW!"

She got out and snatched up the towel she'd left on the nearest reclining chair.

My own towel was still with my backpack and clothes I'd left on the table.

The one where the figure was sat.

"Jesus," I muttered, shaking my head. I lifted myself out of the tub. The towel wrapped around her, Roxanne stood hunched, shaking from what looked like a toxic mixture of the cold temperature and her own indignation. Her teeth were bared as she glared at me.

I walked towards Shelton.

"Hey," I began, but then the figure's face came alive in the sudden glow of a struck match, illuminating the impassive face of the clerk who usually sat at the front desk. Despite the night vision goggles, I recognized him.

After lighting the end, he pulled the cigar from his mouth with a thick plume of acrid smoke.

"Don't mind me, kids. I can see you just fine."

Chapter 37

Man, had I fucked up.

Again.

And probably for the last time with Roxanne.

"Let me out," she demanded, when we were on her street.

I pulled up to the house. She opened the door.

"Wait," I said. "One second, let me talk to you!"

"Do you fucking *realize* he could have us on camera?"

"He doesn't."

"How do *you* know?"

I opened my mouth, but before I could answer Roxanne raised her palm. "Great fucking idea!" she spat, sweeping her hand in an exaggerated gesture. "Another one of your great ideas!

"You know, I. . ." She stopped. The anger in her face fell as she looked away, on the verge of tears. *"I didn't deserve it."*

She got out of the car.

"No, you didn't, I'm sorry!" I called after her.

She kept going.

I watched her walk up to the front door, open it, and step inside. The door closed without her looking back.

Chapter 38

I sat on my bike looking at the changing lights of the Ferris wheel on Santa Monica pier in the distance.

Round and round the lights went, changing colors and patterns.

I had taken my bike through the Venice Beach boardwalk, with no real aim other than for something to do while I couldn't sleep and maybe catch the sunrise.

The sunrise would probably be a while yet to come, but this was fine. Now that I'd stopped, I felt no urgency to continue.

Looking at the glowing wheel was oddly calming. It made no sound, but twirled and pulsed. The sole performer left out in the sleeping circus.

I wasn't sure what I'd been expecting coming down here at four in the morning, other than maybe a little danger. I only knew that it seemed like something I needed to do after tossing and turning while listening to Vic's lion-like snoring and, worse, the voices in my head.

But now those voices were quiet. There was only the sound of the surf and the Christmas-y look of the wheel.

I lost track of time as I stared, only becoming alert when I heard shuffling feet or the rapid-card sound of spinning bike spokes behind me. But the few people out and about that passed left me alone.

Finally, I pedaled forward again.

I would be tired by the time I got back: It was about two miles and uphill.

But I felt better, knowing that I'd found what the Author had sent me out here for.

When I got back to Vic's I would finally sleep, and things would begin anew in the morning.

While the residents and businesses slept, the wheel would keep on turning.

There was something comforting in knowing that it would still be there after I left, all day and night, changing and glowing, wherever I was.

Chapter 39

When I walked in to work, Dave and Bill were the only ones there. They were in conversation.

"No, it was the security guy who caught them," Dave said, turning to look at me.

My heart sped up.

"What's up there, Dylan?" Dave asked.

"Hey."

"What's up?"

"What?"

"You looked like you were about to say something."

"Oh, no. What are you guys talking about?"

"Some security guy from around here thinks he might have the Cat Burglar on camera. It's been on the news." Dave pointed to one of the large screens. "They'll probably show it again. They've been replaying it all day."

"What does it show?"

"Some guy carrying stuff out in boxes. You can't really see him. It's gotta be him though. They'll catch that asshole soon."

"I can't wait," Bill said. "I wanna know what the hell he's been doing with all those cats!"

"That's what everyone wants to know."

"That guy's so fucking screwed."

"He's pissed off a lot of powerful people."

"I'm surprised they haven't caught this guy already," I said. "Don't all these places have cameras?"

"A lot do, but I guess a lot of them don't. We didn't have any cameras catching that guy who robbed you, remember?"

"This guy has to be some top-notch pro, too," Bill said. "He got into fucking Tom *Hank's* place!"

"I know," Dave said, opening the register. He handed me

my bank. “That’s what’s creepy about this whole thing. This guy seems to be able to get in anywhere he wants.”

At first, I thought it was a stray dog.

Then I was cruising alongside and saw clearly what it was.

A coyote.

“Whoa.”

Not that coyotes were rare in the hills, but walking a residential street this side of Sunset?

I slowed down. The coyote walked onto the sidewalk and was shielded from view by the parked cars.

“Turn left onto Greta Lane. Then your destination will be on the right!”

I turned, seeing the coyote already a good distance up the street.

“You have arrived!”

Parked, I opened the door and stood up.

The coyote was out of sight.

“It was just outside?”

“About five minutes ago,” I said. “That’s unusual, isn’t it?”

“It is,” said the woman in the yellow dress that moved like a stretched tent. “He must have been hungry.”

“Are coyotes dangerous?”

“They can be. They’ve been known to chase joggers and people out walking their dogs up near the mountains around here, and they’ll stalk little children. They’re especially dangerous to children.”

Walking back with the empty carrier bag I looked up and down the street. No sign of the coyote.

Inside my car, I looked at the credit card slip.

The woman had tipped me $2 on $59.

I shook my head.

Then again, I thought, *better than Lionel Fucking MayWait.*

“Hello Mrs. Frankmeyer,” I said to the familiar short woman who answered the door, rollers still in her cherry-red hair. “How are you this evening?”

Adeline Frankmeyer’s plump face became a raisin of

wrinkles as she smiled. "Fine, dear," she said in her warm voice. "It's nice to see you again."

"How's Mr. Frankmeyer?"

"Oh, he's fine, he's in here. I'll get him down but let me take that off you first."

I handed Adeline the pizza box and salad.

She turned and looked up the stairs. "Mervin? MERV!"

"What!"

"THE PIZZA MAN IS HERE!"

"Yes!"

"He'll be right down, dear." She padded off, her bunny slippers whispering on the marble floor.

Mervin Frankmeyer came down the stairs.

The tall thin man stared as he approached, his expression reminding me of big fishes I had seen at The Steinhart Aquarium—the ones that came close to the glass before bumping it.

"What do I owe you?" he asked.

"Twenty-seven nineteen," I said.

The man's unblinking eyes dropped to his wallet.

"Keep it," he said, handing me the bills.

"Thank you Mr. Frankmeyer," I said. "Good to see you. Have a great night."

The man's tight lips edged towards a smile. "Take care," he said, his hand up in a still wave as I turned away. A moment later I heard the door shut behind me.

The sensor light went off as I passed the parked Lexus under the canopy overhang and the older Mazda parked nearby. I took a few steps in the dark, hearing the soft crunch of sand beneath my shoes.

This was my last delivery of the evening and Dave had already cashed me out. I didn't intend to go straight home, however—after being on autopilot the whole day, I needed a 40oz from 7-11. Then I planned to fall into the welcoming arms of oblivion and sleep.

As I was approaching the open gate, imagining how good that first drink was going to taste, the sensor light came on and illuminated the waiting coyote.

Chapter 40

The coyote didn't move. Just stared, as though curious to find me here.

The sensor light went off.

I brought my hands together in a hard clap, triggering the light on again.

The coyote was gone.

Cautiously, I stepped towards the gate.

The coyote stood in the middle of the road about two hundred feet away, looking over its shoulder.

Back in my car heading down the road, I spotted it again walking alongside another coyote.

The two verged off the road, turning down a bisecting lane.

Was that *another* one further up?

I turned my wheel and began down the lane, following the coyotes. Ahead they were joined by the third. They trotted together, as though they'd been waiting to meet up.

The trio turned left. I sped up.

At the turn, another coyote startled me by running in front of the car, speeding through the shine of my headlights.

A sign read NOT A THROUGH STREET. The short row of houses ended at a chain-link fence with darkness beyond. To the left I saw a building site.

There was a large hole where somebody had peeled the fence back with cutters.

At the dead end I shut off the engine, keeping the headlights on.

I walked towards the fence, casting shadow before me. Moved out of the way so the lights illuminated the hole.

Putting my hand onto the fence, I peered through.

All I could see was a plot of land overgrown with weeds

and grass. I could make out the shape of a lone tree, but that was about it.

I was about to turn back when I heard a yelp.

Kneeling, I squinted into the dark.

A moan.

A hurt, human moan.

Then I was sure I saw movement around the base of the tree.

"Hello?" I yelled. "Is someone out there?"

More moans, but these were unmistakably non-human.

I backed away from the hole.

A low growl from behind quickly turned me around to see a coyote advancing, with its head lowered and teeth bared.

Clapping my hands, I yelled and made a lunge towards it. It turned and ran.

I stepped around the side of my car.

The coyote trotted up the street, then stopped and looked over its shoulder.

"Fuck off!"

I opened the driver's-side door and pressed the lever for the trunk.

I got out the tire iron and my flashlight.

Running back to the fence, I thought, *I must be fucking crazy, whatever I think I'm doing here.*

But someone was out there. Someone who needed help.

"Hey!" I yelled through the fence. "I'm coming! Stay in the tree!"

I ducked under and through the hole and pointed the beam of light towards the tree.

"Oh Jesus. . ."

Now I saw the group of coyotes gathered at the base of the tree. The pairs of glowing eyes told me that the tire iron and I were very outnumbered.

I aimed the flashlight higher, into the wincing face of a girl.

Wearing red earmuffs.

She raised her hand to block the blinding glare.

I started to run, my feet feeling heavy coming up from the gummy earth still wet from rain, but then my foot snagged and the flashlight left my hand as I hit the ground.

Get up!

I scrambled up, off balanced by the weight of the tire iron, as the coyotes erupted in a cacophony.

The beam of my flashlight swirled as it rolled down the slight incline.

"Look out!" the girl screamed.

I saw coyotes racing towards me and raised my weapon.

I was pounced on from behind.

I stumbled forward with the weight of the animal, which just as suddenly bounced off, leaving its snotty growl curling in my ear.

The coyotes circled me, yipping and howling. I turned with them, swinging the tire iron.

Just as one lunged, I stepped forward and raised my leg, meeting the animal's chin with my foot. Its belly flashed as it fell, landing writhing on its back.

I charged another.

The circle broken, the remaining coyotes were backing away.

I turned towards the tree.

One coyote remained at the base. It was larger than the others and its yellow eyes burrowed into me, unmoving.

As I got closer, I could see its face. Its teeth weren't bared and it didn't lower its head.

"Hey fuck-face," I said. "Ready to do this?"

The animal didn't move.

I raised the tire iron.

zzzZIP!

I broke eye contact with the challenging animal and looked up at Earmuff Girl. She was pushing down her jeans. Her skinny, snow-pale legs nearly glowed in the dark.

She turned around, revealing that she wasn't wearing underwear. She lowered her pale rump in a squat, and edged forward.

"Tiisha-tishkah!"

The coyote whirled around and looked up in time for the stream of urine to hit its face.

It yelped, backing away.

I ran forward. Brought down the tire iron onto the coyote's shaking head.

The rest of the body collapsed.

I looked up to see Earmuff Girl straightening. Her thumbs hooked in the side belt loops, she raised her jeans back up her skinny legs, and covered her ass. She turned around and looked down.

"Think we're good," I called up. "Are you okay?"

She nodded.

"Come on, I'll help you down."

She edged forward, looking to the ground, then at me.

"Jump," I said, opening my arms.

I caught her, feeling hardly the weight I expected.

Lowered to the ground, the top of her head came to just below my chest. She looked up, her green eyes cat-like in the dark. She thin lips remained shut.

"Okay?"

She nodded, then turned her cheek, mashing the pad of her earmuff against me as her arms hugged tight.

"That was pretty incredible," I said, "what you did."

The girl said nothing.

Instead, she bopped up, planting a kiss on my lips.

She said something in a light voice that I could barely hear.

I opened my mouth to ask, then realized she might have just told me her name.

I tried to repeat it. "Val-la. . .loll?"

She smiled and said it again.

"Val-la. . .*lou*la?" I knew that wasn't right.

Still smiling, she blinked, and repeated it again, softer and slower. Something about the way she pronounced that last two syllables. I tried, and still didn't get it.

"Val?" I said, shrugging.

She nodded affirmation that it would have to do.

"My name's Dylan," I said. "I've seen you around. It's nice to finally meet you. You're always wearing these." I lifted my hand to pat the earmuffs still in place over her head, but she shrank out of my embrace.

Before I knew what to say, she came back, shaking her head. She jumped up and I caught her, her little legs hugging me.

I laughed.

She turned her face and rubbed her nose with mine.

"Why are you so happy?" I asked, inches from her mouth.

"Because," she said, "You're the first man I've ever said my name to."

I opened my mouth, but she closed it with a kiss.

"Can we go home now?"

"Uh, sure," I said. "I'll take you there."

She kissed me again, then unwrapped her legs as I lowered her to the ground.

I walked over to my flashlight and picked it up, finding her with the beam. Grinning, Val shut her eyes to the light.

Shining the beam over to the tree, I lowered it to the coyote's body.

It took my mind a moment to register what it was seeing: Half of the animal's body melted to bone, with the remaining fur undulating, being eaten by some kind of acid.

Chapter 41

What had she done to that coyote? My mind kept coming back to what I'd witnessed.

"How did you end up with a whole pack of coyotes after you?"

"They can smell me," she said.

I turned to look at her, despite the fact we were moving. "What's that supposed to mean?"

"I shouldn't have been out this late. It's really my fault. This time of year is the worst. We smell ripe to them."

"Who's we?"

"My. . .my family."

"What the hell do—?"

"Go slow, this road is narrow. Daddy has the access to our driveway, but you can park alongside the street over there." She pointed to a row of cars we were approaching on the left side.

Daddy.

How old was Val?

She looked girlish. Yet there was something about her manner that was mature. I had a hard time trying to imagine her going to any high school in Grantwood.

Hell, after that coyote, I had a hard time trying to imagine her using a *bathroom*.

At the end of the line of cars I turned as she suggested, pulling up to the grassy area before a neighbor's fence.

She opened the car door. "Aren't you coming in?"

"For what?"

Val leaned over, her little nose stopping inches from mine. She gazed into me. "Because," she said, "I've chosen you."

Taking my hand, Val led me down the slope of a driveway to a large black gate. I looked up at the imposing barrier, able to faintly see a design made of iron bars over the painted wood.

Val unclasped my hand and walked over to a side door meant for foot traffic. A thick wall of ivy that undoubtedly concealed another wall bordered the door.

Realizing she meant for me to follow, I walked over as she pulled a key from under her sweater to unlock the door. Grinning, she held out her hand.

We walked down a winding tree lined path towards a *mansion*. I marveled at the size. The house was set quite a way back, with a massive lawn area. Unlike the other large houses I'd seen in the area, there appeared to be no lights on. No show to persuade burglars that the place was presently occupied.

"You live here?" I whispered, squeezing Val's hand.

"Yes."

"Big place. You have a big family?"

"Just me and Daddy."

"And where is he?" I asked, uneasy as we approached a curving footbridge. To the right I saw a spacious area flattened with sand meant for visiting cars, but I saw that any visitors still had to walk through this way, the bridge being the only route to the house.

"He's at work," she said. We had reached the bridge. I looked down the side and saw myself reflected on silent water. Behind my peering form the sky was alive with glittering and moving winks of light. The stars were so many and of so many different colors I didn't recognize it as the sky I knew. I looked to my own face, glowing a strange pale purple, and my own wide-eyed puzzlement as Val said, "He works late usually."

I looked up to the sky and again saw the brilliance of otherworldly colors I'd previously associated only with cathedral windows.

Val was tugging my arm. "This way."

As we reached the end of the lawn I let go of Val's hand, jumping as blue flames flared from twin ground lamps on either side of the large front door.

Val laughed.

I watched as she put her hand to the surface of the black door, and it soundlessly opened inward.

She whirled towards me, her face beaming. She took both my hands in hers.

"Please, come in," she said.

I nodded.

After you.

The goose bumps hardening my flesh melted as I passed under the arch of the door. It was like stepping through an invisible wall. My first breath took in the aroma of cinnamon, my exhale felt green and mint-fresh. I couldn't help but close my eyes as I lifted my nose and took more in, as much as my lungs would allow.

"Dylan?"

I opened my eyes and lowered my head to see Val, glowing in the darkness at the end of the passageway and beckoning me to her.

I walked towards her as welcoming heat pulsed up from each smooth tile I stepped on, warming my feet through my socks.

I took Val's hand in mine, and the darkness suddenly blossomed.

"I'm in a dream," I said, looking about.

We were in the middle of an atrium. Colors floated like specks of rainbow dust caught in cider-golden rays of light shining down from three circular windows in the middle of the ceiling high above. Beyond the circle windows that were framed in thick wooden rectangles were more windows in divided rows, curving in the shape of the dome, and through these I saw more of the strange celestial sky I'd observed outside. Below, pale marble arched around tall sentinel doors and more windows on the second storey, with a sparkling golden handrail going round.

All about us at ground level were lush plants and trees, some reaching high towards the ceiling. I marveled at the size of the leaves on one of the plants near me, some the size of coffee tables. From which prehistoric-era had they come?

Something chittered, and I looked up to see a small dark shape like a little monkey leaping from one of the trees.

"Myyap!"

Falling in a downward arch towards the nearest tree, it entered one of the rays of light and turned a glowing neon-blue while at the same time opening into another shape with wings. I watched as the creature floated in the air with the fluidity of a jellyfish, its wings opening and closing in slow motion, until it passed out of the light, where it suddenly turned dark again, dropping fast into the tree with an airy crash and undulation of leaves.

"Oh, I am fucking dreaming," I said.

Val laughed. “Come,” she said, with a tug of my hand. “My room is this way.”

She led me through the jungle of plants to another hallway, where colored flames lit candles in the recesses of the wall as we went. The candles were scented as well, each offering a new aroma. I smelled peaches and roses, honeysuckle, lavender, sandalwood, pumpkin, as well as perfumes I couldn’t name.

At the end of the hall she opened a cream-colored door with the gentle press of her hand, and pulled me inside.

The room illuminated with a dim, rosy glow. It was a mini version of the atrium, filled with plants and trees. The room, however, was windowless and contained a large canopy bed.

Val turned and stood on her tiptoes, kissing me with a soft press of her lips.

“Will you wait for me here, while I prepare myself?”

“Yep.”

She smiled with her perfect teeth, her eyes shining.

“I will not leave you long.” She stepped around me.

After a moment I turned, not having heard the close of a door. It had closed, but there was no knob.

Not seeing anywhere else to sit in the simple room, I sat back on the bed. A small table stood to the right of the door, holding red candles with guttering pink flames that encircled a small vanity mirror. The candles filled the room with a scent I didn’t recognize but liked very much.

While I prepare myself. . .

What did that mean? A shower?

Christ, maybe she had to take another piss.

After a spell of maybe five or ten minutes, during which I’d started to drift into a kind of wide-eyed doze, I suddenly looked up to the silently opening door.

Val stepped into the room, wearing nothing but her earmuffs.

I leaned forward at the sight of her pale, slender body; instantly aroused. Val was small but not skinny: No bony showing of deprivation, rather, her milk-white skin looked very soft. The very sight of it electrified my hands in anticipation.

Val grinned, stepping forward with her arms outstretched.

“Wait,” I said, holding up a hand. “How old are you?”

Val stopped and looked puzzled, then broke into laughter. She put a hand over her mouth, her still-laughing eyes looking mischievous.

Taking her hand away, she said, "I'm quite old enough. Do not worry about that. Do you like me?"

"Yes," I said, lowering my hand. It brushed against the tent in my pants. "As you can see."

But as Val stepped towards me, I held up my hand. "Why are you still wearing earmuffs?"

The grin on Val's face dropped.

"What?"

Slowly, Val raised her hands to the fuzzy red muffs.

Eyes locked on me, I watched a heavy breath rise and fall, then she pulled both muffs back, lifting the band.

Her ears flopped out.

"What the. . ?

Ears the size of my hands dropped like limp flaps of excess flesh, curled and then straightened upwards, the pointy tips inches above the top of Val's head.

She winced and stepped back, nearly losing balance as one foot stepped on the band of the earmuffs. She put her hands to her ears in what had to be an embarrassed, self-conscious gesture.

"No," I said. "Val." I went to her and wrapped my arms around her trembling shoulders, her overlarge ears bending away from me.

"Don't be afraid," I said. "You just surprised me."

"Why do you think I cover them? Why do you think we're always hiding?"

Holding her close, I kissed the top of her head, inhaling her scent. "Shh," I said. "Relax. There's nothing to fear here."

The top of Val's head nodded.

"I've never seen anyone who looked like you. And I want to get to know you so much more."

"They don't scare you?"

"No, they don't."

Val looked up, her eyes glittering.

"I knew," she said.

"Knew what?"

"I knew the moment I saw you coming to my rescue that you were the one. The one I've been waiting so long for."

Val backed up out of my arms, her ears settling at a more relaxed angle.

Suddenly the room changed color from rosy red to glowing green. I looked to the table with the candles and saw green flames rising.

"How do you do that?" I asked, but Val was no longer in front of me.

She was climbing onto the bed. On hands and knees, she crawled up, then looked over her shoulder.

"Do you feel as though you've been waiting for me, too?" she asked.

"Yes," I said, fascinated.

Something about the room then changed.

The many plants and small trees were moving as though stirred by a breeze. But there was no wind in the warm room. Only a sighing sound, that quickly subsided.

I looked back at Val to see her raising her rump, having parted her legs and lowered her torso to the mattress.

"Then mate with me."

As Val and I lay together, her head resting on my chest, I watched glowing moth-like creatures hover about the room, the largest grouping drawn to the candlelight. They were changing colors every few seconds. I hadn't noticed any before, but now they were everywhere.

They must have come from the plants and trees, at some point during our mating.

Mating. That was what Val had called it.

My penis still tingled from being inside her. Though I was spent, I still felt like I was being pleasured—like the soothing and fresh feeling of tea tree oil, only warm.

"Are you awake?" Val asked.

"I don't know," I said.

Val chuckled.

"But if I'm not, don't wake me."

Val lifted her head and looked at me.

"Can I ask you something?" I said.

Val smiled, her precious eyes answering.

"Why me? I know I helped with the coyotes, but why do you say you feel like you've been waiting for me? You're beautiful, magical. Obviously of, um, a certain class.

"I guess what I'm trying to get at is. . .you know, we're in *Grantwood.* And I am ambitious. I am. But right now, I'm just delivering pizza for a living. Did you know that?"

"I know what you are trying to say," Val said. "There are a great many wealthy men to be found here. But you must understand that so many of them are also, how would you say it?"

"Douchebags?"

"Yes. Without much essence."

"And I have essence?"

"Yes." Val kissed me. "You are a true spirit."

"A true spirit with essence. I should add that to my resume."

Val suddenly pushed off my chest and turned towards the door, her ears up like a rabbit's.

Before I had the chance to ask what was wrong, a booming voice roared from the other side of the door.

"WHOSE SHOES ARE THESE?"

Chapter 42

"Get under the bed!"

Val strode towards the door without getting dressed. She put her hand to the door and the light of the room changed back to its dim rosy red. The color-changing moths had scattered. "Take all your clothes with you in case he comes in!"

She opened the door and slipped around it. It closed without sound.

I went to grab my clothes, but froze at the sound of the voice.

"JENNIFER! HAVE YOU BEEN SLEEPING WITH SOMEONE?"

Jennifer?

I could hear Val answering, but she spoke so fast I couldn't understand a word of what she said.

"THESE ARE MAN'S SHOES!"

Me and my stupid habit of removing my shoes!

As I got onto my hands and knees, I realized I was trapped in a very large, strange house with a very angry and large-sounding father. *Daddy.*

Or could she have meant sugar daddy?

This wonderful dream was fast turning into a nightmare.

"SPEAK TO ME IN ENGLISH! WE SPEAK *ENGLISH!"*

As Val's voice got more agitated, I could hear that she was not speaking English. It was a language I didn't recognize at all.

Now both voices sounded like they were getting closer.

Pushing the clothes under the bed, I got onto my belly and followed. I turned my head toward the door, hoping the overhanging comforter would cover me from view if the man should walk in.

The man suddenly roared in the same unknown language.

What are these people?

After several minutes of agitated back-and-forth, both voices lowered in volume. Whatever the hell Val was saying, her argument seemed to be working. Gradually the voices retreated from my line of hearing altogether.

What am I doing hiding? How old am I?

Even if the man came ready to destroy me, is this how I wanted to go out—cowering?

I got out from under the bed and got dressed.

I was stepping towards the door when I saw it open.

Val slipped around it.

"Quick!" she whispered. "I have him distracted, but it might not be for long. He's not in a good mood, you must leave for now.

"Head straight down the hall to the front door. It will look closed when you see it, but I have opened it for you. Just touch it with your hand, and leave the front garden as quickly as you can. I'd rather him not see you like this."

"I understand," I said. "What about you?"

"I will remain here. Now go!"

Val moved aside and I slipped around the door.

The candles in the wall were all burning at a low yellow. As I neared the atrium, I became aware that the scents had changed as well—now they all smelt like something burning.

At the end of the hall I crouched and peered around the corner.

I saw a faint purple light emanating almost directly opposite of where I was, at the far end of the open space. Nothing else in my line of vision moved. The plants and trees were dark abstracts.

I waited, listening for any sound above the hammering of my own heart.

I heard nothing.

Go!

Looking only ahead, I jogged forward in what felt like slow motion.

I made it to the front door and was about to put my hand to it, when it occurred to me to grab my shoes.

They were not where I had left them.

Daddy had taken them when he'd gone to confront Val.

Oh forget the shoes—just get out!

I raised my hand again, but still hesitated.

They were my wedding shoes.

"Damnit," I muttered.

I crept back up the hallway and peeked around the corner.

Forget it, man.

Wait.

I saw a small black shape that looked like a shoe lying on its side, with the other one next to it.

On the balls of my feet, I approached, glancing up to the purple light.

I was about six feet away when the shoe lying on its side looked up at me.

Throwing my arms up, I lost balance and fell back, landing hard on my hands and ass as the dark shape lifted into the air, turning a glowing magenta as it spread its wings, its flat face and belly reminiscent of a stingray's.

I scooted away in a backwards crab-walk.

BURRRP!

Then saw the purple light darken with the coming of a large shadow.

Clack-Clack-Clack. . .

I scrambled for the nearest potted plant and ducked under and behind, the container just large enough to conceal me.

Clack-Clack-Clack. . .

Had he already seen me?

The clacking footsteps seemed to be coming towards me.

The man could have a gun in his hand. Ready to blast the intruder in his home. Ready to blast the guy plugging his "Jennifer."

I looked to my left, measuring how far I had to go.

Go go go go.

Putting my hand on the container, I swiveled and leaned forward into a sprinter crouch, my head forward. I wasn't waiting for the gun.

BURRRP!

The footsteps stopped no more than a few feet away.

My mind screamed I was too late. If he had a gun, I was toast.

Slurp!

The man was drinking something.

Slowly I leaned forward, my muscles trembling as I edged past the pot to take a peek.

The man's gaze was towards the ceiling as he held a large clay jug up to his mouth, slurping. He was naked and hairy, with long frazzled silvery hair sprouting from the sides and back of his otherwise bare head. He was quite short, but he had an enormous swollen gut—the largest on any man I'd ever seen.

My knees hit the ground as my stomach loosened, having seen what had been making the loud clacking sounds.

The man had hooves.

Dropping the flabby arm that had been holding the jug, the 'man' looked right at me, dark liquid dribbling down the layers of his chin.

His glowing yellow pupils went wide.

I scrambled to my feet and ran.

The roar nearly shook me off my feet as I made it to the hallway, where the light suddenly turned red, the candle flames rising like sharp spikes in the wall.

Slamming my hand against the door, it opened.

I ran into the night.

Chapter 43

Hooper answered the door wearing a Christmas sweater and Bermuda shorts, looking genuinely happy to see me.

"Glad you could make it."

"Hey, thanks," I said, shaking his hand. I lifted the bag with my other. "I brought you some beer."

"Oh, thanks! We've already got some too. Come on in."

The apartment was full of stuff. On the dining table was a colored donkey piñata with its eyeless face propped up against a stack of books; the rest of the surface was taken up by junk mail and bills, the chairs also piled with books and sheets of adverts. Beyond the table, the counter tops of the narrow kitchen were stacked with tins and packaged foodstuffs. Boxes took up all the space beyond the door until a couch bordered off the living room, where the space opened up somewhat. I saw a coffee table with a bong next to a laptop, and another couch facing a large flat screen TV. The wall space was lined with shelves of books, board games, DVDs, CDs, and videogames. A rubber chicken hung from a string tacked to the ceiling.

"Welcome," Hooper said.

"Your girlfriend here?"

"She just left for work," he said. "And it's my day off. So I said fuck it, I'm going to get stoned. See if my buddy Dylan wants to kick it."

"I gotta work at five," I said. "But I'm real glad you texted." I'd awoken to the memory of fleeing Val's strange house but not the drive home. I was still clothed, lying on my small section of floor, opening my eyes to the grim figure of Vic hunched over his desk.

The events from the night before felt too strange, too wonderful, and too disturbing to have been anything other than a vivid dream.

And yet I found a skeleton key in my pocket; an ancient-looking thing with a ribbon of script containing a series of hand-drawn numerals. Whatever doubts I had from the night before, *this* was real. Val must have slipped it into my pocket before I had taken off my clothes, knowing I might have to take a quick exit.

Vic hadn't acknowledged me, and I'd decided not to tell him my story after getting mostly one-word responses when I tried to initiate conversation. I'd decided anywhere was better than his dark apartment.

I'd been unable to reach Carter, and had been on my way to him when I got the text from Hooper.

And here I was, still feeling half in a dream.

"You okay?" Hooper asked, his usually impassive face looking concerned. "You seem kinda upset by something."

"I had a very strange night, to tell the truth."

We sat down, Hooper on the other couch. I opened a beer and held it out.

"Thanks," he said, taking it.

Cracking my own, I took a swig. The cool liquid felt good going down my throat. Closing my eyes, I began to gulp.

I only stopped when it began to burn.

"Damn," Hooper said. "You must be Irish or something. So tell me about last night."

"Well, it's like this," I said, leaning back and wiping my chin. "This is going to sound crazy. I mean. Like really."

Hooper nodded. I looked from his staring eyes, to his closed lips, then to my hands squeezing the bottle.

"Right. There's this gal with red earmuffs. She's always wearing them. Since I started working at Taste Testers I've seen her about Grantwood, okay? Have you seen her?"

"Uh, no."

An image of the monkey-thing that had turned into a glowing jellyfish once in the golden light replayed in my head, and I laughed. Lowering my head, I ran my fingers through my hair, groaning as I clawed my scalp.

"Um. You okay?"

"No." For the first time in my life I had my own true story of the supernatural, and was unable to tell. Partially because I felt so tired my brain seemed frozen.

"You down to smoke a bowl with me?"

I looked up at Hooper.

The first rip from Hooper's bong sent me into a coughing frenzy that made my eyes feel like poached eggs. A couple rips later I felt more than fine and told my story.

When I finished, I looked at Hooper and was surprised to see him looking away, staring at the TV as though it were playing something only he could see.

"I really don't know what to say to any of that," he said. "You sure that girl didn't slip something into your mouth that could've been acid?"

"Like while we were kissing? That never occurred to me."

"That's about all I can think to say. I'm sorry."

"But then there's the key! What about that?"

I handed Hooper the key. "This was in my pocket when I woke up this morning."

Hooper turned it over in his hand. "I'm guessing that's a phone number. Have you tried calling it?"

"No."

"Do you want to? Like, now?"

"What, to see if Val is real? I know she is. Even if that was an acid trip, I've been seeing her around for months."

Hooper shrugged, and handed the key back.

"I am going to call that number. Just not right now."

"I wish you would. She might invite us over." Hooper grinned. *"I'd* like to see that house. Sounds trippier than EDC. Maybe she has an Elvish sister? With even bigger tits and ears."

I laughed. "Maybe she doe—wAAAH!"

Something had jumped up and tapped my hand.

Hooper erupted into laughter. "That's just the cat. You sounded like an old woman screaming!"

I looked over the armrest and saw the behind of a cat scurrying away. It disappeared into the jungle of boxes behind me.

"He's always playing in there," Hooper said. "He likes to sneak up on people, so watch out. But don't worry, he's declawed."

Laughing, I sat back onto the couch. I coughed and cleared my throat. "That tripped me out."

"Thought maybe you were hallucinating there for a second?"

"More like I thought it was a Muppet come to get me."

"You like the Muppet Show?"

"Oh yeah. Haven't seen it since I was a kid."

"You wanna watch some episodes? I have the first two seasons. It's always good to watch when you're stoned."

"Sure."

Later, I staggered down the hallway, having to take a piss really bad, my stomach hurting from laughing.

I was really high.

Unlike the rest of the apartment, the bedroom Hooper shared with his girlfriend was very tidy, with a queen-sized bed and nightstand taking up most of the space.

"Find it?" Hooper called.

To the left I saw the toilet through the open door. I went in and flicked on the light.

As I was trickling, I checked the time.

"Shit," I muttered. I would have to lie down soon if I was getting any rest before work.

Back in the hallway I noticed several framed pictures. I stopped and looked at one of Hooper and his girlfriend, arms around each other and smiling for the camera. She was blonde and pretty.

Good for you, Hoop.

Back in the living room, Hooper wasn't there.

"Hoop?"

"In here, one second," he answered from the kitchen. I sat back down on the couch and picked up my beer. I drank the rest of it down.

Hooper came in carrying plates. "I made you a sandwich," he said, setting a plate down in front of me.

"That's real nice of you."

"No problem. You want more beer, I've got lots in the fridge."

"No more beer for me," I said, picking up the plate. The sandwich was toasted, and Hooper had added a handful of corn chips. I picked up the sandwich and bit in, closing my eyes at the flood of hot melted cheddar. Only then did I realize I was ravenous. Before I could stop my mouth, I'd eaten half the sandwich.

"That good?"

"Hell yes. What is this?"

"Grilled cheese with pear slices."

"Pear? I've added tomatoes, but never pear. Man, it works!"

"Glad you like it."

Finished, I started in on the chips. They tasted salty and good.

After setting the empty plate down, I rubbed my hands together and leaned back. "That really hit the spot."

Hooper looked at me. "You want another one?"

"I want to say yes, but I think what I really need is a nap. You mind if I doze off here for a bit before I head?"

Hooper shook his head and gestured at the couch. I suddenly wanted to say to Hooper, *you know what? You're a really cool guy.*

Instead, I said, "Thanks man. Can you wake me up at four?"

"You got it."

Son, wake up.

You come back to me.
Taylor. Hey!
You come back to me, you
Don't be doin us no good dozin off like that.
hear?

"Chuck?"

My heart sank at the sound of my name. The way she said it like a little squeak. Like her sweet little heart was just breaking. And all the night and day long she'd been calling me nothing but Pvt. Taylor. Even at the official goodbye with the family.

I turned and walked back up the porch steps for the I-don't-know-how-manyth time, still checking the dark windows. I grabbed her up in my arms.

For the last time, I told myself.

But this time she said nothing. No more whispers in my ear. Just held me as tight as she could. I heard the crickets.

"I have to go," I said.

Dorothy backed out of my arms, and as I looked at the top of her vulnerable head to where her long auburn hair parted, I wanted to start crying.

Instead, I cleared my throat, nodded, and was about to

leave when her hand reached up to my face.

"You come back to me. You come back to me, you hear?"

Looking into her sparkling eyes, I nodded.

"You hear me, Charlie? You bring this back."

She put something into my hand. As soon as she closed my fingers over it, I knew what it was.

Our penny. The first steel one we'd ever seen—the one piece of change we'd gotten back from the soda-jerk on our first date; the lucky penny we had passed back and forth in so many ways over the year.

"Let this be your barrier against evil."

I turned and went down the steps.

"I love you, Chuck."

I ran down the road, knowing it in the dark.

Wake up. Hey. Wake up!

I opened my eyes to see the big shape of Hooper looming over me.

"It's four," he said. "Who's Dorothy?"

"Huh?"

"You talked in your sleep. I heard the name Dorothy."

"I don't know," I said, moving my leaden legs over the edge of the couch. Sitting up, I rubbed at my eyes. When I opened them, I saw bits of colored light dancing about the dim room. I felt very tired, and the effects of marijuana.

I stood up.

"Thanks again for everything," I said. "Thanks for listening. It's been fun. We should do this again sometime soon."

"There's something I've been meaning to ask you."

"What's that?"

Hooper stared at me with that look of quiet confusion I was used to seeing on his face. "Why aren't you wearing shoes?"

I looked down.

"Oh, shit!"

Walking to my car, I looked down at the purple Converse that Hooper had lent me. They were too big for my feet, and looked ridiculous beneath the tops of my black slacks.

I had left Vic's, walked a few blocks towards Carter's, then back to my car, and driven all the way over here without knowing I wasn't wearing *shoes*. Because they were back at Val's.

Inside my car, I sat back and sighed, wanting to close my eyes. Instead, they drifted over to the wheat penny.

(Let this be your barrier against evil)

Reliving the bittersweet emotion from the dream, I smiled sadly.

It had been like recalling a memory.

(You bring this back)

I wondered if he had.

He must have, for it to come into my hands this side of the water all these years later.

"All right, you can do this," I said.

I looked again at the wheat penny. Put my finger to the tape and pressed lightly. "But help me get there anyway."

Finally seeing a break, I pulled out onto the road.

You're driving while stoned, scolded a voice inside my head that resembled Vic's. *Not cool, dude.*

Hooper does it all the time, I countered.

I was about to find out what it was like walking a day in his shoes.

Chapter 44

"You're all set, Dylan," Taylor said as I walked in. I grabbed the dispatch and picked up the bag.

As I was heading around the corner my head turned at the sight of a woman walking a large shaggy dog. The thing looked like a small pony. I noticed too that the woman, all in black and wearing a ball cap and shades, was incredibly shapely.

"Hello!" she said.

"Hi!" I smiled.

"How are you, Dylan?"

My mind connected the voice with the woman's warm smile.

Stacey Noeltner.

"Lovely dog," I said. "How come I haven't seen him before?"

"It's a she. I keep her in the back when I have deliveries."

"She's a beaut."

"You can pet her, she's friendly." To the dog, she said, "That's our pizza delivery man, Dylan."

The dog looked up as I lowered my free hand to the top of her head, her mouth open and panting. Her black eyes narrowed like they were smiling as I ran my hand down her soft fur.

"Well, it was nice to see you!" Stacey said. "You better get those people their food."

"Always nice to see you, Stacey."

"Happy Holidays!"

I continued on towards the stairs down to the garage.

Stacey Noeltner.

It really was always nice to see her.

"Oh, *Jeez. . .*"

The Body Odor Building. Here I was again, and the stench hadn't improved, even with the doors still wide-open.

If it smells like this all the time, how the hell do people live here? Surely you couldn't ever get used to this smell?

I walked down the blue-carpeted hall, the light coming in from the windows glaring off the shiny white walls. At the end of the hall, I found the apartment and knocked on the door.

I stepped back, remembering how the stench from last time had knocked me out of my socks.

If it wasn't the same apartment, which had seemed to be the source of the stench, I was going to ask this tenant what it was.

The door was opened by a woman with short hair and glasses, wearing a gray tank top and gym shorts over her fit but less than feminine figure. She looked at me with a measuring gaze and an expression that was otherwise blank.

"Guy," I said.

The woman blinked. "Excuse me?"

I put my hand to my mouth and coughed. This breathing only through my mouth wasn't going to work.

I shook my head, and took a breath in through my nose, resigned to the fact that I had to smell the horribly stale air.

GOD that's rank!

"Hi," I repeated, this time with unhindered annunciation. "Sorry," I said.

The woman's eyebrows arrowed to a V as I handed over the pizza. Her eyes didn't leave my face as she set it aside.

"How much was it again?" she asked, talking louder.

"Oh," I said. "Uh. . ."

"What is your fucking problem?"

"Hm?"

"Why are you making disgusted faces at me?"

"I'm not making faces at *ghou. . .*" Screw it. I wasn't going to smell any more of this. "I habba cold."

The woman put a hand to her hip, looking me up and down. She suddenly showed her teeth in what would have passed for a smile if not for her eyes. "How much, pansy-cake?"

"Gay-teen sixty-nine."

The show of teeth vanished, like it was slurped back into the woman's face. With pursed lips and sharpened eyes she glared, then turned and reached out of doorframe, revealing a pull-up bar hanging from another doorframe inside. She stepped back, threw a twenty, and slammed the door.

Snatching up the bill, I ran towards the exit.

"Whuh!" I dropped the carrier bag onto the sidewalk and put my hands to my knees, my heart hammering. I'd run the whole way without taking in a breath, nearly tripping, thanks to Hooper's oversized shoes.

Raising my head, I sucked cool, *fresh* air into my lungs. After a few deep breaths, I started to breathe in through my nose again.

Well, that was one awkward encounter.

Not that I hadn't had a few.

Speaking of which. . .

After I had crossed the street to where my car was parked, I spotted the tree where I'd encountered the creepy Berry-Eater guy.

(They're *so* good. They're great on your cereal.)

I saw the tree, but no Berry-Eater.

"Fuckin weirdo," I muttered, opening my car door.

Going down the ramp into the garage, I noticed a police car just outside the back exit.

After parking, I saw the police car slowly rolling through the alleyway in the same direction a certain bandito had gone off running nearly two months ago.

Nice to see you said a bitter voice in my head. *Come here often?*

But then I remembered the officers who had responded to the call, particularly the one who had gone into the bathroom with me to help flush out my eyes. They'd been great. They couldn't be everywhere at once.

And now they were on the lookout for a certain Cat Burglar, the source of misery for so many people.

"Go get em fellas," I said, getting out of my car.

Topside, I saw Jeffrey and Ryan sitting on the wall facing the ice cream shop. Both of them were wearing delivery jackets, which was strange because Ryan was a cashier.

Ryan turned at my approach and gave me an expression I hadn't ever seen on his perpetually dour face—a smile.

"It's so slow," Jeffrey said.

"Who worked day," I asked, "Joel?"

"Yeah, and it was his last day."

"What? Joel's gone?"

Jeffrey nodded. "He'd put in his two weeks notice, and today was his final shift."

"Oh," I said, surprised Joel hadn't said anything. I'd thought we were friends.

"And Paul too, we think. He hasn't shown up or answered his phone."

"He's missing," Ryan said. "Cat Burglar got him."

As for Paul, I couldn't care less. *For sure, bye bro.*

"I'm a driver now," Ryan said. "I took his spot."

"Congrats," I said. "Now you get to really be in harm's way."

"Yeah, and make some money."

I looked up to see another cop car waiting at the light.

"Notice all the cop cars in the area?"

"They must be close to catching that guy," Jeffrey said. "Either that or they're really watching things now."

Either way was fine with me.

I went into the store to check back in.

Lewis had joined Melissa behind the counter. Seeing only two tickets up, I hurried back to my car, determined to catch another quick nap.

Knock-knock!

I opened my eyes to the steering wheel, then looked up and saw Melissa looking in.

I opened the door.

"Hey you're going to be up in like a minute," she said.

"Okay, thanks."

"Wait a second." Melissa went around my car, reappearing at the passenger window. She pulled the door open, and got in.

"Hey mind if I sit for a sec?"

"No."

She dropped her purse down and reached into it, pulling out a pack of cigarettes. "Mind if I smoke?"

"Yes."

"It's cool. How's your day going?"

"Fine."

"I'm on break," she said. "That's why I came down, cause I was coming down anyway to smoke. So I said I'd tell you that you're up and save them the phone call.

"I still owe you for the cookies."

"You don't owe me anything."

"Can I ask you another favor? My ride tonight bailed. Could you take me home?"

Christ, all I wanted to do after work tonight was go home and SLEEP.

"Where is it?"

"Santa Monica, but it's only like two miles from here. You don't have to take me all the way."

I rubbed at my face. "Sure."

The phone rang.

"Oh that's you!" she said.

Monique Debbenfield was waiting for me at her door, smiling, her round pale face glowing like a little moon in the lamplight. I smiled back, feeling again the touch of imagined fingers between my shoulder blades as though a benevolent spirit was massaging me.

"I knew it was going to be you," she said.

"I didn't know it was going to be you, but I'm glad it is. How are you this evening?"

"Blessed to be here. No trouble finding it this time?"

"None."

"That's good." Monique stared. I stared back, without feeling self-conscious. The woman had an uncanny way of putting me at ease.

"You've had a few adventures," she said.

"Yes, I have. Are you psychic?"

Monique blinked for the first time. "Perhaps. But I can for sure see the soul in someone's eyes."

I smiled and nodded.

"I'm a little worried for yours."

I had been sliding the box out from the bag, but my arm suddenly felt weak.

Monique stepped out from the doorway. "I got it. Oh, it's nice and hot. I'll trade you," she said, taking the pizza box from me while handing back the limp carrier bag.

"What'd you mean?" I asked, as she turned and walked inside. Like last time, I noticed many lit candles in the room.

She came back with her money pouch.

"There's a dark cloud over this city right now, can you feel it? It's been hovering over us for some time. It's not long until it bursts and. . ." Monique looked down at her pouch, pulling it open. "Rains down badness."

I pictured a giant dark cloud spreading in the sky like polluted god-smoke, like something from the climax of *Ghostbusters.* Only instead it was hovering over Grantwood.

"You're talking about all the robberies that have been happening?"

Monique handed me the money. "There's more to it than that. It's something very evil and it wants to hurt us."

"So what's been keeping the storm from starting? What's holding it back?"

Monique grinned, without pleasure.

"Nothing," she said.

At first I didn't recognize the gal coming towards me in dark clothes, long hair swishing from side to side, a backpack slung over one shoulder, until she said, "All finished?"

Melissa. I'd forgotten about her.

"Yep. Ready to go?"

"All set. I wasn't waiting long."

We walked to my car. I unlocked it. Melissa got in while I put my hat and uniform in the trunk.

"What's that?" she asked as soon as I got in, pointing to the wheat penny.

"My barrier against evil."

"Huh?"

"It's a real lucky penny, from the World War Two era."

"Oh wow. Is it valuable?"

"I think so."

"Does it bring you luck?"

"I happen to believe it does," I said, starting the engine.

"Thanks again," Melissa said. "You really have no idea how much I appreciate this."

"Where to?"

"Okay. Trying to think, from here. . ."

"I have this," I said, showing her my phone. "Just tell me the address."

"Okay."

I tapped open Navigation, hit the voice command, and held the phone over to her.

Melissa pulled my wrist closer to her face as she said her address.

The phone made its happy sound in acknowledgment, and I pulled it back towards me, while Melissa didn't immediately let got of my wrist.

"Here we go," I said, backing out of the parking space.

"So you have a girlfriend?" Melissa asked.

Roxanne.

"Nope."

Val.

"But I'm kinda seeing someone," I said.

"Is she pretty?"

"She's pretty magic."

Melissa looked forward.

"Turn right on Montana Avenue!"

A moment later I saw Melissa turn towards me. "She's lucky. She's fucking lucky."

"Huh?"

"Your girl."

"Thanks. I'm lucky t—"

"I had a guy like you I'd be balling you every night."

"In a quarter mile. *Turn right to stay on Montana Avenue."*

"Then I'd wake you up every morning with a blowjob. Just to wake you up."

"Oookay," I said.

"Continue on Montana for one and a half miles."

"Then I'd turn around and give you my ass for breakfast. You'd eat pussy every morning before getting out of bed."

Approaching the stop sign, I glanced to the right, not being able to help looking at Melissa as I turned.

"Does your girl do that?" she asked.

"Uh, no."

Melissa sat up from her seat. *"Really?* HA HA!" I grimaced at her forced laughter. "You poor boy! You must be so frustrated."

"Not really, no."

She put her hand on my crotch. "Aw, poor poor guy."

"Stop it," I said.

"That's not what he's saying. I can feel him standing up. Ooo! *You ready to get out of there, big man?"*

"Stop it!" I glared at Melissa, who was leaning forward, inches from my face. "I mean it."

"Just relax and watch the road, and I'll give you head."

"That's it."

I signaled and turned off the road, quick enough to make Melissa fall back into her seat.

I put the car in park. "You said half-way's fine. Here you go."

Melissa's mouth was trembling.

"Out."

She reached down and pulled up her backpack. Then she turned and the overhead light came on as the door opened. She stepped out.

I looked to my rearview mirror.

"WAIT!"

Melissa slid back into her seat. The door shut.

"I'm sorry," she said. "Really, really sorry. I know you're never going to want to talk to me again. I just really like you and I knew this was going to be my only chance."

"Look," I said, "We don't ever have to talk about it. Okay? I like you too. I'm just very tired."

Melissa smiled.

The smile I gave back felt strained. Turning towards the windshield, I shook my head. "You seriously wouldn't believe the last two days I had."

"It's all good," Melissa said. "And thanks." Her hand patted my lap.

"Okay."

"But seriously, how bout a quick blowjob?" Her hand went to my crotch, rubbing in fast, vicious circles. "I got skills. I can make a guy cum in less than four minutes."

"Ah, fuck, Melissa. . ."

"You can cum right in my mouth." She closed her eyes and opened her mouth wide, tongue touching her chin. "Mmnah."

"Get out, now!"

Melissa squeezed my penis through the fabric.

Grabbing her hand at the wrist and jerking it back, I raised my fist.

"You can hit me," Melissa said, bobbing her head. "Hit me! Mmnah mmnah."

"GET OUT!" I yelled, squeezing her wrist. "GET THE FUCK OUT NOW!"

Letting go, her head bonked against the glass of the passenger window. *"Ow!"* she yelped. "That hurt!" She put her hands over her face. *"Ow-how-how ow."*

"Christ," I muttered, looking at my rearview mirrors. All I needed now was for a cop to drive by and have Melissa say I hurt her.

"FAGGOT!" Bolting up, Melissa slapped at me with both hands. I turned away, catching the light blows.

The overhead light came on. Followed by the slamming of the door. I looked up to see Melissa crossing in front of my headlights, giving me the finger. She ran across the street.

I sat up. Put the car back into drive, signaled, and did a U-turn.

"Turn right!" Sally commanded, making me jump.

Chapter 45

When I finally got up from the floor, it was past two in the afternoon.

Staring at the closet door, it seemed like a colossal effort to get up and put away my sleeping bag, comforter, and pillow—the daily routine.

Vic wasn't around. I'd put on the coffee first.

By the time I'd finished my mug, I'd decided I was going to head out to a diner rather than try to put something together from what I had left in the fridge. Then it would be nearly time for work.

What time was that again?

Today was, what?

Tuesday.

Street cleaning day.

"Oh shit!"

I put my mug on Vic's speaker and scrambled up.

"Shit!"

There was a parking ticket under the windshield wiper.

I pulled opened the envelope.

The penalty was more than I usually made on a good night.

Shaking my head, I turned and walked back to Vic's.

As soon as I opened the door my phone rang.

My parents, calling from the home phone. I hit talk. "Hello."

"Hey Dylan," Dad said. "How are you?"

"Good," I said, stepping over to my comforter and sleeping bag. I threw the ticket down. "How are you guys?"

"We're doing fine. Haven't heard from you, so we thought we'd check in."

"I'm sorry," I said. "I've had a very hectic couple of days. . ."

Minutes later, I went back outside to move my car to find that there was a new ticket on the windshield.

Disbelieving, I pulled it out.

I sat in and put the envelope on the passenger seat.

Guess this ain't my lucky day, I thought, going to put the key in the ignition.

Then I pulled my hand back, seeing the clean space surrounded by dust next to the steering wheel.

The wheat penny was gone.

Melissa!

She must've knocked it off during our scuffle.

Opening the door and moving my legs over, I looked beneath the steering wheel. Grit and a few dried leaves, but no penny or tape.

I looked in the legroom of the passenger seat.

She must have swiped it. I had told her it was valuable, hadn't I?

I slammed the door and started the car.

Maybe it was only a penny with no more significance than that I gave it, but it was mine. And I would get it back.

I reached into my pocket for my keys, then saw that Vic's door was ajar. He had returned.

I knocked, then pushed the door open.

Vic swiveled around in his chair. "We need to talk!"

"What's up?"

"What's this?"

He pointed to the ground where I had my sleeping bag and comforter still spread.

"I was just going to do that," I said. "I'm coming back from moving my car. I got a ticket because—"

"It's three o'clock! Why haven't you made your bed yet?"

"Don't fucking yell at me. I just went outside to move my car. I slept in."

"What are the rules?"

"Why are you asking me?"

Vic blinked like I'd just slapped him. "The rules are you make your bed as soon as you get up. No later, no exceptions!"

I stared at Vic, at the small angry eyes in the puffed-up face, and knew I was done being bossed around.

"Look," I said. "Let me make this easy. We've got on each other's nerves. I think it's time I moved out. That will solve the problem here."

He jabbed a finger at me. "What you need to do if you can't follow the rules, you need to leave *tonight!"*

"I'm paid up for the month," I said, stepping around him. "I'm not leaving any time sooner than the month ends."

"You can stay till the end of the month, *if* you follow the rules!"

"No, Vic," I said, in a calmer voice than I felt, as I put my things in my allocated spot. "I can stay till the end of the month whether you like it or not."

When I turned around, Vic was looking at me like I had just stepped out of the closet wearing a Gestapo uniform.

Now I pointed the finger. "What you need to do, is stop taking your frustrations out on me, and stop talking down to me because *you* feel small. I don't do anything around here to piss you off on purpose."

"Yes, you *do."*

"No, I don't!"

Vic stood and puffed out his chest. "Now you're yelling. And you're getting aggressive."

"I'm getting out of here," I said, stepping to the door. "Save it for your patrons."

Chapter 46

I sat in my car, waiting to be called in for a delivery, staring at the blank square where my lucky penny had been.

Not only had I not found the gray Lincoln, I'd just gotten word that Melissa had quit Taste Testers. According to Dave, they had planned on firing her anyway, but she'd beat them to the punch by calling in an hour before her shift.

That meant the chances of me seeing my lucky penny again were slim.

All because I had to be Mr. Nice Guy and give her a ride home.

I already missed my little ornament.

Never mind that, what are you supposed to do now about your living situation?

If I knew Vic at all, he'd choke dead on his cereal before apologizing. He would expect me to apologize to him, and then he'd relish the petty power of accepting, but only with his condition of et cetera.

Nope. I wasn't putting up with his bullshit anymore.

But I still needed somewhere to sleep.

I could ask Carter.

(CARTER KEEP IT DOWN! *FUCK YOU!*)

Yeah, maybe not.

How about Val?

Only problem there was a certain satyr, who was more likely to have *me* for dinner than have me over for dinner.

But then again, she might have smoothed things over by now. Maybe he would be different this time?

Still, it was time I tried that number.

I pushed the button on the glove box and took out the key.

"Somebody's got a spring in their step."

I smiled at Hooper as I came up to the wall. He was sitting with Ryan.

"What's got you so happy?" Ryan asked.

"Do I look happy?"

"Look like someone just buttered your toast."

"What does that mean?" Hooper and I asked Ryan simultaneously.

Ryan just shook his head.

"Maybe I got a certain young lady's phone number here in Grantwood, and she's given me the key to her house so that I can stop by whenever I happen to be delivering in the area for a little quickie?" I gave Hooper a knowing wink.

Ryan's eyes widened. "No shit, you bagged a customer? Way to go, Dylan."

Way to go, indeed, I thought, walking in to the store.

Val couldn't *wait* to see me!

Bill was packing up the order, with Lewis behind the register looking none-too-pleased to be there—most likely because he'd been called in to cover for Melissa on his day off.

"Think that's everything," Bill said, checking the computer. "Yeah, you're all set. Can you send in Ryan?"

I picked up the loaded bag and carried it out.

"So Dylan," Ryan said as I walked up. "You going to tell us the story?"

"Can't now," I said. *And trust me, you'd think I was lying.* "Later. You're up."

Ryan got up.

"I take it you called the number and she answered?" Hooper asked.

"Oh yeah."

"Well, I'm glad," he said, smiling. "You let me know how that goes."

"I will."

"And if that house is still acid-y, you gotta invite me over. How are my shoes working out?"

"They're a little big, but I'm getting used to them. I'll buy a new pair on my day off and get them back to you."

"No worries. Use them as long as you need them."

"Thanks."

"Everything went well yesterday? I was a little worried for

you when you drove off."

I shook my head as I walked. "I don't know how you do it."

As I was pulling out from the parking structure into the alley, I waited for Sally to kick in.

"Turn right onto Gorman Avenue!"

Looking both ways, I drifted to the open part of the sidewalk exiting onto the narrow street. Parked cars on the left made visibility bad, but I glimpsed an oncoming car in between vehicles. I waited. Not seeing it, I inched out, thinking maybe it had just been turning to park on one of the apartment driveways.

"Turn right!"

Sure that even if the car was coming they could see me; I stepped on the gas and saw the car coming and slammed on the brake.

The other car jerked to a stop.

"Damnit," I muttered looking at the car, a turquoise Cadillac.

The car waited.

They were letting me go.

I waved, and turned the rest of the way onto Gorman.

The light turned green and I signaled left, driving to the intersection of San Clemente. I began to turn the wheel.

The turquoise Cadillac was suddenly right beside me in the oncoming lane, blocking me. I looked at the driver, a white-haired man wearing dark glasses and a golfing hat, his mouth moving.

I rolled down my window.

"ACCIDENT!"

"What?" I yelled back.

"YOU ALMOST GOT ME IN AN ACCIDENT!" the man yelled.

I opened my mouth, not knowing what to say.

"YOU ALMOST GOT ME IN AN ACCIDENT!" he yelled again, his straight white teeth chomping.

"So?" I yelled back. "What do you—?" I was cut off by a cacophony of car horns. Behind, I saw two lanes of waiting cars. I looked back at the man. "You wanna have a conversation about this *here?"*

Blaring horns cut off the man's response, but he turned his head, his square jaw moving as he turned his wheel enough that I could continue.

Moving forward, I saw the turquoise car keeping pace. I heard another yell and looked over.

"I KNOW WHERE YOU WORK, YOU WORK AT TASTE TESTERS!"

I gestured my hand to say, *so, what?*

Another horn honked, this time at the man for driving too slow in the fast lane. He turned away, and I turned back to face the road, putting up my window.

My heart was pounding in anger. I shook my head, hardly able to believe the man.

Sally told me to turn right ahead, the turquoise car continuing on.

Almost every estate on Mannerville Canyon was now decorated with Christmas or Hanukah lights. Driving was like going through a circus.

Headlights fast approaching from behind lit my car, and I looked in the rearview mirror, wincing at the sudden blinding of high beams. A horn blared. Seconds later, a black stretch limo was moving alongside me in the oncoming lane. I slowed, wanting it to pass.

A low rumble diverted my attention from the road to the nook where my phone nestled.

I picked up the phone, and looked up again to see the limo speeding ahead.

I looked at the phone in my hand and hit the on button.

Jesus, tell me I imagined that.

My phone had just growled.

Chapter 47

Marveling at Val's naked bottom slamming back, our flesh clapping, my hips went mad. My head shot up as I closed my eyes and saw a glowing celestial flower blooming behind my lids as I came into her, my hands pulling at her long ears. Val let out a moan that filled the room, and I heard myself like an echo from another valley. I collapsed onto her, Val's hot skin beneath me.

Stay awake, my whirling mind warned, *you've got to go.*

The very last thing I felt like doing.

I rolled off Val and onto my back.

Val put her hand on my hammering chest. Her lightly touching nails circled, coolly igniting the hairs. "You've got to go," she whispered.

"Unfortunately. I just had to see you so bad."

"I understand. I'm glad you came."

I opened my eyes and turned my head.

Val's face was grinning in the dim rosy light of the room, her cheeks glowing.

"I can come right back in an hour," I said. "I'll stay then as long as you want."

Val's lips peeled back in a smile. "I want that. But not tonight. Daddy's coming home soon. I've explained things to him, and all is well. He's very eager to meet you. But we should do it appropriately. I will introduce you in a respectful manner, rather than him coming home and you already here in his house again. Do you understand?"

"Yes. I'm eager to meet him too, you know. We'll get together for dinner or something. My treat."

Val nodded. "Yes. Though it will be his treat."

"Whatever seems proper to you."

Val leaned in and nudged me with the soft touch of her

pointy nose, then kissed my forehead. "You have to go."

She got off the bed and gathered my clothes while I stared at her body.

"This reminds me," she said, coming back with the pile. "I have some bad news. I'm afraid you're not getting your shoes back." She bit her lower lip. "Daddy ate them."

For a moment, I could only look at Val. Then I picked up my slacks. Standing up, I began dressing.

"Were they important to you?"

"Yes." I put on my undershirt. Then my uniform shirt.

Stepping to Val, I lifted her chin with the side of my index finger.

"But it was time I stopped walking in them, anyway."

Val smiled. We kissed.

"Gotta go!" I said. "Call you later, okay?"

I turned and jumped, swatting playfully at the neon moths fluttering about the ceiling. Val laughed.

I ran down the hall, suddenly wondering just how late I was.

Even Lionel May-Wait deserved his pizza, eventually.

Chapter 48

Dave was at the register, counting money. He looked up at me.

Expecting to be asked why I'd taken so long; Lionel had looked none too pleased when I finally showed up at his door, but the tip reaffirmed that I had done the right thing by making him wait, I had my excuse ready.

"I got a last one for you," Dave said. "They called at nine on the dot, so I still had to take it. You're my only guy left."

"That's no problem," I said. I wasn't looking forward to spending the night in my car, anyway. "I'm in no hurry."

"I'm going to cash you out again so you can just go home after. Soon as I finish counting this, give me a second."

He slapped his hand onto the now empty display case. "You can just put the bag here."

I did as he said, then stepped over to the table against the front window and sat down.

Bill came out from the back with a mop.

Outside, two cop cars were waiting at the light across the street.

"So many cops," Bill said. "It's crazy."

"Right?" Dave said, "They think they're going to catch the Cat Burglar in the act, or something?"

"Dude's a pro," Bill said. "This guy's been getting away stealing from estates with cameras and shit."

"That's what I'm saying. You're not going to catch this guy, or *guys*, just driving around."

I looked over at Dave. He looked at me as he continued. "I mean I'm glad they're making their presence known, but it's not enough. That guy's probably moved on already."

"You think so?"

"Oh yeah. Smart as he is, he'd be stupid to keep doing it.

He's way too high profile now—it's nationwide news. Everybody in the area's on high alert for him. I was talking to a cop the other day came in here, and he said they've been getting so many false alarms. People calling in cause they see someone walking around their neighborhood looking suspicious and shit?"

Bill laughed. "That's funny. They all arrest some fucking girl scouts going door to door."

Dave laughed. "Yeah! I can see Jehovah's witnesses standing in line like The Usual Suspects."

"No, seriously," Bill said. "He's like the Grantwood Bogeyman."

Dave nodded, looking up at one of the screens mounted above me. "Seriously."

I turned and looked back out the window. The cops were gone, the light now green.

"You have arrived!"

Dropping the phone into the nook, I opened the door.

Looking up and down the street, the oft-visited Frankmeyer residence something like a quarter-mile up, I saw no one coming, and crossed.

Stepping onto the sidewalk, I looked beyond the gate of the big dark house in front of me, looking for a house number. There was none that I could see.

I continued up the sidewalk to the next house. This one was illuminated in the front, and there was light shining from behind the cream-colored curtains of some of the windows.

The windows that I could see, that was. This house also had a gate around it more akin to a wall.

I pushed the button on the call box.

While I waited, I happened to glance down and see a piece of paper on the ground below the box, with a long piece of scotch tape attached that had now affixed itself to my shoe.

Straightening my back, I bent my knees and lowered the heavy bag to the ground. Pulled the paper from my shoe. I looked at the message written in thick black marker and highlighted in yellow.

PLEASE!!! DO <u>NOT</u> PUSH BUTTON
CALL PHONE BUTTON BROKEN!!!!

"Oh, whoops," I said, dropping the note.

My hand went to my back pocket and flattened it.

"Ah, hell," I groaned, looking at the dispatch slip in my hand.

The customer, a Lori Lyngarth, had even left a message in the notes section.

CALL CELL DON'T PUSH THE CALL BUTTON!!!!

As I was about to return to my car to retrieve my phone, I heard a click from the callbox.

A small red light glowed from the box, indicating that the line was open.

I waited a moment to be greeted, then called out, "Hello?"

I heard a voice answer in what sounded like a questioning grunt.

"It's the pizza guy," I said.

There was a pause. Then the red light winked out as the gate began to open.

Guess the callbox is working after all, I thought, picking up the heavy bag.

I stepped inside.

The big white house was all lit up, with every window on the bottom floor blocked by curtains, and black iron bars on the outside. To the left was a manicured lawn. . .with a broken gazebo.

What the hell happened? I thought, staring at the crushed wooden structure as I walked. It looked as though one of Steven Spielberg's dinosaurs had stepped on it.

Just before I reached the steps to the porch, I got a whiff of something rotting.

Glancing up at the house, I took a few steps to the left where the driveway continued. In front of the garage I saw a dumpster.

I knocked on the door, wondering what sort of people needed their own dumpster, as I noticed cracks above the front door.

The door swung open.

A bulging belly filled the doorframe. I looked from the belly button, to the waist and legs in red pajamas, then up at the jiggle of man-breasts.

The legs were slowly shuffling back. The ground murmured beneath my feet as his chin came into view.

I swallowed, trying to find my voice, as I looked at the

man's face; his hairless, oval-shaped head looking remarkably small sitting on top of his gigantic shoulders.

The man's eyes were wide, his mouth puckered, a chain of drool escaping.

"Gurnng?"

"Um." I swallowed. "Did you order—?"

"MMYARRR!"

Before I could even think, I saw the man coming out with one arm winding back. I watched as the arm rotated with the hand coming towards my head.

Chapter 49

"There, there," soothed a woman's voice. *"Wake up, sweetheart."*

Something hot was slithering down my head.

I opened my eyes.

A face filled my vision, the features sharpening as it backed away.

It was a kind-looking woman in a light blue bathrobe, with butterscotch hair curling beneath her ears.

"You're okay," she said, sounding out of breath. Her face broke into a toothy smile as she sat back in her chair. "You're okay!"

"What happened?" I croaked.

"I'm so sorry. So, so sorry, oh gosh! Lorris isn't supposed to answer the door."

I suddenly remembered the giant, his arm spinning around to hammer down. My heart began to palpitate. I touched the hot wet thing on my head, feeling it slide off. The woman picked up the face towel from the ground.

"How is your head?"

"Fine, I guess."

"Does it hurt?"

"Uh. . .no. Just kinda foggy. I was. . .wait, I was knocked out. How long was I unconscious?"

"Only a few minutes. I heard the commotion and came right down. You've been laying here about five minutes. You're very lucky he just grazed you, or you wouldn't have a head left."

"MUMMY?"

The woman whirled around as I slid up the mound of pillows behind me. We both watched the door that had been slightly ajar, open. The massive belly of Lorris filled the doorframe.

"Lorris, out!" Lori commanded, jabbing a finger in his

direction.

"MUMMY MUMMY?"

"Go playtime Lorris, until Mommy says so!"

The big belly turned and sobbed, stepping back out of sight. "Henng-heng-hyengg. . ."

Lori went to the open door, peeked around, and then shut it.

"Don't be afraid of him, Honey. He's completely under control while I'm here."

"Shouldn't he be on a leash or something?" I asked, sliding back down the mound of pillows.

Lori grinned. "Oh he is. It's just not a physical one. I couldn't do that to him anyway. He's a human being." She flinched. *"He's my boy!"* Both hands came up and cradled her head. She let out a moan.

The sound tugged at my heart—it sounded an awful lot like the moans I'd heard from my own mother at the time of the funerals.

"Hey," I said. "Why are you crying?"

Lori looked up, her lovely face glistening with tears. Her nose had begun to run as well.

"Please don't," she whispered.

"Please don't what?"

"Please!" she yelled, throwing her arms back. "Don't take my baby boy away from me!"

Before I could say anything, I felt the ominous rumble of Lorris approaching.

"MUMMY?"

I scooted back up the pillows.

One of Lori's hands shot up in a clenched fist.

I saw the veins of her wrist press out, like she was squeezing something in her hand. The door shook, then I heard Lorris retreating.

"Don't worry," she said. Her arm dropped back to her side. "I told you," she said, "You're safe from him as long as I'm around."

I nodded, in complete misunderstanding.

Lori closed her eyes. I watched the heavy rise and fall of her breasts pressing out from her robe. She appeared to be trying to calm herself.

"What did you just do?" I asked.

Lori exhaled, blowing out her cheeks. "I used this," she

said, opening her hand and revealing a small red ball.

She threw it to me in a gentle underhand. I caught it and squeezed it like a sponge.

"A clown nose?"

Lori smiled. "I call it a Lorris ball."

"I don't get it," I said.

"Squeeze it."

I squeezed it a couple of times in my hand, then looked up at Lori.

"Did you hear anything?" she asked.

"No," I said, squeezing it again.

"I don't hear anything, either," Lori said. "But Lorris does. He hears a special frequency. A special command."

"Are you kidding me?"

"Not at all. Look." Lori gestured with her head. I followed the direction and noticed for the first time all the little colored balls about the room. They were scattered about like oversized gumballs. "I've got them all over the house, and I carry them with me at all times.

"They're color-coded for different commands. That red one you have there means 'Stop'. Now." She produced another ball, an orange one, and tossed it to me. "Try that one."

I did as she asked. Immediately Lorris let out a roar. The house began to shake.

"Oh SHIT!" I yelled, but Lori looked calm, holding up another red ball. I looked down at the one still in my hand, and squeezed.

The pounding footsteps stopped, only feet away from the door.

They retreated.

"You see," Lori said. "I do have him on a sort of leash. I have to. But it's more effective and lot less cruel than if I were to chain him up like some. . .monster."

"I see," I said. I looked down at the balls I held. "So I guess orange means 'Come Here'?"

Lori smiled. "It means 'Come to Momma', but yes. You get it."

Looking at the other balls scattered about the floor of the room, I saw green, purple, pink, white, yellow, and brown. I wondered what they could all command (though I thought I had a pretty good idea what yellow and brown meant).

"But you know what I don't get?" I said. "Why would you

think I would take him away?"

The smile dropped from Lori's face, and again I saw a very frightened woman. Her lower lip trembled.

Lori's eyes narrowed, then she looked away.

Oh, I get it.

"You think I'm going to sue you?"

Lori's face crumpled. "No! Please don't! They'll take him away from me!"

"Calm down," I said, holding up one hand to gesture 'Stop', realizing as I did that I still was holding one of the balls. I turned my wrist; saw that it was the red one. I turned my wrist back, and made a show of squeezing it as Lori. "Okay? I'm not going to sue you."

"Whatever you want. My credit card?"

"I want you to sit down in that chair and calm yourself."

Lori nodded. She took a seat.

"You must think I'm a nutcase," she said. "I guess I am too. I'd do anything for my son. It's not just that I love him for being my son—most mothers love their kids. Wait, do you have kids?"

I shook my head.

"You don't understand then. You couldn't. Until you're a parent, you don't know what fear is. You see how disadvantaged he is. You see how much harder his life is going to be, especially when I'm gone."

"I understand," I said.

Lori shook her head, as if to say again, no, you don't.

"I know what's it like to fear for someone every day. Even on the happiest of days. I had a wife. For a short while."

Lori looked at me.

Her lips twitched up in a grimace of understanding. Mine did the same.

After a moment, I said, "Look, I'm not someone you need to worry about. I am going to ask you for something though, and tell me if it sounds fair. I feel fine right now but, maybe just to be safe, I should go to the doctor soon just to be sure my skull's okay, make sure there's no internal bleeding or whatever. If you'd help me out in paying for the doctor visit, I'll call it square. Fair enough?"

Lori nodded. "More than fair."

"Deal, then."

This time Lori really did smile.

"Well," I said. "If you don't mind then, I think I'd like to be going home."

Lori's eyes widened. "Oh! But what are we going to do about your work? Are you going to be in trouble for being out so long?"

I sat up. "Luckily, no. You were my last delivery, and the manager said all I had to do was go home after I delivered your pizza."

Lori got up out of the chair. "Pizza! God, I'd forgotten I'd even ordered them."

As she turned, I stuffed both hands into my pockets.

Lori opened the door.

She waited as I got up off the bed and went to her.

"Don't worry," she whispered, as I followed her out the door. I followed her through to the living room, where she shrieked to see the remains of one of the pizza boxes and my carrier bag on the floor near the front door. The cardboard was pulled apart. The carrier bag lay deflated, the flap partially torn off.

I turned to see Lorris across the living room in front of the large TV. He had one hand in his mouth, like he was sucking his fist.

"What about Mommy, Lorris?" Lori stomped one foot.

Lorris pulled his fist out, making a loud wet pop.

"Mum-mumm?"

"You were supposed to wait. You know you always wait for Mommy, even when she's not in the room."

"MUMMY!"

"Yes, Lorris, I—"

"MUMMY MUMMY!"

Lorris bounded forward, shaking the whole house. I backed up, jamming one hand into my pocket.

But before I could pull out one of the balls, Lorris had grabbed Lori.

He flung her straight up into the air.

"WHOO-HOO!" Lori bellowed, almost to the high ceiling, her legs and arms flailing. Her bathrobe followed her down like a fuzzy parachute, leaving nothing of her body to my imagination.

Lorris caught her, and flung her up again.

"HA-HAH!"

This time I noticed a couple of dents in the high ceiling as I followed Lori's flight up.

Lorris caught her, and again threw her towards the high ceiling.

I watched as Lori whooped and came back down.

Lorris bear-hugged her to him, cackling.

"Put me down!"

Lorris did as told.

"That's. . .my good boy," Lori said staggering back, out of breath. She turned to me, her face red, and smiled. "I'd like you to properly meet. . .my son." She turned. "Lorris? Be my good boy now and. . .say hello. . .and you're sorry. . .to our nice pizza man."

Lorris came towards me as I backed up to the wall.

His belly an inch from my nose, I smelled butter and cheese mixed with the bready smell of body odor.

He stuck his index finger into his mouth, then pulled it out with a wet *bloop.* He brought it down and gently wiped it across the top of my shirt where it covered my shoulder.

"Nice to meet you too, big guy," I said.

"Now go into your room!" Lori called out.

A moment later, Lori and I were alone again, in a trembling house.

Lori got her purse and gave me her business card. "Call me as soon as you need that doctor appointment and I'll take care of everything."

"Now I don't know where my receipt went, but you still owe me some money for the pizzas."

"Oh gosh! You're right. Sorry."

Lori turned away, and I watched as she hunted through the mess that Lorris had made of the pizza boxes.

"Here we go." Lori dug into her purse, and produced a hundred dollar bill. "The rest is for you, of course."

"Thank you, Lori. Thanks for taking care of me."

"Oh my gosh, no! Thank you for being such a sweetheart. I can't tell you how sorry I am for all the trouble. But hey, at least you made some friends out of it."

"That sounds good to me."

"Oh my gosh! And I didn't even get to try your pizza."

"Well. . .there's always Denny's."

Chapter 50

The fellow who answered the door wearing a black hoodie looked like he'd had the life sucked out of him.

Carter didn't acknowledge me. Just slowly turned his stiff body, leaving the door open for me to follow.

I stepped inside the dim apartment, into stale-smelling air, and shut the door.

"You hung over?"

Carter moaned, shuffling towards the couch.

Normally I would've laughed, but I didn't feel full of sunny weather myself.

It had been one uncomfortable night, trying to sleep in the reclined front seat of my car. I'd tossed and turned as much as the space allowed, and kept opening my eyes to the glare of the streetlight overhead. What sleep I had managed had been plagued with bizarre and disturbing images. The last dream had been of Lorris chasing me through the streets while I ran in slow motion, trying to get away.

Carter fell onto the couch. His head angled towards the ceiling with his eyes closed.

I sat on the loveseat. "Got any beer?" I asked, looking at all the empties on the coffee table.

Carter's face contorted. "Stop it," he said, his voice plummy.

"I thought you weren't drinking. Or was it smoking? With you I can never tell from one day to the next."

"Fugg you."

I smiled. I hadn't seen or spoken to Carter in days, but it felt longer. It was good to be back in his living room. "We have some catching up to do. I know I got a lot to tell you."

"Gah!" Carter expelled, opening his eyes. "I gotta stop

doing this."

"Drinking?"

Carter closed his eyes and shook his head slightly. "Bein un-Tao."

"What?"

Carter said nothing.

I waited a moment.

"Well, you want me to go first?"

"I went out with Mike last night after work."

"Yeah?" I hadn't heard from Mike since the Halloween party. "How's he doing?"

"Same old."

"So, what happened?"

"Got fucked up. Went out to a few bars in Westwood, then ended up here. I think the cops came again. I don't remember."

"You want to grab some breakfast, or something?"

He groaned.

"Or do you need to yark?"

"I just need to not move. Not do anything today. What's going on with you?"

"Oh, man," I said. "There's been a *lot* going on. I'm not sure you're in the right frame of mind to hear it, though."

"Ngh. Shoot."

"This might take a while."

"I'll listen. Just keeping my eyes closed cause my head."

"You want me to run over to Ralph's and get you some ibuprofen?"

"You know we don't believe in that shit. Fuckin aspirin killed Bruce Lee."

"So I think last time I was over here me and Roxanne hadn't gone on our last date yet, right?

"When you ate the cookie."

"No, with the hot tub."

"No, how'd it go?"

Carter's demeanor brightened as I rattled on, his eyes opening the more I got into my final misadventure with Roxanne, but after Val and the details of the night we met, he only listened as I continued with my encounter with Melissa, my falling out with Vic, and finally of Lori and Lorris Lyngarth.

"*Now* what do you think of my so-called life?"

Carter stared, his mouth in a tight line.

"Why you looking at me like that?"

Carter shook his head, and looked away.

"Uh. I really like the first bit. Sorry things didn't work out between you and what's her name. But this shit about a fuckin elf, and Greek Devil Daddy? And a *giant?* I mean, it's a good story n shit. But I don't know what you're really trying to tell me."

"I'm really trying to tell what fucking happened!"

"Don't take this the wrong way! But for a bit there I was kind of wondering, that thing you told me about your wife and sister?"

"Wondering if I was making all that up too?"

"No! No, I believe you there."

"Just not here."

"I mean. . .well, what do you *want* me to say? What the fuck would you say if I told you all that?"

"So what are you saying? That I made it all up? That I'm fucking crazy?"

"I, *you. . ."* Carter sat up extending his arm, then swung it back, falling onto the couch with the movement. He put his hands over his eyes. "Oh my gosh."

His face was red when he pulled his hands away, his already hurting head obviously not relishing this added tension. "Oh look, just forget it man. I believe you. Okay? But you just gotta realize that's the craziest shit I've ever heard from anyone who wasn't on drugs."

"I realize it sounds crazy. Believe me, it all seems surreal as hell to me. But I do have better things to do than be making up stories. For starters, I'm out of a place to live. I don't want to be tip-toeing around Vic any longer than I need to."

"Yeah."

We sat together for a moment without speaking.

"I thought my life was going to get interesting when I moved out to LA, but not like this."

When I looked at Carter, I was relieved to see a smirk on his face. His eyes had a glint in them.

"When you going away?" he asked.

"To visit my parents? Next week. Well, just a couple a days now."

"Let's get together for an action movie night. A little early celebration of the end of the year."

I couldn't help but smile. "You thinking a little Van

Dammage?"

"I'm thinking a lot of Van Dammage. I'm thinking some Jackie Chan, maybe a dose of Steven Seagal."

"Sounds like a plan."

"We'll order a pizza."

"No, fuck that!"

Carter laughed. "Some other kind of takeout then. Something classically unhealthy and sashy-ating, to give us energy to get through a buttload of kung-fu movies!"

"Sounds good to me. You'll have to get over your hangover first."

"Ugh! No. I've decided. That's it for me for this year, and for a while. I'm not drinking till I have a full six-pack back."

"You'll just be getting stoned out of your mind, then?"

"I need to cut that shit out too. Fuck! I need to get back to Zen."

"In the meantime, I can't wait. This'll be a good send-off."

"I think you really need it too, man."

"I agree."

"No, I think you really need to be studying our grandmasters—so *this* doesn't keep happening." Carter was pointing to a spot on his head just above his left eye.

I leaned forward, squinting.

"I don't—"

"Bro, check yourself in the mirror."

Chapter 51

Dave looked up from counting money at the register. "What happened to you last night? You were supposed to call me."

"Oh, that's right!" I said, smacking my forehead.

Ow.

"I completely forgot."

"Whoa, what happened to you?" Dave's eyes narrowed. "Did someone attack you again?"

"No, no. I just ate shit getting out of my car."

"You tripped getting out of your car?"

"These shoes are too big for me, and one of them got caught as I was getting out."

Dave stared. "That sucks. You're lucky you didn't get a concussion or something."

"Yeah."

"Or get scratches or gravel under the skin."

"Yeah."

"You just look like you landed on something, like a fist."

Taylor came up from the back. "Hey Dylan, go ahead and clock in, we got something for you in just a minute."

"I'm done here," Dave said to Taylor.

"All right brotha. See you Friday. You at the Beverly Hills store tomorrow?"

"Yeah," Dave said without enthusiasm. "Can't wait."

"All right brotha. Let me get you your bank, Dylan." Taylor turned and went to the far register.

"Come here real quick," Dave said, stepping past me towards the soda fountain.

He pulled out several napkins from the dispenser. Then filled a water cup with ice.

He tilted some ice onto the napkins, bundled it, and

handed it to me.

"Keep it iced. It's swelling."

"Thanks," I said.

Dave put a hand on my shoulder. "I used to be a bouncer, I know what a fist to the face looks like. Let me know if you want to talk about it."

I nodded as he stepped past me. "See you guys!" he called.

"Later!" Taylor called back. "All right, Dylan, here's your bank. What the hell happened to you?"

"I tripped getting out of my car last night," I said, taking the money. "Luckily I landed on my hand."

Back on street level, I looked up at the swollen cloud cover. I sat on the wall, feeling the wind billowing around my jacket.

Jeffrey joined me, and after I explained my face, he told me about the impending storm—the weather forecasters predicted an unusual amount of rain over the next few days.

This'll make sleeping in the car more interesting. . .

I thought of what Monique had told me, about an impending storm.

Of *badness.*

You have arrived. . .

My mouth dropped open at the sight of an all-too-familiar face.

She looked equally shocked to see me.

"Dylan?"

"Oh. Hi."

"I didn't expect to see *you!"*

"Didn't expect to you see you, either." The name on the dispatch had said Richard Sanchez.

Ella laughed.

I looked from her white teeth—*shark teeth*, as I'd always thought, to the large breasts pushing out from her purple T-shirt, to her gray sweatpants, the toes of her bare feet peeking out from the bell-shaped bottoms.

Weird seeing Ella dressed so casually, with her hair down.

"You don't have to look so nervous," she said. "I'm not your boss anymore."

"No, you're not." Meeting Ella's eyes, I grinned. "How've you been?"

Ella's smile faltered. "Good. Um. Would you. . .come, come in for a second!"

She stood aside. "Please," she added.

I stepped in. She shut the door.

"So how've you been?" she asked looking over her shoulder, leading me down a hardwood hallway that smelled of pine.

I glanced up from the big oval of her moving rump. "Good," I said.

"You got a big ol' bruise. Someone beat you up?"

"More like a stupid accident."

A light flicked on, and the hallway opened on the right to a small living room area with a couch facing a mounted flat screen above a bare mantelpiece. "I like your place. Nice space."

"Just set it down right there."

"So how's things at JB's?" I asked, opening the flap.

"I quit."

Setting the lone box onto the marble counter, I looked up.

Ella smiled without showing teeth. "Yeah. It was time."

"Oh. You're moving on to another job, I take it."

Ella nodded towards the ground. "Moving on is right."

She turned away from me.

"Um. . .how much is it again?"

I looked at the papers in my hand.

"Oh, it's already been paid for," I said. "I just need you to sign."

"Okay."

"Ella?"

"What?" Ella had her head in her hands. She let out a pained sob.

"Are you okay?"

Ella whirled around.

She hugged herself to me. I felt her hot wet face press against my cheek as I put an arm around her.

"I'm sorry," she blurted. "My husband just left me!"

My life gets more surreal by the minute, I thought, as I tried to comfort the sobbing woman.

A woman I'd detested. Ella had been like no boss I'd ever had—she'd been the worst.

(She'd also been the prettiest, which had made her seem more evil)

But it was hard to see her as *Ella* now. She was a human being, and she was hurt.

Her body shook like some living thing was fighting its way up her throat.

"I'm sorry!" She stepped out from my arms. She smacked her hand against her forehead. "I just don't know what to do! I want to fall apart and die!"

"I'm sorry, Ella."

"I'm supposed to drive down to my Mom's tomorrow, but I don't know if I can! I don't know if I can even do *anything!"*

"I know that feeling," I said. "You wake up every morning and you feel like you just want to die. Just switch off."

Ella continued. "I don't know how I'm supposed to go see a lawyer and look at papers and be all business-like, like. . .like it's a fucking *business! Not everything I had. . ."* She raised her contorted face towards the ceiling.

"I'm so sorry. That's so tough."

"The life we had is over. My life is over."

"I understand," I said. "More than you know."

Ella looked at me like she was noticing me for the first time. "Why did he leave me?"

"I don't know," I said, soft as I could.

"Why did he?" Ella lowered her eyes, like she was getting a revelatory thought.

She suddenly smiled.

Not the shark smile. A real Ella smile.

I realized that Ella wasn't just pretty—she was beautiful.

"You know what, Dylan? He left me for one of his co-workers. He'd been fucking one of his co-workers. Can you believe that?"

"Oh God," I said, putting my hand on her shoulder. "That's awful."

"Do you know how that makes me feel?" She put her own hand on top of mine.

"I can't imagine—"

"Like I'm so undesirable. So unattractive."

"Well, that's certainly not—"

"It's left me feeling empty. And aching. You know? Empty

and aching inside."

Ella was staring at my chest, the fingers of her hand massaging mine.

"You know what's so weird? After all that I still love him. And I want him so bad. You know, if I got the chance, I would just fuck the living shit out of him right now. Almost like I had something to prove, you know?"

She looked up at me. "Is that weird?"

"No. No, I'm sure it's only natural to—"

"I mean *you* find me attractive, right? You just said so."

"Right."

"I remember when we used to work together, I used to feel your eyes all over my ass. You liked the way I looked in those tight pants, didn't you?"

I smiled in embarrassment. "Yeah. I guess, yeah."

"So now we don't work together anymore, do we? Has anything changed?"

"What do you mean?"

"Do you still like my ass?"

Ella's eyes shined from the center of her long, damp eyelashes.

"Sure."

"Yeah?"

She removed her hand from mine, and I took my hand off her shoulder.

"What is it about my ass that you like?"

"Uh, I don't know, it's. . .well. You have an ass like a Miami music video."

She smiled.

"You still wanna fuck it, even though it's no longer about power?"

"What?"

Ella pushed against me and I felt the soft press of her breasts. Felt her arms wrapping behind.

"Do you wanna fuck me?"

"Uh. . ."

Ella pouted her lips.

"Ella, I'm . . ."

Really turned on!

". . .going to go. I think you're having a real rough time, and I'm sorry. I think you're confused."

Ella blinked, and looked away. Her cheek was so close to

my face, I saw a little freckle I'd never noticed.

She unwrapped her arms, letting them fall to her sides. "Yeah," she sighed. She stepped back and turned away. "Sorry."

"Don't be," I said, following her to the front of the couch. "It's okay."

"Can you just sit for a second?"

"Sure."

I sat back onto the couch, feeling the uneven push of square cushions.

Ella stood with her back turned, the shirt stretched tight at the shoulders.

She wasn't wearing a bra.

And I looked down. At her *ass.*

It was incredible up close. So full, pressing so tight against the pants.

Ella looked over her shoulder.

"I'm sorry, Dylan. You must think I've really gone crazy. Well, I'm not. I'm just really feeling a lot right now, okay?"

"I understand."

"No you don't!"

"Ella, I don't think you know this, but—"

Ella lifted her T-shirt over her head, her hair sprouting out. She threw it aside and turned around.

Her bare breasts looked fantastic, her dark brown nipples the size of half dollars.

"Let me make myself clear," she said, lowering her sweatpants. "I'm horny, you little twerp." She stepped out and flung them aside.

I looked at Ella's warm-looking thighs the color of gingerbread.

They walked towards me, the mound between her legs divided by a sliver of dark trimmed hair.

Ella stopped inches from me and turned around, her naked ass jiggling.

I felt her fingers on the back of my head push me forward as she bent over.

"Eat *this,* you insubordinate little shit!" she said, mashing my face.

I heard my phone ringing from a distance.

Opening my eyes, I sat up from the bed.

Ella was lying naked beside me, asleep.

I walked out of the room, down the stairs and into the living room, where our clothes were scattered. Following the panicky sound of my ringtone, I found my pants and pulled out the phone from my pocket.

"Hello?"

"Dylan where the hell are you?"

Taylor.

"Sorry, man. I'm okay, I. . .got into a sort of accident."

"Oh *shit*," he said, his tone changing to concerned.

"I bumped my car into the side of the road. I mean, a *wall*, and punctured my tire. I had to change it."

"Wait, but you're okay, right? Nobody's hurt?"

"Nobody's hurt. It was just me."

"Wait, so, did you deliver the pizza?"

"Yeah," I said. "It happened on the way back. I should have called you. I just got so frustrated. It took me forever to change the tire."

"Man, you are the poster boy for bad luck. Okay, well I'm glad you're okay. You're on the way back now, right?"

"Yeah!" I said, turning towards the hallway. "I'll be there soon."

"Okay, listen," Taylor said, resuming his former angry tone. "When you get into an accident, you need to let us know. Okay?"

"You got it. Really sorry."

"Get your ass back here. I wanna go home."

"On it," I said, and hung up.

Gotta make this a real quick exit, I thought, putting my left leg in my pants. With any luck, Ella would stay dozing.

"Jesus," I muttered, shaking my head, as I bent to pick up my uniform shirt from the floor.

I couldn't believe I'd just fucked my former boss.

Without a condom, too.

Clothed, I began walking down the hall, then realized I was forgetting the carrier bag.

I snuck back to retrieve it from the kitchen, then headed back down the hall on my tiptoes towards the door.

I put my hand on the knob.

You should say goodbye, at least. Wish her luck.

Dropping the carrier bag, I went up the stairs.

Ella was sitting up in bed with her legs spread, her eyes closed as she stretched her arms over her head in a yawn.

I looked at the moist cleft between her legs, where I'd licked and plunged. I could see my sperm on her thighs.

She yawned, dropping her arms.

Reaching between her legs, she glided a finger down her parted lips, pressed her finger in, and brought it out with a wet click. She put the finger in her mouth.

Pulling the finger out with a wet pop, she opened her eyes.

"Hey," I said, "I just came to say goodbye."

Ella smirked, and turned onto her side, stretching her arms. "Bye."

"Sorry I have to run off, but I'm still at work and they're calling me."

Ella said nothing.

I looked to the top of her large dresser, where there were several framed pictures. I saw Ella with many friends, smiling and making faces.

"I hope you felt a little better, just there."

"It was all right." Ella sat up.

That *had been only all right?*

"Well, you take care of yourself. You hang in there, okay?"

Ella said nothing. Raised her arms over her head in a V-shape.

Not sure of what else to say, I looked again at the little pictures in little frames arranged about the dresser. I took a step closer, looking for any sign of her husband in them.

I didn't see any man in the pictures.

Ella must have put them all away.

She yawned.

"Well Ella, I hope Richard realizes—"

"Huh?"

"Your. . .husband."

"My husband?"

"Yeah. Richard, right?"

Ella's mouth opened, then shut. She smirked. "Right!" she said, turning away. "My husband. Rich."

She sounded like she was trying not to laugh.

"Wait a second," I said. "You're not married?"

"Nope." She got up, smiling.

That chilling shark smile I hated.

"But I got a boyfriend named Rich who really likes me. He's the one who ordered the pizza, and he's on his way over here. Maybe you two would like to meet? I'll introduce him to my pizza boy!"

I felt my own teeth baring as I stepped towards her, clenching my fists. "You mean you made all that up?"

"You fuckers think you're the only actors in town?"

I stared into Ella's shiny black eyes.

She smiled back with her teeth.

I shook my head. "You're really disgusting."

I backed out of the room, and turned. Went down the stairs.

"Dylan!" Ella yelled. "Have you been checked for STDs?"

I looked back up at her peeking around the corner. "What? Why?"

Ella showed her teeth.

"You might want to now."

Chapter 52

I woke thinking, *somebody's outside,* and saw the purple glaze spattering my windshield like so many small gasping mouths. Thick-looking water, like syrup, washed in the streetlight from above.

It was just the rain. Really coming down.

The car rocked with a gust of wind.

This must be it, I thought. *The start of the Storm.*

At least I only had one more shift to get through and then I was driving up to visit my parents for Christmas. It'd be a nice break.

Then I would come back and sort things out, get a new place.

Plus I had my little get-together with Carter before work to look forward to. It wouldn't be the all-night Kung Fu movie-a-thon he'd suggested, but it'd be fun, whatever we ended up doing for the few hours before I had to go to work.

I smiled at the thought.

Carter. My lunatic buddy.

You just gotta get a few more hours sleep first. . .

Closing my eyes, I turned onto my side and waited, listening to the rain.

Chapter 53

"Damnit, Carter."

I hammered on the door.

The door pushed open under my fist and I could hear Carter and Maddy yelling at each other.

"You said so long as I did the floor, and I did!" Carter yelled. "Quit being a cunt about it!"

"Don't call me a cunt, you asshole!"

Maddy was walking in to the living room in a white T-shirt and green shorts. She looked startled to see me. "I tried knocking. Okay if I come in?"

"Dylan, can you please take him away from me?"

"Hey, we're not done here sister diddle!" Carter yelled, walking in to the room and pointing his finger. He was wearing a karate uniform tied with a black belt and a red bandanna on his head.

"Well I'm done, and your friend is here," Maddy said, stepping through the hanging beads into the kitchen.

Carter followed her into the kitchen, seeming not to have noticed.

"OH WASSAMATTA WASSMATTA HONEY? ISSIT CAUSE YOU KNOW I'M RIGHT?"

I picked up the bag and brought it inside, shutting the door behind me.

"Stop yelling at me, Carter! They're going to call the police!"

"YOU STOP YELLING! YOU'RE YELLING!"

"GET OUTTA MY FACE CARTER! GO TALK TO DYLAN!"

"GET OUTTA MY FACE CARTER! GO TALK TO DYLAN!"

"HEY!" I yelled. "CARTER!"

The hanging wall of beads parted and Carter came out.

He got into his fighting stance.

"I've been trying to call you," I said. "I brought some beer."

"Oh! Fulacho?"

Carter came towards me with open arms. "Come here baby."

I stepped in to his embrace.

His wet tongue darted into my ear.

"Ahhgh!" I pushed him back.

Carter cackled into a backwards somersault, his feet slamming the wall.

"CARTER!"

The beads rustled.

Maddy looked at Carter lying on the floor, and to me. "Please Dylan. Just get him out of here, he's shit-faced. That guy upstairs has probably already called the cops."

I shook my head. And I'd been worried about hurting Carter's feelings by not being able to stay for an all-night marathon. "I don't know where I can take him. I only came over to hang for a little while. I have to work soon."

Carter rolled to his knees and whipped his head up, grinning like a maniac.

"I'm going to call the police if he keeps this shit up."

"Sorry Maddy," I said, as she turned and stepped back into the kitchen. "We were just supposed to hang and watch a movie."

"Kung Fu Movie," Carter intoned in imitation of a wizened Master.

"Hey bud," I said. "So what's happening?"

Carter got up, brushing himself off.

He came over to me and put a hand on my shoulder. "Bro, look." He turned his head towards the TV, and the stack of DVDs standing a foot high.

"You rented all those?" I asked. "How many did you get?"

Carter grinned, nodding. "We're going to have a *good* night."

"Ah, man. Dude. We're not going to have time for all those."

Carter's face fell.

"I got to work in about an hour and a half, and then I'm driving up to the Bay Area tonight."

"You mean, you're working? The pizza job?"

"Yeah. At four."

"Where you got the pizza, you bring the pizza?"

"What?"

"Where's the fucking pizza you said you were going to bring?"

"I don't know what you're talking about. I didn't say that."

Carter stepped back, splaying his arms. "Are you fucking kidding me? We were supposed to do this! I've been getting ready!"

"I can see that," I said. "You look wasted. Let's sit down. I got time for one. What's your favorite movie?"

I reached into the bag and pulled out a beer for myself. I didn't bother offering one to Carter.

"I'm going to put these in the fridge," I said, picking up the bag.

In the kitchen I found Maddy sitting at the little dining table in the corner, eating what looked like a calzone on a paper plate.

"What's going on?" I whispered.

"He's fucked up," Maddy said, looking wounded. "He's been drinking since last night I think. He keeps talking about some stupid Kung Fu thing you guys are doing today. What the hell did you tell him?"

"I didn't tell him anything. He wanted to have a day where we'd watch Kung Fu movies and have a few drinks, but I have to work and leave for home afterwards. I'm only here for a little visit."

"Why does he always get this way when you come over?"

"What do you mean?"

"He starts acting like an idiot."

"You mean he doesn't always act like an idiot?"

"When *you're* around he's even worse."

When I came back out Carter was on the couch drinking my beer.

"You fucker!" I said, turning around.

When I came back out again with another beer he was glaring up at me.

"What the hell's the matter with you?" I asked.

"The dayye," he said, doing his Christopher Walken impression, "It's ruined. You ruined it. My frehnd. I'm disappointed."

"Let's watch a movie."

"Hey," Carter whispered leaning towards me, a glint in his eyes. "You wanna get stoned?"

"No, man." I set my beer onto the table. "I'm not even going to drink much. Tonight's going to suck out there on that road, and I'll need to be alert. You can," I added, thinking it might put him to sleep, a mercy for Maddy.

"Nope! Not doing it then. Fuck you."

"All right, so what movie—?"

"Nope!"

I wasn't going to talk to him while he was like this, so I downed my beer and walked back into the kitchen.

"Maddy, I'm getting out of here."

"Hey!" Maddy shut off the running faucet and turned towards me. Her mouth hung open.

Just then I felt a little sorry for her.

"Can't you just take him somewhere? I'm all alone with him today and I have errands to do and he won't leave me alone."

"Would if I could, I can't take him to work with me."

Maddy gestured to the fridge. "Take all that beer with you, then! Please."

The beads rustled and Carter stumbled in. "Hey. . .wassa what you bitches bitchin?"

He swayed on his feet.

"Look, buddy," I said. "I gotta get going. I need to pack my suitcase, so I'll leave you to your merry-making. Merry Christmas, man."

Carter opened his mouth, then closed it. His eyes seemed to be swimming in his head.

"You be a lot nicer to Maddy, okay?"

"Fulachos machos?"

"I'm afraid so."

"No no. . .poquitos?"

"No stayo," I said. I turned towards Maddy. "You take it easy, and have a Merry—"

Maddy shrieked and ducked as brown glass exploded onto the counter.

"Shit!" Carter said. "I was aiming for the trash can. My bad, sissy."

"WHAT THE FUCK YOU ASSHOLE!" Maddy screamed.

"STOP YELLING!" Carter yelled.

"Hey!" I said, putting my hands onto Carter's shoulders. "Let's go!" I steered him backwards into the wall of hanging beads.

On the other side, I steered him towards his room.

"This is like goin backworss."

"Keep moving," I said.

Keeping one hand on his shoulder, I pushed the door

open.

Carter collapsed onto his fold-out hammock in the middle of the junk-ridden room, cackling.

"What the hell man? You could have really hurt her!"

Carter rolled onto his side. He had covered his face with his hands as though he were crying. Now he peeked out at me, his face red and smiling. "No I couldn't have."

"Yes you could've!"

"Dylan, you don't—"

"Shut up and listen! You're drunk as fuck and you're being an asshole! Now I'm leaving. I don't want Maddy to have to call the cops on you. You stay right where you are on that fucking bed and pass out. You hear me? Don't leave this room."

"Okay."

"I'm serious! You got it?"

"Yep."

"What you going to do?"

"I'm a gonna. . ." Carter draped an arm over his eyes.

I waited.

He began to snore.

I shook my head, looking about the little room.

What the hell had gotten into him?

I looked into the corner of the room where Carter's maroon yoga ball sat with one of his shirts draped over it.

Well. Merry Christmas, bud.

I closed the door.

Maddy was in the kitchen, sweeping up the broken glass.

"Hey," I said. "He's passed out."

Maddy looked up at me.

"What?" I said.

Maddy shook her head.

"I'm going to go now," I said. "Think you can manage by yourself?"

"What, without you?" she said with biting sarcasm.

"Have a good one," I said, turning. "You can keep the beer. Why don't you have some?"

"Fuck you, no! You're taking it with you!"

I went through the beads.

"HEY!"

I walked towards the door.

"Here!"

I heard Maddy's footsteps on the hardwood floor and

looked behind me as I was turning the doorknob.

She dumped the two six-packs onto the couch with a loud clang of glass that made me cringe. "Take it and get out!"

She walked around the couch, and turned her back to me.

And stumbled back with an airy *bounth!*

Carter cackled as he came in, darting around the couch towards the kitchen holding the yoga ball.

"I'M GONNA KILL YOU!" Maddy shrieked.

Carter bounced the ball and it hit the ceiling.

On its way down, he chopped it towards Maddy. It hit her and bounced off.

Carter turned and ducked into the beads. Maddy followed.

I opened the door and stepped out, hearing Carter shout, "I WILL BUM-WIPE YOU TO INFINITY. . ." as I closed it.

My head lowered in the rain, I crossed the street, the wind blowing hard against me.

I opened the car and sat in. The door slammed with the extra push from the wind.

I stuck the key in the ignition.

Ran both hands through my wet hair.

I turned around in the street, then slowed at the stop sign, signaling right.

The sudden hammering at my window made me jump.

The passenger door opened, and Carter got in.

"GO!" he yelled. "SHE'S GOT A GUN!"

Ducking, I sped forward.

A block up I saw a stop sign coming fast and stepped hard on the brake, lurching both of us forward, Carter bonking his head on the curve of the windshield.

We shot back into our seats as we came to an abrupt stop.

I looked over my shoulder. No headlights or people running up the road, from what I could see in the rain.

"What the fuck, you asshole!"

"You okay?" I asked.

"What the fuck was that?"

"What do you mean what the fuck was that?" I said, continuing on through the intersection. "Is she chasing us?"

"No."

"What?"

"No, it was just inside, we're clear."

"But she pulled a gun on you?"

"It was more like a wooden spoon. But that shit can be deadly too."

"What?"

Carter cackled.

I pulled the car over.

"Get out you drunken asshole!"

"Hey, I'm sorry man!"

"Get out! You're drunk!"

"No, I'm not!"

"OUT!"

"Wait," he said. "Chill, man. Okay?"

He looked at me soberly.

"I'm really not drunk," he said. "That beer you gave me is the only one I've had today. That was all an act."

"Shut the fuck up."

Carter slowly smiled, his eyes looking steady.

He pursed his lips and blew. "Smell alcohol?"

I stared at Carter. The rain pattered loud.

"You son of a bitch," I said.

Carter turned and clapped. Bending forward, he cackled towards his knees.

"That was *all* an act? Why?"

Even as I asked, I felt the tickle of amusement bubbling up my throat.

"I was just trying to make her leave," he joyfully whimpered, shaking his shoulders. "So we could be alone and do our shit."

"Jesus, Carter."

We both laughed.

"But I don't give a fuck," he said. "I can watch those movies later. Let's get something to eat now. Come on, I'm starving."

"All right," I said, flicking down the turn signal to the left. "Why are you such a holy terror to Maddy, though?"

Carter sighed, and sat back.

"I gotta move out, man," he said. "I don't like the way she talks to me sometimes."

After taking Carter through a McDonald's drive-thru, he wanted to utilize my employee discount.

"Come on, man! I haven't even tried your pizza!"

"How the hell could you possibly still be hungry?" I asked.

"I'm fuckin starving."

"Are you stoned?"

"No!"

"I gotta take you home now, otherwise I gotta take you to pick up the pizza, and by the time it's ready I won't have time to take you back. So you'll be stuck walking miles back in the rain."

"Fuck that. Let's order the pizza. You can drop me off when you're delivering close to my area or just when you're finished."

"What the hell are you talking about?"

"I'm going to ride along with you tonight!"

"No you're not!"

"Why not?"

"Because. We can't do that."

"Who's going to see when we're out and about?"

"They'll see us when you're getting into my car, in the garage. A lot of the employees hang out down there. Especially tonight with the rain."

"If anybody asks, just say I'm your visiting cousin."

"Yeah, we look related."

"Who cares? They complain, just go oh I didn't know, sorry. Then I'll walk home, okay? How bout it? Ride along! Ride along!"

I didn't like the possibility of being reprimanded at work because of Carter, but I did like the idea of him keeping me company during what was sure to be a dreary few hours.

"Okay," I said.

"YES!" Carter clapped. "Ha-ha! This is going to be fun! We'll be the fumachos of the night!"

"But you're going to have to keep a low profile while I'm waiting for deliveries."

"I gotcha, Sriracha."

"Which, I think is going to be a challenge. Have you forgotten one thing?"

"What?"

"Don't you think you might attract a little attention wearing a fucking karate uniform on a night like this?"

Carter looked down, then shrugged. "I'll just stay in the car. Anybody comes up and tries to fuck with me, they're gonna find out exactly why I have this."

Chapter 54

My car windows were fogged, making it impossible for anyone to see who was sitting inside—the result of Carter and I having been in the car for an hour and a half.

Slow, slow night.

Here I was with my first delivery (a double), and my shift was more than halfway over.

I was glad now Carter had accompanied me.

I was even glad that we had ordered the large pizza.

Opening the backseat, I set down the two bags. Shut the door.

Opened my door and sat in.

"Okay," I said. "Here we go."

"We going far?" Carter looked at me with bright eyes. How the little guy stayed so energetic with all his intake of food was beyond me.

"We're going to the hills," I said. "Here, hold this and give me that." I handed him my dispatch slips over the pizza box on his lap.

"Yes!"

I started to lift the box off Carter's lap, then realized I couldn't hold it on mine with the steering wheel in the way. "Just hold it," I said, lifting the lid. There were three slices of the deep-dish pizza left. "Jesus, man. Where do you put it all?"

Then I noticed the crumpled wrapper off to the empty side of the box.

"What was that?" I asked, taking a slice.

"What?"

I bit into the pizza. The cheese had gone cold, enlivening the spices and the salty taste of the sausage and pepperoni. I closed my eyes at the feel of the soft dough yielding between my teeth.

I chewed, swallowed. “The wrapper in the box.”

“Oh! Cookie.”

Carter cackled as I turned to him, mouth open.

“God damn it, Carter,” I said again.

We had been moving very slowly up Sunset Blvd towards Mannerville Canyon.

Now I saw why. Up ahead, a tree had fallen into the road.

Carter kept laughing beside me, already feeling the effects of the pot cookie.

Remembering how his other cookie had affected me made me feel sick to my stomach.

“Seriously, Carter,” I said, as we slowly merged into the left lane. “What are you thinking?”

“Come on,” he said. “I didn’t realize you were going to be working tonight and I’d planned for us to share this. But since I ain’t driving. . .”

“Once was plenty, thank you.” It was the reason I’d given Carter back the other cookie.

“Aw, *foo-foos!”* He reached out and tickled under my chin.

“Stop that!” I said, jerking my head to the side, turning the wheel slightly to the left.

“Doritos?”

“Seriously Carter, cut the shit!”

“It’s okay, baby. I got your chi.”

On the other side of the obstruction, I returned to the right lane and stopped behind a car in front.

“In a quarter mile. Turn right onto Mannerville Canyon Road!”

“Oh-*ho!”* Carter picked up the phone and raised it to his face. He mimed cunnilingus.

“Put it down!”

“Hey, when am I going to hear the sexy voice?”

“You won’t. Put it down.”

“How do you make it talk in the sexy voice that leads you to the girls? I want some sexo.”

“It’s just a glitch, now put it—”

“OINKY-BOINKY!” Carter shouted into the phone. “OINKY FUCKIN BOINKY, *haha!”*

We both jumped at the blast of horns behind us.

There was growing space of empty road ahead.

Carter lowered his window as I let up on the brake.

Leaning out, he shouted. "HEY! OINKY-BOINKY!"

I heard another honk from behind.

"Carter!" I yelled, "Sit down!"

Carter sat back into his seat, leaving the window open. I was going to tell him to close it, but the cold air coming in felt invigorating.

Instead, I said, "Chill out. I'm serious. Or I'm pulling over and leaving you here. You got it?"

"Turn right onto Mannerville Canyon Road!"

I signaled, slowing. "This is the road where Arnold Schwarzenegger lives. Enjoy the lights."

We continued on Mannerville, travelling through what seemed like a carnival tunnel of flashing lights and moving decorations, until the first stop sign, where Sally told us to turn left.

As we began up the hill, Sally told us to continue for one and a half miles.

"What do you think?" I asked after a few moments of silence. "Do you like it up here?"

"Eh," Carter said, unimpressed.

"The view is incredible. I guess you have to really see it during the day."

"Eh."

"You all right?"

"No, I need to. . ."

"What?"

Carter leaned out the open window. *"Na nah nana naa. . ."*

"Is that supposed to be the theme from Jurassic Park?" I asked, laughing.

Carter cackled, then continued with his off-key version.

"Stop it!" I said, after we passed a man on the side of the road by a parked car. He had stared at us. "Remember, I have a glowing topper on top of my car that advertises where I work." I pressed up Carter's window.

We continued up the road, winding around sharp turns and passing signposted driveways, my headlights sometimes lighting on parts of the luxurious homes not concealed, making the windows look like large opening eyes with glowing pupils.

"Where'd all the Christmas lights go?" Carter asked.

"I don't know," I said, suddenly wondering the same thing.

"In a quarter mile. Your destination is on the right!"

Slowing, I pulled off to the side of the road, glancing down at the display screen of the phone. There was no trouble finding parking up here, but some of the houses were spaced quite far apart.

"You have arrived!"

"All right," I said, parked. "I'll be right back."

I got out from the car.

The wind blew hard against me, billowing my open jacket. It felt cold now.

I got the first bag out from the back.

A wooden post with iron numerals told me I was at the right house.

The driveway angled down, and the house seemed to be settled on the edge of the hill, giving its occupants a wide view of the area and hillside opposite.

However, its occupants weren't much concerned for *my* view: There was no porch light on, or any other form of illumination. There appeared to be no front windows either, which I thought strange.

These folks must like their privacy, I thought.

I stumbled forward, nearly dropping the bag. Looking down, I realized the uneven ground was the result of my right foot having stepped off the driveway and onto the edge of a lawn.

Folks are assholes, not to leave any light on for me.

In the shadows to the left, however, I could make out two parked vehicles.

Stepping cautiously, I went up a set of steps. At the top, a large dark rectangular shape announced the door.

Not seeing a doorbell, I raised my fist to knock, then hesitated.

I looked behind me at the vehicles.

This doesn't feel right.

I turned and walked along the side, but saw no other door. I did see a pair of windows though, but they showed nothing of the inside, their blinds pulled down, which was why they had blended in with the dark exterior from a distance.

I walked back to the door and knocked.

After a moment, the door opened.

"Hello," I said, not being able to really see the person, though I could tell it was a woman from the shape revealed by the faint illumination of the active fireplace in the darkened room.

"Hi," she said in a disinterested voice.

"How are you tonight?" I asked, handing her the box.

"Not so good. One second, okay? *Dad,"* she called.

"How much is it?" asked a grumpy voice.

A moment later, a short bearded man in a white sweater and shorts stepped into view with a florescent light affixed to his head. Suddenly, I understood.

"How long has the power been out?" I asked, handing him the receipt.

"All day," he said, shoving a collection of bills in my hand. "Keep it."

"Thank you, sir. I'm—"

The door slammed in my face.

Must be very difficult to have to go without power in that big, big house for a few hours.

I walked down the steps.

Back at the car, I was relieved to find Carter still sitting in it.

"Now," I said, climbing back into the driver's seat. "On to number two."

"Poo-poos?"

"They're without power," I said, starting the car. "That's why we haven't been seeing any Christmas lights. This whole area must be without power. Hand me that," I said, indicating the dispatch in Carter's hands.

Carter gave me a blank, open-mouthed look, then looked at the paper in his hands and twitched, as if coming awake. He handed it over. "Bro, I think this shit is starting to kick in."

I looked at the address on the dispatch. It was on Maplewood Road.

I signaled, and turned around.

The grass blew wildly at the side of the road, the wind rocking the car. At least it was no longer raining.

"What's this guy think he's doing?" Carter asked.

I saw the man standing by the car ahead.

As we came down, he stared at us, scowling. He was wearing a windbreaker and black slacks, standing with his arms folded.

The car behind him was blocking the entrance of a driveway.

"That is kind of weird."

As we went further down, I noticed more and more cars parked in front of open driveways, parked parallel so as to block anyone from entering.

And I understood.

These people had a lot to lose; with the power out they had even more reason to fear intruders. Especially with the Cat Burglar.

We turned a corner and there was a large white van with jacketed men moving about. We passed them fast, but it looked like they were from the power company.

"Why aren't you using the thingy?" Carter asked.

"Oh, I forgot." I pulled over to the side of the road.

I picked up the dispatch and spoke into my phone.

"Five-six-one, Maple—"

"Hey make it do the sexy!"

"Goddamnit Carter, you asshole!"

The phone chimed with the wrong text.

I cancelled, and reset back to the Navigation menu.

"Now don't say anything until I'm done talking this time," I said.

I hit the microphone icon and raised the phone to my face.

"Five-six-one—"

"SEXY YUM-YUM!"

"SHUT UP!" I punched Carter in the shoulder. "You do that one more time I'm giving you the death-punch and leaving you out here!"

I picked up the phone and again held it close to my mouth, my other hand blocking Carter. "Five-six-one. Maplewood Road. Grantwood."

"Sex. . ." Carter whispered.

The phone chimed, but this time without Carter's addition.

"In a quarter mile. Turn right onto Mannerville Canyon Road!"

All the lights on Mannerville now seemed mocking, coming down from an area without power.

We had turned onto Sunset. A loud blast of cool air made me jump and look over at Carter. He was lowering his window.

"HEY!" Carter yelled. "HEEEY!"

"STOP IT!" I yelled.

A yellow Mustang sped forward.

"Follow them!" Carter yelled. "Those girls are horny!"

"I'm not following them. We're—"

"In one mile. Turn right onto Barrel Road!"

"What she said," I said.

"Dude! What the fuck? You're. . .hey! Take me to the

magic castle!"

"What?"

"Your elf chick!"

"Don't call her that again, her name is Val."

"I wanna meet her!"

"You will meet her. Not tonight."

"I want us to skewer her!"

"What?"

"Skewer her with our cocks!"

"What?"

"Does she have pointed pussy lips?"

Keeping one hand on the steering wheel, I punched Carter in the shoulder.

"LET'S MAKE LOVE TONIGHT IN THE MAGIC CASTLE!" he screamed in my face.

"SHUT UP!" I yelled, aiming another punch at him, but this time my fist only felt the loose fabric of his uniform.

"LET'S FULACHO HER CHACHO!" he screamed back.

"CARTER I'M GOING TO FUCKING—"

"Turn left onto Barrel Road. Then turn right onto Maplewood Road!"

Turning the corner, I saw the red light ahead and pressed on the brake. Carter continued to laugh as we slowed.

Having come to a stop, I turned towards him. "Look man. I know you're getting high but you seriously gotta be cool while I'm driving."

"I feel ya."

I burrowed into Carter with my eyes. After a few seconds, he looked away.

I turned to face the windshield and opened my mouth, but before I could say anything, I was interrupted by a guttural voice.

"Go-*ink* leffgh. . ."

A horn honked and I looked up, turning to Carter. "Did you fucking hear that?"

"Yeah I heard it, go!"

"But did you hear—?"

"The light's going to turn!"

I scooted into the intersection, feeling blood swell up my neck from my pounding heart.

"Go, fuck!" Carter shouted.

I turned the wheel, onto Barrel Road.

And immediately turned right onto Maplewood, even as the voice below said, **"Go-*ink* roighttt. . ."**

"What the hell is that?" Carter asked.

"We're turning around," I said, speeding up the road. "We're being misdirected."

"What do you mean?"

"That's the goddamned Demon Voice! We don't want to follow where it tells us to go. Trust me."

"Why not?"

"Because it means we're in danger."

Ahead the road widened. I let up on the gas.

"We're in danger?" Carter asked.

"If we don't—"

"Danger of getting *THIS?"* His tickling fingers under my chin made my hands jerk, turning the wheel.

I hit the brake and winced at the screeching even as I saw the oncoming blur of clothes and realized it was too late.

Chapter 55

The person had rolled up the windshield and over the roof with a *KA*-THUMP *BUMP* before we hit the curb.

"Oh my God," Carter said. *"What just happened?"*

I put the gear in park and got out.

The figure was stretched horizontally, just a few feet back.

The child-sized figure.

"Oh, no. . ." I groaned, stepping over.

It looked like a boy, though I couldn't be sure—the clothes were baggy, and a white helmet sheltered the head.

The kid suddenly sat up.

"Hey!" I said, bending at the knees.

The boy looked up at me with wide eyes.

"Are you okay?" I asked.

He blinked, shaking his head. "What happened?"

"You mean you don't remember?" Carter said from behind.

The boy looked to Carter. "Um. No."

"Are you hurt?" I asked.

"Um. . .I don't think so."

"Can you stand? Here." I put my arm around him.

He got up without seeming to need my support.

"He looks good!" Carter said. "You're good!"

The boy looked around the ground. Spotting my topper lying nearby, he made to move towards it, then to me. "Have you guys seen my board?"

"Were you skateboarding?"

"Yeah, I was on my way home, and. . ." The boy's eyes suddenly widened. "Oh my God," he said. "I remember now!"

"You do?"

"You were on I Fought the Law and Lost! That's where I know you from—you were the bad guy!" The boy smiled. "Wow!

How come you're dressed like a pizza delivery guy? Are you filming something?"

"Never mind that for a second, I just want to make sure you're really all right."

"Don't worry about me, I take falls all the time. Comes with being a skater. You wanna see a crazy scar?"

"Here it is bud!" Carter said, coming back with the skateboard. He handed it to the boy.

"Thanks. Are you an actor too?"

Carter smiled. "I am!"

"You really know karate?"

"I only use it for self-defense. Why, you wanna spar?"

I grabbed Carter's arm. "Can I talk to you? We'll be right back," I said to the boy.

"It's all good," he said. "I'm gonna roll."

"Just wait a second, please."

I brought Carter around the car. "He doesn't remember what happened."

"Really? That's great."

"I'm not sure that's so great. He might have a head injury. We better take him to a hospital."

Carter made a contorted face that I would've found comical in other circumstances. *"Are you kidding me?"* he whispered.

"We have to!" I whispered back.

"Look at him! He's totally fine. If he doesn't remember, that means he doesn't even know you hit him!"

"If he's fine I got nothing to worry about. But if he's not, I'm responsible!"

"I'll take him home. Hey, kid!"

The boy came over, the board swinging by his side. "Yeah?"

"What's your name?" Carter asked.

"Brandon."

"Brandon, you said you were going home. You live close?"

"Yeah. Like a half-mile or something."

"Great! Here's the deal. I know you got your skateboard, but my friend and I saw you take a bad fall and want to make sure you're okay. So now he's got to deliver the pizza, so I'm going to just walk with you home. Just to make sure you're okay. How's that sound?" Carter looked at me in question.

"Uh, that's okay. I'm fine."

"Do you remember falling?"

"Yeah?"

"No you don't. And that's why I'm escorting you home. If you've hurt your head, you might get lost."

"I'm not going to get—"

"Hey!" Carter gestured Stop. "It's what I'm doing."

"Okay, I guess."

Carter turned to me. "I'll take care of him. You go drop that off and meet me when you're done."

"You're not walking him home," I whispered.

"Bro," Carter put his hand on my shoulder. *"Do you know how lucky we are? That kid could've been killed because of me."* He swallowed. "This is my fault. Let me fix it. I don't want you getting any trouble because of me. So go do your thing, and let me take him home. I'll make sure he's fine, I promise."

"Yeah, but Carter." *You're high,* I mimed.

Carter shook his head. "No, that was pretty sobering."

Carter and the kid turned the corner out of sight. I picked up the topper and walked back to the car.

Better get to the other side quick. I backed up and returned to the right lane without incident.

I turned the bend.

Suddenly my heart was pounding.

I pulled over, putting the car in park.

What are you doing—you just hit somebody, and you let your friend who's ingested a fucking pot cookie take him home?

What kind of person are you? That kid could be hurt, and you're delivering pizza?

A flash of light from the nook drew my attention.

My phone's display had come on.

"You have arrived!" Sally announced. "You haaaaaave*uuuh. . ."* The screen turned red. **"Go-*ink* to *DIIIE.*"**

I picked up the phone. It was almost burning hot.

"What are you?" Squeezing, I held it up. "What the hell are you? What are you doing in my *phone?!"*

The phone vibrated and made a low growl.

I opened my door.

"Shoulda done this. . ." I threw the phone. "A long time ago!"

The phone landed on the street with a crack, patter-patter.

"Good fucking riddance."

Yeah, great, but now you have no phone. No way to contact Carter or work, or anybody.

Sighing, I got out of the car.

A strong gust of wind blew my hat off.

It rolled in the air, landing on the ground at the edge of a vacant lot adjacent the car that was partially obscured by bushes and trees.

I turned back to the road.

Spotted my phone.

Another strong gust made me stumble as I reached the middle of the road.

The night suddenly brightened and the wind grew louder.

Not the wind, a car!

It came tearing around the corner towards me.

The horn blared, followed by the screech of brakes.

I got out of the way just in time as the car swerved, crashing into my car.

"Oh, shit!" I looked at the red lights of the car's rear-end, smelling burnt rubber.

Looking both ways, I began walking towards the car.

The driver's door of the turquoise car shot open, and a white-haired man in a golfing hat stepped out. He shut the door and quickly stepped around to the front of the vehicle.

I followed him.

My car was no longer on the street: The man had slammed right into Ozzy and knocked him over, rolling him down into the vacant lot, which I now saw was at a steep incline. I couldn't even *see* Ozzy, only the splintered wood in his wake.

The man moaned. He was bending forward in front of his Cadillac, hands on knees.

"Are you all right, sir?" I asked.

"My car. Look at it." The man shook his head.

Slowly, he turned his head. His face was streaked with tears.

His torso shot up. "YOU!" he screamed, pointing his finger. "YOU GOT ME IN AN ACCIDENT!"

I stared at the man, and recognized him.

"I think you crashed into *my* car, fucker!"

The man lunged at me, but I stepped aside in time.

He whirled around, and we faced each other.

The man came towards me, baring his teeth. "DO YOU KNOW WHO I AM?"

"The guy whose ass I'm about to kick!"

"YOU DON'T EVEN KNOW!" he yelled.

I slapped my hand onto my pocket, feeling the square-bulge of my stun gun.

Just a little closer, you piece of shit.

The man looked to where I had my hand.

"You in a fightin mood, Pops?"

He took a step back.

"What's the matter, asshole?"

The man turned and went to his car. He opened the door and got in.

What's he going to do, try and run me down?

I took a few steps back.

The man came out with a black object in his hand.

A gun.

I turned and ran.

The hairs on the back of my neck crawled as I pounded the pavement, weaving from side to side trying to make myself less of an easy target.

Get off the road, quick!

I saw an open gate to my right and ran up the large driveway, triggering a sensor light.

As I followed the driveway around the left, I recognized the house.

The Frankmeyer's.

Only one car was parked beneath the canopy overhang: The brown Mazda.

Even if they were home, I'd be corned by the time they answered the door.

I ran to the front of the car and crouched.

Then noticed another sand path leading towards a gate. The gate was a closed barrier of wood, low enough to scramble over.

Fuck it—I'm not waiting to see if he's coming.

Ducking low, I scurried to the gate.

I jumped and grabbed the edge. Pulled myself up.

One leg over, I looked back.

The man was trotting up the driveway.

Swung the other leg over, and jumped.

Landing in darkness, I felt the bite of sand on my palms as I rolled, onto damp grass.

I tried to stand, but my right leg buckled at sudden pain

from my ankle.

Keep moving!

Putting the weight on my left, I found the path, and began towards the back of the house.

Ahead I saw a faint glow of orange light, coming from the window of a large shed or bungalow.

I stepped onto something spongy and almost lost my balance.

I scraped my foot, but still felt the extra pad of something beneath as I reached the little building, seeing up close the window that had guided my way. It was covered, the light shining through fabric from inside.

I knocked on the door, looking back towards the gate.

The man would probably figure out quick I had jumped the fence.

Was he willing to jump it?

I knocked again, harder.

"Come on," I muttered, going around to the window. I knocked on the glass.

As I stepped back, I looked down and could see something dark covering my sneaker in the glow.

Bending, I raised my foot.

The something had fur on it.

I touched it with my fingers. Soft.

Gripping, I pulled it off my sneaker and held it up.

It was the skin of a cat's head, the ears hanging limp on either side of my fingers. I'd had my foot inside it from the back.

Tap-tap-tap!

I looked up at the window.

A bearded face was leering out and waving.

Dropping the pelt, I turned and started to run.

And saw the shadowed figure of a man running towards me in front of the fence.

"COME HERE TURKEY!" yelled the man with the gun.

I whirled around and ran back up the path, turning the corner away from the little building towards a veranda at the back of the house, where I could see the glowing lights from a Christmas tree behind large glass doors.

I ran up the steps to the door.

Pulled at the handles, shuddering the glass.

They were locked.

I hammered on the glass.

"AH HA!"

The man was walking towards me, his shoulders rising and falling in exertion, aiming the gun. "YOU. . .DON'T RUN. . .FROM ME!"

The man stopped a few feet from the concrete steps. His teeth glowed in the dark.

"NOW. . .BACK DOWN!"

A sliver of yellow light behind the man caught my eyes—the door of the little building began to open.

"YOU'RE COMING WITH ME. I'M GONNA—"

I didn't hear what the man said next, as all my attention focused on the *thing* emerging from the little building.

Something dark and large walking on all fours, like a bear.

But with the hairless face of a. . .

My back slammed against the glass.

"Woof."

The man whirled around, swinging the gun.

"Ho!" He jumped back, landing on his ass, the gun smacking the ground.

The thing galloped towards him.

"No!"

The creature pounced onto the man, knocking the back of his head onto the step with a hideous *thok!*

The jowly mouth opened, heaving a cloud of visible breath onto the man's face as it sank down over the neck.

There was a wet tearing sound as the man's eyes went wide, looking at me. Blood gushed from his mouth, his head shaken by the frantic growling maw.

I turned and grabbed at the door handles, pulling and pushing.

Laughter from behind.

A man dressed as Santa Claus emerged from the little building.

I looked at the blood-spattered creature, looking up as it chewed a hanging piece of flesh, then turned back towards the doors.

I took a step back, then kicked at the frame.

The doors thundered open.

I ran inside into a dim room lit only by a Christmas tree.

Which way, which way?

Passing a kitchen, I ran to a hall, missing my chance to grab a knife. But I had no intention of fighting this maniac and his hound from Hell. All I needed was to get out of the house from the front.

Ahead, I saw three closed doors.

I made it to the end and yanked the last door open.

And looked right into fluorescent lights.

"Heww meh."

Opening my eyes, I looked down and saw a bloody naked woman, squirming on the ground, her feet and hands tied together.

She opened her mouth in a complete look of pain. Several front teeth were missing.

"Heww meh."

I stepped back, out of the room.

The door beside me opened and light exploded. I felt myself slam into the wall.

Santa came at me with brass knuckles over a gloved fist that doubled with my vision, both rotating around each other. The fists slowly cocked back, and I looked at Santa's face as it turned to two, each of them smiling.

With vampire teeth.

Chapter 56

Clack-clack-clack. . .

He was coming.

Oh God, this was it.

And I'd managed nothing more than discovering that I was in a windowless room, all the while looking back through the windows of my life.

Seeing the people I would never see again. The people I loved, the people who had touched me, who had taught me. . .

And my regrets. To think that my dreams of becoming a writer and an actor would never be realized. At the end of the line, they'd only been that: Dreams.

The last several months had flashed through my mind, and what I wouldn't give to step back in. Now that I realized how truly good and wonderful it had all been.

I wished I could thank everybody. Wished that I hadn't left Vic on bad terms. Carter too. If only he were here—we'd turn this horror show into an action flick where the good guys won.

The door opened, spilling light in from the hallway.

Vampire Santa filled the doorframe.

"Rise n shine! Cow-tippin time!"

He flicked on the light.

"You awake yet, bud?"

My whole body tensed as he stepped towards me.

He went to the bed and sat down on the edge.

"How you feelin, pardner? Like one unlucky bastard?" He laughed, slapping his knee. He was still wearing the brass knuckles. "Well, that you might just be. But then, maybe not. I like to look on the bright side of things. You're an actor, right?"

I groaned. The throbbing in my head. The bright light made it even worse.

He grinned, baring his fangs.

"Course you are, like every dipshit workin a joe-job in this town. But I never asked you before. You probably don't recognize me, but I sure as heckfire recognize you. *I* never forget a face, nor a name. Here. . ." He tugged down the white beard then lifted it up over his head, pushing off the hat with it. "How's that, now?"

"Duh. . .Dee?"

"D-G, dumbass! Motherfucker, how many times do I have to goddamn tell you? You're the one with ADHD, I tell you."

The jovial and friendly customer I'd known as DG Santos looked none too pleased now.

"Why's you don't just call me Dave, okay? That's what it stand for anyway. *Dylan.* Dylan, what?"

I stared at Dave.

"What's your surname, pussy-juice?"

"Mur. . ." I began. Then groaned.

"Oh, now. You don't want to tell me? Really? I thought you actor fags was supposed to be obsessed with yourselves. I ain't no agent—I'm only asking cause I figured you might have a stage name or something. How bout Dylan Deadfart? Like that?"

He laughed as he stood up.

"I ain't no vampire neither," he mumbled, putting a gloved hand to his mouth. He pulled out the fake teeth. "Thing's makin me thirsty." He dropped them into the large pocket of the costume.

"How'd you like the costume, by the way? Ain't this neat? Ain't even mine. Belong to the two old farts is own the house. They got a whole lot of costumes they do, upstairs. Kinky motherfuckers. Makes me sick to think. . .hey! We could dress you up as something. What would you like to be, actor boy?"

"DG?" I groaned as he came towards me. "Dave?"

He stopped about a foot away from me.

"What? This the part where you start beggin like a little bitch? Why, cause you think you know me? You don't know me. You think just cause I like your pizza, that I was nice to you those times I ordered I'm gonna cut you a break now? Well, I am. Sorta. Though. . ." He laughed. "It probably ain't the kinda break you expectin, boy. Come on now."

He took hold of my ankles.

I tried to kick out of his grip, but he was strong. My ankles being tied together made my legs feel so much weaker.

"Hey! Hey, now. You wanna give me trouble? Don't make me put you on my lap, boy. I already know what you gettin for

Christmas.

"Thanks for the gun, by the way. Appreciate it. Not that I don't already got me several, but it's always nice to add another with somebody else's prints and registration. Can't say I exactly like the package it came with, but." He chuckled. "Woofus sure did."

Dave dragged me out of the room and the short distance to the one I had entered. He knocked on the door.

"Julie?" he called. "Honey pot? You decent?"

Laughing, he opened the door.

I was dragged in. Dave let go of my ankles and stepped around me. I raised my head as I heard the door close. The woman was gagged and sitting up with her back pressed against the wall, and I noticed a bloody towel wrapped around her breasts.

The woman's eyes were bruised and swollen, making her look very tired even though her shoulders heaved. She was certainly wide-awake.

"Jules? Meet your boy-toy, Dylan." Dave stepped around, blocking the glare of the light above me. He leaned down and planted his hands on his bent knees. "Whadda ya think, bud? Bet you weren't expectin *her* for Christmas! Huh? Do I deliver or what?"

"What are you doing?" I asked.

"I'm putting you in a movie with her!"

"Movie?"

"How'd you like to fuck her, little bud? How'd you like to fuck *Julie fuckin Juggs?"*

I said nothing.

"You're not an actor *fag,* are you?"

"No," I said.

He kicked me in the side, rocking me up. "Then show some enthusiasm, asshole! Not everyday someone lets you fuck a porn star! Don't tell me you don't recognize Julie Jiggle-Juggs. That's J-U-G-G-S, and the original too, from the nineties. Not that new fat bitch. Here, look."

He stepped over to her. "I know she's all bloody now." He bent down. The woman groaned.

He stepped aside and turned to me. "There! Recognize her now?"

I suddenly did.

The poor battered woman with blood smeared across her face was Stacey Noeltner.

"You do recognize her! She's great, right? Well, she was until she retired and got those fucking plastic implants. Bitch! Ruining already perfect breasts! You know what, though? I do kinda like them as souvenirs." He turned and bent towards Stacey. "I plan to sleep on them at night."

He turned to me. "I've improved her, see? Cut out those fake jellow joppers and removed her teeth." He showed me the fist with his brass knuckles. "That wan't nothing pleasant I tell you, but I had to. For precautions. But it actually really worked out well! Now she can *really* suck on dick. It's like putting it to her twat. Trust me, I know. God damn. . ."

Dave straightened and made a show of clapping his gloved hands. "You ready to see, boy? Ready for your big scene?"

He came towards me. Kicked me in the side, rolling me onto my stomach.

I felt his knee in the middle of my back as he whispered into my ear, affecting a gentle tone. "I'm taking these off you now," he said, wafting milk-sour breath into my nose. "Untying your ankles too. But that don't mean you do nothin, you hear?"

The knee pressed hard, making me cry out.

"You hear?"

I nodded.

"Mmkay. Hold still."

My body shook as he opened the cuffs, keeping one wrist squeezed in his hand as he worked, then the other, all the while reminding me that his knee was on my back.

I heard a *clank* as the cuffs were thrown in the corner.

"Now," Dave said, pressing the cold brass knuckle to the back of my neck. "Slowly. Put your arms out in front of you where I can see em."

I did as he ordered.

The knee pressed off.

I heard a click.

"That, my friend, is my Glock forty-five aimed at your nuts. Mmkay?"

He untied my ankles.

"Now, fuckles, I want you to slowly stand with your arms raised and turn around to me."

I did as he ordered.

"Now. Back up to the wall, but away from the door."

I did as he ordered.

But I knew he saw me look towards it.

"You can run for the door if you like. Risk gettin shot an all. Then you'll just have to get past Woofus, and you're home free." He laughed. "No problem!"

Beyond the door, I heard *Woof.*

"Take off your clothes."

I looked at Dave.

He aimed the gun down. "Ten seconds."

I pulled off my uniform shirt, then my T-shirt. Pulled open the button of my jeans, and down the zipper.

I pressed my hands to the sides of my pants.

Gone.

"Looking for this?" Dave held up my phone-styled stun gun. "Do we need to make a call to someone?"

The end of it buzzed.

I shook my head, and lowered my pants.

"What about your socks? You cold?"

I took my socks off.

Dave laughed.

"I love this. You carry this in case you need to use it. Sure little good it did you!"

Dave lowered the stun gun and raised the hand holding the gun to my face. "Get on your knees and walk into the center."

I did as ordered.

Still aiming the gun at me, he turned his head away. "Now, baby. I know it's been a long night. But I got one more favor."

He turned to me. "Don't move."

He dropped the stun gun into his pocket. Holstered the Glock in his belt.

He stepped over to Stacey. She dropped her head and whimpered, her shoulders jumping. Putting one hand on her shoulder and the other on the back of her head, he pushed her away from the wall, onto her knees.

How much time would I need to get to the door? I wondered, looking away. Could I make it just in time before he pulled that gun?

I thought I could.

But then that goddamned *Dog!*

Lumbering as it had looked coming out from the little building, I'd seen what it could do.

It would still have to catch me, though.

"HEY!"

Dave stepped away from Stacey and over to me. "Don't move!" he yelled even as I backed up a few paces on my knees.

He reached into the inside of his red jacket and pulled out a large black-tinted knife.

He aimed its point towards my head. "Don't move," he said. "Not a twitch."

Bending slowly, he lowered the knifepoint closer to my face. "Look towards that door one more time. . ." The blade came to my eye. I shut it.

I felt a prick on my eyelid.

"I cut this eye out and have Woofus eat it in front of you. Do I need to make myself clear?"

"No," I said.

"All right, then. You can open your eyes."

I hesitated. Then slowly opened them.

"Get back into the center where the light is." He went over to Stacey. *"You* get back into the light," he ordered, pointing the knife.

Stacey shut her eyes and arched her eyebrows in a pained look. She slowly shook her head, whimpering.

Dave grabbed her wrist and pulled her hand off her knee. He ran the knife across her arm.

Stacey screamed from the other side of the gag.

Dave let go and pushed her forward.

"Go."

Shaking her head, Stacy came towards me on her hands and knees.

"Right there's fine. Hold up, you two."

As Dave adjusted the lights, Stacey and I looked at each other. I didn't dare say anything, and Stacey couldn't. She looked at me with pleading eyes. I tried to tell her through mine that I would do what I could when I saw the chance.

"Whoo! Getting hot in here."

From the other side of the lights I saw Dave take off his Santa coat and throw it onto a chair in the corner. He wore no shirt beneath. He bent and picked up something from the ground and came back to us.

It was a video camera.

"All right, kids. Ready to have fun?"

Dave stepped in between the lights behind Stacey, his hairy, flabby belly wobbling. He had removed the gloves, but not the brass knuckle—it was in his free hand. He gave her a light kick in the rump. "Scoot just a little forward, honey. There we go."

He aimed the camera at us. I saw a pinprick of green light. "Lookin good! All right. Now." He lowered the camera to his side. "So. You two are in a room together. It's a little tense. You've got a guy who will shoot the fuckin shit outta you if you don't follow his directions. So, you wanna act like your life kinda depends on it, okay? Any questions before we begin? Oh, and Julie baby, you know from before you can make as much noise as you like without fear of bothering anybody. I only had you gagged cause I wanted to explain things nice and clear to Dylan-boy here without your constant interruption. Mmkay? You too Dylan. You won't wake your parents here, so moan if you mean it."

Planting a foot onto Stacey's back, he lowered his brass knuckled fist to her face. Stacey turned away. He ripped off the tape with his fingers, turning her head back. He stuck his fingers into her mouth and pulled out a large swab of cloth as red drool spilt out of Stacey's mouth.

"Yuck." He threw the cloth aside, then wiped his hand down his black jeans.

"Scoot forward some more, Julie. . .perfect. Now arch your back just a little. I wanna see that big bloody booty. All right. ACTION!"

Stacey whimpered.

"What's your name, son?" he asked me. "HEY! Look into the camera when I'm talking to you!"

I looked into the camera, then at Dave. "My. Ngth. . ." I couldn't talk. My whole body was shaking.

"Oh that's good. Real emotion. I like it. Okay, so Dylan? First I want you to say Hi to your Mom. Then you're gonna grab this bitch by the hair and shove your little peckerwood deep into her throat. Mmkay? Go!"

I looked at Stacey who was looking up at me between the swollen lids of her eyes. Her mouth was closed tight and lined, her chin seeming to sag.

"I'm sorry," I whispered.

Stacey blinked.

"HEY!" There was a *schink* as Dave pulled out the knife from its sheath. "I didn't tell you to say I'm sorry, I told you to say Hi Mom!"

"HI Mom!" I yelled.

I put my hand to the back of her head and scooted

forward. I felt the sticky warmth of Stacey's mouth as she took me in.

"There you go! Have that bitch suck your dick. Ram it down her throat!"

Stacey put her hand to my hip and leaned in, taking me in all the way.

I grimaced as I felt myself growing hard, with a sick feeling in my lower belly that felt like the flutter of poisonous butterflies.

"There you go! Aw don't that look uncomfortable. You love it but you don't wanta, you fuckin lil perv!" Dave laughed.

Stacey suddenly gagged, squeezing me between her toothless gums.

Dave was bent forward, angrily fingering her. "Yeah ain't she a hot little slot-pocket! Mmph!"

I lowered my hands to where Stacey's breasts used to be, to the damp cloth and tape covering her wounds, and moved my fingers over to her armpits.

If I could suddenly lift her with enough force to tumble her backwards onto Dave, I had a chance of knocking him off guard. He'd have his hands busy and all I had to do was get to him before he could draw either weapon.

Dave stood up.

He lowered his zipper.

"Guess what Jules? You've gone and done it again, you gorgeous whore. Look what we have here." He pulled out his erect penis.

He held the knife in his other hand and pointed it down at me. "Put your hands on her neck and hold her head up."

I did as he asked.

"Can you see her face, Dylan?"

I looked down at Stacey even as I felt her hot tears running onto my thumbs.

"Puh-eese," she whispered.

"I want you to look at her face while I stuff her butt and see how much she loves it. Then when I say, I want you to start squeezing that neck. Squeeze until I say stop. You got it?

"Get ready for the ass-pounding of your career, Julie!" He clamped the knife between his teeth and lowered himself behind Stacey.

I watched him aiming the video camera while directing his penis in with the other hand.

Stacey screamed between my hands as her body was

thrust forward.

"Shut up bitch!" I yelled.

Dave looked up and smiled around the knife, chuckling. I raised my hand for a high-five.

Dave gave me a no-touching fist-bump, then clamped his other hand onto Stacey's waist and continued to thrust.

I had hoped to twist his wrist.

Knife still in mouth, Dave gestured for me to start choking.

I nodded.

Pushing Stacey's head down, I leapfrogged across her back and punched Dave in the nose. The knife ejected from his mouth in a burst of spittle as he slammed into the wall while I lost my balance, turning with the momentum. I landed on my elbow with my other arm going across his jean-clad thigh.

Pressing onto his leg, I raised the elbow up and into some part of Dave, colliding with an explosion of nerves.

Rolling away, I heard a bang on the floor.

Facing the door, I saw Stacey scrambling for it.

"No!" I yelled. "Wait! Don't open—"

Stacey flung open the door.

Then screamed, jumping back.

"Sta—*gagh!"* My whole body seized in red stinging pain.

After several long heart-pounding seconds, I opened my eyes and saw Dave's hairy back wobble, kicking Stacey on the ground by the light stand.

He raised a foot, then brought it down onto her head.

I shut my eyes and tried to roll away, but my movement suddenly halted.

Dave was straddling me. He leaned down; his eyes furious, his teeth bared, a trail of snot running onto his mustache.

I felt the pain again as I heard the buzz of the stun gun, and screamed.

When I opened my eyes, I was on my belly, being handcuffed.

"You wanna fuck with me?"

I was rolled onto my back.

Dave grabbed me by the throat.

"All right, pretty boy," he snarled. *"Wanna know why they call me the Cat Burglar?"*

Dave steered me out the door with the Glock to my back.

Looking up from the hardwood floor dotted and smeared with Stacey's blood, I saw Woofus standing in the hallway halfway down. I pressed back, the gun painfully digging between my shoulders.

"Keep moving."

Woofus waited until we got within feet, giving me ample time to see him for the first time in proper lighting, before turning around. He lumbered forward, breathing like a bear, showing me his large testicles.

I couldn't begin to guess what mix of breeds the dog had come from, but the way the fur was missing from the head had given the face a horrible all-too human look from a distance. Now that I could see the creature's scarred and meaty face in the light, I was even more afraid.

As we entered the living room Woofus ambled to the right, to the Christmas tree in the corner.

Dave steered me to follow.

An old stained comforter was spread at the foot of the tree. Woofus stepped onto it, turned, and sat down.

"Sit!"

"Woof."

"Not *you*. Dylan, sit your ass down by Woofus." Dave pushed me onto my knees. I sat Indian-style.

"Get comfortable." Dave stepped back, aiming the gun with one hand. "How do you like my Christmas tree?"

I nodded, looking down at my lap.

"Naw, naw, I don't think you looked yet. Look."

I raised my head and to the right.

Strung around the tree were so many cat heads, some still with fur, lights glowing from the mouths and eye sockets, while others were picked-clean-skulls. Tails, tied together, were looped around the tree between the heads. At the very top a white kitten was wired to look crucified.

"You can bet those two old scrotums ain't expectin this when they get home!"

Woofus grunted.

I got a whiff of something dead and digesting, and turned away, gagging.

"You don't like it?" Dave laughed. "I thought. . .ew. Woofus, you asshole."

Dave's boots clacked away.

He screeched in surprise.

I looked up.

"Jesus pickle! I didn't see you. You're like a fucking *phantom."*

A figure was standing in the kitchen.

Dave gave a nervous chuckle. He wiped his brow with the back of his wrist. "Are we all set?" He had affected the friendly and eager-to-please tone I'd previously associated with his 'DG Santos.'

The stranger wearing the black vest and white shirt didn't answer, but looked down. He had something in between both hands.

"Caddy's off the road?"

The man turned his hands in opposite directions, and there was a wet-sounding *gop!*

"What about his car?" Dave asked, hooking a thumb back at me.

The man stepped forward, past Dave. His hair was tied back, long enough in a ponytail. His big nose and lanky figure reminded me of Ichabod Crane from the cartoon I'd loved as a kid.

He sat onto the chair already pulled away from the table facing the patio doors, and put the jar onto the table. He took some of the contents and put it to his mouth. His fingers came away with a wet smack.

Chewing, he said, "Hidden enough where it is. It'll keep for tonight. You won't be around when they find it."

I tried to make out the man's features from where I sat.

That mumbly voice sounded familiar.

"All right," Dave said. "We're good to go then."

Dave turned and looked at me, then forward again. "I'm gonna go out to storage for a minute."

"Pizza guy," the man commented, pulling out another something from the jar.

"Yeah! From Taste Testers."

His mouth rotated in chew, then he swallowed. "Good pizza."

"Damn good pizza. Order that shit all the time. I'll be back."

Dave set the Glock on the table with the stranger, then went to the patio doors. He went outside.

Woofus groaned, prompting a startled turn of my head.

The dog appeared to be asleep. The flaps of his jowls hung over the sides of either paw like the wings of a dead stingray, touching the ground. I stared at the uneven pulpy flesh around his mouth; at the strangely mottled skin about his face, like sickly freckles and moles.

I wondered what sort of horrendous abuse the animal had endured to look like it did.

Not that I had to wonder what sort of abuse it was capable of.

I looked up to see the man soundlessly coming over; holding the chair while his other hand clutched the jar.

The man turned the chair around and sat down with its back facing me.

He held out the jar.

"Would you like one?" he asked.

I opened my mouth.

It was at that moment that I recognized him. He was the creepy Berry-Eater I'd met before.

Only it appeared he'd gotten a face-lift—his skin looked smooth and waxy, not to mention pale. "You've got to try these. They're so good. . ." He reached into the dark jar.

He held out his thumb and index finger, showing me the circular object pinched between them.

He had it turned so that I would recognize the cat's eyeball. "They're like berries. Little cherries. They taste like the soul of a little creature going down."

"Woof."

I heard the windy sound from outside as the patio door opened announcing the return of Dave, aware of the minute sense of relief that brought me.

"Woofus? Num-nums!"

Dave was carrying two cages: One a gray plastic pet carrier, the other cage looking like an airline tote purse with see-through fabric and a pink trim.

He set both down in the middle of the room.

The Berry-Eater got up from the chair and turned towards him.

"I'm going to feed Woofus," Dave said. "Take care of this guy, and then I'll be ready to hit the road. Do you want to, uh, could you start packing, or?"

The Berry-Eater walked past.

"Car's parked out front, right?"

The Berry-Eater put the jar down on the counter, then said without turning, "Going to now."

"All right. Meet you soon."

Dave turned back to me. His eyes looked rabid as his lips peeled in a Cheshire Cat smile. *"Woofy ready for some moresome?"*

The dog responded with a grunt.

Dave squatted, shooting his arms out with his hands clawed. He stepped towards me in this walk-like-a-monster pose. "Now Dylan yer gonna get to see jes why I steal em cats. I steal em cause my little doggie here jes loves the taste of pussy! Dontcha, boy?"

"Mroow."

Dave turned. Stepped over to the cages.

He peered into the pink carry-on.

"Mroow."

"Oh yeah? You think so, shit-face?"

"Mroow."

"Come here." Dave opened the carrier bag. "Yes, yes, I know you're hungry." He reached in.

He pulled out a cat by the scruff of the neck. The cat was gray with a white belly, its body thin.

"You see this?" Dave said. "This little faggot here tried to scratch me. Hissed at me. But see? Don't feed em for a few days, and now he's a cooperative little boy. Aren't ya?"

"Mroow."

Dave turned the cat, smiling while his other hand reached behind.

He lowered himself into a squat, lowering the cat onto its shaky legs.

"There ya go." Dave let go of the cat.

He mashed it with his hand as he slammed onto his knees. He raised the knife and plunged it into the cat's back.

The cat screamed.

Dave pulled the knife out in a squirt of blood, and brought it down again as the cat rolled its torso onto the side with its paws flailing. The cat made a surprised choking sound that sounded all too human as Dave buried the knife into the side of its neck.

Dave looked up with excited eyes. "Hungry boy?"

I looked at the poor creature making spasmic sneezing sounds, its eyes open and draining, and looked away.

I looked at Woofus.

The bags beneath the dog's eyes sagged so much there was about a half-inch of red showing, while the yellowy pupils regarding Dave and the cat looked bored.

"Here you go, Woofus. Nums-nums!"

The limp body of the cat landed next to me with a wet splat.

"Jesus!" I blurted, scooting away.

Dave slapped the back of my head.

"No sudden movements," he said, stepping to my side. "You back off from Woofus, he'll give chase."

Woofus, however, didn't look like he was about to give chase to anything.

He looked down at the dead cat splayed on its back, its belly sliced open like a gutted fish. He lowered his nose, sniffed. Raised his head. The yellow eyes rolled up at Dave.

"What? That ol sandbag from earlier got you filled up? That was just an appetizer! Come on, you got this."

Woofus remained couchant. If he'd still had a tail, I was sure it would be wagging in agitation.

Dave crouched. Putting his free hand onto the cat's face for purchase, he dipped the knife into the slit and grunted as he made jerking movements with his arm. He brought the knife out clinging pieces of guts. He tapped the side of the knife at Woofus's closed lips, making the animal blink, leaving a red smear.

"Eat!"

The jowly mouth opened, showing a stretching membrane of saliva between sharp browned teeth. Dave jerked his wrist, slinging in some of the guts. The dog's mouth closed with a click of teeth and began to chew.

Dave pushed the carcass, then stood up. He stepped over to me.

He wiped the side of the knife down my shoulder and arm. "Give you a little flavoring."

I looked at Woofus, who now had his face in the cat's stomach.

As Dave walked towards the other pet carrier I pulled at the handcuffs behind my back.

Maybe now that the dog is distracted. . .

Down the hallway, I knew where two of the three doors led, but the other one that Dave had come out of had to lead outside.

If I could get there before Dave shot me, I could kick it open.

The Berry-Eater would be outside watching the front. But if I could get past him. . .

I'd seen no evidence that he was armed, but even if he was, if I could get onto the road before he could draw, I had a chance of outrunning him. The guy might not risk chasing me where there could be other cars on the road. I was in handcuffs after all—people would stop for me.

"Here kitty. . ." Dave had turned the gray cage towards me. He pushed it so that I got a look at its occupant, a black cat. "Say hi to your little friend, Dylan Dingles. He's going to be your wittle fwend who lives wiff you in Woofy's tum-tums."

The black cat regarded me with curious green eyes.

"Mm. . .roow?"

"Woofy? Ready for some dark puss?"

Woofus had his mouth over his cat's back as he dug in with his teeth. The way the bag-like flesh of his mouth undulated, it looked like he was sucking the juice out of an orange.

Orange?

Orange. . .

The little ball I'd had in my pocket!

Was it still in my pocket?

Dave had opened the cage. "Come on out little bud!"

The black cat dipped its head down. Surveying its new surroundings.

"Come on, fuckle-dum."

The cat took a step forward, and Dave snatched it up by the scruff.

"Mm. . .roow?"

Dave smiled at the creature. "Do that again."

The cat's mouth opened, a small hole of pink. *"Mmmroow?"*

"This little fucker's only got one tooth left. That's funny. Makes you look kinda evil there, bud."

"Hey, Dave?" I asked.

The smile dropped from Dave's face as he looked at me. "Did I say you could fuckin talk?"

"Where's the little ball?"

Dave lowered the cat. Its legs pedaled.

"You know, the little orange ball I had in my pocket?"

"What about it?"

"My wife gave it to me," I said, putting Darlene's face in my mind. "I had a wife once, but she died a few years ago, and. . ." My voice faltered with the swelling of emotion. "I always carry it with me. I squeeze it and pretend it's her hand." My vision blurred.

"Please!" I blurted, spilling hot tears down my cheeks. *"Let me hold it again as one last thing!"* I dropped my head and sobbed.

Dave was silent a moment.

"Well, gosh darn."

I looked up at him.

Dave's face was somber. "I'll be butt-fucked in a supermarket if that wasn't a decent performance."

"Mm. . .roow?"

Dave looked at the cat. *"Shaddap!*

"Tell you what, I give you a glowing review for that one. You can die knowing you weren't that bad an actor. Mmkay?"

"Please Dave!"

"Please Dave!" he mimicked. "All right fine, fucker!" He sheathed the knife. Put his hand into his pocket. I heard the jingling of keys or change.

He pulled out the orange ball. "Will this make you shut up?"

"Yes!" I said.

"Fine. What're you going to do for it? Suck my dick?"

"I. . ."

"Oh, no? You mean you're not a faggot? Well sorry, only dick-sucking faggots are getting orange balls tonight. You're outta luck."

"Please."

"Say you're a faggot! Say you're a dick-sucking faggot! Say it!"

I dropped my head and shook it in despair. "Just don't squeeze it."

Dave was silent.

I looked up.

And wished I hadn't. Dave's lip curled in a dangerous snarl.

"What the fuck is this?" he asked, holding the ball up. "This spray some kind of shit? Huh? You tryin to trick me, you little shit?"

"It's just a soft ball. Squeeze it if you want, okay, or don't. Please just let me hold it one last time!"

Dave turned the ball in his hand, inspecting it with narrowed eyes. He brought it to his nose and sniffed.

Just squeeze it, you fucker!

"Woofus!"

The dog looked up from the ugly bundle of guts and fur

beneath its paws, blood dripping from its mouth.

Dave tossed the ball over to Woofus, who stopped it with his nose, sniffed, then closed his mouth over it. He lifted his head as his giant jaws snapped together.

I looked at Dave. The cat had turned over and was trying to scramble away as he pressed onto its back with his knee. He slammed the back of its head with his brass knuckles.

"Little fucker," he growled, grinding the knuckle into the back of the cat's head.

The lights flickered.

Dave looked towards the ceiling, mouth open.

"Woof."

He looked at Woofus.

There was a boom in the distance.

"Storm's back up," Dave mumbled, looking over his shoulder towards the shuddering patio doors as rain pattered.

Ding-dong!

Dave looked towards the kitchen.

His brow furrowed.

Ding-dong!

Maybe it was the cops! Somebody had seen or heard something.

Which could mean that even now they were surrounding the house. I looked hopefully out the patio doors.

Ding-dong!

There was another boom of thunder. Louder. Woofus raised his head and looked towards the patio.

"Let's get a move on, shall we?"

The cat lifted its head with its eyes wide and mewled in pain as Dave adjusted his knee. He wrapped his fingers around the animal's neck.

"Did you ever see that movie about the alien hunter? Watch this. . ."

Pressing his other hand onto the cat's shoulder, Dave pulled.

The cat peeled back its lips, showing the one sharp tooth. I heard the scream trying to escape.

"Come on. . ." Dave's tongue stuck out as he scrunched his face and grunted.

I saw the cat's outstretched trembling paws, and looked away.

I looked at Woofus.

The side of his face opened, baring teeth as he rose to his feet.

"Woof."

"Guh!" Dave sat back, slamming one hand for balance, the cat limp in his other.

Sitting up, he wiped his forehead.

Leaving the cat, he stood up. He pulled the knife from its sheath.

"Woof."

"One second," he said, leaning down. Lifting the cat's head, he stuck the knife in, and began cutting into the back.

"Woof."

"What the hell are—?"

An explosion of thunder boomed so loud the house shook. Dave stumbled back.

Woofus tensed, reddened saliva running out from the sides of his torn face.

He was growling towards the patio doors.

Boom—Boom—BOOM!

I saw Dave slowly turn even as I saw the pale boulder coming out of the darkness through the sheets of falling rain with swinging limbs.

The glass doors exploded, knocking Dave over with the wooden table and chairs, and me onto my back.

"MMYARRR!"

Pain shot into my wrist from the handcuffs as I rolled to my side. My face smacked into the wet floor.

Sputtering, I struggled to a sitting position.

Lorris was gazing down at his shirtless belly covered in blossoming blood from the shattered glass.

Woofus galloped towards him.

"Lorris!"

Lorris looked up as Woofus leapt at him.

Lorris smacked the dog on the head, flipping Woofus onto his back.

The giant slammed onto his knees, shaking the whole house.

He pummeled Woofus with his fists.

I looked to Dave, who had sat up. Mouth open, he shook his head.

"HYUN-HYUN-HYUN." Lorris had his eyes closed in a childish look of fear as gore flew up with the boxing movements of his arms: He was tearing the dog apart with his hands, tossing pieces of Woofus over his shoulders like red chunks of grass from the ground.

A giant tentacle shot up from the dog and roped around Lorris's head.

Lorris opened his eyes. Grabbing hold of the dog's intestine with both hands, he got to his feet and turned, flinging a big bloody chunk of Woofus-guts into Dave.

Spattered in blood, Dave wailed.

Lorris joined him.

"Lorris!"

Ignoring me, Lorris rubbed his gore encrusted hands up his face and onto his scalp.

"Lorris! Get HIM!"

Dave was getting to his feet.

Teeth shone through a face drenched in blood, he planted his feet shoulder-length apart, the knife sticking out in front of him.

"Hey!" he yelled. "Lorris!"

Lorris dropped his hands, splattering blood at his sides.

"Come here, bud. It's all right."

He blinked at Dave. "Dynng?"

"That's right." Lowering the hand that held the knife, he beckoned with his other.

Lorris opened his arms.

He began shuffling towards Dave, arms back, massive belly jiggling.

"Lorris, NO!" I yelled.

"WAAAH. . ."

Dave crouched, then shot upward, burying the blade to the hilt in Lorris's overhanging stomach.

The boy's eyes bulged.

Dave pumped and pumped the hand with the knife.

"AH-Ah-*AAAH. . ."* Lorris stumbled back.

They crashed onto the remains of Woofus together, Dave disappearing from view in the rebounding blubber of Lorris.

The vibration knocked me onto my back.

My face again landed in blood. I rolled onto my side, wondering if I had broken my wrists.

I lifted my head and spat out the metallic taste.

Blood!

The cat's blood was pooled below my face.

Enough to lubricate my wrists out of the cuffs?

I struggled to a sitting position.

Dave was crouched over Lorris's massive belly ramming the knife down and out with both hands, geysers of blood shooting up. "Sloppy-joe eatin mother fucker!"

Scooting back, I found the wet spot, rocking the cuffs. I felt the liquid on my wrists.

Dave was getting to his feet, holding on to the handle of the knife sticking up from Lorris's blood-soaked belly with both hands.

His feet lost traction and he slipped back, smacking his face onto the belly before slipping off.

Grabbing the edge of my left cuff with my right, I leaned forward and pulled with both arms.

Come on!

I closed my eyes as I felt tearing pain.

If I had to break my hand, I was getting out of that cuff.

Dave was crawling, the bloody knife clamped between his teeth.

He stopped and dropped his head, shoulders heaving. His breath was snotty gurgles around the knife.

I knew I had only seconds left.

Closing my eyes, I pulled and pulled.

"Too late," I heard Dave say.

An earth-shattering scream called out and fireworks exploded behind my eyelids, before yet again, I landed on my back.

When I opened my eyes, I saw Dave standing, facing the space where the patio doors had been.

Towards the white figure standing at the top of the steps just outside in the rain.

And I knew who I'd heard screaming.

"Carter!" I yelled.

Carter stepped forward. He slightly shook his head, waving his rain-drenched hair, his eyes wide and manic.

Puffing his chest, Carter raised both hands to his ears. He pulled his hands slowly away into fists, and screamed as he squatted.

"YAAAAAH*ghaah. . ."*

"Watch out, he's got a knife!" I yelled.

Carter glanced at me, then back at Dave. "YAAAAAHg*haah. . ."*

He got into his fighting stance.

Dave took a step back and got into a matching stance.

Holding the knife back, he reached out with his other and beckoned, his bloody face zipped back in a smile. "Bring it, Bruce!"

Carter stepped forward, turning with his other foot.

Dave lunged with his arms up, and threw the knife.

It slammed into Carter's belly.

Carter's body tensed as he grabbed the handle.

I struggled to my feet. Still smiling at Carter, Dave jammed a hand into his pocket and pulled a Saturday night special.

As Dave took aim, I saw Carter look up, his face scrunched in surprised pain.

Dave shot.

And shot.

Carter fell onto the crimson mound that had been Lorris, and slicked down to the ground.

I stepped up to Dave with my hands behind me.

Dave turned aiming the gun, his eyes amused.

I whipped my right arm around, knocking the gun from his hand with the empty cuff as a shot went off.

Dave jumped back, shaking his hand.

I was ready to beat the living shit out of him as an apparition rose above us, red white and spinning. . .

Carter's Van Damme helicopter-kick connected to the back of Dave's head. Time slowed so that I could see his eyeballs knocked to the limit, as his cheeks puffed out, then wobbled, spraying droplets of spit. . .

He fell onto his belly, as Carter landed onto his side with his right leg still stretched wide.

I snatched up the gun, turned around, and aimed it at Dave.

Dave didn't move.

Carter sputtered, coughed.

I went to him.

Tears filling my eyes, I knelt, putting my hand to support the back of his head as he tried to lift it.

Carter's eyes darted from side to side, glazed.

"Hey," I whispered. *"Hey, buddy."*

Carter's face contorted. I felt a jolt roll up his spine and he spat up, the wad of blood splattering onto the side of his face. He turned his head into my palm.

"Hey," I said, moving his head back as I felt a hot tear drop.

"We did it. We kicked ass."

Carter's eyes closed, and bloody lips grinned.

"Let's get out of here."

Dave was still sprawled, unmoving.

Aiming the gun with my free hand, I put my arm under Carter. The handcuffs jiggled.

Carter coughed as he tried to sit up.

The blade was still in him, the handle sticking out just above the knotted belt. Carter put his hand over it.

"Don't try to pull it," I said. "We'll get the ambulance here in a sec."

As I said it, I heard sirens in the distance.

Thank *God.*

I looked back at Dave.

Put a bullet in the fucker, make sure he doesn't get back up!

As I aimed, I looked at the light little gun. After three shots, there might only be one left. And they obviously weren't of high caliber; they hadn't been enough to keep Carter down.

What happened to the Glock?

I looked to the broken remains of the wooden table and spotted it among the splinters.

"Hold up."

I stepped over to the gun, unable to avoid stepping on glass fragments. I felt them sting like so many pinpricks on the bottoms of my bare feet.

I picked up the gun.

Aimed it at Dave.

Now I had the real show-stopper.

I gave the little gun to Carter to hold while I got his other arm around my shoulders. Together we got up.

Keeping my eyes on Dave, we walked slowly to the exit.

Outside was like stepping into a cold shower. I hurried us down the steps.

The remains of the man who had followed me from the Caddy were nowhere in sight. I looked up from the grass to the little building directly across. The dim light from within still glowed behind the covered windows.

I hoped the Berry-Eater wasn't inside.

Where the hell had *he* gone?

I gripped the Glock as we turned the corner.

A figure dislodged itself from the darkness ahead of us but

even as I raised the gun, I recognized him by his clothes.

"Hey what's going on?" The skateboarder's eyes went wide as he looked me up and down. In a timid voice he asked, "What happened to him? Why are you naked?"

I stopped.

Stacey.

She was still in the house. With Dave.

She could still be alive.

"Here," I said to the boy, "Can you take him? I have to go back inside, someone's still in there.

"Sure. Oh my God!"

"He's been stabbed and shot. Be very careful with him until the ambulance gets here. Don't let him pull the knife out, or he'll bleed to death."

I transferred Carter to the boy. The boy was shaking like he might crumple.

The wooden gate had been knocked down by Lorris.

"Make it onto the road. If you see any cars coming before the ambulance or police, flag them down, okay?"

"Okay!"

"Hey," Carter croaked. He looked at me with dazed eyes. The Saturday night special dropped from his hand. "Somethin I gotta tell you."

"Wait till I get back."

"No iss impornant. . ."

Carter's head rolled. Then shot up, like he was trying to stay awake. "Where'd tha girl in the wheelchair go?"

"He's hallucinating. Get him help, I won't be long."

I ran back up the path, to the corner of the house.

Gun ready, I peered around.

With the patio doors destroyed, the back of the house looked wall-less.

Keeping wary of the little building, I approached the patio.

Went up the steps.

Dave was no longer sprawled just inside—he was gone.

I looked to the bloody bulk of Lorris lying in the glass, wood splinters and dog parts, to the cat-head Christmas tree that had fallen over.

A thump.

It had come from the hallway.

Grimacing, I stepped inside, feeling the sharp bite of glass on my bare feet.

Maybe this isn't such a good idea, I thought. Confident as I was with a Glock .45, I suddenly realized that Dave could also have a gun. He'd already surprised us by pulling the Saturday night special.

The wail of the sirens had gotten loud enough to be just outside.

Maybe you'd better let the police take over from here.

And maybe if I did, Stacey would die in the meantime.

Around the corner, I found Dave by the three doors, leaning against the wall, hands on knees.

His head slowly turned, face red with blood, his dark hair hanging.

I aimed the gun. "Don't move, asshole."

Dave bared his teeth.

He slowly straightened.

"I said, don't fucking move."

He raised the fist with the brass knuckles and took a step towards me.

"One more step. . ."

He took one more step.

The door behind Dave swung open with the blinding white light from the fluorescents.

Dave screamed and fell forward.

He screamed again, convulsing on the ground while a red figure crawled over him.

Stacey looked at me. She was wearing the Santa jacket.

She smiled, baring Dave's vampire teeth.

She turned Dave over onto his back. Zapped him again with the stun gun.

Reaching into the open zipper of his jeans, she yanked out his penis.

Dave's head jerked up, involuntarily nodding.

Stacey's face turned ferocious, saliva dripping from her mouth, as she lowered her face to his crotch.

Dave's head snapped back and howled. His eyes bulged, then squeezed shut, oozing tears.

Stacey's head jerked up with a gush of blood.

She spat into her palm.

Straddling Dave, she dangled his detached member over his face.

She grabbed his neck.

"Your turn to eat dick!" she hissed.

Pinching his nose, she shoved her hand into his open mouth.

Dave's bloodshot eyes bulged.

Stacey got off him.

We looked at each other.

Stacey wiped her mouth, then nodded.

Aiming the gun at his face, I said, "Oinky-boinky," and pulled the trigger.

Epilogue

I began writing this memoir five years after the infamous night of December 23, 2013. My therapist encouraged me to write about what happened after it was becoming apparent that the nightmares and frequent flashbacks I experienced on set had begun to affect my work, culminating in my widely-reported breakdown on the set of *Dixie Danish* (contrary to popular belief, I did not call director James Hammond a “dick-guzzling flatulent dog,” though I do admit to the hurtful things said in the heat of my outburst—I'm talking about the one caught on tape in the widely circulated clip).

The idea scared me at first. I thought I'd been doing more than fine moving on. After my one-season tenure in *Heroes in the City of Angels*, I went on to star in the series of successful romantic comedies for which I'm known. I'd been keeping very busy and living the life I'd dreamed of. Why should I go back now and revisit scenes from that horrible night? Scenes I'd block out forever, if only I could.

In the words of Dr. Lange: “Because you can't just lock them away, like ghosts in your attic. You still hear them, whether you like it or not. So go up there and face them! All you have to do is hear what they have to say. It doesn't mean you've got to dwell there, live there. It means you've got to own your own house.”

Easy for you to say, Doc, I remember thinking. The ghosts I got up there are scary as Hell.

But I agreed.

After all, it was just a journal. It was just for me. It wasn't about impressing anyone. It was about looking into the mirror that can be the blank page and being honest with it. As much as I knew it would stir up hard emotions, I thought it would ultimately do me some good.

So I sat down one morning and began writing.

I began as though I were writing a fictitious story, myself as the main character. I didn't know initially why I chose this method rather than doing the Dear Diary—I thought at the time it was because I'm such a movie guy that I think in 'movie-mode,' or maybe it was just because the aspiring writer in me never really died. Now I think it had more to do with how I think of God as being The Author, and decided I wanted to do my best to see myself as The Author might—looking down at it all, experiencing it, but from a distance. In any case, I stuck with it. And here you have it.

Why do I say 'you?'

Because I've decided that what I have written here is something I'm willing to share. I want people to know about this part of my life. Many celebrities want to hide away those years of struggle before the limelight, but I don't. I want you to know that I'm human. I want you to know that I wasn't always 'Jared Manning.' A lot of it is very unflattering and might get me into trouble, but it is the truth.

All of it.

I say that knowing that parts of my story seem fantastical, or maybe just plain made up. (I can just imagine Dr. Lange congratulating me on my use of symbolism) But I can only promise you that I've told the truth from my point of view as best I remember it.

Okay, some events may be out of order, and I'm sure some of the building numbers I picked because I couldn't remember them exactly. But otherwise it all comes straight from my memory banks.

I would've been the one to say that truth is stranger than fiction, if someone hadn't beat me to it.

Another reason for wanting to share this is because I don't like the way the mass media has turned the despicable David Gunston into a pop culture villain/icon, allowing him into that same club with Manson, Bundy, Ramirez, etc. The David Gunston I had the displeasure of knowing would have liked that just fine.

Seth Tomkins' best-selling book *The Grantwood Grinch* is also a shameless money-grab.

In case you're not familiar with the record, David Gunston was apprehended by police minutes after the events I described (unknown to me, the Glock's magazine had been empty the entire time). He lived for less than a year before being murdered in prison (what can I say—the guy had many powerful enemies). I don't think it particularly matters that he didn't live to see trial.

That he lived so long afterwards without his cherished organ in a state of mostly solitary confinement seems just punishment for his atrocities.

And he was able to shed some light on how he got to be so aptly named.

Born in a south Texas community, Gunston showed aptitude for computers as a child and later became something of a whiz. After attending college in Austin for two years, he dropped out following the death of his mother (popular myth now has it that Gunston's hatred of cats began with the knowledge that his mother's body, dead for weeks when finally found, had been partially eaten by the five cats she had kept as companions, but I have it on good authority that this is yet another one of Tomkins' many fallacies). He travelled the country and under the radar for years scamming people and subsiding on what he could from his burglaries. Over time he began to utilize his computers skills, and was eventually able to hack his way into a limousine's software company, where he gained access to the intimate information of close to one million customers. This included the security codes of many buildings and affluent houses, as well as sometimes detailed information about secret entrances originally designed for discretion. Gunston himself posed as a limo driver, and used the vehicles to transport stolen goods.

It is unknown where he acquired 'Woofus,' or why he fed cats to the dog. Speculation is that the media coverage made him cocky, Gunston already having become far more daring in Los Angeles than anywhere he'd been before, and he began to enjoy his new role as media-hyped villain.

During his residence he kept several rented rooms, using most to store his stolen goods. He had been renting the Frankmeyer's guesthouse where I later encountered him with the pretense that he was a music producer. The Frankmeyer's had allowed him to sound-proof the building, and had been trusting enough not to venture inside during his lease, not knowing that the sound-proofing was to keep the many stolen cats from being detected.

Gunston steadfastly maintained that he was a 'Lone Wolf' at all times, denying ever having known a man who the media dubbed The Berry-Eater (my given nickname—I'm good at giving nicknames, you might have noticed). I can attest that the men must have worked together.

But as of this writing, The Berry-Eater remains at large, his identity and exact role in the crimes unknown.

You might be wondering how my friend Carter was able to find me and come to my aid.

Well, if there's a part of this story that *I* find hard to believe, this is it.

According to Carter, he got a phone call before he and the skateboarder could arrive at his residence.

From my phone.

But when Carter answered, it wasn't my voice he heard. It was a woman's.

The woman told Carter that I was in serious trouble. She would not identify herself; she only insisted that Carter run to my aid. The woman described the location and told Carter where he would find me. She assured him that the police would be coming, but not before Carter did his duty.

Before hanging up, another woman's voice, slightly younger-sounding, broke in.

"Hey Carter! Can you tell Dylan that we're okay? Can you tell him that we love him?"

And then the call ended.

Carter says that even as he began to run, he tried to call the number back, only to get the message that my phone had been disconnected.

I can't tell you how many times I have asked Carter if he is *sure* that this happened. That it wasn't a dream he had later. That he isn't telling me this for some kind of comfort.

Carter remains steadfast that not one word of it is a lie.

And the skateboarder, whose name I am omitting for his privacy, also maintains that Carter got a call that promptly turned them around.

Carter is alive and fine. That guy is one tough son-of-a-bitch. He was in the hospital a long time, but he made it out. We're no longer what you call 'boozin-buddies' (neither of us drink anymore), but we remain friends to this day.

You know him as Charlie Wing. But back then, before his stand-up routine made him famous, I knew him just as Carter. The guy I used to work with at that god-awful restaurant.

Stacey Noeltner had a very difficult recovery, but I'm happy to say that as of this writing she's doing very well and has become a great friend of mine. I wish it didn't have to be the shared trauma of a horrific event the thing that brings us together, but we are there for one another. We are not what happened to us.

Lori Lyngarth moved up to Canada to start a new life. The road has been extremely rough on her as well, but she's a strong, wonderful woman. We're always a phone call away from each other.

Victor Mapu and I haven't spoken in years. I tried to keep the door open in honor of what had once been a good friendship, but after so much time passed with emails and phone calls going unreturned, I decided to move on. Who needs friends like that?

Val and I are still together, and consider us married, though no legal document would prove us such. She's been described as a mystery woman by the media because she does not appear in public with me (her choice). Some assholes go so far as to say she's imaginary, but she's very real and, trust me, very very magical. We hope to start our own family when the time feels right.

As for my phone, it was never found. Funny, huh?

I do know that the young man who sold it to me was investigated by police and was determined to have no knowledge of any potentially harmful program installed on it.

Horizon Wireless, of course, remains blameless.

I guess I'll never know exactly what it was.

I do like to think that if it was somehow able to pick up malevolent frequencies, it was also able to transmit others.

I'd like to close by thanking the residents of Grantwood. I've met and known so many wonderful people there. I'd love to have all the time in the world to get to know them better. It really is an amazing place to live, if you should be so lucky.

Oh, speaking of luck—I almost forgot.

The Wheat Penny.

I never got it back. Which is too bad. I really liked that little thing. If you should find it, or you're reading this and you have it, I suggest you hold on to it.

Whether it actually grants Luck. . .
Only The Author knows that one for sure.

Acknowledgements

Special Thanks to LeeAnne Rowe, Nia Ireland, Larry Hansen and zenrage, Thomas M. Baxa, Omero Nunez, Michael Calabria, Janet Joyce Holden, Bill Shafer and Hyaena Gallery, Kieron Connolly in loving memory, Dane Caldwell-Holden, my friends in The Horror Writer's Association, Los Angeles, and Joe Satriani's music for being my constant companion while writing this book.

Ronan Barbour is an actor and writer based in Los Angeles.
visit: ronanbarbour.com

Made in the USA
Columbia, SC
08 July 2022